PRAISE FOR CHRIS CANDER

"A dynamic and insightful storyteller, Cander imbues her work with such poignant character detail, as a reader, I felt I'd all but moved into Martha's neighborhood. As a documented lover of tales of complicated relationships between women, I must say that *A Gracious Neighbor* is among the best."

—Chandler Baker, *New York Times* bestselling author of *The Husbands*

"I couldn't stop turning these witty, suspenseful pages. What new lengths would the endearing and exasperating Martha go to in her pursuit of friendship? This is a sparkling and deeply satisfying novel."

—Margot Livesey, author of *The Boy in the Field*

"Fast paced and affecting from start to finish, *A Gracious Neighbor* offers keen insight into modern-day loneliness and takes a good, hard look at what often lurks behind picturesque houses and perfectly manicured lawns. Chris Cander's skill and empathy make this one of those rare novels that feels like a character study but reads like a thriller."

—Matthew Norman, author of *Last Couple Standing* and *All Together Now*

"Even upscale Houston neighborhoods, filled with families, can hold secrets and dangers. And even those lucky enough to live in them can feel like outsiders in their own lives. Cander navigates the complexities of female friendship and the power of an extended hand with deep insight and empathy. I was completely riveted!"

—Stacey Swann, author of *Olympus, Texas*

"Moving seamlessly between a thriller, a comedy, and a study of the everyday, *A Gracious Neighbor* conjures the universal. Love, jealousy, social anxiety, and our endless foibles are displayed with warmth and hilarity. Cander's characters come to life and leave us turning the next page. This isn't simply a Houston novel but a novel about the collective 'us.'"

—Mark Haber, author of *Deathbed Conversions* and
Reinhardt's Garden

"Anyone who wishes they could choose their neighbors will relate to this simmering suburban drama. Chris Cander pits the power of compassion against the pressures of uniformity in this hugely entertaining drama. Cander explores the high cost of privacy, the insecurity behind our efforts to maintain appearances, and the risks we take to find out what's really going on behind closed doors."

—Christina Clancy, author of *Shoulder Season*

A Gracious Neighbor

A Gracious Neighbor

Chris Cander

A NOVEL

Little
a

Published by Little A, New York

www.apub.com

Amazon, the Amazon logo, and Little A are trademarks of Amazon.com, Inc., or its affiliates.

ISBN-13: 9781542039178 (hardcover)
ISBN-10: 1542039177 (hardcover)

ISBN-13: 9781542039154 (paperback)
ISBN-10: 1542039150 (paperback)

Cover design by Faceout Studio, Amanda Hudson

Printed in the United States of America

First edition

This book is for my family
and friends
and all my gracious neighbors

GRACIOUS /ˈgrāSHəs/

adjective

1. courteous, kind, and pleasant
2. elegant and tasteful, especially as exhibiting wealth or high social status
3. condescendingly courteous, especially to inferiors
4. merciful; disposed to forgive offenses and impart unmerited blessings

A NOTE FROM THE AUTHOR

I had never heard of the Pulitzer Prize–winning writer Susan Glaspell until my daughter, Sasha, shared one of Glaspell's short stories with me. Sasha's English literature teacher at her women-only high school had assigned the haunting "A Jury of Her Peers," which was written and set in the early 1900s, a time when women's lives were restricted mainly to domestic concerns. The teacher wanted the young women to contemplate the myriad ways the female characters were disenfranchised. Sasha told me, "Mom, you have to read this story. You'll love it." I did.

In the story, Martha Hale accompanies her husband, the sheriff, and the sheriff's wife to investigate the home of Minnie Wright, a quiet, reclusive woman accused of murdering her husband, John. Looking around at the unkempt kitchen, the men see evidence of Minnie's shortcomings as a wife, but the women begin to understand that the disarray is a reflection of Minnie's mental state. The men instruct the women to gather some of Minnie's things to take to her in jail, then leave them to inspect the crime scene upstairs. After discovering clues about John's oppressive, abusive tendencies toward his wife, Martha and the sheriff's wife reach their own conclusions about Minnie's guilt and judge her actions to be justified. They understand Minnie's plight because they've dealt with versions of male domination in their own lives. Martha Hale says, "We all go through the same things—it's all just a different kind of the same thing!"

The story brilliantly explores male subjugation of women, gender inequality in and outside the home, the effects of social exclusion and isolation on people's emotional and mental states, and the obligations neighbors have to help and support one another. While sexism and misogyny are the central concerns of Glaspell's story, I was also intrigued by the matter of gender loyalty. Instead of defaulting to understanding and support, the women had to overcome their initial assumptions and judgments in order to feel empathy for Minnie. Once she does, Martha reproaches herself for avoiding Minnie for years because the Wright home "weren't cheerful," saying, "Oh, I *wish* I'd come over here once in a while! . . . That was a crime! Who's going to punish that?" Her comments suggest that in the story, as in life, there are many "crimes" that women commit against one another that aren't punishable by law: scrutiny and social neglect, competition and condescension.

That these issues are as prevalent and relevant today as they were over a century ago is what compelled me to write this novel. I decided to set it in my own neighborhood, West University Place, in Houston, Texas, because we'd just entered the early days of the COVID-19 pandemic, and like everyone else, I was experiencing social isolation at home. For the first time, the room where I'd written all my other novels seemed too confining, so I wrote most of this novel in my backyard—keenly aware of the irony of examining the relationships people have with their neighbors and neighborhoods at a time when most of us were confined to our residences. (An interesting coincidence: Glaspell's story was published in March 1917, a few months before the 1918 flu pandemic. I started writing this novel just weeks before the outbreak of the novel coronavirus pandemic of 2020.)

Lastly, although my novel departs from the original story in many ways, I decided to honor its origins and underscore the timelessness of its themes by using Glaspell's and other turn-of-the-century names for my contemporary characters.

Thank you so much for reading *A Gracious Neighbor*. I'm truly grateful for your support of my work.

Warmly,
Chris

Prologue

We never imagined there would be a murder. We'd never even suspected. But why would we? We live so close to each other, and we live so far apart, going through different kinds of the very same things.

We worked so hard to hide our shame, our secrets, and our insecurities. We emulated other women to try to fit in, to be part of a community, only to discover that even with our manicured lawns and beautiful houses and high expectations, we were still lonely. We could still hurt and be hurt by each other.

Would things have turned out differently if we'd behaved better?

We know this now: if we could go back, we'd have looked more carefully. We'd have tried harder. We wouldn't have been so quick to judge.

One

Martha Hale thought the first Monday in February was early to prune the scraggly crape myrtles in her yard, but as she drove home after dropping her son off at middle school that morning, she noted that most of the others throughout her tidy neighborhood had been topped already. Several years before, someone had delivered full-color flyers to homeowners demanding they "stop crape murder," extolling the virtues of the trees' natural growth habits and pointing out that the ugly, swollen knobs at the unnecessary cut sites were like arthritic knuckles they wouldn't otherwise develop, but that campaign went largely ignored. Residents of West University Place, Texas, liked their gardens neat. The shaped hedges and trimmed trees symbolized their owners' expectations of cultivated, undiminished beauty.

Frankly, Martha wouldn't have minded leaving hers alone, except perhaps a little deadheading later in the season to coax a second round of blossoms. But she would do so only as long as everyone else did, too. Her family stood out too much as it was. They were among the few who didn't retain a professional lawn crew to maintain their yard, and since her husband, Lewis, suffered from chronic back pain—due, she thought, to his posture and increasing belly size and not to his brief experimentation with weight lifting as he claimed—the gardening duties typically fell to her. But she would much rather spend a few sweaty hours in the garden, even with an unwieldy electric chain saw, than have her neighbors think them sloppy. Their circa 1940 bungalow might be small, but nobody could've accused her of not keeping it clean and trim.

She pulled her minivan into the driveway and examined the trees for mourning dove nests. The doves had been cooing and twitterpating lately, and just the other day, Martha found a dropped egg on the sidewalk beneath a live oak across the street. Satisfied that she wouldn't inadvertently also hurt an innocent bird as she lopped the limbs off her trees, she went inside to change out of the pajamas she'd driven Harry to school in again. Nearly every day, she vowed hopelessly to start getting up early enough to put on real clothes before it was time to leave and hoped this wouldn't be the day her car broke down. She put on her comfortable overalls and a sun hat to protect her fair complexion even though the day was overcast and cool, and went to the garage to gather the necessary tools.

By the time she trudged out to the front yard, someone—the Realtor, presumably—had added a bright-red SOLD plaque to the for-sale sign in front of the enormous new house next door. Martha felt a clutch of nervous excitement and squeezed her garden shears as though in a quick embrace. Ever since her dour old neighbors were moved into an assisted-living facility the year before and their lot was sold to a custom-home builder, Martha had been thrilled by the possibility of new friendship with whoever would someday move in. Would it be a young family with children close in age to her fourteen-year-old son? Maybe empty nesters who wanted an upgraded house with room enough for their visiting grandkids? In any case, she imagined how pleasant it would be to have someone she could share a chat with in the glow of evening as they waited for their husbands to come home from work or while the kids played in the street, or lend a cup of sugar to, or linger with over a cup of coffee in the mornings after school drop-off, perhaps in that glorious, light-filled kitchen she'd fallen in love with as it was being constructed. Sometimes she even dared to imagine that the two husbands might become friendly, enough that they could invite the new couple over for laughter-filled dinners, maybe even progressive ones that started at the Hale home with the main course and ended next door with dessert and coffee. She told herself that whoever would buy such a big, bright home would certainly be just as expansive and welcoming as the house itself, and she could hardly wait to meet them. Now, after almost eleven months of anticipation, it was finally going to happen. With renewed enthusiasm, she climbed up on the stepladder to perform crape murder on the thin, bare branches of her trees.

~

Martha and Lewis Hale moved into West U, as the tiny, incorporated city within a city was colloquially called, when she was three months pregnant with Harry. Except for the four years Lewis spent in Vermont at Middlebury College studying geography, they'd both lived in Houston their whole lives, a fact that many people found unusual. Most of their friends from high school had scattered like dandelion seeds in the wind, ending up anywhere but their hometown. Houston was the fourth-largest city in the United States, but only a tiny fraction of its residents considered themselves native, or even wanted to be. "So, where are you from?" was typical small talk among Houstonians, the expectation being that everyone there started out somewhere else originally. Of course, there were some deeply rooted families whose pride and permanence in the city was evident, whose surnames appeared on roads, shopping centers, airports, and medical center and university buildings: Cullen, Hermann, Kuykendahl, Hobby, Heyne, Moody. And despite the city's radiating, decades-long sprawl, there were certain geographic enclaves that were protected from overgrowth by zoning and historic preservation that kept the home values high and attracted affluent, educated homeowners, whether they were white-collar families with kids or seniors who loved the area too much to move on when their children left. West U—with its own city government, police, and fire departments; extensive park system; nationally ranked elementary school; and central location near Houston's medical center, sports arenas, and theater and museum districts—was one of them. The only barrier to entry was the expense: fourteen years after the Hales moved in, the median price for a home was over $1 million. Martha knew that the new house next door had been on the market for almost two. She also knew that she and Lewis were lucky to have gotten into the neighborhood when they did; they wouldn't be able to afford even a dirt lot if they tried to buy in now.

~

Martha had grown up with her mother; stepfather; younger sister, Bessie; and older stepbrother, Thomas, in a small Houston subdivision called Larchmont. She'd gone to Mayflower Elementary, Samuel Adams Middle School, Stonewall Jackson High, and then to the University of Houston Honors College for her BFA in photography/digital media. She didn't meet Lewis, who grew up only six miles away in Briargrove Park and went to Hermann High, until after they'd both graduated college and were waiting tables at the same Tex-Mex restaurant while they searched for professional positions. One of the things that both set them apart and drew them together was that they loved the Bayou City and had no desire to live anywhere else.

Maybe because they were the only college graduates on the waitstaff, they gravitated toward each other right from the beginning. They sat next to each other at shift meetings. They chatted while they waited for the bartender to fill their customers' drink orders, in between waiting on tables or running food, and at the end of a shift when they calculated their tips. Lewis wasn't particularly handsome; his hairline was receding already at age twenty-three, his teeth seemed a bit too large for his mouth, his physique was sturdy but unathletic, and he tended to sweat more than average. But he had a nice smile that reached all the way up to his kind brown eyes, a sharp wit and easy laugh, and was preternaturally calm, even when customers were rude or an order got mixed up or he had to take over another section and his workload was suddenly doubled. He never showed up late, never went out drinking with the younger waiters, and never made lewd or tacky comments about the women he worked with or served.

So, a month after they'd begun working together, as they sat side by side rolling silverware before a Sunday brunch shift, Martha took a deep breath and blurted, "Do you want to go see *The Sound of Music* with me at Miller Outdoor Theatre Friday night?" When he turned to look at her, she thought she saw alarm on his face, and she felt her cheeks inflame. She hadn't had a date in more than a year, but she'd told herself it was because she'd been too busy with her studies and graduation and her job search and not because—as she'd worried since high school—she was plain looking or dull. She flipped a red polyester napkin in half, stacked a knife and fork, and began to roll with vigor. "Oh well, you usually work Fridays and Saturdays, so of course you can't. Or wouldn't want to, probably, since that's when we make the most tips." She tucked the loose end into the roll, dropped it in the bin, and reached for another napkin. "I mean I *think* you work Friday nights, I don't actually *know*. It's not like I memorized your schedule." She managed a laugh, which sounded more like a hiccup. "I mean, I haven't even memorized *my* schedule." Stack, roll, tuck, drop. "You know what, forget I said anything. It's supposed to rain anyway, and who wants to sit on the lawn in the rain? I'm sure tickets for the covered seats are probably gone by now, and besides, you probably don't even like *The Sound of Music*." Stack, roll . . .

He put his hand on hers to stop her, and smiled, all the way up to his eyes. "Actually, I do like it," he said. "And I'd love to go, even if it rains."

7

Martha wasn't surprised that Lewis was the first of the two of them to get a position in his chosen field. For a while, she'd fantasized about becoming a photojournalist or working as a staff photographer for a big company or even starting her own wedding photography business. But although her undergraduate portfolio was technically impressive, it lacked the creative spark that everyone seemed to be looking for. Lewis, on the other hand, accepted an offer to be a geographic information systems analyst at an oil and gas company for what seemed like an exorbitant sum. In reality, his annual salary was only slightly more than what he earned waiting tables, but his total compensation package included health insurance, two weeks' paid vacation, retirement-savings matching, possible year-end bonuses, and opportunities for growth.

To celebrate, he invited Martha to dinner at Anton's—a place neither of them had ever been to but that had loomed large in Houston's elite culinary culture for decades. Martha had heard her mother, Evelyn, remark more than once, in a mocking singsong, "Oh, they went to *Anton's*. Well la-di-da. I can't imagine why anyone would want to spend that kind of money on a meal anyway." Martha understood that her mother's derision was really envy in disguise—Evelyn had often intimated that she'd been deprived of the upper-class lifestyle she felt she deserved—so Martha didn't offer any details about her plans with Lewis, though she would've liked some advice on what to wear to such a place and whether she needed to be aware of any special dining etiquette.

She solved the first problem by driving to the restaurant a few days before their date and watching patrons exit their cars at the valet. Then she borrowed an old black velvet skirt from her mother's closet—even though it was mid-March and therefore felt like summer already—and paired it with a white chiffon blouse she'd bought on sale at the off-price department store where she normally shopped. She didn't realize until Lewis was about to pick her up that her outfit looked like her waiter uniform, but with nicer fabric.

After they'd eaten their burrata and gourds (with slow-grilled acorn squash, candied pumpkin seeds, twenty-five-year-old balsamic, and Piedmontese honey that was so delicious Martha would never forget it), shared a salad (spinach, cucumbers, hearts of palm, tomatoes, avocado, red onion, and blue cheese), and splurged on two filets mignons (Martha gasped at the thirty-nine-dollar price per steak, but said nothing, it was a special occasion, la-di-da), the waiter brought out their dessert (Texas blackberry crostata) on a plate covered by a silver cloche. Lewis, who'd been unusually quiet throughout the meal, abruptly stood. Large spills of sweat worked their way down his sleeves, and Martha noticed for the first time that he was wearing one of the starched button-downs that he wore to work—there was a small guacamole stain on the cuff. The waiter lifted the cloche, and as Martha gasped at the tiny glint of a diamond on top of the pie, Lewis knelt by her side.

"I know it's only been eight and a half months," he began.

Martha, who'd never felt desired by any man before, not even the one she'd lost her virginity to on a dare their senior year in high school, nor by the drunken fraternity boy she'd given a ride home to and then spent the night with her sophomore year of college, nor by the assistant professor who'd screwed her after every Fundamentals of Sculpture class the spring semester of her junior year but never took her out on a date, dropped from her chair and knelt down in front of Lewis.

"Yes," she said.

"But I didn't even ask you."

"Ask me what?"

"If you'll marry me."

"Yes!" she said, and laughed. Lewis laughed, too, relieved if confused, and took the ring from the pie and placed it on Martha's finger. They kissed, still kneeling beside the table like petitioners, and the onlookers, who'd appeared concerned at first by the unusual disruption, clapped politely.

Martha's parents were delighted by the announcement of their engagement, even though they'd met Lewis only twice and the couple was so young—Martha, twenty-two, and Lewis, twenty-four—because he came from a good family, and also, for as long as anyone could remember, Martha's greatest ambition was to get married and have babies. Lots of them. At least five, she'd always said. Her biological father had died when Martha was only two, and for many years, it was just Martha; her sister, Bessie; and their mother. When her mother remarried seven years later, Martha begged her and her new stepfather to have a baby. Her mother laughed. "Are you kidding? I'm almost thirty-eight! That's what obstetricians call 'advanced maternal age.' I'm practically a crone."

Martha figured that she'd need to start early if she was going to have five children before she reached advanced maternal age herself. As she got older, however, and emerged from her awkward preteen years into yet more awkward teen years, she worried that she might not find someone to have all those babies with. "Of course you'll find someone, honey," her mother would tell her. "There's a lid for every pot. Even you." Martha remained cautiously optimistic until the sculpture professor told her he couldn't see her anymore because he'd started dating someone. After that, she wondered if her parents would let her continue living at home indefinitely, and if she should put aside money for eventual sperm donation.

With their parents' blessing, Martha and Lewis set a date for a wedding the following spring. Her mother was thrilled; finally, she'd have a chance to throw a party that people would talk about long afterward. If they did things right, it might even end up in Shelby Hodgkin's society section of the newspaper. Right away, her mother and future mother-in-law made plans to get the families together, and offered to help scout venues and shop for wedding gowns. Evelyn called the church to reserve a date, and wanted to schedule a brunch for Martha's bridesmaids, insisting that it wasn't too early to get their input on things like color schemes and dresses. But while Martha appreciated the attention and enthusiasm, she was a little overwhelmed by the fanfare that lay ahead. Besides her sister, she didn't know who she'd ask to be a bridesmaid. Her cousin on her late father's side, maybe. She didn't have a lot of close girlfriends. She was friendly with her coworkers but didn't think of them as friends. And because U of H was considered a commuter school, she hadn't had what she thought of as a "real" college experience: a roommate and suite-mates, sorority sisters, fraternity parties. For the most part, students were on campus only during classes and then went home or to work afterward. And since she didn't stay in touch with anyone from high school, she couldn't think of how she'd assemble a whole bridal party.

The truth was, for all her fantasies of motherhood, she'd rarely thought about the future father of her children. She wanted a husband, of course. Wanted a whole family, not just the babies. Maybe it was because of the many years she'd spent without a father, or maybe it was because she hadn't had much experience with romance and boyfriends, but for whatever reason, she'd neglected to imagine her own wedding. Which was why, at a cake-tasting luncheon with their mothers two months after Lewis proposed, Martha whispered, "Why don't we just elope?"

His eyes widened and a look of great anticipation came onto his face. "Really?" he whispered back.

She nodded and they giggled like children. She felt as relieved as Lewis looked, and the following Friday afternoon, with their disappointed mothers and other family members in attendance, they said their "I dos" at the county courthouse.

Almost a year later, on the night of the first anniversary of their engagement, their son, Lewis Harrison "Harry" Hale Jr., was conceived. Almost immediately, Martha started house-hunting. Their rented duplex in the artsy Montrose area was affordable but too small for a nursery. Lewis, who liked to consider all options before making any important decisions, suggested they drive systematically to all of the communities on their list to get a feel for each; then they would narrow it down to two or three neighborhoods before searching for any homes. Martha, who'd long since anticipated this next phase of their lives, already knew that she wanted them to live in the Eden of West U, but because of the exorbitant home prices there, she wisely plotted for Lewis to come to the same conclusion on his own.

She bought tickets to see Puccini's *La Bohème* at Opera in the Heights on a Friday night, and suggested she pick him up from his office early so they could check out the historic Heights neighborhood and have dinner beforehand. If they'd gone on a Saturday, Lewis might've been enchanted by the tree-canopied esplanades and the walkable shopping district, but because they sat in bumper-to-bumper traffic on the notoriously congested I-610 freeway for forty-five minutes just to travel seven miles, Martha had only to say, "Oh, I'd hate for you to have to make *this* drive twice a day" before Lewis scratched it off their list. Likewise, after driving around the southwest subdivisions of Braeswood, Meyerland, and Willowbend during a heavy rainstorm, Martha expressed concern about flooding. "All the commercial development upstream is eventually going to affect how much stormwater these areas can soak up. Someday we're going to get another Tropical Storm Allison—or worse." After dinner at his parents' house one evening, throughout which his mother talked nonstop about the baby, and schools, and outfits, and how she'd like to be very, very involved with everything, Martha suggested they drive around his childhood neighborhood as well as nearby Memorial and Spring Branch. "What, and give my mother unfettered access to our daily lives? No, thank you."

All along, under the guise of other interests, Martha had been leading Lewis through West U—taking the scenic route to her OB-GYN appointments in the medical center, to have dinner at the cantina on Buffalo Speedway, to swim slow laps at Colonial Pool to alleviate the aches and pains of early pregnancy. She offered to drive, insisting that he relax, that he'd been working so hard all day, that he should leave the navigating to her. And in this way, passively gazing out the window, he observed the tree-lined streets and the unbroken sidewalks where helmeted children rode tiny bicycles with their neatly dressed parents or friends, and families and couples walked their well-behaved dogs whose droppings they picked up with little biodegradable trash bags. He saw neighbors chatting at the seams between their yards, which were bursting in bloom with pink and white azalea bushes, fathers playing catch with their kids, smoke rising from backyard grills. As she detoured around one of the many parks, he took in the dozens of children screaming with delight as they swung or clambered along on the playground equipment.

After one of these trips, he turned to her and said, "You know, maybe we should consider West U."

She lifted a shoulder. "They do have one of the best public elementary schools in the country," she said as casually as she could. "And I know the home values have only gone up, even during recessions. But isn't it out of our budget?"

"Well, we'd need to tighten our belts some," he said, and then laughed. He placed his hand against the pooch of her belly. "As much as we can anyway. But we have the no-wedding money your parents gave us plus what we've been saving. I think my parents will loan us enough to cover a decent down payment. And if all goes well, I'll be getting a raise this year. So, yeah, I think we should take a look."

They saw ten houses of various styles and ages that following Saturday, from original bungalows to mideighties Colonials to contemporary stucco mansions, eyes wider each time they entered one. It wasn't just that the homes were more stately or beautiful than the ones they'd grown up in, although for the most part that was true; it was the awareness that they were on the cusp of crossing a much more significant threshold than mere homeownership—they might actually be moving into one of the oldest and most exclusive neighborhoods in Houston, which their perky real estate agent called "a modern Mayberry, USA." In spite of her meticulous daydreaming, research, and planning for this opportunity, Martha hadn't quite actually believed it could happen to her—ever, really, but especially so early on.

It was the tenth house they saw that day—and the least expensive, miraculously on the market for only $1,000 above their maximum budget—that caused Martha to press herself up against Lewis's soft chest, before they'd even looked inside, and say, "Buy me this house." Facing south on a six-thousand-square-foot lot on Alcott Street between two other older houses, the cross-gabled bungalow had white shiplap siding, double-hung windows with black fixed shutters across the front, and Chippendale railings leading up to a small covered porch. Four crape myrtle trees with bright-fuchsia flowers were interspersed with neatly rounded boxwoods. Tucked into the louvers of the circular gable vent was a small bird's nest that brought to mind Martha's favorite childhood book, P. D. Eastman's *The Best Nest*, and made her almost weep with tenderness at the idea of a little flock of baby doves incubating above the entry of what she felt in her heart should be their own child's first home. It didn't matter to Martha that it was small, only fifteen hundred square feet. There were three bedrooms and two full baths, a decent-size kitchen, plenty of room for their burgeoning family. There was an old oak tree in the backyard that cast a lovely shade, and a two-car garage with a finished guest room above it that had been built just the year before.

Lewis seemed to be as taken with it as she was. He stood on the sidewalk with his fists on his hips, appraising the exterior as though they already owned it. "There's a slat missing on one of the shutters, but I think I can fix that."

"If anyone can, it's you," Martha said, wrapping her arms around him. The truth was, of course, that if anyone could fix it, it was her, but she didn't mind giving him the credit, the same way she didn't feel bad complimenting him on his hair or dress or the way he scrambled eggs. She wouldn't want to build a house on top of fibs like these, but such small untruths were like spackle filling the tiny holes in otherwise sturdy walls.

Just as she entered her second trimester, Martha worked her last shift at the restaurant, relieved to be finally done with waiting tables even though she still hadn't found what she thought of as a "real" job, and they moved in on a typically sweltering weekend in July. Lewis wanted to hire professional movers, but after getting three different quotes for more than $2,000, Martha insisted they could do it themselves. "I'm four months pregnant, not an invalid. Mom and I'll pack while you're at work, and we can get the dads to help get the heavier stuff on and off the rental truck," she said.

It was much more exhausting than she'd thought, especially with the heat. More than once they had to stop, even while holding an obviously heavy item, to avoid running into one kid or another zooming down the sidewalk on their bike. Did these children have no manners? Did they not see Martha and Lewis standing there? As they made trip after trip into the house, she couldn't help thinking that one of their new neighbors would surely come over and offer help, or at least a glass of lemonade from the stand some kids had set up down the street. She made an effort to stick her stomach out, hoping her pregnancy might inspire someone's empathy. But as the hours wore on, nobody even stopped by to introduce themselves and welcome the Hales to the block. Only when they were nearly finished did a woman emerging from the large Colonial across the street with her dog seem to take notice of them. Martha waved at her with great enthusiasm and called out, "Hi, neighbor!"

The woman looked startled, but after a moment of apparent hesitation, she walked over to the truck. "Hello. Are you moving in?" she asked. Martha could tell by the way she spoke that she wasn't a native Texan, but she was trying hard to sound like one.

"We sure are! I'm Martha Hale, and that's my husband, Lewis, and my father-in-law who just went in the house."

"It's amazing y'all are moving yourselves. Good for you," the woman said with a curl on her lip that Martha hoped was genuine. "We moved in last year and I refused to touch a single box. I'm Lillian Mickelsen. My husband, Daniel, and I have two girls, Madeleine and Noelle. Do you have any kids?"

Martha patted her stomach through her overalls. "In six months, we will! A boy. Oh, we're so excited to be here. Are your girls old enough to babysit? Not that we'll need a babysitter right away, but it's good to know there's someone close by who might be able to help out when the time comes. Or maybe a mother's helper? I'm not really sure what the right age to start babysitting is these days. I babysat for the neighbors starting around thirteen, I think, but that's been a while! Well, you're ahead of me—I don't mean in age, of course. Well, maybe you're older, I have no idea, but if you are, then I need to know your secrets, you look amazing." *Oh hush, Martha.* She wanted to sound as self-possessed as Lillian seemed. "Anyway, I meant you're ahead of me in the kid department, so maybe you can give me some tips on babysitting and, well, anything kid-related I guess!" Martha's laugh sounded nervous even to herself. Lillian shifted her weight and gave her an uneasy smile. Martha bent down to pat the dog's obviously coiffed white pouf of fur. "What's your poodle's name?"

"It's Beignet. And he's actually a bichon frise."

"Oh right," Martha said. "Of course."

"We need to get on with our walk before I melt out here, but it was nice meeting you."

"Yes, very nice meeting you, too, Lillian. I hope we'll get to know each other. Thanks for coming over!"

"Of course we will," Lillian said, and then tugged on Beignet's leash, waving over her shoulder as they walked away. Martha noticed how trim and tanned Lillian's legs were beneath her white shorts, how straight and silky her light-brown hair looked, even in 90 percent humidity. As she smoothed her own sweaty, reddish-blonde hair back into its ponytail, she could feel how frizzy it was.

~

As it turned out, however, she and Lillian had only a handful of interactions in the almost fifteen years since. Their life stages were off by the wrong number of years; her daughters were too young to babysit but too old to be interested in little Harry, and even as the children grew, their ages and genders kept them from overlapping in school or sports. Anyway, especially right after Harry was born, Martha was too busy at home to think about Lillian or anyone else. She enjoyed chatting with other young mothers and their babies at the West U library for story time, and at the fast-food place near the medical center that had family nights with face painting and clowns, and at the park, where they spent hours nearly every day. But she discovered how difficult it was to do anything for herself while caring for a newborn. Even when Harry got to the toddler stage, just keeping them all fed, and the house clean, and the laundry done seemed like an impossible goal. Many days she couldn't find time even for a shower, much less for cultivating meaningful friendships with other women.

Then as they began trying for a second child—Martha hoped for a girl next—without success, and endured one miscarriage and then another, and sought treatment for what seemed to be a fertility issue, and put all their hope into each of three IVF attempts, Martha watched the bellies of those other women at the library and the park begin to swell with their second and third pregnancies. She smiled and congratulated them when they returned, pushing fresh babies in their strollers as their older children walked and toddled alongside. But their fecundity made her feel self-conscious, so instead of trying to join their playgroups and book clubs, she focused on her family, taking excellent care of her son and husband, improving her cooking skills, keeping house, trying to make the best of things. When she was desperate for female support and company, she had her mother and her mother-in-law, and for a long time, that passed for enough.

Which was why, when a huge moving truck parked in front of the house next door on the late-February Saturday two weeks after the SOLD sign went up, Martha dashed into her backyard to harvest four large Meyer lemons from her tree and went inside to make a batch of lemon bars from a recipe she'd been practicing for the occasion. She'd failed to make a friend out of Lillian, and this was her chance to try again with someone else.

"The new neighbors are moving in!" she told Lewis, who was reading a copy of *Geographic Information Systems Monthly*.

"Oh good," he said without looking up.

While the lemon bars were baking, she quickly showered and dried her hair, applied a bit of makeup, which she rarely ever did anymore, and put on an outfit that felt far too dressy but which many women in the neighborhood seemed to wear almost as a uniform: white skinny jeans (hers seemed to have shrunk since she wore them last), a denim shirt (by itself or over a tank top), and flats. Martha had outgrown her version of the other neighborhood uniform of yoga pants with a sleeveless top and maybe a light wrap, so that wasn't an option. It seemed like everyone was always on their way to or from a studio class or the gym, and not just because of their wardrobes; the average clothing size in West U was at least three smaller than anywhere else in Houston. For the past fourteen years, Martha had been trying and failing to lose the twenty pounds she thought made her still look like she didn't belong. She didn't own a lot of jewelry, but she was proud of what she had. She put on her grandmother's diamond studs and the turquoise necklace Lewis had given her for Christmas the year before.

"How do I look?" she asked. She waited a beat. "Lewis!" His head snapped up. "I said, how do I look?"

"Oh. You look great. Why are you so dressed up?"

"I told you, the neighbors are moving in."

"Wait, I don't have to change, do I?" He looked down at his old T-shirt and gym shorts that were snug across his waist. "Are we supposed to be doing something with them?"

"I just wanted to make a good impression is all." She sighed.

"Okay, good," he said, and went back to the article he was reading.

By now she knew that nobody hauled their own furniture into their new West U home, so she peered out the window on the west side of her living room, ignoring the hired men carrying load after load, and waited for the new neighbors to appear.

Finally, long after the lemon bars had gone cold and she was getting hungry for lunch, a white Lexus SUV pulled into the driveway between the two houses. Martha clasped her hands together and called out toward Lewis, "They're pulling up!"

"Marty, you shouldn't stand there gaping out the window," he called back. She rolled her eyes, even though he couldn't see her.

When a tall, slender woman with long blonde hair and oversize sunglasses hopped out of the driver's seat and walked around to the other side, Martha felt a pinch of uncertainty; the woman looked impossibly elegant, even in what looked like a silk robe over baggy jeans. The kind of chic that looked effortless because it probably actually was. She also looked familiar. There was a forward slant to her long gait, as though she were inhabiting not just the space she walked through but also what was just in front of her. It made her look powerful, even predatory, which oddly contrasted with her delicate hands and the gentle tilt of her head. She'd known someone who moved like that once, long ago.

"No way," Martha said, pressing herself first closer to then away from the window.

"What?" Lewis called.

"I think I know her."

The anticipation of making a new friend had been building steadily inside her since the day the house was sold, but suddenly a sense of possibility ballooned as though with helium, and she felt like she was lifted off the ground. There was some anxiety, too, as an unpleasant memory involving this woman returned, as it had occasionally over the years. It felt like some sort of karmic sign. She grabbed the plate of bars— not a disposable plastic container; a real plate ensured the neighbor would have to return it—and jog-walked across her small yard. "Minnie Foster!" she called out, nervous but beaming with delight. "Is that you?"

The woman had just pulled a small birdcage from her front seat and spun around toward Martha. Her face was as lovely as ever, smooth and clear skinned as though the past two decades had passed by without touching her. She smiled at Martha, but when she pushed her sunglasses on top of her head, her eyes were obviously searching for the connection. "Yes?" she said.

Martha leaned forward, as though examining the detail on a statue. "For half a second, I thought I was wrong. You look a little bit different, but it *is* you."

Minnie's hand flew up and touched her nose. "And you're . . . ?"

"It's me! Martha Pagnell! Well, now it's Martha Hale, but back then it was Pagnell."

"Martha . . ."

"From high school! Stonewall Jackson, I mean, not the one you went to in California."

Minnie winced, even as she smiled with her lovely white teeth clamped tight. "God, I'm sorry. I just can't quite place you. Forgive me."

As quickly as it had swelled, Martha's excitement deflated. Why did she think Minnie Foster would remember her? "No, no, of course." She tried to laugh it off, to hide her disappointment as much from herself as from Minnie. "I mean, it's been a while. We graduated twenty years ago, for goodness' sake! So much has happened since then, how can we possibly remember everybody we went to school with? Although I was on the yearbook committee, so I might actually remember everybody. I took a lot of pictures of the classrooms and clubs and pep rallies and stuff."

Minnie studied her for a moment. "Wait! I think I remember you now. Were we in English together?"

Martha scrunched her nose. "No, but we were in choir together junior year. And Spanish and chemistry senior year. And I took your portrait for Most Beautiful Senior."

"Of course! Martha Pagnell. I remember that picture. It was really great, the composition and lighting. It was more like an oil painting than a photograph. My dad kept it in a frame on his desk until he died."

Martha blushed and smiled—Minnie did remember her! And she had liked her portrait! Then she remembered her manners. "I'm so sorry to hear about your father."

"Thanks." Minnie looked down at the bird inside the cage.

"Mine died, too, when I was a toddler. He choked on a piece of steak, of all things."

"My, that's awful."

Martha made a dismissive gesture with her free hand. "It was hard for my mother, of course, but I don't even remember him. My stepfather raised me."

Minnie paused, nodded. "Anyway, it's so nice to see you. I'm guessing you live nearby?"

"I live next door! Can you believe it? What are the chances? Oh my gosh, I can't believe it's you!" Without thinking, she leaned forward to embrace her just as Minnie shifted the birdcage so that it was directly between them. Martha backed away, embarrassed again.

"Sorry," Minnie said. "This is Bonnie." She cocked her head and said to the delicate-looking yellow-and-blue parakeet, "Aren't you, my beautiful girl? Bonnie the budgie. I'm going to put you down for just a second, don't worry." She placed the cage carefully on the driveway and turned to Martha. "I'm sorry I didn't recognize you at first. I think

21

I might be losing my mind. It's been crazy with the move back to Houston. We've lived in Seattle for the past eight years, but when my husband got . . . when he got a new job here, everything happened kind of fast. Tying up loose ends, packing, selling the house, all that." Minnie spun the large diamond ring around and around her wedding finger. "With all the sudden newness, it's nice to see a familiar face."

Martha relaxed and returned to a feeling of anticipation. Minnie Foster was going to be her next-door neighbor! She smiled and handed Minnie the tinfoil-covered plate. "Here, I made these for you. I hope you like them. They're so easy, really, and I grow my own lemons, so if you want more, just let me know."

To Martha's great delight, Minnie accepted them and gave her a warm hug. "That is so sweet of you. Thank you."

"We'd love to have your family over for dinner soon. Do you have kids?"

Minnie gave a weak smile. "No. Not yet, anyway."

"Oh boy, that's tough," Martha said. The way Minnie had emphasized the word *yet* made Martha want to reach out and hug her again. "We only have one, a boy. After he was born, we tried for years for another but it didn't work out. I developed endometriosis after my C-section, but the doctor said it was only stage two and probably wouldn't cause problems, but I guess it did. I finally gave up just before my thirty-fifth birthday because by then, I'd be in the high-risk age group." Just then it occurred to her that she and Minnie were almost exactly the same age. Martha sucked in a breath of air and clamped a hand over her mouth to keep any more words from flying out of it. "Oh, forgive me! I can't believe I just said that. I'm such a dummy. It was too late for me, but I didn't mean to suggest it was too late for you, or that you were too old. I've got to learn how to keep my mouth shut."

"No, it's fine," Minnie said.

"It's not! I'm so sorry. It's just that by then, my son, Harry, was already ten, and really that was why I stopped. The age difference would've been too big is all. Plenty of women have babies at our age. Lots of them in this neighborhood, actually, because of their careers. They get started later." Martha took a desperate breath and let it out. "I'm sure you'll make a wonderful mother."

"Thank you. You're sweet."

Martha didn't feel sweet at all, but she was grateful to be let off the hook so kindly. "Okay, well, we'd love to have the two of you over. You and . . . ?"

"John. I'm Minnie Wright now. He works a lot, you know, so it's hard to find time, but we'd love that." Minnie squeezed Martha's hand. "I'd really love that."

Martha felt like she'd just been crowned homecoming queen after years of disregard. She wanted to squeal, to grab Minnie's hands and dance in a circle. Instead she forced herself to simply smile and nod. "You're busy, I'm sure. I'll let you get settled—that is, unless you need any help?—and then we'll pick a night for you and John to come over. You'll meet my family, Lewis and Harry. And I can't wait to hear all about your life. It must be so exciting. I've never been to Seattle. We'll do it soon, okay?"

"Thank you. I'll be looking forward to it." Minnie's face was calm and lovely as she picked up the birdcage. She looped her index finger into the ring at the top and laced the others into the wire grill with such force and care that her fingers grew pale at the knuckles. She lifted the cage slowly toward Martha. "Say goodbye, Bonnie."

"Goodbye, Bonnie!" Martha said, echoing Minnie's singsong voice as she noticed, then disregarded, Minnie's odd, tenacious grip on the cage, and the two women laughed.

Two

M innie Foster arrived at Stonewall Jackson High School, home
of the Jackson Generals, six weeks into her junior year. On
Minnie's first day, Martha watched from the sidewalk as she maneuvered her metallic-blue BMW among the trucks and used family sedans
into the seniors-only parking lot, something on the pop radio station
blaring through the open windows, and found a space close to the
athletic field. Normally, the upperclassmen who hung out there before
the first bell would shout at any newcomers or underclassmen who
dared try to sneak into their lot until they moved. But when Minnie
unfurled herself from her car, tucking her flipped-up bob behind her ear
and looking around at her new campus from behind dark sunglasses,
she exuded an air of casual glamour that seemed to outshine the bright
October morning. Staring, no one said anything when she walked past
them toward the main entrance, and when she lifted her hand in greeting, they each did the same in return.

The gossip started immediately.

"She's from California," someone said. "Her license plates said
Marina del Rey."

"Did you see that car? It's brand new. Must be nice, huh? But man,
why would you buy it in that hideous blue color?"

"She's from Hollywood."

"She was from Houston originally, but they moved to California when she was, like, six or seven for her mom's job."

"I knew her in kindergarten at Briarpatch Elementary. I remember one time she got mad at this kid named Ryan and she hit him in the face with the chalkboard eraser."

"I heard she was a model. She looks like a model."

"Her mother is an actress. Or maybe it was a director. I don't know, but she had something to do with the movie *Se7en*."

"She was in the movie *Se7en*!"

"She's friends with Brad Pitt."

"She's a total rich bitch."

"I think it's just her and her dad. My grandmother knows her grandmother. Don't say anything, but I think her mom's dead."

"Wait, y'all. Did she kill her own mother?"

"I hear she's going to try out for cheerleader."

"We tried to talk to her after chemistry, but she barely looked at us. What a snob."

"Somebody said she was making eyes at Charlie Baxter. Who does she think she is that she can just walk in and start dating the hottest senior guy on her first day of school?"

"She thinks just because she's from the West Coast she's so much better than us."

"I guess that's how they do their hair in California."

"Her locker's three down from mine and I swear I smelled pot."

"Probably the reason she never talks to anybody is because she's totally stoned. Either that or she's stuck-up. Or maybe both."

Martha contributed her own opinion. "She's in choir with me eighth period. I don't think she's conceited. She smiled at me when I accidentally bumped into her."

As her reputation was dragged through the mud that first day and for the rest of that week, Minnie seemed to float through the halls completely unaware of what was being said behind her back. She spoke only when spoken to directly, and even then it hardly counted as conversation. Each of these interactions, in which she demonstrated her unusual sangfroid, further provoked the other students' pique and solidified the general opinion that Minnie had clearly forgotten her southern roots, if she'd in fact even had them at all. They didn't quite know how to deal with someone who refused to slot herself willingly into the hierarchy, so after they'd exhausted the creative limits of their slanderous claims against her and found her still unresponsive, they gradually moved on to other petty concerns.

Martha was as fascinated by Minnie Foster as the rest of them, but for different reasons. She didn't think Minnie had killed her mother, for goodness' sake, or was even capable of hitting a fellow kindergartner. Sure, she might've been rich—what sixteen-year-old who drove a new BMW wasn't?—and she was really pretty, but that didn't make her a bitch or a snob. And in the middle of third period, under the guise of needing to use the girls' room, Martha had sniffed the metal slats on Minnie's locker. She had heard that marijuana smelled like skunk, and Minnie's locker definitely did not smell like that.

To Martha, Minnie was like the clouded leopards she'd always loved glimpsing in their habitat at the zoo: slinky and private, they preferred to remain alone and hidden from view. Because of that, their activity patterns were virtually unknown. Minnie's seemed to be as well: she didn't eat lunch in the cafeteria; she didn't hang out in the bleachers after school. Martha wasn't a solitary creature by choice, nor did she think of herself as elegant and mysterious as a clouded leopard, but she knew what it was like to live on the outer edges of the in-group.

For this, and virtually no other reason except the brief smile Minnie had given her in choir, Martha sensed an unlikely kinship with the new girl. The only problem was that, because she wasn't good at socializing, she didn't know how to let Minnie in on it.

What Martha was good at was observing. When she was young, her mother put her in ballet and karate classes, signed her up for swim team and soccer and Brownies, bought her a bike and urged her on most Saturday mornings to go out and make some friends. She wanted Martha to be like she'd been: pretty, popular, the belle of the ball. But Martha wasn't good at sports or dancing or convincing strangers to be her friend. "I don't know why a chatterbox like you has such a hard time talking to people your own age!" Evelyn had said, exasperated. Martha wasn't bad looking, but even her mother conceded that she wasn't a classic beauty. She looked like a scaled-down version of her biological father, who'd been an offensive lineman for the University of Texas football team. When all else failed, Martha's mother enrolled her in an improv workshop, suggesting that if she couldn't be the pretty girl, she could at least be the funny one. It all made Martha want to hide in her room.

But on Martha's fourteenth birthday, her stepfather gave her a Minolta 600si and ten rolls of film and spent a weekend teaching her about exposure, depth of field, and composition. She hardly had a bad day again after that. Not only did she love the mechanical and creative aspects of photography and printmaking, but a camera was an ideal prop in social settings, as either a shield she could hide behind or an excuse to engage with people she'd otherwise be too intimidated to approach. Sometimes she didn't even click the shutter because film and developing were expensive, but she carried her camera everywhere and looked through the viewfinder to practice, playing with the settings, imagining the final image. When she did make pictures, they often turned out better than she expected, and occasionally, much better. She liked the quiet power that came with photography, too: the ability to both capture and expose.

All she wanted for Christmas that year was film and money for processing, which she received. At the end of her freshman year, she talked the art teacher into establishing a photography club. By the end of her sophomore year, she had converted an old supply closet into a darkroom and was the main photo contributor to both the school paper and the yearbook committee with a budget that covered her expenses. Though still not the popular girl her mother imagined she'd become, everyone was used to seeing the plump redhead whose frizzy bangs were always clipped back with a bobby pin, who wore clothes that always smelled like fixer, and who had a camera perpetually pressed against her right eye.

Nobody seemed to notice or care, then, when Martha turned her quiet focus to the exotic and elusive Minnie.

~

Juniors weren't allowed off campus for lunch, but they were allowed to go outside to the plaza or the lawn to eat. Someone had mentioned seeing Minnie wandering around the far edge of the campus alone the first couple of days, listening to her Discman. (*No wonder she's so thin*, they said, when they were still overly preoccupied by her. *She walks instead of eating. Has anyone actually seen her eat?*) So, on the Monday of Minnie's second week at Jackson High, Martha, who often spent that hour in the darkroom, screwed a telephoto lens onto her camera body and went out to look for her.

Beyond the track and football field was a small stand of cedar elms that provided a broad canopy of shade but where a year or so before, a four-foot-long green snake had dropped out of the branches and onto the captain of the girls track team. The entire team had erupted in shrieks that could be heard across the athletic field while the captain frantically swatted at and shimmied beneath the nonvenomous and probably equally startled snake until it fell from her shoulders and slithered away. The girl had to be taken to the hospital for her hysteria, and nobody had ventured anywhere near the trees since. But that's where Martha spotted Minnie, weaving among the tree trunks, looking up into the swaying boughs and singing.

She couldn't hear her, of course; she was too far away. But even at a distance, Martha could see that Minnie's shoulders were relaxed and her arms were moving in a graceful rhythm. She could imagine the beauty of her voice, rising and falling on the wind. Moving to the side of the field house where she wouldn't be easily seen, Martha lifted her camera and focused.

Unguarded, Minnie's face was even lovelier than Martha had previously thought. Walking through the halls, or in class, or at her locker, Minnie's eyes were usually downcast, her brow furrowed, her full lips pressed into a straight line. But now, through the camera lens, she looked happy. Untroubled. Approachable. Martha clicked the shutter.

Immediately, she felt guilty, as though she had taken something that didn't belong to her. She'd taken hundreds, maybe thousands, of photos of students, but always with permission. Strangers or people who showed up in backgrounds didn't count because she didn't feel a connection to them. But now she had glimpsed Minnie in a private, unguarded moment, and trapped some part of her forever on a thin layer of gelatin emulsion containing microscopically small silver halide crystals. For the first time since she'd owned her camera, she recognized the power she wielded: to shoot, to capture, to expose.

She used an entire 36-exposure roll of black-and-white film on Minnie, zooming in on her facial features as she moved through the dappled sunlight, on her hair as it played in the breeze, on her hands as they conducted whatever song she was singing. Guilt notwithstanding, she'd have liked to have taken more, but she'd brought only the one roll. Instead she just watched Minnie through the viewfinder until the bell rang and it was time to go back to reality.

The next afternoon, Martha developed the negatives and printed her favorites. After she clipped the dripping photographs to the drying lines, she examined each of them in the red glow of the safelight. Together, the images revealed a very different person from the one the other students had identified: someone who loved nature and music, who was comfortable in her own skin, comfortable being alone. There was one in which Minnie was gazing upward at something, and Martha pulled it down to look at it more closely. When she'd taken the photo, Martha hadn't noticed what Minnie had been looking at but now could see that it was a plump little bird, maybe a goldfinch or a blue jay, and it was gazing right back at Minnie. There was a look of profound tenderness on Minnie's face that made Martha feel a prick of jealousy. She'd have liked to have been that bird, preening under Minnie's lovely gaze. But almost as quickly as the thought arrived, Martha shook her head as though to rid herself of such a ridiculous idea, and clipped the photograph back to the line.

She did allow herself to feel a little special for having seen something in Minnie that nobody else at school that week either could or would. Martha realized that *they*, in fact, were the jerks, so ready to ostracize someone for being unusual. It made her feel a sudden stir of protectiveness toward Minnie, as well as a renewed determination to become her friend.

Maybe she would propose doing a feature on Minnie to the editor of the school paper, and offer to conduct and write the interview to go along with some pictures. Martha might suggest to Minnie that they go out to the elm grove, where they could talk privately, and where she could re-create the images she'd already taken. She couldn't use those; it might look like she'd been spying. Maybe later, after they'd become familiar enough to share their secrets, Martha would show her the images. Minnie wouldn't think Martha had done anything wrong or weird; she'd be flattered that someone had cared enough to seek out and recognize her true self.

But first, Martha imagined, they'd do the interview, and as they talked, Minnie would get to know Martha, too. She'd learn that Martha was a good and sincere person, a fellow creative spirit, and someone who was also misunderstood by the conformists and snobs they went to school with. Maybe Minnie would suggest going to her house to hang out. Martha could already smell the interior of Minnie's shiny sports car, feel the October air flowing across her arm as she draped it on the open sill, hear the sound of their commingled laughter as they tooled around town. They'd go to the movies and the mall. They'd sneak off campus to get ice cream at the parlor next to the stripper club, and on Sundays sneak up to the rooftop pool at the Galleria to lay out, like all the cheerleaders allegedly did. Together, they'd become a force. People would invite them to their keg parties and sleepovers, and they'd be a package deal: What are Minnie and Martha doing? Did you ask Martha and Minnie to come? Even Martha's parents would come to expect Minnie at their dinner table or to join them on their weekend jaunts to their cabin in the country eighty miles northwest of Houston, where they'd swim in the lake, visit the old Czech cemeteries, and play pool and drink Cokes at the Welcome Store. It was so clear in Martha's imagination, it was like it had already happened.

~

The following day, the choir teacher asked Martha to meet before class to talk about doing headshots of the singers for the school's upcoming winter concert program. The lead soloist, a girl named Nellie whose mother always donated the props for their performances—including her own brass bed for a scene in *Hairspray* their freshman year—and who'd been working on her rendition of "Santa Baby" and "Winter Lullaby" for weeks already, had just come down with mono and was going to be out for the rest of the semester.

"There's nobody else who can sing like Nellie does," the choir teacher said as she paced the length of the choir room, her hot-pink cowboy boots kicking out from beneath a full prairie skirt. Her teased platinum-blonde hair was a decade out of style and sprayed into the kind of submission she expected from her students. "It's not that she's good, particularly, just that she's *invested*. Or I thought she was, before she went and got herself infected with the kissing disease, that little slut. Now I'm going to have to change everything. Everything! And obviously we'll need another headshot, as soon as I can figure out who to replace her with."

The words were out of Martha's mouth before she'd fully considered the consequences. "Have you heard Minnie Foster sing?"

The choir teacher stopped and narrowed her eyes. "The new girl?"

Martha nodded. "She's really, really good."

"Are you sure? How do you know?"

Martha looked away from the teacher's eager stare and swallowed hard. "I heard her," she said. It wasn't really a lie, just more like an assumption.

"This is excellent news. Excellent. I'll audition her today."

Martha nodded again. The truth was that she'd only heard Minnie whispering the words to "Jingle Bells" in class. It had sounded in tune and pleasing—but perhaps, she had to admit, only to her. When she'd found Minnie among the trees, Martha had filled in the quiet space between them with imaginary talent—but she didn't know for sure that Minnie was actually any good. What if she wasn't? Oh, but of course she was. Minnie had appeared to be—using the choir teacher's word—*invested*. People who couldn't sing didn't wander around pantomiming a serious performance if they couldn't make good on it.

The bell rang.

Students poured in, excited by the encroaching final bell and the fact that this was their easiest class of the day. Martha took her place on the third riser, nearish to the spot Minnie seemed to have assigned herself. Sure enough, when she arrived just before the second bell and dropped her messenger bag against the wall, Minnie climbed up and stood at the far end of the row. Martha tried to catch her eye to give her an encouraging smile, but Minnie only looked down at her interlaced fingers as everyone settled in around her.

The teacher rapped on the music stand with her conductor's baton, and the room grew quiet. "Y'all know Nellie's out for the concert, right?" A small murmur rose and she pulled her left hand in, closing her fingers to taper away their noise. "Well, apparently we have a gifted replacement right here in our midst. Minnie Foster, come down here a minute."

Minnie jerked her head up so fast her hair actually bounced. Her lips parted and her eyebrows pulled her eyes open wide.

"Come on down here, sugar." The teacher patted her thigh as though beckoning a dog.

Minnie darted her glance around the room, but again not at Martha, whose eager smile was ready just in case.

"Minnie, I know you're new, and you don't know me yet, but rest assured I suffer no foolishness under any circumstances. I have it on good authority you can sing, so get down here right now."

Very slowly, as though moving through floodwater, Minnie made her way to the front of the room. Once there, she stood with her head down, staring at the shoes of the boy on the first row. Martha felt the smile slide off her cheeks.

The teacher handed Minnie a sheet of music. "Everybody knows 'Rudolph the Red-Nosed Reindeer,' but nobody ever remembers the first stanza with all the names, so just sing off that. Ready?" She made a show of bending down to peer under Minnie's curtain of hair, then lifted her chin with a single finger. Nobody made a sound, but there was a wild pulse of energy in the room. "All right now, Minnie. You can do this. And a-one, and a-two, and . . ."

Nothing.

"You want to be shy, that's fine. But singing in my class is not optional. We all have to put up with things in life that make us uncomfortable. That's how we grow. You understand me?" the teacher said. Minnie nodded almost imperceptibly. "Okay then. I'll sing along with you, get you started, all right?" Minnie nodded again.

"And a-one, and a-two, and . . . 'You know Dasher and Dancer and Prancer and Vixen'—louder!—'Comet and Cupid and Donner and Blitzen.'" The teacher's face was animated and her voice rang big and velvety, while Minnie kept her eyes on the sheet music and mumbled the lyrics. "Louder, Minnie! 'But do you recall . . . The most famous reindeer of all?'" She scooped her hands up as if to lift Minnie's voice out from her constricted throat and began the chorus. But in the middle of the third stanza, right after the part about how the other reindeer laughed at him and called him names, the teacher abruptly stopped singing, forcing Minnie into a solo performance.

Her voice was higher and more nasally than might've been expected, given her sultry appearance and grounded demeanor, and also seemed to stumble along in search of the correct pitch like a drunk attempting to walk a straight line. As she sang through the hopeful part about Santa wanting Rudolph to guide his sleigh and the reindeer loving him, tears rolled down her cheeks and dotted her pale-blue T-shirt. It was such a shock to witness her distress that not a single student so much as snickered under their breath. Martha felt Minnie's obvious discomfort—the flushed cheeks, the sweat beading along her neck—as if it were her own. She couldn't bear to watch, knowing it was her fault.

Martha inched directly behind the girl in front of her to hide from the choir teacher. She could just imagine Miss Taylor calling her out: *What on earth were you thinking, Martha Pagnell, putting us all through a nightmare like that?* Minnie would think Martha had set her up on purpose to embarrass her. She'd never be able to convince anyone that her intentions had been—what, good? Who would think she'd really thought Minnie should audition for the lead? She'd have to admit she hadn't done it for Minnie's benefit, but that she'd done it for herself, manipulating a situation so that Minnie would be grateful to her. They'd think she was selfish or crazy or both. What chance would she ever have of becoming friends with Minnie if that happened? She closed her eyes, clasped her hands, and begged every possible higher power to intercede on her behalf.

When the song ended with a protracted, tearful, "You'll go down in his-to-ry!" Minnie turned and fled the choir room. Martha opened her eyes and saw the teacher's anguished face and three of the girls from the most popular group in school look at each other with similar expressions. Some nonverbal communication must have transpired between them, because the three of them hopped off the first riser in unison and ran after Minnie. The teacher sighed and said, "Harold, you lead everyone through the program while I go clean up this mess."

Martha desperately wanted to go help Minnie, too, but she didn't dare move. If she arrived on the scene, the choir teacher would surely say something in front of Minnie about what Martha had told her. No, the only hope she had was that the teacher would forget how it had happened and focus instead on making Minnie feel better. Martha would have to slink through the shadows, as usual, until the crisis had passed.

Three

Early on a Wednesday afternoon toward the end of March, almost exactly a month after the Wrights moved in, the cable technician Martha had been waiting for finally showed up. Over the past few weeks, the Wi-Fi signal in their house had been spottier than usual, to her son's great frustration. How was he supposed to play video games with his squad, as he called them, if the screen kept freezing? Martha couldn't understand the gravity of Harry's gaming concerns—why couldn't he just read a book or ride bikes or pick up a meaningful hobby like she had when she was fourteen?—but the poor connection affected her, too. She delivered all her processed photos electronically, and there had been enough interruptions to her uploads recently that she finally decided to call in tech support.

After setting out a dramatic array of safety cones around his truck, the technician knocked on Martha's door. She let him in, explained the problem, and followed him around as he repeated all the troubleshooting steps she'd already taken, to no avail.

"Everything seems to be okay inside, so it might be the lines coming in are old, or maybe an animal got to them," he told her. "Lot of the new houses in this neighborhood have trouble with weak signals because of their size, but you don't have that problem, obviously. Yours is just old, so it could be the wall construction. Back in the day they used plaster and lath, which has tons of tiny metal nails, and that can cause disruption with the signal."

"But it's been fine up until a few weeks ago," she said, stung. She felt insulted by his description of her house. "Even over the winter break when my son was online all the time, we didn't have any issues."

"I'll check the terminal," he told her. "I noticed the utility pole's behind your neighbor's house, so I'll need to get back there. You know if anybody's home?"

"Which house?"

"That one." He hitched his thumb in the direction of Minnie's.

Martha felt a twitch of glee. She hadn't wanted to bother Minnie with an invitation too early; she knew how long it could take to get settled into a new home, and she didn't want to add any pressure to what was probably a busy time for her. But here was a legitimate reason to check on her. Not a social call, exactly, but maybe it would lead to one. "I'll go over with you and make sure it's okay," Martha told him.

Martha led him across her yard, where the St. Augustine was still mostly yellow and the only vibrant spots were patches of clover, into Minnie's. The Wrights' lawn had been sodded recently with new grass, and it was already bursting a rich, deep green. She made a mental note to apply compost and fertilizer to her grass before it got too warm.

Nobody answered when Martha rang the bell, a resonant chime that she could hear echo through the house even from outside. The gas sconces on either side of the garage were lit, but that didn't mean anything; the Wrights never seemed to turn them on or off. Nor did the absence of Minnie's SUV indicate whether she was home—she and her husband both parked inside the garage. Martha could hardly imagine being able to park even one car inside her own, filled as it was with bikes, Lewis's tinker table, old cans of paint, gardening tools, boxes of Christmas decorations, and the weight bench and dumbbells that had failed to convert her easy-chair husband into an athlete.

She rang the bell again. She tried to look through the glass door, but the sun cast such a glare that she could see only a reflection of herself and the cable tech standing there like a suburban rendition of *American Gothic*. She leaned in and cupped her eyes to the glass just as Minnie swung open the heavy door.

"Hello?" Minnie was barefoot and wearing a long silk kimono over a pair of cutoff shorts and a tank top, her hair in a messy bun. It was a look that Martha knew she'd never be able to pull off but that she very much wished she could.

"Oh goodness," Martha said, regaining her balance. "I'm sorry for peering in like that. I was just wondering if you were home. And you are!"

Minnie looked from Martha to the technician. "Can I do something for you?" The technician explained what he needed and asked for permission to access her backyard. "I'd let you come through the house," Minnie said, "but my husband isn't home at the moment. I'll go unlock the side gate and you can come through there instead, okay?"

The technician nodded and Martha said, "Okay!" even though she was hung up on the idea that John—whom Martha had rarely seen—needed to be home in order for someone to enter their house. Was it just men? Just technicians? Or did it apply to people like Martha, too? Martha had never considered limiting access to her house when Lewis wasn't home. They'd had countless handymen, plumbers, electricians, and appliance repairmen come to fix things over the years, and not once had it occurred to Martha that it might be inappropriate. Was it inappropriate? She'd have to give that some extra thought later. But for now, she followed the technician to the gate, which Minnie had just unlocked and was holding open, and stepped onto the gravel-covered path that led to their backyard and, beyond it, the utility easement where the cables for both their houses joined together.

Of course, it wasn't necessary for Martha to tag along—she didn't know the first thing about cable technology—but she was pulled along as though magnetized. Everywhere she looked—the phrase *feast your eyes* popped into her mind—there was something beautiful. Steps off the stone porch led to a small rectangular pool with turquoise water that sparkled like diamonds had been embedded in the concrete.

"This is the most spectacular pool I've ever seen," Martha said.

"Thanks. It's saltwater, so it doesn't turn your hair green."

On either side were chaise lounges under broad, white umbrellas. Potted flowers bloomed in dazzling colors at every corner. Banana trees were planted along the fence on the west side, while young palm trees and cypress columns lined the fence to the north, presumably for eventual privacy against the imposing three-story home behind the Wrights', whose owners Martha didn't know. There wasn't anything tall along the fence bordering the Hales' yard, however. She supposed it wasn't really necessary; there was only a small window in the guest room above their garage that faced the Wrights' pool. It had been so long since Martha had even gone up there that she didn't think about the fact that the window might yield an invasion of the Wrights' privacy. Evidently the Wrights hadn't either.

Her thought trailed off when she heard a long, insistent whistle coming from the porch.

"I'm here, Bonnie!" Minnie called as she hurried to the large aviary there. Bonnie responded with a series of chirps and trills as she jumped along her perch. Minnie put her finger in between the bars and giggled as the bird pecked at it. "Sing for us, pretty girl!"

As the technician went to work behind the Wrights' garage, Martha approached the aviary. "I've never known anyone who had a pet bird," she said. Then she worried that her statement, which she'd meant to imbue with wonder, might've sounded judgmental. "I mean, it's so delicate. Can you hold it?"

Minnie smiled, still looking at Bonnie. "Of course," she said. "I hold her all the time. John doesn't like her to be loose in the house, but they're very social creatures. Don't say anything"—she turned to look at Martha with a mirthful smile—"but sometimes when he leaves for work before I do, I let her out of her cage and we fly around the house together, singing. Well, she sings. I sort of warble." She leaned in toward the cage and sang, cheerfully but terribly off-key, "'I had a little bird and his name was Enza, I opened the window, and in-flu-enza.' I heard that kids used to sing that about the 1918 pandemic; isn't that funny?"

The image this conjured in Martha's mind was like a punch to her gut. It was peculiar, certainly—what grown woman "flew" around her house with a pet bird? But it seemed awfully lonesome, too, especially because she had to do it behind her husband's back. Suddenly Martha was sucked out of this stunning backyard paradise and back to the choir room at Stonewall Jackson in 1996, watching Minnie cry as she sang so terribly off-key in front of the entire class. How lonesome she'd seemed then, and how wretched. Martha had thought of that moment occasionally over the years, most recently the day Minnie moved in next door, and it always filled her with a kind of soul-sickness. Despite the fact that Minnie appeared to have recovered from whatever discomfort she'd felt in that moment so long ago, Martha felt a slight shock to her nervous system, a zinger of referred pain from some other place that reminded her of her own culpability, innocent though her intentions may have been toward Minnie at the time.

"Are you okay?" Minnie asked. "You look . . . stricken somehow."

"Oh no, I'm fine. I was just thinking back to high school . . ." She shook her head. "No, never mind."

Minnie lifted her hand to shade her eyes. "Never mind what?"

Martha admonished herself for saying "back to high school." She could've said she left the oven on or something. She could have forgotten something at the grocery store. Or better yet, said nothing at all. Her mother had always told her she prattled too much, that she needed to think more before she spoke. *The filter between your mind and your mouth is full of holes,* she'd often said. Martha had always hated the accusation, but maybe her mother was right. Now what was she going to say to Minnie? Quick, quick. What else could she have been thinking back to? She tried to arrange her features into something less panicked, but she wasn't sure it was working.

"Come on, now you've got me curious."

"I shouldn't have said anything. I don't want to bring up any bad memories."

"Bad memories? What are you talking about?"

Well, it was too late now. She'd ruined her chance to be friends with Minnie twenty years ago, and if she had a second chance now, it was probably about to be ruined, too. Resigned, she shrugged one shoulder. "Just that time in choir."

"What time?"

"You know, that time Miss Taylor made you sing 'Rudolph.'"

Minnie dropped her hand, tipped her head back, and released a full-throated laugh that caught Martha completely off guard. "That was so awful!" she said, still chuckling. "I seriously thought I was going to die of embarrassment."

Martha didn't know what to make of the combination of Minnie's words and her laughter. "So, it's not a bad memory then?"

"Oh, absolutely it's bad. The worst." She stopped laughing and cocked her head to the side. "Wait, were you there?"

Martha felt her face grow hot. Was Minnie playing mind games with her? Did she really not remember, which would be insulting but would also be a relief, or was this moment about to get much worse? Was the cable technician going to be a witness to some great humiliation? She glanced at him, but he seemed preoccupied with whatever he was doing. "I was, yeah."

"Well, then you probably remember Mary Margaret and the Jennifers coming out to help me in the hall after I ran out. They were so great. I'd been so depressed that whole first week, you know? I had to leave all my friends in California and I didn't know anybody here when I got back. I felt really uncomfortable starting school in the middle of the semester, but my dad told me, *Don't worry, it's Texas, it's Houston, everybody's so nice, you'll probably have ten best friends by the end of your first day.* Nope. Everyone just stared at me like I was diseased. Nobody asked me to sit with them at lunch or offered to help me find my classes or anything. But after my singing debacle, the girls took me to the bathroom so I could wash my face and cheered me up, and after that we all got to be really good friends. So even though it sucked in the moment, it was the thing that saved my social life."

At lunch the day after Rudolph, Martha had gone out to the athletic field, searching for Minnie among the cedar elms. She planned to offer a shoulder to cry on, to commiserate with her about how mean and, frankly, tacky Miss Taylor was with her pink cowboy boots and bleached hair. She hoped that Minnie didn't know the whole thing was Martha's fault, but if she did, she would just deny it. There wasn't any proof—nobody else had been in the room and Miss Taylor was known to be more than a little scatterbrained. Martha wanted to tell Minnie that she'd hated seeing her cry and wanted to make an overt offer of friendship, one outcast to another. But Minnie wasn't outside. She was in the cafeteria, sitting at the popular table, drinking a Diet Coke and eating Peanut M&M'S just like the rest of them.

It wasn't long until Minnie was on a first-name basis with half the school, even the kids the popular crowd never noticed: the theater people, the debaters, the math and science nerds. She was still quiet, often shy, but nice—if distant—to everyone, even when her newfound rank afforded her to be otherwise. She further ingratiated herself with the girls by refusing an invitation to homecoming with a senior that one of the Jennifers had a crush on. By the end of their junior year, she was a member of the Spirit Committee, the Critters-n-Creatures Club, the tennis team, and was the secretary-elect of the Hospitality Guild. Martha simply went back to eating lunch in the darkroom. As much as she'd have liked to have been part of Minnie's life, she never figured out how to get inside the circle. She just watched Minnie's rise to social stardom from afar.

"I'm glad it worked out for you," Martha said, forcing herself to mean it.

"It was fine. Anyway, let's don't talk about all that anymore. What about you? Do you still take pictures?"

Minnie sat down on one of the chairs near the aviary and crossed her legs. On the table was a sweaty glass of something—iced tea, it looked like—and a splayed-open issue of *ARTnews Magazine* that looked like it had been read more than once. She didn't invite Martha to join her, but she was asking a question that demanded a reasonably detailed answer, and it might seem awkward for Martha to remain standing while she spoke. Perhaps she didn't think Martha needed an invitation; perhaps it was obvious that she should sit and make herself comfortable. That's what neighbors did, right? Most of the time, anyway. Martha sat down in the other Adirondack chair, which was in the full sun. After just a few seconds, the hot wood made her bare thighs very uncomfortable. She tugged her shorts down as discreetly as possible, both to protect her skin and try to conceal her plump, pale legs. Also, she didn't like sitting in the direct sun without a hat; her fair skin tended to burn and freckle if she wasn't careful. She wondered if it would be rude to move her chair into the shade, where Minnie was. She decided to give it a minute, and then do it.

"I still love photography, but I don't spend as much time on it as I'd like, not with my real camera anyway. I'm spoiled by having a camera in my pocket all the time," she said, and held up her phone. "Now everyone's an amateur photographer, even me. I've been demoted!"

What she was too embarrassed to say was that in spite of her early interest and college degree in it, she hadn't ever pursued a serious career as a photographer. The only photography she did was taking snapshots of her son. She had, however, established herself as a reliable postproduction freelancer for several well-known wedding and portrait photographers in town. They had so much work they couldn't keep up with their own editing, but Martha was as meticulous and efficient with her retouching as she was with her housekeeping, and could cull and process as many as four thousand images in a week. She liked that she could work from home—she had her computer set up in the living room—whenever and wearing whatever she pleased. Every time she drove through the Museum District on a day it wasn't raining, there were dozens of bridal or quinceañera parties at the fountain or the park, and the photographers were always loaded down with equipment and sweating as they tried to position everyone before they lost the light. No, sitting in her air-conditioned house wearing her pajamas or loungewear was so much better than having to herd groups of fifteen-year-olds along Main Street in the blazing sun. It was, however, a bit lonesome. Harry, now on the cusp of puberty, was busy with school and lacrosse and possibly even girls, though he was too private to tell her about much of anything these days.

"You should get back into it if you have the time," Minnie said. "You were really good."

Martha smiled, then scooted her chair under the covered pergola until she was practically knee-to-knee with Minnie. "You really think so? It makes me so happy that you remember my work!"

"I mean, I only remember that one photo you did of me. But I'm sure the rest of it was great, too."

Martha refused to feel slighted, and instead took the compliment. She had been good! She'd gotten a bachelor's degree in it, for goodness' sake. Maybe her work wasn't hanging in the Center for Photography or the Menil Collection—of course it wasn't!—but she'd been more than competent. "Thank you!" Martha said, still smiling. "You know, you're right. I should get out my old darkroom equipment and start using film again. I'd forgotten how much I love working in black and white. It's so raw and stripped back. Honest."

Minnie stuck her finger into the aviary and wiggled it. "Maybe you could even take a portrait of Bonnie sometime. I do watercolors of her, but I'd love to have a photograph. In color, of course—her markings are so special."

"Yes, she's a very beautiful bird. And I'd love to take her photo." Martha thought that Bonnie's markings would actually look terrific in black and white, but what did she know? Maybe color would be better.

"I'll pay you, of course."

"Oh no, no payment." Martha flicked her hand, then dared a suggestion: "I never let my friends pay me for my work."

"Okay then," Minnie said, and smiled, which Martha took as a sign of victory. Then she reached out her hand. "Let me have your phone, and I'll put my number in." Martha handed it over, growing shy all of a sudden, thinking of her budding friendship with Minnie, imagining as she had all those years ago of the possibilities that lay ahead: not sleepovers of course, but dinner parties, and afternoons by the pool, and cocktail hours in the Adirondack chairs. But before she could suggest their next meeting or even a date for Bonnie's portrait, the cable technician ambled out from behind the garage and announced that he was finished.

"Okay, thanks so much," Martha said, and waved at him, so lost in the moment that she almost felt like Minnie's yard was her own and he was interrupting one of their usual visits.

He shifted his equipment and waited. "I'm going to need to get back in your house to check the signal," he told her after a moment. Minnie laughed, and he smiled at her.

"Silly me, of course you do!" Martha jumped up, unsticking her skin from the chair so quickly it felt like the one and only time she'd had her legs professionally waxed. At least this time she didn't scream. "Thanks again, Minnie," she said, ostensibly for the utility access, but also for not blaming her for being forced to sing in front of everyone, and for complimenting her work, and for wanting her to photograph her bird.

From her seat, Minnie handed Martha back her phone. "Don't worry," she said cheerfully. "It was nothing."

Four

Martha's son had started playing baseball when he was barely six years old. His first team was the Diamondbacks in the Rookie division. The Diamondbacks team—as all of them were—was volunteer-coached by two of the players' dads. Unlike the older teams, which were drafted, this one was comprised of eleven boys handpicked from Harry's kindergarten class.

The thing about their local Little League was that it wasn't just a casual neighborhood club. Over the course of their sixty-five-year history, they had won numerous state titles, regional titles, and even a World Series crown, beating international teams from Africa, the Middle East, Europe, Asia, and Australia. There were some parents—mostly fathers—who, even starting at the Tadpole division, had great expectations of not only the players but the coaches. It wasn't necessarily common, but at least once every season, within every division, there were screams from and strong words exchanged in the aluminum bleachers beneath the live oak trees at the main fields. There were even the occasional brawls, pugilistic fathers on opposing teams duking out what they considered unfair calls or insults hurled across home plate. The worst example of their competitive spirit was having to take up the coach-fathers' phones so they couldn't cheat during drafts.

But mostly, participating in the league was an opportunity for players and families to come together via a wholesome, childhood-honoring

spring season of baseball that would most likely not lead to a professional sports career. The concession stand, called The Wheelhouse,
offered snow cones and hot dogs as well as gourmet fare from area
restaurants: Thai spring rolls with peanut sauce, pizza from a pair of
Sicilian cousins, jacket potatoes that rivaled what could be procured
in London's Covent Garden. Mothers loved game nights for many reasons: it was a chance to socialize with old and new friends, they got to
watch their sons play, and they didn't have to cook dinner. They sipped
cocktails hidden inside water bottles, and handed out dollar bills faster
than drunk businessmen did on prime rib night at The Gentlemen's
Club, and seemed not to care in the least if all their kids ate was candy
and popcorn. Younger siblings tromped up and down the stands and
ran around the batting cages like packs of wild animals, grandparents
cheered, dads talked shop, and the setting sun cast a benevolent glow
on the games.

To make an organization like this one—which supported twelve
hundred players in eleven divisions from Tadpole all the way up to
Seniors—work as well as it did required a vast network of volunteers
with a willingness to submit to an authoritarian hierarchy and near
militaristic protocols. Every parent was required to perform one or more
jobs per season: team parent, scorekeeper, field coordinator, auction
representative, carnival/concession shift manager, photo coordinator,
sportsmanship representative, and cleanup crew. Each parent was also
required to work two, two-and-a-half-hour shifts in The Wheelhouse,
serving, cashiering, or cleaning. In addition, there were agents and board
members who organized and administrated the league throughout the
year, and a Liaison whose affiliates assisted with league operations and
fundraising. Along the way, someone had the brilliant idea to make this
discretionary servitude an honor by requiring that new recruits to the
Liaison be nominated, thus elevating the countless hours of free labor
to a form of exclusivity.

Every season that Harry played, Martha offered to be both team mom and photo coordinator. She worked extra Wheelhouse shifts for parents who called in sick or had other conflicts. She organized the end-of-year parties and argued successfully each time that there wasn't anything wrong with rewarding the boys with trophies, regardless of their final standings. But even by the time Harry had six of them on his shelf, Martha still hadn't been invited to join the Liaison. When he decided to quit after his Minor AAA season, the penultimate game of which he emptied his full bladder onto his white pants after being hit in the privates by a foul ball, Martha was brokenhearted. Many boys quit—or wanted to—before reaching the Majors at age twelve because that was when things started to become seriously competitive. She'd had no illusions that her son would make it all the way to the Little League World Series the following year as the best of the select players would; that dream had been forgone years before, when Harry proved to have only average skills at best. The reason she didn't want him to quit was because she hoped that by then she'd finally earn her spot in the volunteer ranks.

So, though it was highly unusual to do so without having a registered player in the league, Martha continued to offer her unofficial help each time a new baseball season rolled around. Since she didn't have a team job and wasn't on Liaison, she gave herself over to the dregs of Little League society: the auction committee.

Even in a universe where unpaid labor was considered the height of existence, nobody wanted to be responsible for the annual gala and auction. It required a ridiculous amount of work to negotiate a venue, find entertainment, procure a caterer, collect and catalog donations for the silent and big-board auctions, set up the bidding and payment procedures, and more. Of course, there were committees and subcommittees, but those required leadership, meetings, and oversight. Perhaps the easiest action item was selecting the theme, around which everything—decorations, menu, drinks, logos—revolved. In the past they'd had "Biker

Madness," "Havana Nights," "Disco Inferno," "Great Gatsby," "Roller Derby," and "Hippie Chic." Most everyone in attendance got into the spirit, dressing accordingly, often with creative, expensive, even outlandish results. For the league's sixtieth anniversary, someone suggested a witty "Diamonds Are Forever" motif, and everyone wore their most glamorous attire. This year's theme was both more casual and more perplexing: "Smart Denim." Martha wasn't entirely sure how, but since most of her wardrobe was denim, surely she could find a way to smarten it up for the party.

After months of preparation, hundreds of emails, and thousands of man-hours, the night of the gala finally arrived. The first Saturday in April bore down with the kind of heat and humidity that would inspire many Houstonians without a party to attend to bemoan the onslaught of summer and languish in their living rooms with cold cocktails or glasses of wine. Not Martha. She'd pitched in that day by hauling donations to the venue and helping decorate the tables and set up the vast silent auction offerings, chattering happily with anyone who happened to be nearby. Instead of fatigue, by the end of the afternoon, she felt a buzz of anticipation at being part of an important social event and enjoying a glass or two of champagne—maybe more if she felt like going wild. Lewis wasn't excited about having to get dressed up, even in the jeans-based outfit she picked for him, and talking to a bunch of guys he didn't know well and had little in common with.

"It's that whole Tesla club," he said through the shower curtain as Martha was putting on mascara. "They're going to talk about their investment portfolios and couples' trips to Mexico or wherever they go and when they're going to trade in their Model Xs for the new Cybertrucks that are allegedly coming out so they can all caravan to dinner together."

"Lewis, you sound downright petulant right now," Martha told him. "If you were the Tesla type, you'd fit right in with those guys."

"That's just it, Marty, I'm not the Tesla type. For one thing, it's not in the budget, and even if we did have that kind of money lying around, I wouldn't spend it on a car."

"What would you spend it on?" It was a game they sometimes played, talking about how they'd spend an imaginary fortune. Every Christmas, Martha put twenty-five Lotto Texas tickets into Lewis's stocking and couldn't help but get excited by the idea that they might actually win.

He turned off the water. Martha could hear him drying off. She knew he'd become self-conscious of his belly and didn't like her to see him contorting himself during his toilette. He emerged with the towel wrapped in an effort to conceal his midsection, and turned to squeeze past where she stood at the pedestal sink, her small stash of makeup piled on the sliver of available counter space. "I'd get this bathroom remodeled," he said, smiling at her. "Of course, if we're talking Performance-Model-S-with-Ludicrous-Mode money, I'd do the entire house."

She leaned in and kissed him on the cheek. "For someone who claims not to be a Tesla type, you certainly know a lot about them."

"I'm a man, baby," he said in his best Austin Powers voice. "It comes with the equipment." He giggled and tossed his damp towel at her before closing the door.

~

Even though it was muggy outside and valet was included with their ticket, Martha suggested to Lewis that they park at the big-box store behind the venue and walk. "That way we won't have to wait in line when we're ready to leave," she told him, but that wasn't exactly true. His comment had stuck with her, and she worried that he might be embarrassed if they pulled up in her minivan, which they'd driven so she could haul away any unclaimed auction items at the end of the night and store until they could be returned. But Lewis wasn't the kind of man to put his own insecurities above his wife's comfort.

"Don't be silly," he said. "What if we end up winning a giant stuffed animal or one of those fancy gift baskets? Besides, didn't you say your shoes were uncomfortable?" He pulled into the valet line. As the attendants were opening their doors, he took her hand and kissed it.

Right away, Martha knew she'd made a mistake with her outfit. Not a grave one, but as she looked around at the other women emerging from their cars and standing in the check-in line, she realized that her interpretation of "Smart Denim" was perhaps a bit too literal. She'd opted for a full denim skirt that she thought looked festive and one of Lewis's old Middlebury College T-shirts—the "smart" part of her ensemble—which she'd cut into a V-neck and decorated with rhinestones. She thought it was okay that she was wearing Lewis's school colors and not her own; had her family had the money to send her to an out-of-state college, she was confident that she could've gotten in. She cinched in her waist with a wide patent-leather belt, meant to represent a panther, Middlebury's mascot, and wore patent-leather heels that were indeed a bit too tight. To tie it all together, she wore her favorite denim jacket in spite of the heat and a sparkly barrette in her hair. Until they'd arrived, she'd been pleased with her creativity. Now she wished she hadn't tried so hard. It seemed that most everyone else had simply elevated the neighborhood standard to some version of skinny jeans, a cute top, and wedges.

As if reading her mind, Lewis squeezed her hand and whispered in her ear, "You look beautiful." Then he led her in and handed her a glass of wine from a server's tray.

The gala chair, a bossy woman who'd been an accountant before her sons were born and who presided over everything with a vaguely disappointed air, saw Martha and greeted her with a beckoning wave. "Thank god you're here," Patty said as Martha blushed. "Listen, Emma was supposed to be in charge of selling rings but she had to cancel at the last minute. I'm not surprised; that woman is hardly a paragon of responsibility. She's probably at home nursing either a hangover or a bottle of wine or both. Anyway, can you do it? All you have to do is go around to the tables hawking them in the name of charity. People will love you, you're very cheerful." Patty waved a hand up and down Martha's visage without expression. "Besides, who could say no to someone who's dressed so ironically?"

And so, Martha inherited a large basket filled with bumpy, stretchy silicone rings with flashing LED lights that made her squint as she went along from table to table. It wasn't terrible; it reminded her of her waitressing days, when she'd approach a group engaged in conversation. At first, back then, she'd clear her throat and shift her weight and hope for someone to graciously allow her to take their order. As she gained experience, she learned that she had to take the bull by the horns, as it were, and command the moment without fear. "Listen up, y'all!" she said now to the five couples who only glanced at her without breaking conversation. "These seriously ugly rings are twenty-five dollars apiece, but each one not only gets you an entry into the raffle for a real diamond ring, but it's a way to show off your generosity and support of less fortunate boys in our brother league. All the raffle proceeds go to them to buy uniforms and equipment. Table sixty-two bought two apiece. Y'all don't want to be the only ones without a ring, do you? Who's in?"

To her immense pleasure, she sold out of the rings before the silent auction even opened. All it took was to challenge their altruism and engage their intrinsic sense of competition. Each of the husbands at all of the tables bought not two but three rings, two each for their wives and one for themselves, which they wore, laughing at their ridiculous accessories because they could. As a group, they were beyond ridicule. They could wear tacky, LED-powered rings or drive matching cars because their power lay in their unity. Martha smiled as she scanned their barcoded bracelets, and when one of the husbands offered her one of his purchased rings, she accepted it and gave it to Lewis, who knew what she was up to and wore it anyway.

A half hour before dinner was served, someone announced over the loudspeaker that the silent auction was open. Martha patted Lewis on the forearm and said, "Let's go check it out." Although she'd been there most of the afternoon, there had been so many items to arrange she hadn't even seen them all. But Lewis was deeply engrossed in a conversation with an antivaxxer about the recent outbreak of measles in Orthodox communities in New York. She knew he wouldn't relent until the other guy acknowledged the extraordinary victories of science over disease, so she took their sheet of bidding stickers and wandered over to the vast display of goods and offerings.

There were things like a dove hunt in Argentina, a weeklong stay at the Four Seasons in Costa Rica, a dinner party in the high bidder's home for thirty people, a reserved parking spot near The Wheelhouse, an opportunity to be mayor for the day, portrait sittings, spa retreats, jewelry, and much, much more. The first package Martha bid on was ten copies of local author Chris Cander's latest novel, *The Weight of a Piano*, plus an in-person visit to the winner's book club. Martha had always wanted to be part of a book club, and she thought this would be the perfect opportunity to start one. She put down a bid sticker, then worked her way around the giant U-shaped arrangement, examining each item, smiling and making small talk with other bidders, accepting fresh glasses of champagne from servers who maneuvered silently through the crowd, until she arrived at a clot of women huddled in front of a small, original watercolor painting of a rainbow-colored parakeet.

"What's that?" Martha asked, wedging herself closer. The painting itself was delicate and realistic: a small, thoughtful-looking bird with a yellow head and soft blue breast looked out from a neutral background. Martha's forearms prickled with goose bumps at the bird's eerie stare, as though it were not just looking at her but judging her as well. "Who painted it?"

A woman whose son had been on the same Minor A team as Harry moved over to give Martha room to read the item description:

> "Bonnie" watercolor on paper by art consultant and artist Minnie Foster Wright. Own one of Houston's reputed painters' original works, plus receive a two-hour in-home bespoke experience offering art consulting and fine art appraisal.

"She's apparently a very big deal," said the woman to Martha. "I read about her in *SpaceTown* last week."

SpaceTown was a Houston lifestyle magazine devoted to all the luxury Martha was surrounded by but wasn't part of: fashion, society, the arts, home design, real estate, dining. Each time one arrived in the mail, she put aside anything she was doing and pored over every single page. How had she missed the latest issue? And how had she not known that Minnie was a big deal?

"Who's that?" another woman asked, squeezing in. There was nothing like landing in *SpaceTown* to inspire curiosity and awe.

"Her name's Minnie Foster," someone else offered. "We share a hairstylist. She apparently studied art with Paul Klee at the University of Washington, and now she helps people build their own art collections."

"It couldn't have been Paul Klee. He died in, like, 1940 or something."

"Okay, maybe I got the name wrong. Whatever. She definitely studied art, but she's not famous for her own paintings. Not yet, anyway. But I know the owner of a really important gallery, and he said she had great taste."

"I don't know much about art, but this is pretty good."

"It's not *great*, though."

"It doesn't matter. If she's up and coming, it might be worth something someday," said a woman named Alice. "The opening bid is only three hundred dollars. That's nothing! Plus, a private art consultation. I'm bidding."

Another woman stepped up and put down her own sticker. "Sorry, Alice, but you're right. Who knows what it might resell for down the line? Besides, I think the painting is really sweet. It would look so cute in my guest bathroom."

"Hildy, you bitch!" Alice said, laughing. "Just for that I'm going to go bid up those hideous statement lamps you've got your eye on."

Hildy grabbed at Alice's sticker sheet, but not viciously. "Those lamps are *mine*."

Giggling, two other women rushed to add their stickers to the list, pushing the current bid to $450 in less than a minute. One of them, a woman named Ruth, whom Martha recognized as the mother of a boy Harry was friendly with, sloshed her cocktail onto Martha's jacket.

"Oh wait, is this the woman who just moved here from Seattle? Into that giant new build on Alcott?"

Martha had been watching this small rumpus as though from behind glass, still processing the new information about Minnie. But now she had her own insight to offer. "Yes," Martha said, standing up straighter. "She lives next door to me. We went to high school together."

"Then you probably know what really happened with her husband."

Martha blushed. Of course she didn't know what happened with him. She knew next to nothing about him. She'd hardly seen him, except for pulling in and out of his garage. He never seemed to go outside, not even into his own beautiful backyard. If that yard were theirs, Lewis would be sitting out there every night. "You mean John?" she asked, hedging.

"Unless she's got more than one. Anyway, my husband works in a different department in the same hospital system, but he only heard rumors, so you didn't get this from me." With the muscular coordination of a plague of grackles, the other women all leaned in to hear. "He allegedly had one too many #MeToo moments and got fired. He was pretty high up, though, and they were able to keep it quiet."

"What kind of #MeToo moment?" someone asked.

"He's apparently pretty handsy in general, but he could get away with feeling up his patients here and there. I mean, you go in for a boob job, what do you expect? The surgeon's going to touch your boobs." The women shrugged, acquiescing. "But this one patient said that she went in for a consultation and Dr. Wright offered to do her for free if she gave him a blow job."

"Did she?" someone asked, wide-eyed.

"No, you ninny! She ran out in her hospital gown and told the receptionist to call the police. The nurse had to chase her down to give her back her clothes. The problem was, the woman also had a pretty well-established history of mental illness, and they used it against her, saying she might've made the whole thing up. But I guess it was still enough of a fuss the hospital fired him anyway. Liability and all that."

"Why on earth would a woman stay married to a man like that?" a woman named Gert asked with a note of disgust.

"No offense, Gert, but you're married to a woman so you might not understand how it is," Alice said. An uncomfortable silence fell among them. Everyone knew that Alice's first husband, also a doctor, had cheated on her for years. He'd been discreet about it at first, but eventually he fell for their daughter's ballet teacher and moved her into an apartment not far from their house. He'd been so bold about his affair, taking his lover to dinner at the same Tex-Mex restaurant where he'd taken his family the night before and checking into local hotels with her in the middle of the day, that even someone like Martha caught wind of his indiscretions. Alice was mortified but freely admitted that had he not filed, she'd have stayed with him rather than go through the humiliation of a divorce. "When you're raised Tammy Wynette–style like I was, you're supposed to stand by your man."

"Honey, your mama didn't do you any favors making you think that way. Thank goodness you're not still devoted to that piece of shit."

"Don't forget that piece of shit is my children's father, Gert, but I thank you for your concern anyway."

"Gert's right, though," Hildy offered. "Especially nowadays, women don't have to stay in bad marriages. We have options."

"Hildy, that's easy for you to say. You're married to a lamb. Honestly, has Marvin ever once said a cross word to you?" asked a woman named Hazel, who'd just ten minutes earlier "won" the sleepy brown Labradoodle puppy she was now carrying with a final bid of $16,000. She'd said it was a bargain; the puppy's sibling, which was a lighter shade of beige, went for twenty.

"Only when I spend too much of his money!" Hildy said.

"Bullshit," Alice said. "You're going to spend at least two thousand dollars on those godforsaken statement lamps and he's going to carry them home and plug them in for you." Everyone laughed, even Martha, who in her wildest dreams couldn't fathom paying that kind of money for lamps.

"Well, when it's my time for a lift, I can tell you I won't be going to Dr. Wright, even if he's the best plastic surgeon in town," Hazel said.

"Me either!" said two other women simultaneously.

"Makes me want to peel my bid sticker off," said the woman who mentioned Minnie's status in *SpaceTown Magazine*, glancing at the painting of Bonnie with a sour expression.

"Kinda does me, too," someone else said.

Martha liked to agree with people, often regardless of what they said, but about this she couldn't hold her tongue. "Listen, y'all, not only is Minnie an amazing artist, she's a beautiful person inside and out. You should see their house. And their backyard—it's all stunning." She was flush with pride, her mouth running with information that she did not actually possess but that she felt certain was true. "And John's very devoted to her. They're devoted to each other. I think that business about him is just a nasty rumor." She reached down and put a bid sticker on the sheet, even though it was far more than she intended to spend that night. *Well, it's for a good cause,* she decided.

The women looked at her with vague interest, as if evaluating Martha's authority on the subject. She gazed back, firm in her defense of Minnie's honor, but very quickly she grew self-conscious under their scrutiny. She once again became aware of how silly her outfit was, how tight her belt and shoes were. She reached up and adjusted the barrette near her temple, and she could tell that her hair had become frizzy in the warm air. She would very much have liked another glass of champagne but didn't know how to break the briefly interminable spell she was under.

Fortunately, Alice broke it for her. "Anyway," she said, shrugging. "Rumor or no, the optics aren't flattering. But maybe she's right. Let's go check on Hildy's lamps." The whole group drifted off, the moment already forgotten.

Martha stayed behind, gratefully accepting a glass from a passing server. She wanted a moment to compose herself before returning to Lewis at the table, so she pretended to browse the rest of the items. She was a little tipsy as well as a little unnerved from the whole business about the Wrights. What if she'd been wrong? What if the rumor was true? Martha admonished herself: What business did she have making any claims one way or another? She went back to the painting of Bonnie and thought about how friendly Minnie had been to her when she followed the cable tech into her backyard. It wasn't fair of those women with their perfect clothes and puppies and lamps to spread malicious gossip when there wasn't any proof. Martha was pleased to see that her bid was still in the highest place. There was a perfect spot in her living room where she could hang the little watercolor. When Minnie came over for the in-home consultation portion, she'd be so pleased to see it right when she walked in the door. Martha wondered if she should paint the walls, perhaps something bold but soft, like the robin's-egg blue of

Bonnie's breast feathers. Maybe Minnie would help her pick out new colors. The thought filled her with pleasure, and she went down the row with new optimism. A sparkling necklace caught her eye: a gold teardrop-shaped pendant studded with tiny green gemstones—peridots, according to the description—on a delicate chain. It was a little plain and far outside their budget, but something she wouldn't mind Lewis buying for her. So, without too much consideration, she put down a sticker for the opening bid of $800. The act made her feel fancy and bold, like buying property with play money, especially because she wouldn't win. The auction would be open for another forty-five minutes, plenty of time for someone else to bid on it.

By the time dinner was over, the silent and big-board auctions closed, and many of the attendees had left, Martha was far beyond her limit. She couldn't remember how many glasses she'd drunk, and had only a vague recollection of the meal. It was clear to both Lewis and Patty, the gala chair, that Martha was in no shape to help with the breakdown or cleanup.

"Just get her home safely," Patty told Lewis as she walked with them to the valet. "I'll make sure you get the stuff you won."

"What stuff?" he asked. "We didn't bid on anything."

"I did," Martha said, swaying next to Lewis. "Many, many things."

Patty scrolled through an app on her iPad. "Actually, only three," she said. "A book package, a painting, and a necklace. But you only won the necklace."

"No Bonnie?" Martha mumbled, looking dismayed. "No Minnie?" They both ignored her.

"What was the damage, if you don't mind me asking," Lewis said.

"Not bad. Only eight hundred. It's quite beautiful if I recall. It has peridot stones in it."

"Good lord."

"Go easy on her, though. I know my husband would kill me if I were in her place. A lot of husbands go nuts when this stuff happens."

"Don't kill me, Lewis," Martha said, and lifted her hand as if to keep him away.

Patty leaned in and whispered, "Since she's probably not going to remember, maybe you can save it, give it to her for her birthday or something."

~

With the valet's help, Lewis stuffed his soon-to-be unconscious wife into the passenger seat. He gave the valet an extra tip for his troubles and waved to Patty.

"Eight hundred dollars?" he said, though not harshly, when they were alone inside the car and pulling away from the venue. He glanced at her sleeping form: head back, mouth open, and snoring. He knew from long experience that she'd be profoundly embarrassed in the morning and already felt bad for her. "But don't worry, nobody's going to kill anybody over a necklace," he said, and patted her on the knee.

Five

Her hangover lasted only one day, but it took almost two weeks for Martha to recover from her shame. Lewis reassured her each time she asked if she'd said or done anything terribly embarrassing—or worse, rude—that she had not. She worried that he was withholding some humiliating truth, even though he was the most forthright and honest person she knew. He reminded her that half the gala attendees were drunk on their feet, pointing out that sober people do not pay $20,000 for a dog, no matter how genuinely altruistic they might be. Still, Martha couldn't bring herself to face anyone who might've seen her, and so she hardly left the house except to drive Harry to and from school. She even set her alarm clock for five in the morning to go to the grocery store so she wouldn't run into the usual crowd.

Eventually her dismay subsided such that she could look back on that night—if she had to—with little more than the usual regret. She woke up on a dry, sunny Saturday morning in mid-April realizing that it was one of the few remaining days of decent weather before the air turned to soup, so she decided to go out and enjoy it.

She made chocolate-chip pancakes and fried some thick-cut bacon, and served it for a late breakfast on the tiny back patio off the driveway. A hearty breeze teased the new leaves on the pecan tree behind the garage and lifted the scent of jasmine off the fence. Lewis explained to Harry how thermal imaging technology worked as they devoured their food, and Martha reveled in a sense of untroubled contentment, feeling as placid as the great puffy clouds that floated along overhead.

"Y'all want to do something today? Drive to Galveston, maybe? Or rent kayaks on the bayou?"

"Maybe later," Harry said. "I'm meeting Jimmy and them online at eleven for a game."

"I think you should say, 'Jimmy and friends.'"

"Why? It's not technically wrong."

He had a point. "It just sounds awkward, I guess." Martha took a long breath. She didn't want him to be any more awkward than he already was.

Lewis patted her on the hand. "I've got some work to do, too," he said. "I'll do the dishes, though, so you can rest."

Martha didn't want to rest. She wanted to go for a walk or a bike ride with her boys, to enjoy the day as a family. It seemed like they hadn't done anything like that in a while; everyone was too busy with their own activities. Times like these she especially wished she had a close girlfriend she could call up and make spontaneous plans with. Well, she wouldn't let it ruin her mood. There was plenty she could do on her own. She went inside to lie down on the bed and made a list of options: exercise, call her mother, go to the farmers' market, get a pedicure, do some gardening, read. They were all very pleasant in their own way, but the breeze coming through the open window combined with the effort of creating the list made her drowsy, full as she was of bacon and pancakes, and despite not wanting to, soon she fell asleep.

She awoke hours later, and carried the remnants of her nap like a warm shawl around her shoulders to the kitchen. Lewis had gone to the store; the receipt was on the counter for her to file, along with a bowl of washed grapes. A note revealed that Harry had gone to his friend's to play video games and Lewis had run to the office to pick up some seismic maps. The day had warmed, but there was still a lovely breeze that made her modest backyard look like a dance party with all the swaying foliage and crashing leaves. As she snacked on grapes, Martha noticed that her lemon tree was once again full of fruit. Spring had been generous that year.

Buoyed by an appreciation for the day and a recognition of her own general contentment, Martha decided that she would be generous, too. She dumped a load of laundry that she'd been meaning to fold onto her bed and carried the basket outside, making a mental note to buy an extra one next time she was out doing errands. She picked all the ripe lemons the tree had to offer, even the ones that required a stepladder to reach. Even after putting aside a bowlful for her own use, she still had quite an impressive bounty left.

Martha had a stash of wine bags with her gift-wrapping supplies that she'd long ago bought on sale in case they were invited to someone's house for a party or for dinner. Her mood suffered a fleeting dip when she inventoried the unused bags, but her happiness returned as she dropped a half dozen fat lemons into several of them. She pulled out Harry's old markers and paint pens, and took her time decorating plain gift tags with individual illustrations and messages for her neighbors: *When life gives you lemons, make lemonade* and *From my home to yours* and *May these bring some joy to your day*, all signed *Love, Martha Hale* along with her address and phone number. Then she tied them each up with ribbon—five bags in total—and stood back to admire her work.

By then it was already almost three o'clock. She wanted to deliver all her gifts, allowing time for visiting, and be back in time to start dinner for Lewis and Harry, so she opted not to shower. Instead, she rummaged through the clothes on her bed and found something slightly more formal than pajamas to change into, brushed her teeth, and pulled her hair into a ponytail. At the last minute, imagining herself through Minnie's eyes, she applied a swipe of mascara and some lipstick.

She didn't want to carry all five bags at once; it would be too awkward, especially if she were invited inside anyone's home. But she also liked how all the bags looked together, very intentional and artistic, like something someone on a home-decorating show might do. Then she remembered that Harry's old Radio Flyer wagon from a decade ago was somewhere in the garage, probably holding up a large stack of storage bins. With not a small amount of effort, she unearthed it and was dismayed by how chipped and filthy it was, and how unlike a magazine-worthy image it would create in her neighbors' minds. After a flash of inspiration, she found a couple of unworn silk scarves her mother had given her suggesting—rudely, Martha had thought at the time—that they might liven up her wardrobe, and draped them artistically over the wagon, then nestled the bags inside. It was so charming she took a photo of the arrangement, thinking she might post it to her social media account. She'd mostly stopped using it after Harry asked her not to post any more pictures of him; that was really all she'd liked it for. Sometimes she liked having the ability to peer into her acquaintances' and neighbors' lives, but she'd learned early on that looking too long or too closely generally made her feel terrible about herself. Besides, knowing someone through social media didn't feel earned or special the way it would if the person had shared their stories over coffee, just the two of them.

With a cheerful lightness to her bearing, Martha set off, pulling the wagon behind her. No sooner had she stepped onto the street than a car coming up behind her honked its horn. Assuming that everyone was feeling as sunny as she, she turned to wave with a ready smile, thinking that it was just someone saying hello or honking approval at her errand. Instead, a shiny Jeep Wrangler yanked itself into the oncoming lane to pass her, its teenage occupants looking at her disapprovingly as they zoomed past. She let her hand drop to her side. She hated seeing teenagers drive so fast down the neighborhood streets; it made her worry about what sort of citizens they would eventually become. She made a mental note to talk about it with Harry, even though he was still nine months away from starting driver's ed. The last thing she'd want to hear from a neighbor was that they'd seen Harry zipping around West U like his hair was on fire, risking his safety and reputation just to get to the next stop sign a little sooner. Well, she didn't need to worry about that right then, and anyway, Harry had always been a good, respectful boy. For that, she mostly credited herself and Lewis with their good parenting, but she also thought that living in such a nice area must've had something to do with how well her son had turned out.

Her first stop was to the house directly behind hers. The family had lived there since before she and Lewis moved in, and they'd never been particularly friendly. Early on, when Harry was still a newborn and Martha was feeling rather housebound and lonely, she pushed him in his stroller around the block and knocked on the door to introduce herself. They shared a back fence after all, and she knew from the sounds they made that there were at least two children living there. She'd thought it might be fun to get to know them. Perhaps they might all become friends, and even someday cut a gate into the fence so the children could more easily play together. But when she answered the door, the woman, Anna Devlin, had been very dismissive. "It's nice to meet you but I can't visit now; I've got friends over." The way Anna looked at her made Martha feel terrible. Was it because she was dressed sloppily? Had she broken some unknown rule about knocking on a neighbor's door in the middle of the day? There was no indication in her voice or posture that Martha might be welcome sometime in the future either, so Martha apologized for the interruption and made a hasty, inelegant departure, struggling to get the bulky stroller turned around and off the woman's porch without jostling Harry too much.

A year or so ago, after both the Devlin children were back at college for the fall, Martha was in her backyard pruning her herbs and was startled by a banging against the fence. A moment later, it happened again. It went on long enough that Martha stood a ladder against her house under the guise of cleaning the gutter so she could see what the racket was about. Anna's husband, Frank, was blasting tennis balls out of a Nerf gun for their dog to chase, in spite of the fact that their yard, like the Hales', was only about the size of a large living room and hardly required ballistic force to send a ball from one end to the other. Since they'd had almost no interaction in the fourteen years since their first encounter, Martha knew very little about them, but Frank had never struck Martha or Lewis as particularly bright. Perhaps suffering a dim intellect was why he'd developed such a peculiar hobby. And based on the amount of time he spent in the backyard, it seemed logical to the Hales that Frank had either retired or been let go from his job. In any case, Frank deployed his gun multiple times each day, occasionally, it seemed, even without the dog. Given the age of the fence, which had been new when they moved in, and the effects of Houston's hot, soggy weather, the wood beneath the jasmine vines had become weak, and within a few months of seemingly constant tennis ball attacks, it finally shattered. Anna sent the Hales a letter apologizing for her husband ruining their fence and offering to have it replaced at their expense.

Afterward, Martha felt terribly sorry for the woman, in spite of her chilly demeanor, for having to live with a man like Frank inside an empty nest. Martha's pity didn't extend to an inclination toward friendship, however, and so now she leaned the bag of lemons against the Devlins' front door and rushed back to her wagon without ringing the bell.

Next, Martha stopped at the widow's house next door to her across-the-street neighbor, Lillian. The widow, Mrs. Kashuba, was fond of any kind of animal and spent much of her fixed income on feed for squirrels, possums, and raccoons. Once, when Lillian called the West U police because a raccoon had come through Beignet's dog door and ransacked her pantry, Mrs. Kashuba had rushed out in her nightgown to beg officials not to harm the animal. "I'll vouch for her," she'd screamed, loud enough to wake nearby households. "You can't trap that innocent creature! Studies show trapped coons don't take well to new environments! Just close that damn trap door and let her be and she'll do her job eating vermin and insects. It's not her fault you can't see fit to get up to let your dog in and out with your own two feet, you lazy nitwits!"

In addition to her characteristic spunk, Martha admired Mrs. Kashuba's principles, fortitude of character, and kindness. When Harry was a baby, Martha often stopped to visit when they were out for a walk and Mrs. Kashuba was out front. She was a generous, if unusual, conversationalist and would happily spend hours telling an infant the names of all the flora and fauna in her yard. Over time, as they grew familiar, Martha would often pass Harry to her when he fussed, and Mrs. Kashuba would tirelessly bounce the baby on her hip, carrying him from tree to tree to discuss the shapes of the leaves, or the color and size of acorns, or the characteristic branching of certain trees. She was the one who recognized Martha's postpartum depression and came over unannounced, wanting to know if there was breast milk in the freezer and when Harry had eaten last and telling her to go to bed, that she'd look after him for a few hours. Not even her own mother had been as present as Mrs. Kashuba, and as such, Martha hadn't let a holiday go by in the past fourteen years without inviting her to sit at their table.

"What a dear you are," Mrs. Kashuba said after Martha rang the bell. "I'd love to chat but I'm heading out to do my yoga class with the shelter dogs. When I get back, though, I'm going to make you and my sweet Harry some lemon cake with this. The most irresistible blue flowers are blooming on my Lavandula plant, and they'll be the perfect complement to your Meyers."

Before Martha could protest, Mrs. Kashuba gave her a peck on the cheek and dashed back inside. A moment later she was out the side door with her yoga mat, her long gray braid swinging behind her as she maneuvered her ample backside into her sedan.

Martha rang Lillian's bell next, and followed it with three quick knocks on the door because once, years ago when Harry had been going house to house selling candy bars for a school fundraiser, Lillian's daughters came home on their bikes while Harry was standing on their porch and Martha on the sidewalk.

"Did you ring or knock?" Madeleine asked him.

"I rang," Harry said.

"You have to do both or she'll ignore you," Noelle said.

"Why?"

"She says solicitors ring and beggars knock, so you gotta do both so she won't think you're either one," Madeleine said. Noelle nodded behind her. As it turned out, Harry didn't have to bypass Lillian's system after all; the girls went inside and came back out with enough money to buy his entire inventory. "Don't tell Mama if you see her. She doesn't like us eating candy 'cause she doesn't want us getting fat."

Now Martha could hear Beignet's barking and a female voice telling him to hush. There was more movement inside, perhaps even in the foyer. Martha had the sensation of being watched, as if someone was looking at her through the peephole. But then there was nothing, and nobody answered the door. She contemplated knocking again, and decided against it. Instead, she propped the bag of lemons neatly against the doorframe, making sure the gift tag would be visible right away.

As she turned to leave, however, a teenage boy appeared out of nowhere and dashed up the porch steps toward her so quickly she gasped. "My goodness," Martha said, pressing her hand to her heart.

The boy looked at her from underneath thick eyebrows and long, unkempt hair with a flat expression, then put his hand on the Mickelsens' doorknob.

"Wait a minute there. What are you doing?" Martha said, taking a step toward him.

"I live here," he said with a sneer.

"You most certainly do not, young man. Step away from there or I'll call the police." Martha's heart was pounding in her chest. She'd never been so close to a possible burglar before, but she had no intention of backing down. Lillian may not've been a friend, but Martha wasn't about to let some surly rascal in a ratty T-shirt break into her house, steal from them, or do god knows what to her or her girls.

"Screw you, lady." The boy tried the knob but it was locked. He pounded on the door with a force and tempo that matched Martha's heart. Almost instantly, Lillian opened the door.

"Willy, I've asked you to kindly not bang so hard. You'll put a dent in the wood." Only after Willy pushed his way past her into the house did Lillian notice Martha standing on the step behind him. "Oh. Hello." A flush rose to her cheeks.

"I came by to bring you some fresh lemons," Martha said, pointing to the bag. "Then that boy nearly scared me to death."

"That *boy* is Willy Guidry. My sister's son. He's come here to stay with us while my sister . . . recuperates. She's been ill." She said it with a righteous air, as if her magnanimity were underappreciated.

From inside the house, Willy called out, "Bullshit! She's been drunk, not sick. And now she's in rehab. Again."

Lillian stepped onto the porch, closing the door behind her. "Don't pay any attention to him. He's just going through some emotional . . . adjustments. He'll finish out the school year at White Oak Middle." She picked up the lemons and went back inside, dismissing Martha with a curt "Have a nice afternoon." Lillian had failed to thank her for the fruit, but Martha forgave her, assuming that she was probably distracted by her nephew's crude behavior. The boy did seem to be quite a handful. Martha made a mental note to warn Harry to stay away from him.

The family on Lillian's other side was Martha's penultimate delivery. Triplet boys around age three were behind the driveway gate playing in a blow-up pool and a slide, screaming in delight as they sprayed each other with the hose. Martha couldn't see their mother, Beatriz, a semiretired attorney in her midforties who always looked faintly stoned. There had been some scuttlebutt about Beatriz, who'd moved into the redbrick Colonial a few months before the boys' second birthday along with her elderly mother and a nanny. The boys' father was rumored to be a prominent Fifth Circuit federal district judge in San Antonio, whose heiress wife had given Beatriz more than enough money to raise and educate the children as long as she agreed to return to her native Houston and never so much as think about speaking to her husband or even crossing into the Balcones Fault Zone again. If her recycling bin was any indication, Beatriz relied on a steady flow of wine, vodka, romance novels, and benzodiazepines to get through her days.

It was usually the nanny who supervised the boys outside, but when Martha pulled the wagon up to the gate and called out to the boy holding the hose, "Charlie, sweetie, is Teresa back there with you?" it was Beatriz who wandered out from beyond the porte cochere to greet her.

"Oh hi, Marta."

"Martha," Martha said.

"Of course. Martha. I'm sorry," Beatriz said, holding on to the gate for support with one hand and trying not to spill her drink in the other.

Martha didn't hold the mistake against her. As much as she'd wanted more children, she couldn't begin to imagine how hard it would be having triplets, especially those three. It wasn't uncommon for one of them to escape the yard, like they were indoor-only cats desperate for a taste of freedom. Teresa or Beatriz or both would rush outside, hollering for the stray child in both English and Spanish while trying to keep the other two corralled. Most of the time one of the neighbors would scoop the fugitive up as he fled, sometimes promising cookies or ice cream as a reward for not kicking too hard as he was being carried home. Even the West U police knew to keep an eye out, ever since Billy figured out how to unlock the front door in the middle of the night the year before. After the alarm went off and the police dispatched, they found him sauntering down the middle of the street like he knew where he was going but was in no rush to get there.

"I brought you some lemons from my yard," Martha said, pushing the bulging bag through the iron bars. She wasn't sure Beatriz was sober enough to make it all the way back up the driveway and through the house to the front door, so she would have to transfer them here.

"You must've been reading my mind, amiga! Teresa just freshened my drink and told me we were out. You've saved me," she said, hugging the bag to her chest. "Do you want to come in? I'll have Teresa make us a fresh batch." She turned and called, "Teresa! Ven acá!"

When yelled at high volume in a drunken slur over running water and youthful screaming, Martha supposed, it was possible to confuse the name "Teresa" with "Charlie." Charlie must've thought so, anyway, because he laughed and ran toward his mother with the hose on full blast.

Martha, who normally relished the opportunity to spend time with other people, didn't hesitate for a moment. "Not today, but thank you so much! I hope you enjoy the lemons," she said as she spun the wagon around. "See you later, Beatriz. Bye, boys!" She made it just out of the water's reach as Charlie, with his brothers laughing beside him, drenched his shrieking mother.

Martha had saved Minnie for last, of course. The light was at a flattering slant, low enough to signal the calm arrival of evening. How nice it would be to sit down in Minnie's backyard, invited this time, and continue their conversation from a month ago. She'd become so busy with the auction shortly after the cable-tech appointment and afterward in a state of self-imposed isolation until her hangover and embarrassment completely subsided that she hadn't followed up with Minnie on her offer to take Bonnie's picture or otherwise pursued their burgeoning friendship. In fact, she now realized, she hadn't even run into her on the driveway or seen her coming or going in all that time.

She was gripped by a sudden panic. What if something was wrong? What if Minnie had become sick? Well, she had her husband, of course, but it's always nice to have a friend stop by to bring homemade soup and gossip magazines or just make sure there's nothing someone else can do. Years ago, the elderly neighbor two doors down had fallen in her kitchen, just out of reach of the telephone, and lain there for two days before her out-of-town daughter had the police go down to check on her. She was alive, but unconscious and badly dehydrated. Martha felt terrible even now that she hadn't thought to stop by when she noticed two days' worth of newspapers on the old lady's sidewalk. Watching the ambulance pull away, Martha vowed that she'd keep better watch on her neighbors from then on, and here she'd let a month go by without knocking on Minnie's door. She wouldn't make that mistake again.

She left the wagon at her own house and hurried to Minnie's. After ringing the bell, she stepped away from the door, not wanting to embarrass herself or startle Minnie by seeming to peer inside again. She noticed then that the previously clear glass had been frosted and felt a small prick of humiliation. What if they'd done it because of her?

Just then Minnie opened the door. She was wearing a long silk caftan printed with oversize florals that seemed to float around her, so delicate that it didn't settle into place until a moment after she did. "Hello, Martha," she said with such warmth that Martha immediately forgot her worry about the new opacity of Minnie's door.

"I was feeling so guilty that I hadn't been by before now," Martha said in a rush. "But you look wonderful, not sick at all. I'm so relieved!"

"Why would I look sick?" Minnie looked genuinely concerned, almost embarrassed, as though she'd been caught at something.

Martha laughed awkwardly. "I didn't mean it like that. It's just that I hadn't seen you in a few weeks and who knows, you could've been sick or hurt or lying unconscious on your kitchen floor or something, and I felt terrible that I didn't make sure you were okay. I mean, sometimes terrible things happen, so we all should look out for each other, right?" She noticed that Minnie's forehead had furrowed out of sync with her smile. "Anyway, I brought you some lemons. I had a million of them, and so I thought I'd share. I don't know if you bake, but you could use them for garnishes or even just put them in a bowl in your kitchen for decoration. Speaking of which, I'd love to see what you've done with the place. I haven't been inside since the Realtor's open house." Her mind flitted back to the frosted glass. "If your backyard is any indication, I'm sure you've decorated it beautifully. In fact, it's so nice out today, if you wanted, we could make some lemon drops and sit out on your porch—or mine, whichever. I have an unopened handle of vodka; I can run home and get it. Or iced tea if you're not interested in cocktails. What do you think?" Martha thrust the bag at Minnie, took a gulp of air, and waited.

"Bless your heart," Minnie said, accepting the lemons. "And I wish I could take you up on your offer, but right now's not a good time. I'm getting ready for a party."

Martha swatted once at the air, a *no-problem* gesture. "Rain check, then! And I owe you that portrait of your Bonnie, so just call me when it's a good time. I put my number on the tag there. Or text, whichever is easier. I hope you have a great time tonight. You look fantastic."

"Thank you. And thanks for the lemons," Minnie said. "It was so nice of you to think of me."

Martha detected a hint of surprise mixed with the sincerity in Minnie's voice that made her wonder, for the first time, who Minnie's friends were. She hadn't noticed anyone coming to visit, but of course she wasn't always watching. Still, Martha was reminded of Minnie's first week at Stonewall Jackson and how lonesome she'd been until Mary Margaret and the Jennifers hijacked her. Maybe Minnie was lonesome now, too, in a new neighborhood, back in a city she'd been away from for many years. She sounded genuinely happy that Martha had stopped by with the gift, and that made Martha feel doubly good. It had been such a nice day in so many respects. She waved at Minnie and turned to go. Behind her, the door closed with a soft click. Martha looked over her shoulder, but all she could see through the door was a warm glow of light.

~

After dinner, Martha suggested they go for a walk before settling in to watch a movie. Leading her husband and son down the driveway, enjoying the fading sunlight and dry breeze, she paused after noticing a parking service stationed on the sidewalk in front of Minnie's house.

"Are they having a party?" Lewis asked, stopping beside her.

Martha squared her shoulders, inhaled deeply, and continued walking. There was a tang of ozone on the air, suggesting an approaching storm. "It appears so," Martha said. A knot formed in her stomach as they passed the stand with a sign that read PRIVATE EVENT. COMPLIMENTARY VALET. Minnie hadn't been getting ready for just any party; she was getting ready for her own. Then, trying to justify her lack of knowledge, not to mention her lack of invitation, Martha said, "Maybe it's a work thing."

As hard as she tried to pretend she wasn't bothered, Martha found it difficult to keep her tone light during their walk. Her own reaction frustrated her; her utterly delightful day now seemed tainted. Had she misinterpreted Minnie's reaction to her visit and the gift? She'd seemed so appreciative. Or was she only being polite? Minnie *was* a southerner, after all, even if she had spent the better part of a decade on the West Coast. Martha replayed their conversation and recalled now that after what had probably been a long-winded salutation on Martha's part, Minnie had responded with *bless your heart*, which was a versatile—and often vicious—phrase in southern vernacular, depending on the tone. Which had it been? A genuine expression of appreciation? Of pity? Or had it been a honey-covered *fuck you*? No, it couldn't have been the latter. Minnie was too benevolent, and besides, Martha most certainly didn't deserve such merciless disapproval as that.

But what if it'd been pity? Martha felt her heart constrict. Maybe it was Minnie who felt sorry for Martha instead of the other way around.

"Hey, slow down, Marty, we're not running a race here, are we?" Lewis said, taking her hand. "Did you hear us? Harry's been asking if we can get some ice cream before starting the movie."

Martha slowed and took several deep breaths, forcing herself to calm and reorder her thoughts. What did it matter if Minnie was having a party? It probably *was* a professional event. She was a "big deal" in the art world after all. And her husband was a fancy plastic surgeon, complex reputation or not. Maybe they were doing a fundraiser for some charitable cause. It didn't mean Minnie didn't care about Martha just because she and Lewis hadn't been invited. It didn't take a genius to guess that the Hales weren't floating around in that kind of socioeconomic stratosphere. In fact, it was probably a gesture of kindness they hadn't been included; they wouldn't feel pressure to make a contribution or a purchase they couldn't comfortably afford. Yes, surely that's what it was. Minnie wasn't excluding her; she was protecting her. Her mood lifted as that logic settled in.

"Yes, of course. Ice cream sounds great. Absolutely perfect," Martha said, taking Harry's hand. She gave Lewis a squeeze with her other, and they walked home like that, arms swinging, Martha comfortable in the knowledge that she was right where she belonged.

Six

It wasn't until Martha heard an unfamiliar bark coming from Minnie's side of the fence that her curiosity flared up again. Because she worked at home, Martha was accustomed to the routine sounds in and around their house: the near-constant leaf blowing by lawn crews, freshly frozen ice cubes dropping into the receptacle in the freezer, the AC condenser fan turning on and off, creaks when stepping on certain sections of the hardwood floors, the pentatonic wind chimes Lewis had given her for their fifth anniversary that she'd hung outside their bedroom window, and of course, the tennis balls blasting against the new wooden fence between theirs and the Devlins' backyards. She was also familiar with the various barks of the neighbors' pets and their typical locations, so when she heard what sounded like Lillian's now-elderly dog, Beignet, whose signature sound was one high-pitched woof followed by three short yaps, she cocked her ear toward the noise. It was so distinctive that when Harry was ten years old and memorizing both the NATO phonetic alphabet and Morse code for fun, he told Martha that Beignet's bark represented the letter *B* and said his owners must've been very smart to name him accordingly. Shortly thereafter, when they'd been outside at the same time, he said as much to Lillian, to which she'd remarked, "Aren't you a strange little boy?" and gone inside.

"I'll be back," Martha said. She handed Harry the bowl of popcorn and swung her legs off Lewis's lap.

"Want us to pause it?" Lewis asked.

"No, you keep going," she said. They didn't object as she heaved herself off the couch. How the two of them could be so engrossed in *Die Hard* after seeing it at least ten thousand times was beyond her.

She went outside to see if Beignet had gotten loose. She looked up and down the street, but all she saw were dozens of parked cars and the two valets leaning against their stand.

"Excuse me," she called to them. "Did you see a little white dog running around out here?"

As if rehearsed, they both quickly hid their cigarettes behind their backs. "No, ma'am," one of them said.

Then the other one looked at him and said, "You think she means that scrawny one that came over here for the party?"

Martha approached them. "Old and skinny? Kind of ugly with a wonky-looking eye?"

"Yeah, that was it," one said, and the other nodded.

Martha thought she might be sick. "Beignet . . . went to the party?"

"Yes, ma'am. But not by itself. It came with people. On a leash."

Martha was no longer listening. She turned and jog-walked back across her yard, up the driveway, and to her garage. Damn it. It was locked. She went in to retrieve the keys from the hook and could hear the *Die Hard* German terrorists' voices coming from the TV, one telling the other to get rid of a body and to keep the hostages calm. Martha shook her head; Lewis and Harry probably hadn't noticed she was still gone.

She rushed up the stairs to the guest room above the garage and crouched down in front of the window that faced the Wrights' back-yard. Sliding the lower sash up a few inches, she could hear snippets of conversation, the occasional burst of laughter. There were proba-bly thirty, maybe forty people milling around, lounging on the porch chairs, and standing at bistro tables that had been set up around the pool and covered with gauzy cloths. The pool itself was lit and glowed an otherworldly blue-green. The firepit was blazing softly, and beyond it, a bartender was making and refilling drinks for the guests. And sure enough, there was that stupid old Beignet, wriggling around like a fool beneath the aviary, barking their shared Morse code initial at Bonnie the parakeet.

Martha couldn't believe it. She simply could not. How was it that she wasn't better company than a dog? She watched in horror as Lillian appeared at the aviary at the same time as Minnie, and shared a laugh as Lillian pulled Beignet away and handed him off to one of her daughters. What sort of party was this? Lillian didn't work; her only profession seemed to be guiding her children into a size-four young adulthood. Her husband did something in sales, she remembered, but she didn't know what kind. Martha scanned the group to see if there was anyone else there she recognized. Hildy, her acquaintance from Little League, and Marvin, Hildy's anesthesiologist husband, were talking to an attractive, muscular man in a formfitting T-shirt Martha slowly recognized as John. She scanned the others and saw some vaguely familiar faces, but she couldn't identify them. She assumed Hildy was there because her husband and John were both doctors, but how on earth did Lillian wrangle an invitation? Had she become friendly with Minnie? More so than Martha had? Maybe they'd gotten to know each other through her art-consulting business. Yes, that was probably it; Lillian had probably hired Minnie to find some new art or something, and so Minnie had felt the need to include her.

Martha looked again at John, whom she'd only ever seen in a suit on his way to or from work. She was briefly stirred by his striking masculinity, the way his biceps completely filled his shirtsleeves, how casually he raked his free hand through his gray-blond hair, which was thick enough to need the raking. Well, of course he would be beautiful. Minnie was gorgeous. Didn't people of similar degrees of attractiveness always seem to find one another? Or was it that a particularly attractive partner inspired the other toward self-improvement such that they ended up on the same level? She thought of her dear Lewis, his failed weight-loss attempts and his beer belly that wasn't actually due to beer but to her southern cooking, which usually included generous quantities of butter and bacon. Early on, she hadn't been a very good cook, so she disguised her culinary mishaps with flavors that wouldn't fail. As the years went on, she became quite competent, capable of complex, even exciting fare—boeuf Bourguignon, sausage ragù with creamy polenta, eggs Benedict, savory chicken with crème fraîche—but her favorite recipes always called for her old standby, high-calorie ingredients. She then became aware of her own midsection, which was spilling gently over her waistband as she knelt on the floor. Her mind flitted to their son, who'd been gangly in childhood, but now, on the cusp of puberty, had become what she affectionately considered "fluffy." Now all three of them were a little fluffy, she realized. Not many of their neighbors were. Elsewhere in this country, carrying twenty extra pounds on one's person wouldn't be the difference between the haves and the have-nots, but in West U, it seemed somehow to be part of it.

Her knees popped as she stood. She watched a few more minutes at the window, wishing she had curtains to hide behind—not that anyone was paying attention to her. She tried to imagine herself and Lewis at Minnie's party. What would they be wearing? Who would they be talking with? Lewis would look awful in a formfitting T-shirt, but wouldn't it be nice if he didn't? She closed her eyes and saw herself in a silky caftan, holding a glass of wine, and floating from conversation to conversation, chatting comfortably with various guests.

When she opened her eyes again, she noticed Lillian's nephew, Willy, standing in an unlit corner of the Wrights' yard, picking at the stem of one of the banana plants and kicking the dirt around at its base. *What an awful child,* she thought. She had half a mind to bang on the window or call out to tell him to stop when she saw a man wearing a wildly colorful sport coat glide across the porch and kiss Minnie on each cheek. "Darling, this is fabulous!" He made a sweeping gesture with his arm, seeming to indicate everything in the immediate vicinity. "I'm clearly paying you too much," he said so loudly that even from her vantage Martha could hear his British accent. He and Minnie laughed.

Why was it that some people seemed to go through life so effortlessly? What did they know that Martha did not? She sighed and turned away from the window. What business was it of hers if that nasty Willy Guidry stripped the leaves off Minnie's trees?

She took a slow, deep breath to calm herself, the way she'd learned that one time she tried a yoga class. She'd overheard some of the mothers with children in Harry's preschool talking about a new studio they'd fallen in love with. So that's why all these women were so lithe and calm, she'd thought, and decided to give it a try. She showed up in a pair of sweatpants and one of Lewis's old T-shirts and, at the back of the room, unrolled a mat she'd borrowed from the studio. The only enjoyable part of that hot, miserable hour was the first two minutes in which the bouncy contortionist-yogini instructed them to sit with their eyes closed and set an intention for their "practice." She had them inhale the goodness of the universe through their noses, exhale any negativity out their mouths. In, out. In, out. Martha never went to another yoga class after that, but she sometimes used the breathing technique. In with the good, out with the bad.

Except now, after a couple of deep inhales, she noticed that the air she was breathing smelled stale. Musty. She opened her eyes and looked around their guest room. There was an old desk she'd found at a garage sale that she'd intended to sand and paint but had never gotten around to doing. Harry's old Pack 'n Play that now contained their mismatched set of luggage. The dresser and nightstand from her childhood bedroom. A daybed that had been a hand-me-down from her parents. Martha couldn't remember the last time she'd changed its sheets. She hadn't needed to; they'd never had any guests sleep there.

She glanced again out the window. Perhaps this would be better used as an office for her postproduction work. Harry was always in the living room on the big computer playing his video games. Why did she need to relegate her own income-producing work to the corner of the kitchen counter as she'd been doing? It would be much more comfortable here. The desk wasn't in bad shape, and she wouldn't even need to buy a chair. She could bring up one of the infrequently used ones from the dining room to sit on. It would be quiet, and there would be little to distract her from her work. She might even increase her weekly processing output, and therefore, their income.

There was a rise of laughter from beyond the window. Yes, Martha decided. She would turn this room into her artist's garret. That she'd also be able to see what was happening at Minnie's house day to day—how she and John interacted if and when they sat outside, what they cooked on their grill, who came to visit and what they talked about—would simply be a coincidence. She smiled to herself and went back into the house to finish watching the movie with her husband and son.

~

After Martha made her decision to create a room of her own, she wondered why she hadn't done it sooner. She'd written her high school honors English thesis on Virginia Woolf after all, and was well acquainted with the author's argument for a woman's right—or imperative—to commandeer both a literal and figurative space for her creative endeavors. Even now, she could recall Woolf's statement, which had been the opening line of her own paper: "In the first place, to have a room of her own, let alone a quiet room or a sound-proof room, was out of the question, unless her parents were exceptionally rich or very noble, even up to the beginning of the nineteenth century." Now here she was, at the beginning of the twenty-first century, considering her own right to a quiet room in which to work. She wasn't rich by local standards, though by global ones she certainly was. And of course, she wasn't a writer, but she did consider herself an artist. Okay, maybe not a real one, but at least an assistant to a real one. Perhaps she was an arbiter of art. Yes, why not? It was an apt description. She exerted her own creative influence over a photographer's raw images. She was responsible for producing a final product that would please both the artist and her subject. In that way, she was very much an important part of the creative process. Even an essential part. No bride would be happy seeing images of herself gazing at her dearly beloved with shadows beneath her eyes or her nose illuminated by sunlight when the rest of her face was shaded or her own bodily imperfections—pimples, cellulite, panty lines—pulling a viewer's eye away from her ethereal joy. Martha knew how to adjust a photograph enough to highlight the subjects' best features and minimize their worst without their even knowing why they looked so beautiful, so radiant, so flawless. They credited the photographer or their own loveliness or the magic of their special union. They never knew that Martha had sat at her computer in her pajamas with either a cup of coffee or a glass of wine, working to subtly erase any evidence of imperfection in white balance, saturation, composition, humanity. If anyone deserved a room of her own, it was Martha. And now she would have one.

Lewis was supportive, as she expected he would be. Harry, on the other hand, was elated and offered to help her get it set up. She knew it was because he thought she was too strict about his video gaming and assumed that if she were in another room—especially outside their small house, where she could see and hear practically everything—she wouldn't constantly nag him to turn it down, turn it off, go read a book, or do something that required creative thought. After Harry and she had moved the desk and he was getting her computer connected to the Wi-Fi, she said, "Now, just because I'll be working out here doesn't mean you can play with your video games all afternoon," she said. "I'm still going to mostly work during school hours, so it's not like I won't be in the house."

"Mom, I don't play *with* my games. I just play the games." He rolled his eyes. "Jeez."

Normally, she'd take a moment to discuss his tone of voice, but as she surveyed the freshly cleaned room, the new blackout curtains that would let her control the amount of light she needed as she worked, the new area rug she'd bought on sale, and colorful throw pillows on the washed daybed, she let it go. She inhaled deeply and took in the goodness. Then a thought occurred.

"By the way," she said, turning to Harry. "Have you run into Mrs. Mickelsen's nephew? He's moved in with them, apparently."

"Willy?"

"That's the one."

"Yeah, I met him at school. He's in my PE class."

The contentment she'd felt only a moment ago left her. "Harry, now you listen to me. I have a bad feeling about that boy. I want you to stay away from him, okay?"

"But why? He seems cool."

"I understand how tempting it would be to make friends with him, especially since he's right across the street, but I'm telling you, he's trouble. Okay?"

Harry shrugged and mumbled, "Okay."

Something about the way he said it, though, gave Martha the uncomfortable feeling that he didn't mean it. She made a mental note to keep an eye on him. The last thing she wanted was trouble with one of the neighbors.

Seven

Thursday morning a few days later, Martha woke with a feeling of purpose and ambition. She was out of bed even before Lewis, in time not only to put on real clothes but to shower first, the way a woman who worked outside the home would, because she was now going to be a woman who worked outside her home. Of course, since it was only a few dozen feet outside, she didn't feel it necessary to overdo the moment, forgoing any makeup and letting her hair dry naturally. Still, it felt like a professional accomplishment to drive Harry to school in a pair of jeans, a clean T-shirt, and flats instead of pajamas and slippers.

It turned out to be fortuitous as well, because when she pulled into her driveway, she saw John Wright, wearing a dapper-looking suit and tie, carrying her two blue plastic recycling bins toward her garage. She parked where she was, partially blocking the sidewalk, checked her teeth for crumbs in the rearview mirror, and tried to smooth down her hair.

"John!" she called. It came out more forcefully than she intended, so she tried again. "I mean, hi, John."

He placed the bins neatly next to her garbage bin, then turned to her and smiled. "Good morning," he said as he walked toward her. He took her right hand and shook it, placing his other one on top. Her physical response to this friendly embrace surprised her: she felt like cheese melting between two warm slices of toasted bread.

"What"—she gripped his hand tighter, feeling unexpectedly woozy—"what are you doing?"

He released her gently. "I noticed your bins had been out front for a few days. In case your family was away, I thought it might look suspicious to eager prowlers to leave them out." When he smiled, a dimple appeared on his left cheek. He could've been a movie star. "And it looked a bit messy. I hope you don't mind."

"Oh jeez, not at all." Had she remembered to brush her teeth? "I can't believe I didn't do it myself; I'm usually so careful about that stuff. I do like to keep things tidy, which you and Minnie probably do, too, seeing as how neat your yard always is. The front, I mean. Well, the back, too—I was there with the cable guy a month or so ago. Minnie was there, too!" She remembered what Minnie had said about John not liking strangers in the house and panicked. "We went through the gate, of course. Your pool is amazing." She took a breath. "Anyway, I've been setting up my new office the past few days and I guess I wasn't paying attention. It was so nice of you to bring them up for me. Thank you." She admonished herself for not keeping up her own high standards and vowed not to let it happen again.

"You're very welcome," he said. Then, after a pause, "Doesn't your husband take care of that for you?"

Her face felt like it would go up in flames. "Usually, he does. Of course." She forced a laugh. "He's got a bad back, though, and sometimes it really bothers him. It's no trouble for me to do it; they're not heavy at all." She was proud of her ability to manage her home as well as she did, both inside and out. Maybe John would admire that about her, too.

"Call me old-fashioned. I just think lovely ladies such as yourself shouldn't have to bother with trash, heavy or not."

Another surge of heat, part blush, part shame. What must he think of her doing her own lawn? What must he think of Lewis?

"Well, I'm off," he said. "It was nice to finally have the chance to speak with you one-on-one, Martha." He flashed the dimple at her.

"It was so nice," she said. "John."

"Until next time." He turned to go, and Martha watched him walk. What great posture he had. And chivalry.

"John?" she called, and he turned back. "I just wanted to say, since you're new here and might not know, we don't really have to worry about prowlers in West U. But thanks again anyway."

"Good to know," he said. She couldn't be sure because of the distance between them, but Martha thought he might've winked.

~

Her weekly schedule was flexible, but fastidious. On Mondays, she did a thorough housecleaning: changed the sheets, scrubbed the bathrooms, mopped, and vacuumed. Growing up, her mother had always cleaned the house on Mondays because it ensured a fresh start to the week. Her mother also said that the only decent way to begin a day is by making the bed, because an unmade bed was both a psychic and a moral error, and there was practically no way to recover from that. Even as a grown woman, Martha would rather skip a shower than skip the simple act of making her bed, lest she have to bear the burden of Evelyn's imaginary disappointment throughout the day.

Tuesdays through Thursdays, depending on the number of photos she had to process, she worked five to six hours each day at her computer. After dropping Harry at school, she cleaned the breakfast dishes, then made herself a second cup of coffee, and worked until lunch. After cleaning up the kitchen a second time, she worked again until it was time to pick Harry up, because she liked to be available to help with homework or just spend time with him before it was time to start dinner. It seemed like such a long time ago that he wanted to help her bake cookies after school, or unspool a length of butcher paper on the driveway to paint on, or go to the park to swing and play in the sand-box. These days, he rarely seemed to need her, but even so, she found it difficult to reimagine the structure of her school-day afternoons. She could hardly bear to think too far forward in time, when Harry would go off to college and the scaffolding of her life, which had been built by and for motherhood, fell apart. She kept herself from thinking about it too much by staying busy with other things.

Fridays were when she tended to the yard, mowing or pruning. Her stepfather always did the lawn on Friday afternoons after work, so if they had friends over for dinner or happy hour on the weekends, the yard would be neat and inviting. Martha kept that habit, too, although the need had not been as urgent. Saturdays were for family: relaxing, watching movies, maybe going to the beach or fishing. She didn't usually cook on Saturday nights, but on Sundays, cooking and baking were her main focus. She took inventory of the contents of her pantry and refrigerator, cooked whatever was nearing expiration and composted the rest, planned the week's menu, went grocery shopping, and made a big dinner. Occasionally one or both sets of their parents joined, but most often it was just the three of them. They had long ago stopped going to church, but Martha always led them in a prayer before Sunday dinner: "May all be fed. May all be healed. May all be loved."

Now, with a fresh cup of coffee, she pushed away any stray thoughts about her conversation with John, then settled down at her new desk to begin her day. She had four big batches of images to complete this week, and had only done two so far. April was a boon for event pho-tography. In the almost three weeks since the gala, she'd already edited six weddings and two b'nai mitzvah. She was going to have to work extra today to get it all done on time, and would probably have to work Friday, too, which was irritating. This time of year was also a boon for grass and weeds, and she needed to allocate time for that.

As if she'd conjured them just then, she heard the simultaneous powering up of a lawn mower and leaf blower next door. She stood and watched from the window as a group of men in long-sleeved shirts and wide-brimmed hats methodically swarmed into Minnie's backyard, setting immediately to work. They worked without speaking but in a coordinated, methodical manner that reminded her of a colony of ants. Martha had never bothered observing a lawn crew do its work before, but now she was fascinated by their efficiency. When they were finished and dragging their equipment and bags of cuttings and waste behind them back through the side gate, Martha glanced at her watch again. In just twelve minutes, they had cut the grass, weeded the flowerpots, pulled dead branches from the banana trees, shaped the cypress columns, bagged the clippings, and sprayed the palm trees with something, probably to keep the aphids away. Someone had even quickly skimmed the pool, even though Minnie had a separate pool crew to manage that. Twelve minutes! She could tell by the sound of the machines that another squad in this lawn platoon had been working on the front yard at the same time, and that they'd loaded up and rumbled away again within sixteen minutes of their arrival.

It would take Martha all Friday to do that much work on her own.

She didn't have as intricate a yard as Minnie's, of course. But from February through November, she spent at least two hours per week and usually more on hers. What if all those hours had been poorly spent? Martha opened a new spreadsheet on her computer.

For each photography event she edited, she was given between two thousand and twenty-five hundred raw images to process. For simplicity, she entered two thousand in the first column. Always, before she edited anything, she did a first pass to look through and cull out any low-quality, blurry, unflattering images, and that usually took her down to about 75 percent, or fifteen hundred potentially usable photos. The real work was creative and labor intensive, editing and delivering the finished portfolio, which usually ended up being around 45 percent of the second-pass images or, for this analysis, seven hundred. It took her an average of six hours to complete seven hundred images. It might take her competitors less time—there were editors overseas in sweatshops who could produce twice that number—but the reason she had such steady business is because of her exacting quality standards. A photographer didn't have to go back over her work to make sure they wouldn't embarrass or frustrate a client with poor photographs; they knew whatever she delivered would make the customer happy. For that reason, she charged on the high end: seventy cents per image, which ended up being between four and five hundred dollars per event or, in this example, $490, which came out to $81.66 per hour.

How much did the lawn crew charge? She knew an average cost was $35 per visit for a simple yard like hers. She entered that on her spreadsheet. It didn't bother her that the lawn guys made $140 per hour to her $81.66; they had to split it among them. What bothered her was that for a mere $35 per week, she would've freed up two or even three hours in which to work on her photo editing, for which she could potentially earn over $200. And she wouldn't have to spend those hours sweating and itching and straining herself. She could be sitting right here, sipping coffee, doing all the work she needed with just her hands.

She'd been so proud of that $140 per month savings for so long, but now it made her feel foolish. If she'd done the math when she started working in earnest five years ago—she stared at the calculator—she could've earned an extra $40,000. More than enough to remodel the bathroom. Or buy a Tesla. And she wouldn't have been the only person—the only *woman*—in the neighborhood doing her own lawn. Also, it made her curious: What else had she been doing wrong all these years?

Eight

On the second Monday in May, Martha pulled her minivan into the middle school's drop-off lane just barely on time for the first bell, which frustrated her. Punctuality was one of her favorite traits about herself. She was about to wish her son a good day when the vice principal approached her window.

"Mrs. Hale," he said flatly, by way of greeting. "I wonder if you'd mind pulling into a parking spot and coming in for a chat." He bent down and peered into the car. "You too, Harry."

Martha felt a hot rush of panic, as though she'd done something wrong—had the vice principal somehow gotten wind of her slight intoxication at the gala? The Little League wasn't associated with the public school system, but could that somehow affect Harry's good standing? Would he be dismissed from the lacrosse team? Would she be asked to keep a certain distance from campus? Also, why hadn't she cleaned out the cupholders and gotten a car wash over the weekend like she'd planned? Her fastidious housekeeping did not always extend to her automobile. "Yes, Mr. Summers. Certainly. Of course. Be right there."

She pulled into a spot and checked her hair in the rearview mirror. Thank goodness she was now in the habit of wearing appropriate clothing in the mornings. She'd have died on the spot if she'd been summoned to the principal's office wearing her pajamas. She hopped out of the car, vibrating with adrenaline, and was halfway to the curb when she realized that Harry wasn't beside her. He was still sitting in the passenger seat, slumped down like his shoulders had collapsed, staring at his lap. Martha then realized it had been over a month since the gala.

She yanked open Harry's door and leaned in. "What on earth have you done?" Spittle from her whisper-yell landed on his prepubescent cheek. He didn't even wipe it off, just sank lower in his seat.

Martha had to admit that it was both a great relief not to be the cause of the vice principal's concern, however grave, and so horrifying to know that her one and only begotten son must've done something egregious that she could barely tug him out of the car and onto his feet.

Now it all made sense. Normally, Harry used an alarm to wake up in time to get himself ready for school. They had a dependable, coordinated schedule: every day, by the time the bacon was frying, she heard the hinges on his bedroom door creak open and the shower turn on shortly thereafter. Then he would drop his full backpack by the door and be at the kitchen table just as she was plating his breakfast. Depending on how well he'd slept—which she knew was due to how long he'd stayed up playing with his video games, in spite of her admonitions—he either chatted or grunted as he ate. This morning, however, she'd had to enter his room twice to urge him out of bed. The second time, he mumbled that he wasn't feeling well and couldn't go to school, so she kissed his forehead to test his temperature. It was normal. She pressed the back of her hand to his cheek. Still normal.

"You're fine," she said. Her own mother had never accepted vague complaints of illness, and so neither did Martha.

"I'm not fine," he said, rolling toward the wall. "I'm sick. My stomach hurts."

"Well, come eat something and we'll see. You're probably just hungry."

"I'm not hungry."

She moved to the end of his bed to evaluate him and saw that his eyes were open. If his eyes had been closed, she'd have pulled up his blankets, kissed his cheek, and gone to call the pediatrician. But since that was not the case, she pulled the blanket down and stood over him with her fists at her waist. Yesterday was Mother's Day, and he'd been perfectly fine. He and Lewis let her sleep in, made her a lovely breakfast, then sent her to the nail salon for a pedicure. They ordered takeout for dinner and all seemed perfectly well. Afterward, Harry asked if he could go out to ride bikes with his friends. Feeling a benevolent afterglow from the day, she'd agreed. But now she realized he had a science test this morning, and he'd been out much later the night before than he should've been. Of course he didn't want to go to school; he hadn't studied. She took a sharp inhale, angry at herself for not making sure he'd prioritized his schoolwork.

"Lewis Harrison Hale, it's time to get up now. Your breakfast is on the table. Skip a shower if you need to, but let's not be late to school."

Now here they were, trudging through the parking lot. Harry refused to answer her demands as to what news awaited her, so she simply said, "You did something wrong, that's clear enough. You don't want to talk about it, fine. I'll hear it from Mr. Summers anyway."

With righteous urgency, she pushed Harry ahead of her into the vice principal's office and marched him toward his desk. It wasn't until Mr. Summers asked her to please sit down that she noticed the other people already seated in four chairs crammed along the wall.

"Oh," she said, startled. "Oh my. Hello, Ruth. Hello, Lillian. Boys. Well, this must be something serious."

Lillian Mickelsen pinched her nephew on the arm and told him to get up. Martha clutched her purse to her chest and sank down in the vacated seat. Ruth Miller, who'd thoughtlessly sloshed her cocktail on Martha's jacket at the gala last month, elbowed her son, Richard, and hissed at him to get up, too.

"It's quite serious, I'm afraid," Mr. Summers said. "Boys, come over here and let's discuss this situation."

The three of them shuffled themselves into a row in front of Mr. Summers, but only Harry hung his head so low that his chin practically rested on his breastbone. Richard shifted his weight from one slim leg to the other and chewed on his pinkie fingernail. Cocksure, Willy stood perfectly still with his hands in his pockets, holding the vice principal's gaze. Martha's heart ached. She didn't even know what the crime was, but she could tell just by their body language who was guilty of it.

"Moms, did you happen to notice the tarp hanging on the wall facing the football field this morning?"

Ruth and Lillian looked at each other and at the same time said, "No?" Martha took a moment to recall if she and Harry had driven or walked past that particular area. "No," she finally said.

"There are actually several tarps hung up around the exterior of the school because last night, someone spray-painted . . . penises on the brick walls."

"Penises!" Martha said loudly, springing out of her chair and startling the women beside her.

"Unmistakably," Mr. Summer said. "They were quite . . . detailed. It was urgent that we get them covered up as soon as possible. No doubt some of the girls would've found them disturbing. Fortunately, a conscientious passerby emailed me several photos of the vandalism late last night and I was able to get some of the custodial staff to help me conceal the . . . depictions."

He turned his computer monitor around so everyone could see it. Spray-painted in stark white on the redbrick wall of the middle school was a thick shaft flanked by enormous balls and topped by a distinctive, slouching head. It seemed to grow out of the ground like a giant mushroom, nearly as high as the oak saplings the PTO had planted the year before that stood in a row in front of it. Ruth and Lillian gasped.

Martha strode to the desk and stood facing Harry, Richard, and Willy. "Did you boys do that?"

"Mrs. Hale, please," said Mr. Summers.

"Answer me," Martha said. She was so outraged the room blurred at the edges. None of them said anything. It wasn't possible her son could've had anything to do with such a scandal. It simply wasn't.

As if reading her mind, Mr. Summers said, "The witness also sent me a video." The boys now looked at each other, panic visible on their faces.

In the clip, one boy was spray-painting what looked like a comma into the very top of the graphic, and the other two were pointing and laughing. Then the videographer shouted at them to stop what they were doing. All three of them spun around and looked, deerlike, directly at the camera, with what appeared to be night-vision goggles hanging around their necks. The videographer zoomed in on their stunned faces in the split second before the painter dropped the canister and they took off running. Mr. Summers reversed and paused the video, and let the mothers process what they could very clearly see: Willy and Richard with their eyes wide and mouths open. And Harry, half turned, holding the paint in midair.

Martha, feeling her face go first cold and then hot, returned to her chair and sat down.

"So," Mr. Summers said, looking from one boy to the next. "Whose idea was it to deface our school like this?"

"Harry's," said Willy.

Harry jerked his head up. "No it wasn't!" he said.

"Sure it was. It's right there on the video, isn't it?"

"But that was the only part I painted!" Harry was clearly on the verge of tears. "You and Richard did everything else!"

Willy looked at Mr. Summers. "You only got one video, right?"

"I didn't say that," Mr. Summers said.

"Well, whoever took it yelled at us to stop, so it probably was the first time he saw us—Harry—painting anything. He probably didn't take any videos before that, or else he'd have yelled at us then, right?"

Mr. Summers raised his eyebrows and toggled his head from side to side. "Well, I can't argue with that."

Lillian leaned forward. "His daddy's a criminal defense attorney," she said pridefully.

"It's awfully convenient that the 'only' part you painted was caught on camera, isn't it?" Willy had turned to face Harry, his air-quote fingers still held up between them.

"Willy's gonna be just like him," Lillian whispered to Ruth, who nodded in agreement.

Or like your drunk of a sister, Martha wanted to say, but did not. Maybe having a son like Willy had driven the poor woman to drink. Besides, she felt like she was partly to blame for Harry's participation. He'd come to her while she was doing the dishes the night before, asking if he could go ride bikes with friends. She'd been surprised and then thrilled; her son had been so withdrawn lately, so uncommunicative. Except for his video game opponents, some of whom didn't even live in the same city, Harry seemed to have very little social interaction. She'd assumed that it was just a phase, possibly something to do with hormones, so when he announced he'd been invited to go biking with kids from school, she agreed without even asking who he was going to be with. If she'd asked and he'd told her Willy was going, she'd have said no. And if she'd asked and he'd lied, she'd have known he was lying. She'd known that Willy was trouble. Why hadn't she been more proactive about keeping Harry away from him?

Harry began to openly cry.

"We were just biking around," Willy said. "Then Harry pulled out a can of paint and said he was going to do it and if we wanted to be friends with him, we'd have to do it, too. I think he was trying to take advantage of me being new here. But we didn't do anything. We only watched. I'm sorry, Mr. Summers. We should have stopped him."

"Harry," said Mr. Summers. "Is that true?" Harry only shook his head, crying with his eyes closed. "Richard, is Willy telling the truth? Was this Harry's idea?"

Richard looked first at Willy, who winked at him. Richard flicked a glance at Harry and then nodded.

"Willy! I saw you winking at Richard. What's that supposed to mean?" Martha said.

Lillian turned and glared at her. "Martha, how dare you shout at my nephew like that, especially when your son was the one caught painting in the video. Besides, Willy wasn't winking. He probably has an eyelash or something."

"Ladies, please. Settle down," Mr. Summers said. "I'm trying to get to the bottom of this."

"Or the tip," whispered Willy, loud enough for Martha to hear. Richard giggled.

"Willy Guidry!" Martha said. "That is appalling!"

Lillian stood up, scraping the wooden chair legs against the linoleum floor. "Martha, that's enough. Willy hasn't been in trouble with the vice principal or anyone else since he got here, has he, Mr. Summers?" He shook his head. "Ruth, has Richard ever gotten in trouble at school?"

"Well, there was the one time he set a fire in the chemistry lab," Ruth said, shrugging. "But I think that was it."

"You told me that was an accident," Lillian said.

"Well, that's what he said. Right, Richie?"

"Mom, don't call me that," Richard said.

Lillian sighed and shook her head. "This is exactly why I send my girls to private school. Remind me again why you didn't want Richard to go private, Ruth?"

"He didn't get in," Ruth said, looking at her hands.

Lillian turned back toward Mr. Summers. "My nephew has only been here for six weeks. There's no way he was responsible for this. He'd never even think up something like that," Lillian said. Willy smiled beatifically at her. His teeth were off-white and crooked, but Martha still wouldn't have been surprised to see a light twinkling at the edge of one like in a toothpaste commercial.

"Whereas your son," Lillian said, spinning on her heel and facing Martha so closely she could smell the stale hint of chocolate, which she allegedly refused to let her children eat. "I know for an actual fact that Harry was caught masturbating in the boy's restroom last month. Only a pervert like that would paint penises all over the school."

"That's not true!" Harry said between sobs. "None of it. Willy made it up!"

Mr. Summers stood up abruptly. Ruth realized that she was the only one left seated in the room, and so she slowly stood up, too. "This is the first I'm hearing about a restroom incident," the vice principal said, his heavy brow furrowed.

"I didn't do it!" Harry shouted. "Willy only said that to embarrass me in front of some kids at lunch!"

Martha rushed to Harry and gathered him in her arms. She realized it was the first time he'd let her hold him like that in a very long time, and she, too, began to cry. She didn't care what her son had or hadn't done; she couldn't bear to watch him suffer like he was. He might be growing up, but she still knew her son's character. She also remembered what it was like to be fourteen and under the spell of people with more confidence and power than she.

Still, the video evidence could not be denied. She untangled him from herself and held him out at arm's length.

"Harry, honey, tell the truth now," she said. "Not the bathroom thing. I already know that's bullshit. But the graffiti. I mean, you were on the video. Was it your idea?"

He looked at her with liquid, red-rimmed eyes. His pale cheeks were blotchy like they used to get when she would put him in his room for a time-out and he would beg and cry to be let out. There weren't locks on the bedroom doors, so she would have to stand on the other side, pulling on the old brass knob to keep him from opening the door, watching the interminable three minutes count down on her wristwatch, crying along with him.

"No, Mom," he said quietly. "I painted a little more than just that one part, but it wasn't my idea. I swear."

Martha looked at Mr. Summers. "That's good enough for me. I believe him."

Lillian stepped forward. "Of course she's going to believe him. We all want to believe what our children tell us. Have you ever heard the mother of a serial killer or a school shooter admit that she suspected him all along?" She looked at Martha with what looked like a contrived expression of pity.

"The fact is, Mrs. Hale," the vice principal said, "Willy's right. There is only one video, and in it, Harry is clearly the one doing the vandalism. Without any other evidence, I'm going to have to assume that he was responsible for the entire enterprise."

Martha thought she saw Willy and Richard exchange a fleeting smile. Proof of both Harry's vindication, and also of his defeat. But what could she do? In the court of public opinion, which is where it seemed everything in this neighborhood was decided, Harry—and she—had been beaten.

"Harry, I'm going to give you a five-day out-of-school suspension starting today and a fine of two hundred and fifty dollars to cover the cost of cleaning. I also want a three-page essay on the importance of samaritanism." Then he looked at the other boys. "Willy and Richard, I find it hard to believe you had nothing to do with this, but I can't prove it. However, since you've admitted that you were there voluntarily, I'm going to give you both a one-day out-of-school suspension, and I want you each to write a two-page essay on the dangers of authoritarianism."

"What's that?" Richard asked.

"Look it up," Mr. Summers said. "Everyone, you're dismissed."

~

Martha and Harry left the school without a word. Pulling into the driveway was a jolt; she could hardly remember having driven home. Harry followed her inside and went immediately into his room, very quietly closing the door behind him. Martha had no energy for her usual Monday morning cleaning routine. What did it matter anyway? Who would notice if the toilets weren't scrubbed and the sheets stayed on the beds an extra day? An extra week?

Instead, she went into the kitchen and pulled out the ingredients for a mixed berry tart, Harry's favorite dessert. Flour, sugar, butter. Mascarpone cheese, heavy cream, lemon juice and zest from the last lemon harvested from her tree, apricot marmalade, berries. It wasn't difficult to make but required just enough focus to distract her from the reality of the morning. After she made the dough, pressed it into the tart pan, and put it in the freezer to chill, she made a fresh cup of coffee and went outside to drink it on the stoop. The crape myrtles were filling out again, bright-green leaves thick along new branches, fat clusters of hot-pink flowers at their tips. Martha searched the collars where the branches met, hoping to see a new bird's nest.

A few minutes later, above the sound of mourning doves and leaf blowers, Martha could hear Minnie's garage door scroll open. If she'd had any spring in her legs, she'd have jumped up and gone back inside before Minnie could see her sitting there doing nothing. Instead, she pressed herself against the slice of wall between the front door and the porch railing and willed herself invisible. Anyway, she wasn't in any mood for pleasantries.

It worked. Minnie backed out of her driveway, then slowly headed east, past Martha, without even looking in her direction. From the set of Minnie's jaw and the slack of her profile, Martha thought that she looked as unhappy as Martha felt. Perhaps she was late to work. It was already ten o'clock, and she thought Minnie usually left the house before now. Who knew, maybe everyone was having a bad case of the Mondays.

Martha went back inside to bake the crust and beat together the ingredients for the filling. If the scent from the oven had reached Harry through his bedroom door, he didn't react. After spreading the mixture along the carefully scalloped edges of the crust, she took her time arranging sliced strawberries, blueberries, and raspberries into neat, concentric circles. All over the top, she brushed the warm marmalade glaze. She slid a large slice onto a plate, and along with a fork and glass of milk, set it on the serving tray she always used to deliver Harry's food when he was sick.

He was sitting on the floor against his bed, staring out the window, which yielded a view of nothing but Minnie's new fence. Before the Wrights' enormous house was built, there had been an original single-story bungalow in that lot, whose low profile had allowed a generous amount of afternoon sunlight into Harry's room. Now it was in perpetual shade. Martha set the tray down next to him.

"I'm sorry," he whispered. A couple of tears splotched onto his jeans.

She sat down on the edge of his bed and wiped his cheek with the back of her hand. "I know you are," she said.

He dragged his gaze to her. "I just wanted them to like me."

She sighed and looked at him with an understanding half smile. Isn't that what they all wanted? "Do you think it worked?"

"No." He gave a scornful laugh. "Especially not now."

She resisted the urge to chastise him for going against her instinct and her instructions. The humiliation seemed to be punishment enough. "Well, they don't exactly seem like the kind of friends you'd want, you know? Willy was pretty quick to blame you for everything. And Richard seems like he's just Willy's minion."

Harry shrugged.

"You told me you thought Willy was cool. Were they nice to you before today?"

He shrugged again. "Not really." Slowly, he picked up the fork and took a bite of the tart. After a moment he said, "They called me Harry Balls."

Martha sucked in a gulp of air. "Well." She cleared her throat. "That's awfully rude of them."

He nodded and continued eating, and Martha was plunged into a memory of herself at Harry's age, eating a sandwich in the cafeteria the first week of high school.

A sophomore boy named Leo—who in retrospect was a great deal like Willy—slid into the empty seat next to her. Two summers before, she'd been in a theater camp with Leo's little sister Sarah, and Leo was the one who picked her up every day while their mother waited in the car. Had he remembered her?

Leo helped himself to a chip from Martha's lunch. "What's your name?" he asked her.

Martha could hardly breathe, struggling to swallow the bite in her mouth. Simply put, Leo Parker was beautiful. He had sandy-colored hair, light-brown eyes that seemed almost golden, a smile that tugged higher on one side, dimples. He wasn't very tall, but his charisma more than made up for his stature. Besides, his rich, crackling voice hinted at a forthcoming growth spurt. She'd heard a rumor that he was the best kisser in the entire school. She licked her lips. "Martha," she said, breathless.

"Martha," he repeated, looking deeply into her eyes as he helped himself to another chip. "Why'd your parents name you that?"

Could this actually be happening? She told him the story she always told people who asked about her name. "My mom loved The Beatles. Well, she still does. But when she was, like, sixteen and a half, *The White Album* came out, and she loved the song 'Martha My Dear' so much she decided if she ever had a daughter, she would name her Martha. The lyrics are so pretty. Have you heard it?"

"I have, but I'd love to hear you sing it." He smiled, and his dimples pocked his cheeks.

"Oh, I'm not a very good singer," she said, shaking her head. Leo, she knew, played lead guitar in a band. He could probably sing, too.

"Just a little bit of it, then. Please?"

She glanced around and noticed that a few other sophomores had gathered behind Leo, all of them smiling at her like she was one of them. She nodded at him, took a sip of Coke to wet her throat, and sang the last verse, trying to emulate Paul McCartney's jaunty tone. It had been her mother's wish when she was born that someday, someone would love her the way McCartney loved the Martha of this song. Leo held her gaze as though in a caress. Could it be her mother's wish was coming true? When she finished, she giggled and felt herself go a little light-headed.

Then, abruptly, Leo began to laugh. "Your mother named you after a dog!"

"What? No, she didn't." Martha could feel the swell in her heart drop into her stomach.

"She did! Paul McCartney wrote that song about his sheepdog. Didn't you know that?" He looked around at the other kids and they began to laugh, too. "Martha was McCartney's dog!"

"That's not true," Martha said quietly, because she didn't know for certain. She'd never thought to ask.

"Ew, Leo, don't eat any more of those chips. They're dog food!" some female sycophant shouted.

"Hey, where's her leash?"

Martha grabbed her food and stuffed it into her lunch bag. She picked up her satchel off the floor and rushed away from the table.

"Oh, does Martha need to be let outside? Hurry, before she pees on the floor!"

That afternoon, she'd asked her mother about the origin of her name. Evelyn said, "Don't be silly, honey. Who would write a love song to a dog?"

Martha didn't eat lunch in the cafeteria again after that, choosing to spend her time in the library, and later, the darkroom instead. She was still taunted in the halls, or before and after school, until the fun wore off and the kids moved on to other victims. They may have forgotten it, but she never had.

Now she reached down and ran her hand over Harry's cheek. "When I was your age, the kids made fun of me, too," she said. She didn't mention that even though adults didn't often say it out loud, she still felt like she was on the wrong end of a joke that everyone seemed to get but her. She hoped her son would somehow fare better than she had, that he'd find at least one really good friend, that he'd feel comfortable in his own body and his community, that he wouldn't have to strive so hard to fit in. She didn't tell him those things, though, because she didn't have the experience to back them up. Instead, she offered what little advice she could: "The trick is to try not to let it bother you."

Nine

The week of Harry's suspension was miserable. He hardly wanted to leave his room, not even to play video games or be on his computer. Instead, he lay in bed and read Lewis's old, tattered copies of Ian Fleming's James Bond books and occasionally worked on the essay Mr. Summers required before he could return to school. Martha was happy Harry was reading, but she worried about his mental state. She tried talking to him, making his favorite foods, offering to watch movies together, but he was listless and forlorn. It didn't help that the day after the incident, Lewis had to fly to Denver for a weeklong geospatial conference.

She thought, briefly, about calling her mother. But she could already imagine what Evelyn would say. First, she'd be shocked. Then Martha would have to defend Harry by explaining the larger circumstances, reminding her mother of the typical middle school pecking order, exonerating her son's susceptible nature. Evelyn, decades removed from parenting young teenagers, would no doubt recast her own experience in a flattering light. She was always blameless and outstanding in her selective memories. *You should've demanded more of him when he was a child. You were always too soft, Martha. In more ways than one, I might add. If it had been me, I'd have provided the boy more structure, more discipline. As far as I know, Harrison has never once been spanked. I know you've given up your religion, but that doesn't change the fact that the*

Bible states quite specifically if you spare the rod, you spoil the child. I'm not saying you need to use an actual rod, but it seems to me you've hardly ever punished him. You should demand more responsibility, more respect. If I hadn't held you to a higher standard, who knows what mischief you'd have gotten into at his age. Is he even remorseful? Maybe I should come have a talk with him. Martha shook her head to stop her mother's imaginary tirade, and resigned herself to handling the situation on her own. She just hoped Evelyn wouldn't somehow read her mind and call. Martha was skilled at putting on a good front when she had to, but she'd never been able to hide her true emotions from her mother.

The house was eerily quiet. Their daily routine, gone. Because she often found Harry staring into space, or absentmindedly rummaging through long-forgotten corners of his closet, or curled into a tight ball under his covers, she felt compelled to check on him multiple times throughout the day. She didn't even want to put on the television for company because she wanted to be able to hear Harry if he made any noises, which he rarely did. It was nearly impossible to focus on photo editing because she was both uncomfortable being outside the house in her office and also afraid of getting too absorbed in her work. What if he needed her and she didn't know it? She still went up to her office for a half hour or so here and there, but for the first time in many years, she fell behind on her assignments.

Dragging from lethargy on the warm, hazy Tuesday evening of that terrible week, Martha put a frozen pizza in the oven for dinner and went outside to water her front beds. It hadn't rained in a week and her gardenia bushes were looking parched, the petunias she'd planted in March already wilted. The daytime temperatures were becoming summerlike, grazing the midnineties. She didn't really feel like being out in the heat, but at least she could stand in the shade. Perhaps it was time to have a sprinkler system installed.

Martha froze, midspray, when she heard Minnie's front door slam closed. Martha knew she looked terrible, dark circles under her eyes from poor sleep, her hair a frizzy cloud. She probably smelled terrible, too, not having bothered to shower in two days. But it was only Lupe, the Wrights' housekeeper who came once a week. Lupe walked down the walkway with her handbag and umbrella under one arm and a large Tupperware container in her hands, and greeted Martha with a jut of her chin.

"Hello, lady!" she said. "I'm not stealing! Miss Minnie said I could have!" Smiling, she lifted the container as if to prove her innocence.

Shortly after Lupe started working for the Wrights, she'd come over to give Martha a misdelivered piece of mail—embarrassingly, a mailer for CPAP machine supplies, which Lewis had used for several months to help with his sleep apnea after his weight became an issue. Martha had tried to remove him from the marketing list, but the company continued to send promotional mail, as if assuming he'd eventually need their equipment again. But Lupe hadn't seemed interested in the mailer's message, only concerned that it be delivered to its intended recipient. She'd seen Lupe coming and going often enough over the past couple of months to know she was reliable, and assumed her also to be honest. "Of course, Lupe. I wouldn't have thought otherwise," she said.

"Miss Minnie es muy buena gente," she said. "See you la próxima."

Martha thought it was strange that she spoke to Lupe, albeit superficially, more than the people she worked for. Martha watched her walk away in the direction of the setting sun, worried that Lupe was going to get too hot. The bus stop was at least a quarter mile away. Briefly, she wondered if she should offer her a ride, but just as quickly dismissed it. Driving Lupe to the bus stop might imply that Martha thought Minnie should've offered to do it. But what did she know about an employer's duty to her housekeeper? She'd never had one.

Just then, an SUV heading toward her moved into the oncoming lane and pulled up next to Lupe. Martha dropped the hose, ready to sprint to her aid in case it appeared Lupe was in some kind of danger. But then she saw John behind the wheel of the gleaming white Range

Rover that Lewis had told her probably cost over $100,000. Martha watched as Lupe spoke to him, nodding, then as John handed her an enormous bouquet of white calla lilies through the open window before driving off again. Lupe turned around and walked back to the Wrights' house, looking glum and clearly burdened by the heavy arrangement.

Martha approached her. "Need some help?"

"No, gracias. He just need me to put some water. Ay, Dios mío, maybe I miss my bus." She hurried inside, muttering to herself in Spanish. Martha had studied enough in school to know it wasn't a string of kindnesses.

Martha wondered if something was the matter. Normally, Minnie returned home from work around five thirty and John typically got home an hour later. Today, not only had Minnie not returned from work yet but John was early. Perhaps he was meeting Minnie somewhere out for dinner? Come to think of it, Martha didn't remember seeing Minnie leave that morning. It was possible Minnie hadn't gone to work at all. Maybe she'd been at home all day. Martha tried to recall if she'd heard their garage door around the time Minnie usually left for work. She'd been so distracted with Harry that she hadn't noticed. Not that she always noticed, of course. She certainly had plenty of other things to worry about. She turned off the hose and rolled it back up onto its holder. What did it matter anyway? What the Wrights did and when was certainly no business of hers.

Harry asked to eat his pizza alone in his room, and so Martha ate her own in front of the television. The news was depressing: there were tensions in Iran, in Venezuela, in Alabama. At least the Astros were up against the Tigers, but Martha wasn't enough of a baseball fan to either watch a whole game or be energized by its outcome. Eventually, she opened a bottle of rosé—nothing fancy, just a screw-top one that had a pretty label and was featured on sale at the grocery store, an afterthought on her way to the checkout lane—and went out to sit in the backyard to enjoy the last streaks of orange before they dipped completely behind Minnie's roof.

Apparently, she wasn't the only one with that idea.

"Come on, baby. Come sit down with me."

Martha recognized John's voice, but she'd never heard him speaking quite like that. The sound of it gave her goose bumps. *Velvety* was the word that popped into her mind. *Caramel.* It was simultaneously deep and gentle, almost like he was talking to an animal. Did they get a dog? Martha angled her head, listening for a reply. None came.

"Please." It came out as both an order and a plea. Again, there was no audible response. Martha heard the elaborate squeak of a corkscrew, a satisfying pop, the gurgling fill of one glass and then another. Unless dogs drank wine, John must be talking to Minnie. Yet Minnie hadn't spoken.

Perhaps it was her own malaise that activated Martha's curiosity, or perhaps it was because she had nothing better to do. Very slowly, so as not to cause the aluminum lounger to creak, she got up and tiptoed to the stairway leading to her office. Just as slowly, she parted the curtains and raised the window overlooking the Wrights' yard. The previous owners of the Hales' house hadn't installed a screen when they built the room above the garage, and in all the years they'd lived there, it hadn't occurred to either Martha or Lewis to add one until she was setting the room up to become her office. After considering the effect and the expense, she decided against it. Besides, she liked the unfettered view. Not for spying, obviously, but of the treetops, the clouds. It was peaceful to glance up from her work occasionally and see the wide blue sky. A screen would be just one more barrier between Martha and the beautiful world beyond her.

She pulled the cushion from her desk chair and knelt on it beneath the window, careful not to expose too much of herself. It was well past sunset, but their outdoor lights were bright enough that she could easily see John sitting on the edge of one of the lounge chairs by the pool, holding both glasses of wine. On the table between the chairs was the oversize bouquet of flowers that he'd given Lupe to arrange.

"Minnie, my darling," he said. "Will you please sit with me? I miss you all the way over there."

So, she *had* been home all day.

After a moment of apparent hesitation, Minnie emerged from the shadows of the porch and slowly descended the steps toward the pool. John stood up to offer her the wine. She flinched, then accepted the glass with an outstretched arm. She sat down on the opposite chaise, unsmiling.

"There we go," he said, raising his glass. "A toast? To my beautiful, brilliant, talented wife. I love you. Always and only, you."

To Martha's eye, it seemed that Minnie was reluctant to touch glasses. Did she not agree with him? She appeared to be looking at John's torso, not his eyes. Was she ill? Had she stayed home because something terrible had happened to her at work? Perhaps she'd lost a client or a sale or something; Martha wasn't entirely sure what her job entailed. Whatever it was, she looked disappointed. Petulant, even. She kept her left arm close against her midsection, almost cradling it, like she didn't want to open herself up to him. And yet here was John, not only a handsome, fit, successful man, but evidently a devoted and attentive husband, not to mention neighbor, seemingly willing to hold his glass aloft indefinitely until she could be bothered to meet it.

"Cheers," he said, warm and confident.

"Cheers."

What on earth was wrong with Minnie? She barely looked at John, and instead lay back in the chair and turned her gaze to the sky. What was so enchanting about the cloudy, humid funk hanging above them that could keep her from engaging with her husband?

Martha thought about Lewis, and felt a deep longing overcome her. Lewis wasn't as sexy or sophisticated as John, but he genuinely enjoyed her company, and let her know as much. At least he used to.

And she assumed he still appreciated her emotional and physical labor that made his own domestic life easy. They often had satisfying conversations about more than just their family or work. They even had a decent sex life, if not quite as robust or frequent as it had been in the beginning. She'd heard that lots of couples drifted apart at least physically if not maritally after years of infertility struggles. Even if it was only once or twice a month, they still found each other that way. She made a mental note to seduce him when he came back from his work trip. Their lovemaking always made her feel grateful afterward, lying with her head on his chest, playing with the nap of hair on his belly. Some of the articles she'd come across in women's magazines seemed to indicate that she shouldn't actually be grateful for sex, though. That it was a form of subjugation, and she should instead feel empowered and benevolent for allowing a man access to the temple of her body. Maybe those women were all thin and somehow enlightened beyond her understanding. Maybe that's what was happening now between Minnie and John. She was so lovely, so divine, that she couldn't be bothered by his affections. She could have anyone she wanted. On the other hand, Martha had never had the luxury of being choosy. She truly was—even if she wasn't supposed to be—grateful for Lewis's attention. Over their nearly sixteen years of marriage, they'd rarely spent a night apart, and now, home alone with their unhappy son in his room, she missed Lewis especially hard.

"So, I was thinking," John said. "What if we went away for a long weekend? Napa or Sedona?"

"I don't ever want to go back to Napa," Minnie said, still staring at the sky.

Martha bristled. She'd long wished for Lewis to take her away to Napa Valley for a weekend.

"How about Portugal, then? Algarve's perfect this time of year. I could cancel my clinics, and we could leave a week from today. The beaches won't be crowded until mid-June; we could have the town to ourselves."

Minnie was unmoved.

"Umbria, then. Oh, or Rovinj! Really, babe, anywhere you want to go."

Martha watched him retrieve a blanket from the porch and take it to Minnie. He laid it across her lap like a royal servant would. Where on earth was Rovinj? She would have to look it up.

"Minnie, please look at me."

After a moment, Minnie languidly rolled her head toward him.

Martha copied the movement; paying attention to the sensations in her neck, to what kind of power might be found there.

"Can we go somewhere? Forget about everything for a minute?"

"You said you had some important surgeries coming up."

He reached over and refilled her glass. "Min, look at me," he said. "Minuit. Nothing—and nobody—is more important than you." After a moment of silence, he said, "Look, I said I was sorry. You know I didn't mean to—"

"I don't know why you insist on this new thing, calling me 'Minuit.'" Martha was startled to hear the snap in Minnie's voice, but John seemed unaffected.

"It's French, it's sexy."

"It doesn't mean what you think it means. It doesn't mean *small* or *cute* or whatever. It means *midnight*." She rolled her head away again, and looked at the darkened sky.

"Okay, Melanie," he said, his voice suddenly dropping as he empha-sized the first syllable of her given name. "Would you prefer I call you that?"

She ignored him.

"Fine. If that's how you're going to be, then I'm out." When he stood up, Minnie leaped off the chaise away from him. He made a sound that was somewhere between a chuckle and a growl, and poured the remnants of his wine into her glass. "I'm going to go get a real drink." He put his glass down next to hers, then leaned toward her and said in a quieter voice that Martha had to strain to hear, "Don't you forget how lovely you are." Or was it, "How *lucky* you are?"

He strode into the house. A light in an upstairs room went on. The bedroom, Martha knew, from having walked through it during the open house. Shadows moved across the closed curtains, and then the light went out. Moments later: the sound of an interior door slamming, the roar of his car engine, the grinding scroll of the garage door closing after he'd pulled out of the garage. Throughout those few minutes, Minnie hadn't moved at all. But then, after it had been quiet for a while, long enough to hear the crickets starting up, the first of the season, she let go of her grip on the back of the chaise and went slowly back inside.

Martha stood and rubbed her kneecaps, which hurt from the kneeling. Discord of almost any kind made her uncomfortable, and watching Minnie and John frustrated with one another bothered her more than she'd have imagined. But all couples—even ideal ones—occasionally argued, didn't they? They have a range of emotions. They suffer. That was how they grew. Martha knew this as well as anyone.

She pulled down the sash and went back to the house to make sure her son was okay.

Ten

O n Friday, Harry's final day of suspension, he seemed like he might finally be emerging from his self-induced isolation. He came into the kitchen and laid his head on Martha's shoulder. It wasn't quite an embrace, but she would take it. When she offered to make him lunch, he almost smiled as he nodded.

"Hey, Mom, I'm working on my essay for Mr. Summers. Did you know there are still, like, eight hundred real Samaritans living in a village in the West Bank? It's not just a story from the Bible."

"Huh," she said, trying to imagine it. A whole village of people who would stop to help a stranger who'd been left naked and beaten alongside the road. "No, I didn't. That's really cool." She handed him his lunch, which he took back to his room to eat.

Of course, they probably weren't all as good as the original Good Samaritan, the one who helped the dying man in the Gospel of Luke who even a priest walked past. Still, she couldn't stop thinking about what a kind and gentle world it would be if everyone were like that. There wouldn't even be any victims to pick up and nurse back to health if all the world was good and kind, but they'd all take care of each other in other ways: sharing food, helping with chores, educating and loving each other's children. Martha knew, from several years of Vacation Bible School—which her mother said was part of her spiritual education but was really just free babysitting—that the parable of the Good Samaritan was part of Jesus's response to the question from a lawyer, "And who is my neighbor?" The neighbor, of course, was the Good Samaritan.

The neighbor.

~

She checked her watch: 2:46 p.m. She knew it wasn't her business, but she couldn't help but notice that Minnie hadn't left for work again that day. The unpleasant scene between her and John on Tuesday night had been gnawing at her ever since, possibly because she'd been feeling so glum herself. It was like her melancholy had doubled just by imagining that Minnie was unhappy. Martha wanted to echo what John had said, that Minnie *was* lovely. Lovely and lucky both.

It occurred to her then that nobody had checked on her or Harry since The Incident. It was like she and Harry were both pariahs, strangers left alone to fend for themselves. The one time she'd gone to the grocery store after sunrise, she'd felt other women's fleeting glances on her like hail against her skin. Martha reprimanded herself. Here she'd been so wrapped up in Harry's misbehavior and punishment and her own response to it that she hadn't really considered what was happening to the other people around her. Again. She'd been behaving more like the priest or the Levite after him who ignored the suffering man. She decided right then that she would recommit to holding herself to a higher standard than that. Martha Hale might've been a lot of things, but one thing she refused to be was unneighborly.

She finished kneading the bread she was making for dinner and set it to rise, washed the lunch dishes, changed out of her pajamas, and collected her camera bag. Then she checked on Harry and told him she'd be right next door if he needed anything.

~

Minnie answered the door in a caftan that, while elegant, was more bathrobe than work wear.

"I'm sorry to barge in on you," Martha said, "but I'm having a terrible week. I can't focus on my work and can hardly even sleep. So I wondered—if you were home, and here you are—if you'd like me to take those pictures of your bird like we talked about. Bonnie, of course. I mean, if you're not busy with something else. I brought my camera. Oh, and a loaf of bread. I've been baking a lot of bread lately."

Minnie gave an approximation of a smile and opened the door wider. As she reached to accept the loaf from Martha, the sleeve of her caftan shifted to reveal an ugly black brace on her left wrist.

"Oh!" Martha said. "What happened to your arm?"

Minnie pushed the caftan back down and waved at the air dismissively. "It's nothing. Just me being clumsy. I was hanging a painting at work yesterday and fell off the stepladder. It's my fault for wearing heels. Anyway, it's going to be fine. Come in."

Martha took a deep breath and exhaled it slowly as she crossed the threshold for the first time as an invited guest. Minnie's house smelled glorious. Somehow, it smelled exactly how a photo spread in an interior design magazine looked. It was chilly, too. The Hales kept their thermostat at seventy-eight in the summer to save on their electricity bills. Anytime Lewis or, more often, Harry, left a door open, she called out for them to close it. "Do you want to air-condition the whole neighborhood?" she'd say, Evelyn's refrain familiar in her own mouth. Besides, even if they wanted to keep it cooler it was almost impossible; their house was so old, it was hard to control the temperature.

Martha gazed all around, taking in the expanse and the architecture, which she'd already seen, but now, more intriguingly, the personalization of the space. Giant art pieces—paintings, sculptures—hung in the foyer with lighting on them that was wonderful and somehow just right. There was a silver-toned table along the entryway wall, with a neat stack of oversize books, different-size vases in matching metallic hues, a weird ball that looked like it was made out of moss, and other mismatched, oddly shaped objects that seemed not to go together at all but yet looked like a perfect collection beneath the circular mirror with round metal discs sticking out from its edges. How did Minnie know how to arrange things in this way? Even if Martha owned the same art and furniture and knickknacks—that word seemed too unsophisticated to describe Minnie's things, but she didn't know what else to call them—she'd never in a million years be able to put it together so cohesively. Martha thought of her own small entryway table: a catchall for keys, mail, receipts, change, lost-and-found items. Shoes, backpacks, bags, and jackets were dumped beside it in spite of the fact that she'd put a nice wicker basket underneath it to corral the detritus. She collected the mess every Monday and redistributed it all where it was supposed to go.

Martha was moving so slowly through the foyer, angling her head to read the book titles—ooh, one on Dorothea Lange, her favorite photographer!—and examining the plexiglass sculpture on the wall, that she didn't realize Minnie had gone into the kitchen and come back carrying two glasses of sparkling water.

"Oh, thank you," Martha said. "This looks so nice." She made a mental note to start affixing lime wedges to the edges of her beverage glasses. "It all looks so nice. You have such incredible taste."

"Oh, it's mostly John. He has a really refined aesthetic," she said, chopping her hand through the air. "Want to come sit down? Truth is, I'm not exactly having the best week either. I could use a little company."

Martha smiled to herself, pleased both that her instinct to check in on Minnie had been correct and that she'd made the choice to be a Good Samaritan. She followed her neighbor past the enormous dining room on her left and the glassed-in wine closet on the right, into the living room, which was so large that there were actually two sitting areas between the fireplace and the kitchen. Minnie sank down into one of the large suede sofas. Martha thought of the corresponding piece of furniture in her own home as a couch—that's what her own mother had always called them—but that word seemed grubby now. Minnie's was most definitely a sofa and not a couch. She indicated that Martha should sit in the one across from her. The wall of windows along the entire north wall let in so much light that Martha couldn't believe how small and dark her own house was by comparison. She dragged her gaze from one end of the room to the other like a caress, until she landed on the view outside the two smaller kitchen windows on either side of Minnie's stove. The bottom half was the new fence, and above it, a few inches of the Hales' shiplap siding, which looked dingy, and their roof, which they should've had replaced at least a couple of years ago, not only because it was old but because Hurricane Harvey had done some damage to it. In fact, Martha could see a few patched shingles even from where she was sitting. She shrunk down into the plush cushions. How awful for Minnie to have this immaculate home and have to look out the window and see all that. She would call a roofer immediately.

"That looks pretty awful," Minnie said, as if agreeing with Martha.

Martha felt her face go hot. Had she said all that about her roof out loud? "What?"

"Your knees. Did you fall?"

Martha stuck out her legs and looked down at herself. Below the hems of her Bermuda shorts, her kneecaps were indeed a deep, irritated-looking scarlet—from having knelt at her window, eavesdropping. She'd been so distracted the past few days she hadn't even noticed.

Minnie stretched her good arm behind the sofa and grabbed her purse. "Here, I've got something for that." She pulled out a tube and offered it to Martha.

Martha read the description: *relieves muscle pain and stiffness due to minor injuries, overexertion, and falls; reduces pain, swelling, and discoloration from bruises.* She rubbed the recommended amount into her discolored skin. "So, why's your week been bad?" Martha asked, handing back the tube. Then, thinking her question might be too direct, quickly added, "I mean, you don't have to tell me if you don't want to talk about it."

Minnie gave a half smile and shrugged. "Just work stuff. Mostly." She lifted her injured wrist. Then, looking over Martha's shoulder, said, "This is so weird."

"What's weird?"

"It's Bonnie. She's so quiet. Usually whenever someone comes in, she has a fit, squawking and flying around her cage. But look at her. She's just sitting there, looking at us. I've never seen her act that way before."

Martha turned to follow Minnie's glance and noticed the gilded cage for the first time. It was quite large, bigger than the outdoor aviary, and had many accoutrements, whatever they were for, inside. Bonnie was indeed sitting quietly on a stick, her pale-yellow head cocked to the side, looking at Martha.

"Hi, pretty girl," Minnie said, her voice rising softly into a higher register. "Can you sing for us?"

Bonnie began to trill and chirp, moving her head as though she was actually singing.

"That's her happy sound," Minnie said. "Really, this is crazy. She hates most people. I got her four years ago when she was about two years old from this rescue group in Seattle. There was a huge flock of them that'd been dumped by a pet store that was going out of business. Sometimes they do that if they can't sell them, just take them outside and let them go." She gazed at Bonnie and smiled. "I saw it on the news, actually. All these sweet little birds in quarantine. They had to decompress in a dark room to recover from the stress of being chased by falcons." Minnie looked back at Martha. "Can you imagine?"

Martha shook her head. Before seeing Bonnie, she'd never imagined parakeets either in captivity or the wild, much less going from one to the other.

Minnie sighed and looked down at her bandaged wrist in her lap, and began picking at a loose thread sticking out of one of its seams. "My husband—John—didn't understand why I was so upset about it. We'd been married about two and a half years then. He—we—really wanted a family, and it wasn't happening. We did the whole thing, went to the doctors, did the tests. They said he had low sperm motility. Lord, you'd have thought they told him his dick was going to fall off." She closed her eyes and shook her head. "Oh, don't listen to me. I shouldn't talk about him like that. He just wants a family. He really is a good person, you know. It's not his fault."

Martha leaned forward. "No, of course not. It happened to us, too. We tried for almost nine years without any luck." She lifted her hands.

"I remember you saying that the day we moved in," Minnie said with an expression Martha couldn't decipher.

"Oh, I sure did, didn't I? Jeez, my mother's right—my mouth runs so fast my mind can't keep up. Anyway, at least we have Harry." Then, like she'd been shocked, she cupped her nose and mouth with her hands. "Oh my god, I'm so sorry. I did it again. I don't know what's wrong with me; I keep saying the dumbest things. I can't believe I said *at least I have a child* to someone who doesn't."

"Don't worry about it."

"No, I shouldn't have said that. It was awful and insensitive. I mean, I remember you said you were still trying."

Minnie shrugged.

Martha leaned forward. "Are you? Or did I misunderstand?" Then she shook her head. "Oh jeez, forget I said anything. I mean, it's obviously none of my business. Sorry."

"It's fine. Yeah, technically we're still trying." Minnie chuffed a small laugh and held up her hand. "Fingers crossed. But John's forty-six now, and I'm thirty-eight, so . . ." She shrugged again. "You know."

Martha thought about what her mother had told her so long ago, when Evelyn talked about being of advanced maternal age at thirty-eight.

Martha and Lewis had stopped trying when she was thirty-five. They'd exhausted their savings account trying to conceive another baby. When the stock market crashed in 2008, Lewis panicked and instead of leaving what they had left where it was so they could recover from the loss, he cashed it out. Their property taxes were over $10,000 a year; their mortgage was $18,000. Plus, they still owed Lewis's parents the money they borrowed for their down payment. Realizing that they'd likely never catch up financially, they'd quietly let go not only of the dream of a large family but of having even one more child. "I do," she said. "It's a rough road. I hope it works out for you, though."

"Well, I have Bonnie. And she's like my baby. I imagine she's a lot easier than an actual kid, though."

"Oh my god, yes. The last time I had a pet was when I was eight, right before my mom got remarried. There was an open house at the daycare where I went after school and the director had this litter of puppies she was hoping to give away. I remember begging my mother to let me have one, even though money was tight, but she gave in. I took really good care of him, fed and brushed him, carried him around constantly, set up playdates with other dogs in the neighborhood. It was a ton of work but it was nothing compared to having a baby." Martha slapped her thigh. "I had no idea how hard it was going to be. Harry took up every moment of my life for years. He never napped, and anytime I tried to put him down he cried. He wouldn't even sleep in his own bed until he was ten. I'd wake up and he'd be asleep on the floor beside me on a pallet he'd made out of blankets and pillows. I mean, of course I'm so glad to have him. And it wasn't always terrible. He was—he is—sweet and smart. He's fourteen now, and about to graduate from middle school. For the most part, he's a really good boy." She leaned forward, forced a laugh. "But actually, he's at home right now, this whole week in fact, because he was suspended for painting penises on the exterior of his school."

Minnie raised her eyebrows.

"He was coerced into it. By the popular kids. It wasn't his idea." Martha, suddenly embarrassed as much by her own revealing chattiness as her son's misbehavior, shifted on the sofa to look at Bonnie in her cage. "Anyway, that's why I'm so stressed out and decided to stop by. Can you take her out of the cage so I can photograph her?"

"Sure." Minnie elegantly pushed herself off the sofa, then cooed to the bird as she approached. She opened the little door, and Bonnie stepped onto her extended finger with the poise of a movie star emerging from a limousine onto a red carpet.

Martha took her camera from her bag and checked the settings. "That's great, right there. Can you hold her like that for a minute?" Martha moved around the two of them, framing Bonnie from various angles and distances. "Do you mind if we move into the hallway so I can use that red-and-pink painting as a background? I think it'd be really interesting with her blue and yellow feathers."

Minnie looked at her with an appraising squint. "You have a good eye," she said. "I wouldn't have thought to do it, but that complementary color scheme is a great idea."

Martha looked at Minnie and smiled. "I want to get close to her so I can keep her in focus and blur the background. Will that be okay?"

"You can try. She usually won't let anyone but me get close to her, but she seems to like you."

Bonnie watched Martha as she worked, often looking directly into the lens with first one eye and then the other as she clicked the shutter. Minnie held her out in front of various art pieces, using the vibrant colors and textures to set off Bonnie's pastel plumage. Minnie suggested doing a still life of sorts, using fruit that matched her feathers.

"Here, put down your camera and you can hold her while I set it up."

Martha did as she was told, and nervously accepted the transfer of the bird from Minnie's hand to her own. The brief moment their index fingers were pressed lengthwise together sharing the delicate weight of the bird felt so intimate Martha felt her face flush. Minnie, collected as ever, smiled and turned away to slice pieces of pineapple and pears.

"What if I drop her?" Martha was aware of the preciousness of Bonnie's tiny body the way she was whenever she held someone else's baby. Despite her own years of holding and carrying her son, she always worried that she'd forgotten how to do it, that she'd somehow lose her grip and accidentally maim or murder the child.

"You can't. She'd just fly away," she said. "Anyway, it's just amazing how into you she is. I'm almost jealous." Minnie glanced at Martha with a smile that indicated she wasn't actually jealous at all. She arranged the fruit on a plate, stood back to critique it, and made a few minor adjustments. "Okay, maybe put her down right here. What do you think?"

They worked together like this, shifting accessories, recommending angles. Minnie spoke gently to her bird throughout, and Martha copied her. Bonnie was as placid as she could be the entire time. At one point, Minnie leaned in and Bonnie touched her beak to Minnie's lips. Martha clicked the shutter at the perfect moment.

"Got it!" Martha said, her voice a burst of elation that punctured the calm that had settled over the three of them.

Startled, Minnie jumped enough to unsettle the bird, and Bonnie fluttered away. Minnie stood, composure regained, and extended her palm toward Bonnie. "It was so nice of you to bring your camera," she said over her shoulder as she returned the bird to her cage.

"Did I do anything wrong?" Martha said in a rush.

Minnie turned to face her, looking both startled and concerned. "What do you mean?"

Martha hadn't planned to say anything, but after such a pleasant time with Minnie, she couldn't reconcile what had been nagging her for a month. "Your party. I just wondered if there was a reason, you know, that—" She pressed her hands to her cheeks as Minnie's face turned red. "Oh jeez, this is embarrassing. I'm sorry. I shouldn't have brought it up."

"No, it's fine. I feel terrible about that, really. Especially because you'd just brought me those lemons . . ."

"Don't worry about it," Martha said. She felt terrible having put Minnie on the spot. Most of the time, she'd rather be uncomfortable than make someone else feel that way. And now Minnie would probably never want to be friends with her.

"It was my husband's idea to have a few people over, mostly from his work or mine, sort of a back-to-Houston networking thing." She made an apologetic moue and shrugged.

"That's what I figured, but then since Lillian Mickelsen was there—I mean, I thought I saw her crossing the street when we, my family I mean, were out for a walk—so I thought maybe it wasn't just work. But anyway, it's none of my business." She felt a little nauseated.

"Her husband sold John some medical equipment, I think." Minnie reached over and put her hand on top of Martha's. "I'm really sorry. I wanted to invite you. I wanted to invite the whole block, in fact. I thought it would be a way to get to know the neighbors, but John said we had to keep the guest list to a reasonable number. He insisted."

"Oh well, that makes sense."

"I wish I could've invited you, Martha. I hope you'll forgive me."

It might've been just an excuse, but Martha believed that Minnie was being sincere. She had wanted her at the party, but her hands were tied. That was enough for Martha. She felt nearly as pleased as if she'd actually been a guest. "Well of course I do. I understand how persnickety husbands can be sometimes."

At that, Minnie winced. "Speaking of which, look at the time," she said. "I had no idea it was so late. And I look like such a mess."

Martha followed her glance to the oven clock. It was almost five. How had two hours passed so quickly?

"I'm sorry but I have to get ready." Minnie looked around, flustered, and began to tidy up the kitchen. "John's coming home soon."

"But it's Friday. Doesn't he come home later?"

Minnie looked at her quizzically as she awkwardly scraped the fruit into the trash, trying to balance the plate on her brace. "What?"

Martha realized how strange it must've sounded for her to comment on his schedule. Their pool crew came on Fridays, she knew, because she was often doing her own yard work when they pulled up with their equipment. By chance—not that it was relevant to her immediate concerns—she'd also noticed that John would swim laps after they'd cleaned. So okay, she'd noticed some of their habits, but it was only a quirk that she'd remembered anything specific. Still, she quickly turned away so Minnie wouldn't see the panic she felt and began repacking her camera bag. "I mean everyone, not just John. You know, husbands coming home late in general. After a workday. Sometimes Lewis doesn't get home until after seven or even eight, but of course that depends on meetings and other things." She glanced up to see if Minnie looked upset, but she appeared to be preoccupied by other concerns.

"He doesn't really like Bonnie being out of her cage. He says it's dirty," she said, scrubbing the countertop. "It's not, though. She's very clean."

"Of course," Martha said. "She does seem very clean."

"Do you mind showing yourself out? I kind of need to hurry." Minnie gave her a worried smile. "Thanks for taking the photos. I can't wait to see them." There was something strange about Minnie's shift in demeanor, but Martha decided it was none of her business to pry.

"Of course," she said again. "I really loved shooting her."

"Oh, and about your son?"

Martha stopped and turned back.

"I once drew a nasty picture of Miss Taylor, you know, the choir teacher, and left it on her desk. If she ever found out it was me, she didn't say anything. Your son's just being a kid. He'll be fine." Minnie winked at her.

Martha smiled and tried to wink back, but she felt the entire left side of her face collapse awkwardly onto itself. She giggled first, and was elated when Minnie did, too. "See you soon, I hope," she said, and closed the front door behind her.

~

That evening after feeding Harry an early dinner and making sure he was content in his room, Martha went up to her garage office to work on the raw images she'd taken of Bonnie. She was surprised and delighted at how many really good ones there were to work with. This added another layer of satisfaction on an already pleasing day. She had the feeling that a difficult time was now behind her. Harry seemed to be so much better; he'd finished his paper and would go back to school on Monday. Lewis would return tomorrow, and they would have a lovely family weekend together. And she had finally spent some quality time with Minnie. Even though she'd seemed strange at the end, Martha didn't think it was because of her. If anything, Minnie's behavior inspired an urge in Martha to keep an eye out for her neighbor. She was clearly much more sensitive than Martha had thought. Those earlier fantasies of developing a friendship with her might not be so fantastical after all.

For that reason, she spent many hours culling through the photographs of Bonnie, settling on a dozen that really captured the bird's delicateness, her calm, her curiosity. She was sure to include as many as she could that had been staged by Minnie, although objectively she didn't think they were the best ones. The ones with Bonnie standing next to the fruit, for example, seemed a bit contrived. Her favorite among them all was the final image, of the appearance of a kiss between them. In it, both their eyes were closed, a tender moment between owner and pet—although in this case it seemed more like mother and daughter. It was quite stunning, actually, that she'd been able to capture it. She spent a great deal of time processing that one in particular, adjusting the exposure, the softness, and the cropping to highlight it exactly right.

Chris Cander

When she finally decided it was finished, she glanced at the clock and saw that it was past eleven; she'd been working for four straight hours. She saved all the images once more, just to be safe. Tomorrow, she'd upload them to her favorite color printer's server. He was terribly expensive, but he used archival paper and would print them as many times as necessary until she was pleased. Her idea was to sign them and give them to Minnie as a gift. Maybe she'd even frame the one of the two of them. No, she decided. She wouldn't presume to know what kind of frame to use. Besides, she didn't want to appear overeager; it would be better if she gave them to Minnie in a simple manila envelope. In fact, she'd just slip them casually through the mail slot and wait for Minnie's reaction.

Feeling exceptionally pleased, she turned off the light and went back inside to check on her sleeping son.

Eleven

The following Wednesday morning was Harry's eighth grade pro-
motion ceremony. Despite their rush to shower and dress—Harry
nearly made them late by insisting on doing his own tie—Martha
wanted to slip the envelope of freshly printed photos through Minnie's
mail slot before they left. She dropped it in, then tiptoe-jogged across
the lawn so her heels wouldn't sink into the earth. She was halfway
across the small patch of green between their houses when she realized she should've just used the sidewalk. The Wrights' sprinkler system
must've gone off earlier, and her nice leather pumps were now darkened
with wet.

Because there were over four hundred students in the graduating
class, the ceremony was held inside a stadium field house in southwest
Houston. Together, the student body and their families, who packed the
bleachers, looked like the United Nations. Yet, predictably, the mostly
white clique of which the snotty woman from the gala, Hazel, and the
graffiti-artist Richard Miller's mother, Ruth, and their husbands were
a part of, segregated themselves in a section close to the floor with the
best view of the balloon arc under which the graduates would pass to
receive their certificates. Martha and Lewis sat two rows behind them,
in between darker-skinned families she didn't know. She felt guilty for
not knowing the people sitting beside her, in spite of the fact that their
children had presumably attended school together for the past three

years. She smiled at the parents to her left, saying congratulations and nodding, then to the family on Lewis's right. At the same time, she felt guilty for wishing she were sitting down below, among or at least closer to the people from her own neighborhood, who were talking and laughing at each other's stories and fanning themselves with their programs. Lillian and Daniel were down there, too, along with a man Martha didn't recognize, who must've been Willy's father in from Louisiana. All three of them were scrolling on their phones and didn't seem to be paying attention to each other or anyone else.

"Don't mind the Tesla crowd," Lewis whispered into her ear. Martha could always count on him to know what she was thinking.

Still, as they waited for the administration to finish up whatever they were doing before the event began, she leaned forward, trying to hear their conversations:

. . . fired my maid for asking me if I'd gained weight . . . I most certainly did, right there on the spot . . . don't call Americans gorda *in this country . . . hand over her key . . . the locks changed anyway . . . never know with those . . .*

. . . you reduce downside market exposure because you get your principal back even if the asset's value declines . . .

. . . on sale . . . I know!

. . . Seaside next week. We always stay at this cute little cottage off Tupelo Circle . . .

Sex tape! Are you kidding me? Does Minnie know?

The latter was followed by a loud *shhhhh!* and the little knot of women who'd been talking jerked straight up for a moment, then leaned even more deeply together. Martha tilted so far toward them that Lewis had to grab her arm to keep her from careening into the empty bleacher in front of them. Minnie? There was only one Minnie in the whole neighborhood—that Martha knew of, anyway.

Then the principal's voice came over the loudspeaker requesting that everyone rise for the Pledge of Allegiance.

Martha tried to shift her attention to the pledge and the ceremony after it. While she clapped for each student as their names were announced, her mind kept going back to *sex tape* like a stray thread caught on something. She told herself to listen for the surname Guzmán because Harry would walk shortly thereafter and she wanted to be ready with her camera. Meanwhile, she tried to puzzle out what those West U busybodies could be talking about.

Harry's name was called, and he walked beneath the balloons and across the basketball court to receive his certificate and have his photo taken. Martha took her own photos, and made a mental note to talk to him about his posture. He clomped along in his new clothes bought for the occasion with his head forward and down like he was trying to keep himself from going downhill too fast. At least he had a gold-and-blue honors cord around his neck. It pleased her that Richard Miller and Hazel's son George did not. She took a satisfied breath. Her son, flawed though he might be, had graduated middle school, and with honors no less. But her next breath seized in her chest. Next he'd be going to high school and would have to endure all its attendant humiliations. She could only hope it would be easier for him than it had been for her, but she feared that wouldn't be the case. Lewis reached over and squeezed her hand.

After the final student was announced and the ceremony concluded, everyone spilled slowly out of the arena and into the concourse leading to the main doors. Martha pulled her husband into the throng of West U parents, trying to get close to one of the looser-lipped gossips so she might find out why they'd been talking about Minnie.

"Hazel, hello there!" Martha said, pushing forward. "Congratulations to George on graduating. How's your puppy? The one you bought at the Little League auction, I mean."

Hazel looked at her through narrowed eyes. "Aren't you that boy's mother?"

"Harry?"

Hazel snapped her fingers and smiled. "Yes. That's him, the one with the penis fetish."

Martha opened her mouth but could find no words to speak.

"Oh, come on now," Hazel said with a laugh. She placed a warm hand on Martha's forearm. "I was only teasing. You've got to admit it's a little bit funny."

Martha slowed, momentarily allowing the crowd to absorb her until Hazel was just out of reach. As they moved along, the shock subsided and she became angry. How dare that woman be so haughty? She knew Hazel and her husband were deeply religious. They both taught Vacation Bible School every summer, dropped off pamphlets about the Methodist church at baseball games and track meets, held Bible study at their home every Wednesday night. Martha also knew from the rumor mill that George had been sent to church camp to "pray away the gay" the summer before, which she thought was abominable. Propelled by maternal protectiveness and an uncharacteristic burst of vengeance, she rushed forward again and let her shoulder graze Hazel's.

"Actually," Martha said, pressing her lips into a smile. She hardly recognized the tone of her own voice. "He's not the one obsessed with penises. Not that there's anything wrong with that."

Hazel flared her eyes and pressed a bejeweled hand to her breast as she sucked in a breath of air.

Martha gently pushed her on the forearm and said, "Oh now, don't be so sensitive. I was only teasing." Then she ushered past Hazel, chin lifted and feeling buzzy with adrenaline, Lewis at her rear.

She needed a different tactic if she was going to get any information from these women. It wasn't her nature to be so bold or manipulative, but if Minnie was the subject of a nasty rumor, she felt compelled to do whatever she must to find out what it was.

"Josefina," Martha said, moving next to her. Josefina had been the PTO treasurer all three years her son, Tomás, had been in middle school, and for three of the six years he'd been in elementary. She was also the lacrosse team parent and dance squad parent. In her former life, she'd been a risk adviser for a large finance company, but now she divided her underemployment between volunteerism and gossip. Martha might've tried to befriend Josefina if she didn't have such a penchant for slander. She wouldn't want to accidentally give her anything to talk about. "Congratulations to Tomás. I know how hard he worked to finish strong." According to Harry, Tomás had nearly failed both English and algebra. It was likely that Josefina, who was a generous PTO donor as well as its treasurer, had somehow influenced the administration's decision to pass him. Apparently, they were sending him to military school in the fall.

Josefina looked at Martha over her shoulder. "Thank you. Yes, he worked very hard. And kudos to your son, too." She raised an eyebrow. "I know he's had a rough time recently."

Martha stiffened, but didn't let Josefina's derision sway her from her purpose. "Did you hear about"—she glanced back and forth for dramatic effect—"the sex tape?"

Josefina grabbed her forearm and looked at her with wide eyes. "I know. Isn't it just awful? Bless her heart, she'll never live down the scandal."

"I can't imagine," Martha said, placing her hand over Josefina's in a gesture of commiseration. She couldn't believe how easy it had been to confirm such sensitive information. Perhaps she'd finally be able to penetrate their social circle after all. "How did you find out about it?"

"Oh, you know, it's going around," Josefina said. Then she whispered in Martha's ear, "You know Wanda McHugh, right?" Martha nodded. She knew who Wanda was, though she didn't know her personally. Wanda had married into a well-heeled family and talked incessantly at the boys' baseball games about her dressage lessons at the country club. Josefina continued, keeping her voice low and glancing around to make sure she wasn't being overheard. "Her brother-in-law's cousin, who lives in LA, has a friend in Seattle whose sister—or sister-in-law,

I can't remember, but I think she's a hairstylist—was a patient of John Wright's and then became more than a patient, if you know what I mean, and they made a sex tape together. Honestly, why would anyone do that? It's so gross—and dangerous."

"Really dangerous," Martha agreed. "But was it an actual tape? Do people really do that?" Except for the images of Bonnie, it had been forever since she printed any of her digital images.

"Not usually," Josefina said. "I mean, not that I know of. But apparently, he only had a physical copy somewhere because he was afraid of having anything incriminating on his computer. Anyway, she thought he was going to leave Minnie for her, and when he didn't, she told her sister she was going to sue him to get the tape back. She doesn't really care if anyone else sees it, she just wants to expose him for the scoundrel he is."

"Has she sued him?" Martha whispered back.

"No, this is breaking news. Wanda just got the text this morning."

"So, he has the tape?"

"According to Wanda's brother-in-law's cousin, he's got that one and more of other women. Apparently, he's kinky about keeping and watching them. If this gets out, his reputation will be ruined. And his poor wife. If she finds out . . ." Josefina raised her eyebrows in an inscrutable gesture. "He sounds like a total pervert. And I've heard he's something of a brute, too."

Martha's stomach turned. It was all nearly impossible to believe. "If it's true, then it certainly sounds bad," she said.

"Wait, how did *you* hear about it?" Josefina asked.

Martha turned toward Lewis. He was still tethered to her by their clasped hands but was deep in conversation with someone she didn't recognize. She turned back to Josefina. "We've got to rush off now. Talk later, okay?" Then she veered away, tugging Lewis along behind her.

"What was all that about?" Lewis asked. "Why are you in such a hurry?"

"Oh, nothing. I just want to get Harry so we won't be late for our lunch reservation. You know how fussy my mother can be." That wasn't entirely untrue, so Martha left it there. She didn't like lying to her husband; she was a firm believer in telling the truth because then she'd never have to remember what she'd said. Well, and also because it was the ethical thing to do.

Likewise, she couldn't imagine Lewis ever lying to her, much less cheating. In fact, the idea of Lewis making secret sex tapes with other women almost made her giggle out loud, but then she thought about Minnie. How awful it would be to be in her position. Martha didn't know what Josefina had meant about what would happen if Minnie found out, but she could imagine. She'd be humiliated and embarrassed. She'd worry about what people were saying behind her back, a mortification Martha well understood.

She'd be angry, too, of course. Maybe she'd be so upset that she couldn't forgive John, and she'd leave him. Martha didn't know her well yet, but there was something about being in the Wrights' house the other day that made her think it was more John's than Minnie's. If they separated or divorced, Martha felt sure Minnie would be the one to leave. Now that they'd started to really develop their friendship, she didn't want to imagine Minnie carrying Bonnie's cage out to her car, waving goodbye from the driveway, and following a moving truck to a new destination as it drove away with her things inside. She and John didn't have children; if Minnie left, she could go as far away as she pleased. Martha felt a premature but nonetheless deep sense of loss just thinking about it.

~

It was the idea of Minnie's shame that agitated Martha's sleep that night, though. She had a series of nightmares that conflated her own memories of being avoided in social settings, side-eyed at the grocery store, talked about behind her back. In one, she was giving a speech on a topic she didn't understand to a full auditorium. As she stammered and sputtered along, people filed out, tossing their programs to the floor, clearly annoyed with her. In the end, only Lewis and Harry remained in their seats until, shaking their heads in disgust, they left, too. In another, she sat down at a beautifully set breakfast table loaded with all her favorite foods and was about to take her first bite when she noticed the newspaper headline sticking out from underneath the bread basket. It read **Martha Hale, Horrible Mother to Be Charged for Various Crimes of Neglect.** In the most memorable dream, someone had painted oversize penises all over the exterior of the Wrights' pristine white house, and hundreds of neighbors gathered on their lawn pointing and laughing. Martha, feeling as responsible as if she'd sprayed the graffiti herself, had guided Minnie into the Hales' living room, and held her while she cried. She woke with her heart pounding and hair damp from sweat, and lay there taking slow breaths to calm herself until Lewis's alarm went off.

Fortunately, she had three full days of errands and activities to distract her from unpleasant thoughts. On the Sunday morning of Memorial Day weekend, they would take Harry to meet the bus to Camp Liberty, where he would spend the next three weeks horseback riding, playing tennis, and waterskiing on Inks Lake.

Last fall, she'd received a postcard invitation to attend an informational session about the camp at the home of Violet and Samuel Davidson, an elegant, dynamic young couple who were very involved in local politics and community outreach. Martha hadn't ever seriously considered sending Harry to camp, but she was curious about the interior of the Davidsons' sprawling Tudor-style house and hoped to engage in some interesting conversations with other prospective camp parents. As she'd anticipated, they served delicious canapés and high-quality wine, which alone made the evening worth getting dressed for. She was surprised, however, at how moved she'd been by the presentation, in which counselors talked about the importance of summer camp for instilling independence, confidence, and resilience. A slideshow on the big-screen TV showed images of smiling campers engaged in various activities, arms draped around one another, roasting marshmallows over a fire, sailing, playing field hockey. She loved the idea of her son going tech-free for three weeks, trying these new sports, and making new friends.

At the end of the talk, one of the camp representatives matter-of-factly mentioned the cost. Martha had just taken another bite of a creamy, sausage-stuffed mushroom and nearly choked when she heard the number—a three-week session cost more than her first used car—and tried to stifle her cough by taking a large sip of wine. Everyone turned to look at her, seemingly nonplussed by the exorbitant expense, and she dabbed at her watering eyes and said, smiling, "I'm fine, don't worry. Something just went down the wrong pipe."

She was quite relieved that Harry had seemed only mildly interested in the idea when she went home to tell him about it at the time, but during his recent suspension, she'd called the camp to see if there were any spots still available for the first term. She didn't care if she had to process wedding photos around the clock or mortgage her soul or sell her body to be able to afford to send him. Somehow, she'd figure out how to minimize the impact on their budget. Besides, this wouldn't simply be a fun vacation for him; it was an investment in Harry's character development.

They had a list of items to pack, some of which she could scrounge from her mother's linen closet and her in-laws' garage, and everything down to individual socks had to be labeled. She was busy up until the moment they helped him load his trunk into the underbelly of the coach, and as they waved and waved at the darkened windows long after Harry would reasonably be waving back, Martha felt herself sinking into a state of minor despair. She worried that Harry wouldn't make friends easily or that he might injure himself somehow. What if he fell off a horse? Or twisted an ankle skiing? Or got too many mosquito bites or a bad sunburn? Had she packed a hat? Yes. Two, in fact. She sighed as she and Lewis climbed back into the minivan. Harry had never been away from home more than a day or two at a time, and now he'd be gone for three weeks. What if he couldn't stand it? More significantly, what if Martha couldn't?

"Is it too early for ice cream?" she asked, dropping her head back against the rest.

Lewis smiled at her and started the car. "It's never too early for ice cream."

~

Martha wore herself out deep cleaning the house on Monday. She used the opportunity of Harry's absence to go through his clothes and set aside a pile to drop off at the donation center. They'd go shopping for new things later in the summer, after he had the growth spurt that everyone said boys got between eighth and ninth grades. She emptied Harry's drawers, jacket pockets, and backpack of all the detritus he'd collected: the bits of trash, gum wrappers, pencil stubs, movie stubs, a few french fries that were old but, alarmingly, not yet decomposed. She stripped the bed and pulled it away from the wall to vacuum underneath it, and excavated more random items: playing cards, video game cartridges, the stuffed heart she'd given him for Valentine's Day that had embarrassed him, empty potato chip bags, and candy wrappers. She was more than a little relieved that she hadn't come across anything pornographic or illegal. That business about John had really gotten to her.

She thought of Minnie's flawless-looking home and imagined that if she were to look underneath her bed, there would be nothing but plush, clean carpeting. Even Bonnie's cage had been tidy when she was over there. Martha admonished herself for not taking better care of her son's room, and also for not teaching him how to do it himself.

By the end of the day, Harry's room and closet were spotless, as was the rest of her house. After dinner, she sank down on the couch next to Lewis, exhausted. That would be her plan, she decided. She'd just figure out ways to keep herself busy until Harry's camp term was over in mid-June.

On Tuesday afternoon, while she was taking a break from processing images from a two-year-old's birthday party that was more extravagant than her wedding, her doorbell rang. Hoping for a surprise visitor—even if it was her mother—Martha was disappointed to discover that it was only a package delivery, and worse, it wasn't even for her. The unmarked box on her doorstep was heavy and addressed to John P. Wright. At least by returning the misdirected package, she might have another chance to visit with Minnie. Since Martha had gone up to her office early that morning, she didn't know if Minnie was at home or not, but she decided it would be poor form to hold on to the package any longer than absolutely necessary. She slipped on her shoes and picked up the box.

Lupe was standing on a step stool on the Wrights' porch, one hand pressed against her lower back, the other wiping down the glass on the front door, which to Martha looked spotless already. "Buenos días, lady," she said, turning. "I see you coming." She pointed to their reflections.

"This package for Mr. Wright came to my house by accident. Want me to leave it here?"

"Is heavy?" Lupe asked. Martha nodded. "Can you carry for me please? My back."

"Of course. How did you hurt your back?"

"Working all the time," she said, slowly climbing off the stool. "Getting to be old lady!" Martha didn't think Lupe could be much older than she. Did that mean she was also getting old? Her thoughts drifted along this current as Lupe punched in the code on the Wrights' keypad: 1972. She didn't mean to notice the combination, but now that she had, she couldn't help wondering what it represented. A year? Minnie was born in 1980, same as Martha. 1972 must be John's birth year. Yes, that made sense, she thought as she stepped inside. Minnie had mentioned John's age, forty-six, when they were talking about pregnancy. She followed Lupe down the foyer, and as they approached the living room, Bonnie began to screech.

"Cállate," Lupe called out, though not harshly. Then she said to Martha, "She only like Miss Minnie."

Martha set the box down on the kitchen island and turned to Bonnie. "Hi, pretty girl," she said in a singsong voice the way Minnie did. "Did you like your pictures?"

Bonnie grew quiet and looked at Martha with her head cocked through the gold bars of her cage.

Twelve

Thursday morning, Lewis woke Martha up with a kiss. "Happy anniversary," he whispered. She'd been dreaming again, and struggled against its pull. "I'll be in meetings all day, starting early, but I have a surprise for you tonight. Get dudded up and I'll pick you up at six thirty. Okay?"

"Okay," she said, pushing herself up.

"Love you. See you tonight."

"Love you, too." Martha checked the clock, which also showed the date. Sure enough, it was the thirtieth of May, their sixteenth anniversary. With everything that had been going on lately, she'd completely forgotten.

She dressed, poured a cup of coffee, and because the house felt too empty, went outside to sit on her front steps. The sun was up and the birds were chirping. Everything seemed normal. Soon, she heard the Wrights' garage door open, and Minnie backed out. She paused at the end of the driveway, waiting for another car to pass. Martha could see through the windshield that she was wearing a blazer and red lipstick and had pulled her hair into a sleek bun. She waved, even though she didn't expect Minnie to notice her.

But to Martha's surprise, Minnie waved back, her face breaking open into a slightly lopsided smile. She reversed her car into the street, then pulled up in front of Martha's walkway and rolled down her window. "Good morning!" she called out.

Martha was delighted. She walked down to meet her. "Hi there! How are you? You're off to work early today."

"Yeah, I'm taking a big client on a gallery tour. He's decorating a new office space," she said.

Martha stared at Minnie's mouth. Something looked different, but she couldn't quite tell what it was. "Is your lip okay?" she asked. "Is that a bruise?"

Minnie's fingers flew up to touch the bottom right side, then she angled the rearview mirror to look. "Oh gosh, is it that obvious?" She gave a sheepish smile. "I'm embarrassed to admit it, but I got Botox and a little filler injected yesterday. He must've hit a blood vessel or something."

So that was why she hardly seemed to have aged since high school.

"Anyway, listen, thank you so much for the prints of Bonnie. I just love them. I'm really sorry I haven't reached out to tell you that; I've just been really swamped with work."

"Oh, that's okay! I'm just happy you like them." She felt a great relief. The truth was, she'd been wondering why Minnie hadn't said anything about the photos. Martha worried that she thought they were amateurish or not artful enough.

"Are you sure I can't pay you for them?"

"Heavens no! They're a gift, for a friend."

"You're sweet," she said. "It's just that I deal in art, and I think artists should be paid. Even artists who are friends." Minnie smiled and reached her hand out to touch Martha's, accidentally bumping her with the brace. "If you won't let me pay you in cash, then how about in cocktails?"

"That would be wonderful!" Martha said, and immediately wished she hadn't sounded so exuberant.

"Great. We'll talk soon, okay?" She withdrew her hand and rolled her window back up. She waved as she pulled away.

Standing there waving back at Minnie, watching her car disappear into the distance, Martha thought again about the rumors she'd heard the week before about John having had an affair. The news had been fresh then, but had it traveled all the way to Minnie by now? She seemed too happy to have heard anything about her husband's alleged infidelity. Maybe she was faking happiness? If someone told Martha that Lewis had been cheating on her, she'd be catatonic from devastation. She couldn't bear the idea of Minnie suffering that sort of pain.

As she went back inside to refill her mug, an idea popped into Martha's mind that was so unexpected, so electrifying that she broke out in goose bumps. What if she could find that sex tape before her new friend did?

∼

Martha couldn't help it that she noticed things. She was a photographer, and in general, photographers had good eyes for detail. Also, she had an organized mind, and she liked spreadsheets and tidiness and order. Lewis sometimes teased her that she was obsessive, but she was proud of her systematic thinking and competence and her efficiently run home.

In any household, Martha knew, someone had to keep track of the number of toilet paper rolls available in the bathroom, and the amount of money in the checking account, and when it was time to change the air-conditioning and water filters. Someone had to make sure the children's immunizations were up to date, and birthday presents purchased ahead of a party, and that the driver's licenses and car registrations were renewed before they expired. In order to prepare or provide dinner on any given night of the week, someone had to have a mental inventory of the pantry and refrigerator, to know what food had to be eaten before it spoiled, to shop regularly without allowing too much to go to waste, and to combine available ingredients in a variety of creative and healthful ways that satisfied both the preferences and aversions of all the members of the family. In the Hales' household, that person was Martha.

Lewis was busy doing things like preparing data documentation and analyzing information for GIS projects, and her son was too young and self-absorbed even to recognize the mental load a house manager carried in order to keep things stocked, cleaned, changed, and paid. Most of the women Martha knew in her neighborhood performed this role, but they could then delegate tasks to their housekeepers, nannies, and other hired help. Martha did it all herself.

For the most part, she didn't resent this work or the emotional or physical fatigue it sometimes caused. She was good at it, for one thing. By contrast, Lewis, who was extremely intelligent and capable of remembering any number of work-related demands and special things like their anniversary or her birthday, suffered from a strange type of forgetfulness at home: trash-pickup days, how to load and run a washing machine, when specific bills were due. Even if she thought it would be fair to ask him to do more around the house when he was working as the primary breadwinner, she wouldn't be able to let go of the worry that he'd leave something important undone.

Also, her mother had told her many times that she needed to keep her own accounting of her household, that a husband could die—god forbid—and an uninformed wife could suffer from a lack of knowledge about how her life should hence be conducted. She also advised her to set aside enough savings that she could use in case of a tragedy. Martha had painful memories of overhearing Evelyn crying in her room many nights after her father was gone. Not only was Evelyn mourning her and her daughters' loss and her sudden single parenthood, she was exhausted from trying to find a job and figure out how to do all the things around the house that her husband used to do. Only many years later, after her stepfather arrived, did Martha realize that the reason her mother had lost weight back then was because even while she did the work of two people, she still didn't have enough money to feed both her children and herself.

Martha and Lewis had a traditional division of household labor, with him as the breadwinner, but she knew she was capable of taking care of Harry on her own if she ever had to. She'd have to sell their house, of course—she couldn't even pay the West U property taxes on her salary alone—but she'd figure something out if it came down to that. It was Lewis she worried about. She had a file on her computer labeled "What to Do in Case I'm Dead" so that if she were a victim of a hit-and-run or a pandemic virus or some other unfortunate and unforeseen event, Lewis would be able to step in and take care of their mundanities. It was a literal step-by-step list of where their important documents were kept, who should be contacted, what bills needed to be paid and how, what sentimental objects should be passed down to Harry and the stories that made them significant, and even a link to a private series of videos that Martha had made instructing her son on how to live what she considered to be a good and honorable life.

For these reasons, it wasn't even a little bit surprising that Martha's mind had grabbed and retained the code to the Wrights' front door lock when she'd seen Lupe punch it in on the keypad the other day. Martha didn't have an exceptional memory—she couldn't easily recall phone numbers or dates, and instead relied on her calendar and address book, which she meticulously maintained—so she assumed she'd forget the key code. Then she tried to force herself to forget it. But because she'd understood the logic behind the combination, it was harder to shake than a random sequence might've been. She couldn't make herself not remember that it was John's birth year, especially because while she was trying to erase it, she couldn't help but wonder why they'd chosen his year and not Minnie's, and what that might mean about their relationship. If the Hales had a digital dead bolt, she'd probably have selected something that represented all of them, or at least both her and Lewis.

Maybe their wedding or first date anniversary, or their house number backward. The point was, all that thinking about those four digits seared them into her memory instead of deleting them, which she knew would've been the proper thing to do.

On the other hand, Martha's gift for logistics might just be the thing that would save Minnie from untold pain and embarrassment. Not only did Martha know how to enter the Wrights' house, she knew that on Thursdays, typically nobody would be home until their lawn crew arrived sometime in the late afternoon. Of course, John *had* come home early two weeks before, the Tuesday after Harry's suspension and the Friday Martha had photographed Bonnie, but those seemed to have been the only times.

She sat back down at the kitchen table, then stood up, then sat again. If the rumors were true, and there really was a physical copy of a sex tape, then shouldn't she, as Minnie's friend, try to protect her from whatever fallout might come of it? If she could find it and destroy it, then even if John's patient and alleged lover issued a subpoena or whatever, the evidence would be gone. There would be some public scrutiny, but without proof, John would have plausible deniability. The scandal would be some ugly talk and nothing more.

Of course, it would mean breaking into their house.

Martha sank down into a chair at the kitchen table. Break into their house! She'd never done anything like that before. Well, once—sort of. When she was thirteen, she babysat the infant daughter of a couple who were rumored to be swingers. They always said she could eat whatever she wanted but should never go into the guest bedroom upstairs. This mysterious rule drove her to distraction until one night, after the baby was asleep, Martha gave in to her curiosity. Inside, she found a shocking trove of sexual accoutrements that she later described to her peers in great detail. Though it garnered her a temporary boost in popularity, she felt guilty for having done it. Worse, word got back to the parents and she was never asked to babysit for them again.

In this case, going into the Wrights' house wasn't about curiosity. Not entirely, anyway. She'd seen only the common areas in the Wrights' home since they moved in, so of course she wondered what it was like upstairs. A person's bedroom can reveal a lot about who they are. The mere thought of it made Martha's heart beat as fast as if she'd been running. When she picked up her coffee cup, her hands were trembling. Her mother's voice manifested in her head: *Trust your gut, Martha, dear. The body doesn't lie.*

"Well, what am I supposed to do?" Martha replied aloud. "Let some hooker ruin Minnie's life?"

It wasn't that Martha *wanted* to go into Minnie's house without permission. She had to. And she had to do it now, before the weekend, before anything legal happened. If she hurried, she'd have enough time to go inside and find the tape before anyone might intercept her there.

But how to do so without being seen? Obviously, it wouldn't do to walk right in the front door. Mrs. Kashuba or Lillian or anyone else might happen to see her, and then what would she say? She could dress up in costume, perhaps. She'd worn a platinum wig to one of the galas years ago, complete with bell-bottoms and a ruffled top in honor of the seventies theme. Maybe she could put that and her big swimsuit cover-up on and pretend to be Minnie wearing one of her caftans. Ha! Lillian might have to eat her heart out, seeing "Minnie" returning home from a visit at Martha's. But of course, Minnie was at least four inches taller than Martha, and she couldn't even bear to imagine how many pounds lighter.

Her temporary distress was alleviated by an idea. Martha dashed up to her office and screwed her super-telephoto lens onto her camera body. She pointed it at Minnie's porch, but there was too much glare to see the door. Surely if they had a keyless entry on the front, they'd probably have one on the back. But she didn't want to take the risk of being seen going into the yard unless she was confident she'd be able to finish her mission. She might be able to get a better view through the open

149

window. It was stuck. "Damn humidity," she said aloud. Frustrated, she banged all around the edges to loosen it from the sash, thinking as she did it would be just her luck that she'd miss and smash her fist through one of the panes. But the banging worked. She shoved the window open and leaned out as far as she could, rotating the lens to its longest focal length. Because of her angle, she could just barely see the door's lock and handle through the viewfinder, but it looked enough like the one on the front door to give her hope.

A thought occurred just then that brought a rise of bile into her throat: What if there was a surveillance system? After all, Harry hadn't expected to be seen defiling the school, but he was caught on video doing it. She moved the camera around the rest of the porch, looking for equipment. She hadn't noticed any before, but she knew that some homeowners in the neighborhood outfitted their exteriors with cameras. Maybe whoever had designed the Wrights' house had incorporated them so subtly that they wouldn't be noticed by a potential burglar or assailant, not that there were many to worry about. She didn't see any sign of a security system through her camera lens, and when she swept it around to the houses behind and next to Minnie's, there wasn't anything obvious there either. She put her camera down and closed the window. For the greater good, she'd just have to risk it.

She put on her gardening clogs, which she'd be able to slip off at Minnie's back door so as not to leave any footprints, and went out to water her front beds. She told herself to be relaxed and inconspicuous as she looked around, but her heart was beating so hard she was certain someone standing outside would be able to hear it. A jogger went past her, then a pair of nannies pushing baby strollers. An older man in shorts and knee socks marched down the sidewalk, probably doing his morning exercise, and he saluted her as he approached. She had a moment of panic that he was there in some official capacity, having read her mind and intending to thwart or even arrest her. But he marched on without pause or comment. Then Lillian, as though conjured, appeared, walking Beignet on a leash down the sidewalk on Martha's side of the street. Nervously, Martha waved, and Lillian gave her a strange look that made Martha's heart pound. But a second later, as Beignet urinated on Martha's grass, she said, "Oh, hi. Sorry, I didn't recognize you. I have the worst eyesight." She pronounced it *ah-saht* in what Martha had come to learn over the many years of living across the street was an affectation of Lillian's, who tried to hide her Louisiana roots with a Texas twang. At least she wasn't there to spy.

Finally, there was a lull in activity, and by then the bushes were well soaked, but even though a shallow puddle was forming where she was standing in the grass, she was having trouble convincing herself to move from her spot.

She glanced anxiously at Minnie's house. Should she really do this? Did she really expect to find anything? The answer to both was probably not. But Minnie had been so sweet to her that morning, so gracious and appreciative of the photos. If there was the slightest, albeit unlikely, possibility of helping Minnie avoid humiliation, then she was going to do it. And yes, she was more than a little titillated by the prospect of looking around. Maybe she'd find out something that could advance their friendship. That they liked the same kind of books or towels or something. But mostly, she justified her plan as being an act of altruistic heroism.

Enlivened, Martha turned off the faucet, hurried around the side of her house and across the property line, and with a final look around, let herself through the gate, which, as she'd logically assumed, was unlocked that day so that the lawn crew would be able to access it. She closed it behind her, neither slowly nor quickly, and after quietly setting the latch back in place, she crouched down on the gravel-covered path with her back against the fence to try to catch her breath.

Several minutes later, after nobody had come knocking on the gate to find out what Martha was doing in Minnie's backyard, she was ready to make a break for the porch. No, not too fast, or it might draw attention somehow. She was grateful for the cypress trees along Minnie's fence, which had grown considerably since they were first planted and now offered some of the total privacy they would eventually provide. Martha wondered what the owners of the house behind Minnie thought of this barrier that was slowly rising up between their yards, and for that matter, what they thought of the neighbors on their perpendicular side, the uppity Anna Devlin and her husband, Frank, with his Nerf gun constantly blasting against their fence. It didn't matter now. She just needed to walk casually to Minnie's back door and let herself in like she belonged there so that whoever might be looking from a third-floor window or through a video camera would just assume she did.

She was drunk on adrenaline by the time she got to the porch, slipped off her shoes, and entered the code into the keypad. There was a slow, grinding sound as the mechanism turned; it had worked. Without a look back, she let herself into Minnie's house. Immediately, she regretted her decision to do so. She'd been so concerned about surveillance cameras that she'd neglected to consider whether the Wrights had an alarm system. She heard a high, pulsating peep-peep-peep sound that was similar to her parents' alarm warning, indicating she had probably thirty seconds to disarm the system before the police were notified. Crime in West U was so notoriously low that neighborhood reports included mostly incidences of "found property" or "criminal mischief" for flag-stealing or house-wrapping. As such, when they were called upon—to stop a break-in, for example—the local cops would reliably arrive on the scene in under two minutes. Martha had maybe twenty seconds before the police were dispatched and she was arrested for breaking and entering.

Frantic, she looked for the alarm pad. In her parents' house and every other house she'd seen with a system, the pad was always near the door. But there wasn't one. She patted the walls, as though it might appear out of nowhere. She dashed through the house to the front door to find one there, but again, there wasn't one. Now she likely had ten seconds to get back out the way she came in. As she ran through the living room, about to fling herself back outside, she realized that the peeping had changed to a trilling sound, and that it was coming from Bonnie's cage.

She bent over with her hands on her knees, nauseated from the cocktail of stress and relief. After a few deep inhales and long exhales, she straightened up, brushed her damp hair away from her face, and walked over to Bonnie.

"Hello, Bonnie," she said. Her voice sounded strangled, so she cleared her throat and tried again. "Hi, pretty girl." Bonnie hopped from one perch to another, looking at Martha and trilling quietly. "You scared me half to death." Martha stuck her finger in between the bars and wiggled it. Bonnie hopped closer and tipped her soft yellow head toward it, but didn't peck. Martha felt her heart rate slowing down. The little bird really was such a sweet, calming thing. It seemed such a shame that she spent all day locked in the cage, large and well stocked though it was. It made her think of Harry and wonder if he was as lonesome at camp as she was at home without him. Martha struggled briefly with a desire to open the door and hold Bonnie again, now that she knew she wouldn't hurt her. She longed to feel the bird's small weight in the cup of her hands, to marvel up close at her dainty existence, but decided it was far too risky.

She looked around the room for any interior video cameras. Years ago, when Harry was a baby and she'd been talking with some of the other young mothers at the park, one of them said she'd installed nanny cams throughout her house so she could keep an eye on her daughter's babysitters. The cameras were hidden inside various objects so nobody knew they were being watched, and she'd caught a number of them engaging in misbehavior—falling asleep on the couch while her infant cried on the floor, inviting boyfriends over, raiding the liquor stash. Martha was glad nobody had that kind of equipment back when she was a babysitter. Minnie didn't have children, but that didn't mean she and John didn't have cameras. The apparent lack of an alarm system gave Martha a small comfort, though she couldn't be entirely sure a squad car wouldn't come screaming up to the house any minute, alerted by a silent trigger like those infrared beams that guarded precious museum artifacts in spy movies. She took a deep, fortifying breath. If that happened, she'd just come clean and hope for the best.

But she'd come this far, and couldn't waste time worrying about any of that now. She needed to get on with the mission she'd come there for. Including taking Bonnie out of her cage, she wouldn't do anything inside the house that would make her actions look worse than they already did. "Don't you mind me," she told the bird. "I'm just here to help your mom. I'll only be a minute."

She turned, galvanized by her determination. But where to start? Having no experience with sex tapes, Martha realized she had no idea where someone would keep such a thing. Not at work, certainly. Presumably, people made sex tapes in order to watch them, and they would most likely watch them at home. Josefina had specifically said there was a physical copy because John didn't want any damning evidence on his computer. Of course it wouldn't actually be a tape; if there was one at all, it was probably a DVD. She could certainly find one of those, especially in a house that was so minimalist and well organized. It was just a matter of logic. Her optimism returned as she took stock of the Wrights' living room. There was no television there, and therefore no DVD player. She remembered how comfortable those plush sofas were, and thought what a perfect place to curl up and watch a movie it would be. She, Lewis, and Harry made do on a single old couch that had first belonged to Lewis's grandmother. Maybe someday they'd splurge on something like these.

"Okay, okay," she whispered. She walked toward the stairs near the front of the house. The stairs were exposed to the street by an enormous picture window that extended from five feet above ground level almost to the roofline. She peeked through the glass to see if anyone outside happened to be looking toward Minnie's house, then sprinted up the curved staircase to the second floor. There was a large open room that the real estate agent had called a game room when she'd given Martha a tour long before Minnie moved in. There were built-in shelves and a wet bar, presumably for less formal entertaining. Martha was surprised to see a set of sofas that were nearly identical to the ones downstairs, and an equally formal decor. Along the wall opposite the three windows that yielded a view of their street were three large paintings of the sky, hung close enough together to give the impression of a panorama. It was interesting but impersonal; to Martha it seemed more suited for a gallery or a museum than a game room. But so far, Minnie's house was very much like a gallery: beautiful and slightly intimidating. And cold, too. She glanced at the fancy digital thermostat on the wall. It was set to seventy-eight, the same as the Hales', which was much harder to keep cool. "Huh," she said aloud. Maybe fancy houses were just better at keeping things inside.

Although all the doors were closed, Martha knew from having walked through the house when it was still on the market that there were four spacious rooms upstairs, each with an enormous walk-in closet and its own bathroom. The first one off the hall from the game room appeared to have been designated as the guest bedroom and was even bigger than the one Martha and Lewis shared, with a comfortable-looking four-poster bed and an antique-looking nightstand. Martha wondered if this had perhaps been Minnie's childhood furniture. She stepped inside. On top of the dresser to the left of the door were a delicate brass lamp; a small, framed figure drawing; and a stack of old leather-bound books. While tastefully arranged, it wasn't quite as staged-looking as the decor throughout the rest of the house. In fact, the room itself felt different. Softer. The items in it seemed personal, like they might've once belonged to an older family member. Martha picked up an exquisite wooden box and admired the intricate inlay pattern on the lid. She could tell it was old and probably handmade. A treasure.

She was merely admiring the box when she lifted its lid; she didn't expect to find anything inside. Inadvertently, she'd stumbled upon a private time capsule, a haphazard collection of detritus from Minnie's early years: her National Honor Society membership card, her lifesaving and water safety card issued by the American Red Cross in 1994, her residence hall ID from Whitman College, a tag for a pet named Tiger with a Houston address, a Brownie pin, a tiny copper bracelet, three crisp two-dollar bills, a smashed penny, several swimming medals from middle school, a gift tag marked "To Minnie from Grumps," an old pipe that still smelled like tobacco, a lock of blond hair, a chain with several small mismatched keys, a tin photograph of a grim-faced couple who looked a bit like Minnie, and more. She closed the box and put it down, letting her fingertips trace the design before moving on.

Propped on a small chair in the corner was an old teddy bear with a missing eye, whose fur was mostly gone in places. Martha picked it up, as gently as she would a baby or Bonnie, and held it. "Aren't you a dear?" she said to it before placing it back where she'd found it. She'd kept her own favorite stuffed animal from childhood, a bear-shaped pillow made out of printed blue material that her mother had sewn for her. It was flat and so well loved that the cotton was threadbare and shiny. Seeing Minnie's bear—or what she assumed was Minnie's—made her ache with tenderness. They'd both been little girls at one time, desperately clutching their bears for security.

She peeked into the closet, wondering what a couple with four bedrooms stored. Martha could only dream of having so much extra space. Her heart broke a little bit, though, when she saw a box containing an unbuilt crib leaning against the wall inside. She remembered the happiness she'd felt the afternoon she and Lewis had built Harry's crib and set it up in the room that was still his, the one whose window was almost directly beneath the one in this room. They'd been so happy to have their little home in West U and to be anticipating the birth of their first child that even the lack of an assembly guide hadn't frustrated them. After they'd completed it and Martha made it up with a soft blue sheet and a blanket her little sister, Bessie, had crocheted in between her premed classes at Stanford, she and Lewis had a pizza picnic on the floor of the baby's room. The joy of that memory had carried her through many difficult moments since, and she was stricken that Minnie might not ever have a similar one.

She was jolted out of her thoughts by Bonnie's chirping downstairs. Had one of them come home? She looked at her watch; she'd already been inside for nearly half an hour. How had so much time passed without her even noticing? She took her phone from her back pocket and set a timer for forty-five minutes. Clearly it was easy to get lost in Minnie's house, but she wasn't there to rummage around. She felt terrible for accidentally going through Minnie's treasure box, and besides, if anyone *was* watching, how could she explain herself? She'd give herself less than an hour to find the tape and leave.

The room across from the guest bedroom had been turned into a gym. Not just a yoga mat in a corner; no, this room had rubber-tile flooring and one wall paneled with mirrors. There was a weight set that at one brief time would've made Lewis salivate, a treadmill, a stationary bike, and some contraption that looked like it might've been a medieval torture device. For Pilates, maybe? Martha looked around the rest of the room. There was even a big wall-mounted TV and speakers along the ceiling. She backed out and closed the door, thinking that not even the opportunity to be entertained while working out made that room seem appealing.

Although there was a formal study off the foyer, the third room upstairs had been turned into an office. There was no question whose it was. The dark-gray walls were covered—neatly—with framed diplomas, certificates, awards, and photos of John in formal, social, and sporting settings. She learned more about the man from this tour of his office walls than she had in three months living next door. There was a heavy desk in front of the windows, arranged so whoever was sitting in it faced the door. It took her a moment to realize that something was missing: there wasn't a guest chair or love seat in the room, no place for a guest to sit, unless on the zebra-skin rug in the center of the room. Martha bent down to examine the pattern, but she couldn't tell if it was real zebra or just a printed cowskin. As a Texan, she was used to cow leather, but for some reason, exotic skins distressed her. When she moved to examine his bookshelves, she avoided stepping on it.

First, she looked for DVD cases. She didn't expect to find anything there—surely, he wouldn't keep something as risqué as a sex tape right there on the shelves—but she couldn't rule it out. All she found were medical textbooks and biographies of notable historical figures—Socrates, da Vinci, Edison, Jobs, and others—but none of their own works. There was a small section of one shelf dedicated to World War II–era statesmen and another to JFK and beside that, a number of poetry collections, interestingly only by male poets and all of whose names she recognized. She moved to his desk.

As she expected by now, the surface was uncluttered. There was a traditional leather blotter, a pen holder, a monogrammed notepad, and an in-box with papers and unopened mail she didn't dare touch. Below, she checked the five drawers: a shallow one in the center, and a deeper box compartment and file holder on either side. The first few held nothing unusual: sticky notes and other office supplies, stationery, charging cables, noise-canceling headphones. One of the file drawers contained nothing but blank greeting cards, sorted by occasion: birthday, sympathy, thank you, congratulations. They weren't the cheap kind that came in packs of ten either. She pulled out the thick stack in the folder marked "Sorry" and noted the sincerity of the sentiments, the high-quality envelopes that went with them. It reminded her that she needed to buy Lewis an anniversary card before dinner. They'd never developed the tradition of buying each other gifts, mostly because early on they didn't have the money for it, but they always gave each other a card. She flipped through the tabs on John's hanging folders, and when she got to the one marked "Anniversary," she paused just long enough to reprimand herself for even considering taking one of his.

She closed that drawer and pulled on the one opposite. It was stuck. She jiggled it again. It wasn't stuck; it was locked. She checked the center drawer again, looking for a key, then the others, but there wasn't one. Harry had once watched a video tutorial on picking locks. She'd admonished him at first—why on earth did he need to know how to pick a lock?—but when he insisted on showing her how to do it using two paper clips, one bent into what he called a tension wrench and the other straightened out to act as the pick, she found herself intrigued. That was years ago, though, and she couldn't remember how to do it. Maybe she could find the video on her phone and try to teach herself, but that might take too long and besides, Harry had used pliers to manipulate the paper clips, and John didn't have any pliers in his desk. She'd have to go back home to get her own, which would increase her chances of being seen.

"Think, Martha," she muttered. She imagined her own office space, paltry as it was by comparison. If she had a locked file cabinet, where would she keep a key? Not on her usual key ring; it had too many as it was, and she wasn't in the habit of carrying it around. John probably dropped his own key ring somewhere in the kitchen when he came in through the garage. Okay, so if it were her, she'd keep a key somewhere nearby. Hidden, certainly, but handy. She looked underneath the desk to see if it was taped to the frame—that would've been a very good hiding place, she thought, even though it wasn't there—then again in each of the unlocked drawers. It wasn't in any of the hanging files, not tucked into any of the unsigned greeting cards. She lifted the pile of papers in the in-box to see if it was underneath. Where else could it be? Hanging it behind one of the framed pictures seemed excessive. It had to be easily accessible. She looked again at the bookshelf. One of the titles had briefly snagged her attention as she'd skimmed the books earlier but not enough to stop her at the time. There, between a biography of George S. Patton and one of Winston Churchill, was the only book without a dust jacket, titled *Live from the Battlefield*. Martha pulled it down and opened it. Inside, where the pages had been hollowed out, was a small key matching the brass hardware on John's desk.

Thirteen

Martha's hands were trembling as she inserted the key into the lock. She was thrilled by her own sleuthing skills, but now that she was about to open the file drawer, she was nervous. Josefina had sounded convinced that the information was true, but of course it could've been just a rumor and nothing more. After all, there'd supposedly been a long list of connections between the alleged sex partner and Wanda McHugh, who was a known braggart with a tendency toward exaggeration. Wanda could've gotten the story wrong, or even simply made it up. To Martha, it seemed like people in West U passed around their canards as carelessly as they spent money and often for the same reason—to be admired. Wanda was probably bouncing up and down in her saddle right then, thinking about her name being in everybody's mouth. And hadn't Martha been right there, willing to gobble it right up? She was suddenly ashamed of herself for playing her own part in spreading the news.

Except that if it were true and there really was a tape or video or whatever, then Martha had done the right thing in reacting to the rumor. She was in a unique position to help Minnie. She couldn't stop the spread of gossip—that horse had long left the barn—but she might be able to reduce its impact. Even if Wanda's cousin's somebody-in-law's hairstylist did sue John, there wouldn't be anything to retrieve because Martha would have already retrieved it. That is, if she found it.

She paused, simultaneously wanting both for the tape to be there and also not to be. It wasn't just that she didn't want Minnie to be hurt by it; she simply didn't want it to be true. Martha might not have known John well, but he'd only ever been kind to her the few times she'd seen him. He always waved if he noticed her standing outside, flashing that Ken-doll smile that she had to admit made her feel quite special in the moment. She wanted John to be the devoted and loving husband he seemed to be. The one that took his wife on impulsive trips to Mexico and called her *darling*. Not the kind of man who would cheat on her and lock up a sex tape in his desk drawer.

She pulled it open and looked at all the handwritten tabs filed in alphabetical order: "Affiliations," "Auto," "Finance," "Health," "Home," "Mom and Dad," and more, with many subfolders interspersed between, thick but tidy, going all the way to the back of the drawer. There were so many files inside so many folders that Martha almost missed it, but the very last hanging folder was marked simply "X." X as in *XXX*? Her hand hovered over the contents of the drawer for a moment as she steeled herself. She reached inside the folder and withdrew a DVD inside a paper sleeve. It, too, was marked "X." Martha held it to her chest and closed her eyes. She guessed John was indeed that kind of man. Her stomach roiled.

She locked the drawer, used the hem of her T-shirt to wipe the surfaces she'd touched even though she couldn't see any fingerprints, returned the key to the hollow book, and, at the door, checked to make sure nothing looked out of place. She crept to the stairs and looked out the big window again. A car drove past, then another. Across the street, Mrs. Kashuba was bent over, weeding her garden. Martha held her breath and jogged down the stairs as fast as she could without tumbling. How awful it would be to get this far only to end up sprawled on the floor with a broken something and have to call for help. She hurried through the foyer toward the back door when the alarm on her phone went off. She jumped at the noise—a pentatonic scale that was much louder than she'd expected it to be—then quickly disabled it. From her corner of the living room, Bonnie mimicked the sound of the alarm.

"Shhhhh," Martha said, rushing over to the cage in a panic. "Don't sing that." What if Bonnie repeated it later? Minnie would wonder where Bonnie had learned it. Maybe Minnie would assume it was a sound associated with Lupe's phone and leave it at that. "Okay, it's okay, Bonnie. You're a very good girl." Martha put her finger into the cage again and wiggled it. Bonnie hopped closer on her stick and touched her tiny beak to Martha's fingernail. Martha was beginning to understand why Minnie had such affection for the little bird, and it made her sad for Minnie that she didn't have a child, since she seemed to want one so badly.

"Bye, bye, Bonnie," Martha whispered. With forced composure, she went out the back door, pushed the lock button on the keypad, stepped into her clogs, and walked to the gate. Through the wooden slats, she could see that Mrs. Kashuba was still bent over her rosebushes with her back to the street, so Martha opened the gate just far enough to slip out. Taking a deep breath, she strode all the way across her front lawn and up the driveway without glancing back.

~

In spite of her disappointment in John, her triumphant exploit had made her ravenous. She'd only had coffee that morning, which was wholly inadequate for a task such as this. Lunchtime the last few days without Harry at home had been lonesome, but the DVD lying on her kitchen counter offered an interesting distraction from her solitude. She made herself a large sandwich and iced tea, and ate standing up without taking her eyes off the little handwritten "X." Her mind darted, squirrel-like, among three things: first, the fear that someone had seen her, or that she'd tripped an alarm, or that she'd been videotaped going into and rummaging around the Wrights' house, and would have to account for her actions; second, self-congratulation that she'd achieved her primary goal of protecting Minnie; and third, an unrelenting and increasing curiosity about what exactly was on the DVD. Minnie seemed nearly perfect: smart, stylish, tall, thin. Martha couldn't imagine what kind of goddess this hairstylist who'd tempted John away from her must be like.

But she didn't have time to think about all that. She'd accomplished her errand, and now she had real work to do. A client had sent her an enormous batch of photos of an Indian wedding that would take days to process. And she really should run to the grocery store; they were going out to dinner that night but were low on eggs and orange juice, which Lewis liked to have for breakfast. Plus, she needed to pick up a card, which would require some time. She didn't like to grab the first one she saw; she always ended up reading all of them in the anniversary section to pick the one that reflected the most meaningful sentiment without being mawkish. Last year, she and Lewis had exchanged identical cards, and for weeks afterward felt an even deeper connection because of it. Now, though, she felt extra pressure to select the perfect card, and she was angry at herself for leaving it to the last minute.

Thinking about buying a card made her think about the ones in John's desk, which made her think about the DVD that was now in her possession, and which she would have to hide. But where should she store such a vile thing? She couldn't risk Harry finding it—or even Lewis, for that matter. Not only would they be shocked by the content, how would she explain why it was in her possession? This made her wonder again: What was on it? Stop, Martha, she thought. It's none of your business.

Abruptly, she tossed the last bite of her lunch into the trash and chided herself as she washed her dishes. She would go to the store, then take a shower so her hair had time to dry while she worked in her office. She'd finish up by six, and that would give her thirty, maybe forty minutes to get ready for dinner. Lewis wasn't quite as punctual as she, but he was close.

"Good plan," she said aloud as if to commit to herself. She picked up the DVD and held it under her arm so she could wipe down the counter with a soapy dishrag. As she rinsed and wrung out the rag, started the dishwasher, and microwaved a half cup of leftover coffee, the weight of the object jammed into her armpit seemed to grow heavier and harder to hold. Plan or no, she knew she wouldn't be able to concentrate on the wedding photos or the appropriateness of an anniversary card until she satisfied her curiosity with an answer.

As she slid the DVD into the player in the family room, she glanced guiltily over her shoulder. Of course, nobody was there, nor could anyone see the TV from outside. She sat down on the edge of the couch, and with trembling fingers, pressed "Play."

"Here we go." John's voice was clear even though the video wasn't. It looked like it was shot on a camcorder, like the old Sony Hi8 Martha had before Harry was born. But even the low quality couldn't obscure John's mischievous expression as he smiled at the camera and then moved away from it, revealing the beautiful female body lying on a bed behind him. Martha gasped and reared back, away from the TV screen, one hand clamped against her mouth.

John winked again at the camera before he turned his attention to the woman, whose head was out of the frame. She was lying on her back on top of a plush-looking bed in what looked like a fancy hotel room, totally still—was she even awake?—a thick curl of dark hair draped over one of her breasts. John approached her from the foot of the bed and stroked the inside of her calf. He was kneeling and Martha could only see his upper body: his trim torso and muscled shoulders and arms. He looked back at the camera and made a "shhhhh" motion with his finger, then, smiling, touched the woman's other leg, very gently moving upward to her knee, to the inside of her lower thigh. She jumped when he got even higher and made a startled, moaning sound. "Quiet," he instructed in a sharp voice, slapping her thigh. Then his movements became soft and fluid again. "Don't say anything. Don't move."

Martha leaned forward again.

John teased his way up with his fingers, then with his mouth. She shifted when he flicked his tongue in between her legs, and he slapped her on the hip, quite roughly it seemed, and said, "I said don't move." The woman lay still again. John crawled onto the bed and slowly pushed her legs apart. She seemed not to resist him at all, though Martha could see a red handprint on her thigh. He moved into a kneeling position and Martha could see, for the first time, his very erect penis. She hadn't thought about what John would look like naked, but she realized that he looked exactly like what she'd have expected him to, if she'd been expecting anything at all. Smooth, velvety-looking skin, a sculpted body, just the right amount of hair in the right places: chest, arms, groin. He teased the woman with his penis, moving it in circles, rocking back and forth, his abdominal muscles tensing and relaxing. The woman tried to hold still but her muscles, too, were twitching. The slow friction between the bodies on-screen was building such a heat that Martha felt like she was sitting astride a fire. John's breath became shallower and the woman's chest rose and fell like a pant, and when he finally slipped himself inside her, he threw his head back and the woman wrapped her legs around his waist, and they moved at different rhythms, groaning, until they found the one that matched.

He was like a gymnast or a yogini, moving at various angles without breaking his stride. At one point he shifted his position so that he was straddling only one of her thighs, and the sensation made the woman cry out—in pleasure, Martha assumed—and John, who was facing the camera, said with his eyes closed and teeth together, "You like that, huh?" and reached out to hold the woman's breast. Martha wanted to see her face, not only to know her identity, to see how closely or not she resembled Minnie, to try to guess why he was having sex with her and not his wife, but also to know if the woman was enjoying what was happening, because Martha, in spite of herself, had become very aroused, and she would feel even more guilty about her arousal than she already did if the woman wasn't enjoying what John was doing to her and the rather demanding way in which he was doing it.

"You want a necklace, baby?" John said, panting. "I've got a big, beautiful one for you. You want it?" The woman moaned, possibly in assent, though Martha had no idea what a necklace had to do with anything. John's thrusts grew quicker, his face screwed up in prerelease, and suddenly he yanked himself out of the woman and swung a leg over her abdomen so that he was kneeling over her breasts with his penis in his hand. He let out a roar and at the same time released his semen at the hollow of her throat. Then, in between heaving breaths, he laughed. "There you go, baby. Straight from the bottom of the sea. Wait, let's get a close-up of that fat pearl necklace." He scrambled off the bed toward the camera and grabbed it. The image shook as he turned the camera, then steadied as he pointed it at her breasts and moved it up to her neck. "Don't say I never gave you anything." He zoomed in on the glistening trail sliding away into the woman's dark hair, and laughed. "Do you like it?" he asked. "Let's see how much you do." He laughed again as he guided the camera up the woman's neck. Her hands flew up to cover her face, but Martha thought she could see the corners of her mouth lifting into a smile.

"Don't," the woman said, her voice muffled.

"Don't what?" John pulled at her hands. The woman turned her face away from the camera, but seemed to giggle as she did so. "Don't do this?" He dragged his finger through the slippery trail on her neck and tried to put it in her mouth. John laughed, less playfully this time, and the woman wrenched away from him. Martha wasn't sure which unsettled her more: their strange interaction or the tingling between her own legs that persisted in spite of it.

"You know you love it, baby. Come on now, say you love it." With his free hand, John smeared his semen from the woman's neck onto her face, which she tried to avoid by thrashing from side to side. He slapped her across the cheek. Uncomfortable but transfixed, Martha sat forward, desperate for a glimpse at the woman's expression, but her hair and the jostling of the camera obscured her features. No wonder she wanted to sue him to get the tape back.

"Say it!"

Suddenly the woman stopped writhing and grabbed the hair at her temples. "Fine," she said, as she pulled the dark hair away from her face—and off her head. "I love it!" She threw the wig at the camera, which shuddered and then settled back on her face, her blonde hair coming out of its ponytail. Martha stood up, sucking in a breath, watching the woman stare at John with an inscrutable expression on her flushed face. What shocked Martha, who stood in front of the TV with her mouth ajar even after the video ended and the image turned to snow, wasn't that the woman seemed neither angry nor happy, or that she'd been wearing a wig. What shocked her was that the woman was Minnie.

～

Martha moved through the rest of the afternoon as though in a trance. She went to the store, somehow shopped for and selected an anniversary card, processed several hundred photos, and got herself showered and dressed for her dinner with Lewis—but all the while, part of her consciousness was watching the tape over and over again. Its very existence raised so many questions. Why did John have it? Were there more? Had he really had an affair with a former patient? If not, why did someone start the rumor?

Beyond the presence of the tape, Martha also struggled to make sense of the baffling scene it captured. Because her own sexual experience was so limited, she struggled to understand the dynamic between John and Minnie. She knew the concept of role-playing, of course, but hadn't ever engaged in it. And only when John used the term *pearl necklace* did Martha realize what the boys meant when they'd used the term—laughing and posturing as they always did, always hinting at their conquests—back in high school.

Except for the very end, Minnie had seemed to enjoy what John was doing. That was the thing her mind kept going back to on a playback loop: John on top of her, moving, his muscles, his fair body hair, his ability to take control, to give pleasure. Martha couldn't remember exactly at what point Minnie had climaxed, but Martha was certain that she must have. The more Martha thought about the scene, the more excited and engaged and then satisfied she imagined Minnie had been, in spite of—or maybe even because of—how rough it had been. Maybe John and Minnie had made the tape as an homage to their relationship, the way other couples might keep portraits of themselves. On the first eleven anniversaries of their marriage, Martha had set her camera on a tripod outdoors and captured an image of her and Lewis in the same pose as their wedding portrait. She imagined giving him a book of those photos on their thirtieth or fiftieth anniversary. But the year they decided to stop fertility treatment, she was still carrying some extra weight from the hormones and didn't want to memorialize that experience in a photo. The following year, she'd come down with a late-spring cold and by the time she was well, she'd forgotten about their annual picture. The year after that, she'd decided to cut bangs—a terrible mistake that she regretted instantly—and refused to allow herself to be photographed. And so it went. Now Martha wondered if by letting those photo opportunities slip away, she'd also let go of some of their romance. It had been a long time since they'd had anything more than plain, perfunctory sex. She wondered if she should buy a wig to surprise Lewis with. Maybe it would excite him to pretend she was another woman. Maybe it would excite her.

This idea nagged at Martha as she processed a batch of the wedding pictures. While she was tweaking the luminance on a close-up of the bride and groom, Martha's mind drifted out of her garage office and into the hotel room in the video. She imagined herself in Minnie's place: lying on top of expensive bedding, watching John move his fingers slowly up her legs, feeling him enter her. As soon as she realized how shallow her breathing had become, and that she'd drastically overcorrected the image she'd been working on, she stood up and did a few jumping jacks, which made the window overlooking Minnie's backyard rattle in its pane. Martha was not one who gave herself over to fantasies, especially during the daytime, and never with another man. "That's enough," she said aloud, saved the files that were open, and shut down her computer for the day.

~

Lewis was nearly a half hour late when he finally pulled into the driveway. "I'm so sorry, hon. I got held up in a meeting. I called the restaurant and told them we'd be late," he said as he unloaded his briefcase and lunch bag while holding a bouquet of flowers behind his back.

Normally, Martha would've been counting the minutes in frustration, but today she hardly noticed his tardiness. "They're beautiful," she said, and pulled a vase from a high cabinet.

"Let me pee and we'll go," Lewis said.

She cut away the cellophane, ignoring the grocery store price tag. Some of the roses and their leaves were already wilted and browning, so she hid them in the back of the arrangement. The toilet flushed.

"Ready?" She nodded and he took her hand. "You look great, Marty. Pretty as the day I married you." He leaned in and kissed her quickly. "Let's go. I know you hate being late."

She'd assumed they were going to their usual—a cozy Northern Indian place where they could watch the cook skewering meat to go into the tandoori oven—but Lewis was driving the opposite direction. He caught her puzzled glance and smiled. "I figured we deserved a fancy night out for a change," he said.

"We do?" Martha couldn't think of why. In fact, she felt a sudden rush of guilt-induced nausea, remembering that just a few hours ago she'd broken into the Wrights' home and into John's desk, then watched them having sex on a private tape that they'd made for their own enjoyment. She still didn't know if someone had caught her intrusion on a security camera, or what exactly she'd say if and when she was confronted. Lewis would be so disappointed. Oh god, what if the police got involved? What if it was in the paper? What if her mother found out?

"Well, sure. What with Harry's graffiti and suspension and everything. I know that was really hard on you."

She closed her eyes and fought back the idea that apparently the apple hadn't fallen far from the tree.

"You okay, Marty? You look a little peaked."

"I'm fine. Just thinking about Harry is all." She found a paper napkin from a fast-food restaurant in the glove box and pressed it to her forehead. "It'll pass."

Lewis pulled up to Anton's, where they hadn't eaten since the night of their engagement. "I have an idea. Let's not talk about Harry. Tonight, it's just going to be about you and me, okay?"

Lewis ordered a bottle of pinot noir that the sommelier recommended, and because he knew her so well, said, "Don't worry about the prices. It's a special occasion." They both ordered the filet mignon, although Martha, forever her mother's daughter, couldn't help noting how expensive it was even if she was told not to, and several side dishes to share. Their conversation was easy but unremarkable, its edges worn smooth by so many years together. As Lewis was talking about a project he was working on, something that he'd already told her about in detail and that was still scientifically beyond her understanding, her mind began to wander. She wondered if Minnie ever thought about the cost of things, or if John did. Like the hotel room where they'd made the tape. Had they been on vacation? Or did they go there specifically for that purpose? She wondered how often they had sex in general.

"Marty?"

She blinked a few times, smiled. The wine was tranquilizing. "Yes?"

"I asked how you're liking working in the garage."

"You mean my office."

"Right."

"It's good. I like it," she said, thinking of the view of the clouds, the tips of the cypress trees growing along Minnie's back fence. She thanked the waiter after he topped off their wineglasses.

"That's good," Lewis said.

She took a sip. "It really is. Absolutely delicious."

"Your office?"

"What?" She cocked her head at him as she cut a piece of steak.

"Your office is delicious?"

"No, the wine is." She laughed, enjoying the pleasant sensation in her limbs, as though she was floating underwater. She thought of Minnie's pool, how sexy it would be to swim there at night, with the moon overhead and the turquoise lights under the surface. "But I guess my office is, too."

Lewis laughed along with her, though he didn't seem to understand what was funny. This fact, along with the alcohol, made Martha swoon the way she had early in their marriage. She looked at her husband as if she'd just noticed he was there, as if she didn't know his features by heart. She admired the five-o'clock shadow on his ruddy cheeks and the fullness of his lips, how his eyes shone in the candlelight and the adorable jiggle of his belly as he laughed. She took another sip of wine and realized that she would like very much to have sex with him, and this idea pleased her. They hadn't ever been particularly wild or insatiable during their almost two decades together, but it wasn't too late to try something new. They, too, could be the kind of couple who did exciting things in the bedroom.

After their entrées were finished, the waiter brought out a slice of cheesecake with sparklers and HAPPY ANNIVERSARY written in chocolate around the rim of the plate. As their tradition dictated, they exchanged cards first, and would share dessert afterward.

"Oh, that's so sweet," she said after reading.

"Thank you," he said, looking up from the one she'd given him. "This is beautiful." She had no idea what she'd written, having done so in a distracted state, but she was pleased that he liked it.

"Listen," he said. "I know we don't usually give each other anniversary presents, but I got something for you." He withdrew a small velvet jewelry box from his jacket pocket and, with a shy smile, pushed it across the table.

Inside was a gold teardrop-shaped pendant studded with tiny green gemstones. "Lewis, it's gorgeous." She held it up to the light to see it sparkle. "Wait. It looks so familiar for some reason. Was it your mom's?"

He blushed. "No, it's new. You saw it at the auction a few months ago and liked it."

"That's it!" She couldn't remember having pointed it out to Lewis, but it didn't matter. "Oh, honey, I can't believe you bought it for me. That makes me feel so special." She got up from her chair and went around the table to hug him.

He demurred, patted her on the arm, and, once she was reseated, took a big bite of the cheesecake.

"But why this year?"

"Oh," he said, then swallowed and wiped his mouth. "Well, I've noticed how you've been . . . taken, I guess . . . by the people next door. The big new house and all that. I just wanted you to have something nice, too, I guess. And besides, it's got peridots and I found out that's the stone for a sixteenth anniversary, so there you go."

She fingered the pendant, feeling the texture of the dozen or so tiny gemstones. "Lewis," she said, looking at him intently. "I don't want you to think I'm comparing us to the Wrights. I'm grateful for what we have, for our family. I'm not jealous of Minnie."

Lewis looked puzzled. "No, of course not."

"I mean, she's beautiful and everything. She's got great taste and is super nice, but I can tell you, she's got some problems, too."

"She does? What kind of problems?"

Martha realized she was treading on dangerous ground. Normally she told Lewis everything, good or bad, but she couldn't let him know what she'd done that day. "I just mean regular problems. Like anybody. Point is, I'm not jealous of her. And I don't need to have what she has to be happy." She leaned forward and took his hand. "But I love my necklace."

"I'm glad," he said, though he still looked somewhat confused. A moment later, he asked, "Don't you want to put it on?"

Martha held Lewis's hand on the drive home, aglow with contentment from the wine, the delicate weight of the necklace, and the anticipation of an amorous end to the evening. When Lewis went into the bedroom to change out of his work clothes, Martha opened the bottle of wine she'd bought earlier that day and poured two glasses, then settled herself on the couch in what she imagined was a casual but seductive pose.

Lewis emerged, wearing an old T-shirt and a pair of basketball shorts that he used to work out in. "You're having more wine?" He took the glass Martha held out to him. "I don't know if that's such a good idea. I've got to be up pretty early tomorrow."

"Just one glass," she said, patting the couch. "I thought we could keep the festivities going a little longer." She felt a small thrill at the memory of having watched the tape from that very spot on the couch only a few hours before.

"Okay." He sat down, tugging his T-shirt down over his belly.

She touched her glass to his. "So, I've been thinking. What if we went away for a long weekend? Maybe someplace like Napa. We've never been there."

"In California?"

"Yes, silly. Did you know there's more than four hundred wineries there? We could do a tour. They're famous for cabernet sauvignon."

"We're not really big wine drinkers, though. Except for tonight." He smiled.

"Okay, well, it's not only about wine. They have all these fabulous resorts and restaurants, too. We could go next weekend. Or this one, even! Heck, we could go tomorrow! As long as we're back in time to pick Harry up on the fifteenth, we can be totally spontaneous. We could lounge by a hotel pool, or even go for a hot-air balloon ride if we wanted. I've always wanted to do that. Oh, and June's off-season, so it'll be cheap. Well, cheaper. And it gets down to the midfifties at night. Can you imagine?" Her eyes shone with excitement.

Lewis raised his eyebrows. "Wow, you've really thought a lot about this."

She settled back against the cushions, piqued at his assessment. For some reason, she didn't want Lewis to know how badly she'd wanted to be one of those West U couples who went away for their anniversaries or took weekend vacations with their friends. How much she'd like to be like Minnie and John. "Actually, I haven't. It just occurred to me that we have a chance to do something a little wild since Harry's at camp. I think it could be really fun."

"It would be, I guess." He paused long enough for Martha to grow hopeful. "You know what? Why not?" He clinked her glass. "To spontaneity!"

"To spontaneity!" She made a squealing sound and took a large sip of wine.

"Although," he said, lowering his voice, "I have to check my calendar at work first. We have a quarterly review in a week and a half and I'm going to have a ton to do to get ready for it. That's what my meeting tomorrow's about." Martha slumped her shoulders and sighed. "I'm not saying no, Marty. Just let me check, okay? And if not now, we can do it another time."

"Promise?"

"Promise."

"Okay. But in the meantime," she said, putting her glass down, "I know another way we can be spontaneous." She took Lewis's glass and put it down next to hers. Then she crawled over to him and wriggled herself into a straddling position on his lap, one knee jammed into the cushions and the other mostly off the edge. She leaned down and kissed him deeply. They weren't in the habit of kissing like that, even when they made love. In general, she found his tongue to be a bit too sloppy in her mouth and didn't especially care for the abundant exchange of saliva that it entailed. But now she probed his mouth with her own, trying to go slow and to enjoy the sensations, inviting him to do the same, to do whatever he wanted. Already she felt like they were successfully embarking on a new phase of physical intimacy, and this increased her desire even more. She felt wild and sexy, straddling her husband in the living room on a Thursday night before she'd even brushed her teeth. He seemed to be enjoying it, too, moving his hands up her back and groaning appreciatively.

She pulled away and sat up so that she could remove his shirt. But as she was sliding the hem up toward his chest, he pushed it back down over his exposed belly. "Wait. Let's go to bed."

She teased his shirt back up. "Why? Nobody's here. We can do whatever we want."

He pushed it back down with a sheepish expression on his face. "At least let's turn off the lights."

Now wasn't the time to confront his body-image issues. "Okay. Tell you what." She climbed off him and tossed the old afghan his great aunt had crocheted for them as a wedding gift on the floor. "I'll get the lights and you take off your clothes. I'll meet you down there." She undid the clasp of her peridot necklace, laid it on the coffee table, and began to undress herself.

"I don't know what's gotten into you but I like it," he said.

"Hopefully you will," she said. "Get into me, I mean." She giggled.

Secure under the cloak of mostly darkness—the streetlights shining through the front windows cast strange enough shadows to make the moment still feel impulsive—they settled into a familiar rhythm. What

Lewis lacked in sexual athleticism, he made up for with his generosity. Using one of two proven methods, he always made sure Martha came before he let himself get too carried away. She was too worked up tonight to protest against this routine, though she'd planned to suggest that they try to reach orgasm at the same time. There would be plenty of opportunities for that in the future, though, given this new coital paradigm that was opening up for them. As she was still writhing from her release, Lewis entered her. She watched his expression evolve from satisfied to concentrated to deeply focused, and just before he reached the stage where he looked like he was about to sneeze, she said, "Lewis, I want you to give me a pearl necklace."

"A what?" he said, breathlessly.

"A big, beautiful pearl necklace straight from the bottom of the sea."

His movements slowed and his expression changed from focused to confused, but he continued, his belly slapping against hers with each thrust. He wiped the sweat from his brow before it could drip on her face. "You don't like the necklace I gave you?"

"Of course I do. I love it. But I want another one." She arched her back and touched the hollow of her throat. "A homemade one, if you know what I mean."

Now he stopped moving. "I have no idea what you mean. Am I doing something wrong?"

She swished her hips back and forth, hoping to maintain his erection for him if he wasn't going to. "I want you to . . . to come on my neck." But she cringed even as she said it, thinking it sounded more vulgar than erotic when spelled out like that.

Lewis must've thought so, too, because his penis almost instantly shrank and slipped out of her. "But . . . why?" He looked genuinely shocked.

Embarrassed, she pulled a corner of the afghan across her chest. Lewis moved off her and leaned against the couch. "I don't know. I thought it would be sexy. Don't men like stuff like that?"

"Not with their wives!"

"Wait, are you saying you'd like it with someone else?"

"No! Of course not, Marty. How could you say something like that?"

"But you'd like it if I wasn't your wife?" She wished now that she'd put on the wig from her old gala costume.

"I haven't thought about pearl necklaces since I was about fifteen years old. As far as I know, that kind of thing only happens in teenage fantasies and pornos, and I'm not an expert on either." He pulled on his shorts and sat there, looking at her.

"Lewis, please. I'm sorry. I wasn't trying to gross you out." She sat up, covering herself. "Can we go to bed and start over?"

He scrubbed at his face with his balled-up T-shirt, then put it on. He took a long drink from his glass of wine. "It's okay. I'm not grossed out. I was just surprised is all. We were having such a nice time."

"We were! I'm sorry. Can't we try again? Nothing surprising this time, I promise."

"I'm not really up to it anymore, if you know what I mean." He gave her a half smile and shrugged.

She moved to him on her knees and gave him a chaste kiss on the cheek. "Soon, then."

"Sure," he said, pushing himself up to his usual spot on the couch. He grabbed the remote and turned the TV on. Martha had made sure to turn off the DVD player and set the input back to cable. Now the sports channel came on, the announcer sharing highlights of the Cardinals-Phillies game earlier that day.

"Happy anniversary, Lewis."

He glanced at her. "Happy anniversary, hon."

When had Lewis become so plodding? She collected her discarded clothes and shoes, and left the room wrapped up in the afghan, dismayed, unsettled, and unsatisfied.

Fourteen

Martha woke up the next morning when Lewis's alarm went off, but she pretended to still be asleep. She wished she actually were; her head felt thick from drinking too much, and she'd slept fitfully, waking up several times from unpleasant dreams to gulp down water or go to the bathroom or both. Not only that, she was, for the first time in their marriage, embarrassed by her behavior with Lewis. And even more by his rebuke.

She listened to him moving around the kitchen making himself breakfast. The smell of coffee could usually draw her out of bed, but today it made her nauseated, so she rolled over to face away from the door and covered her face with her pillow. During his shower, she could hear him singing one of his favorite Journey songs, which meant he was in a good mood. Well, he was usually in a good mood. He didn't tend to hang on to grievances or pout about anything, especially where she was concerned. But still.

Even with her eyes closed, she knew exactly what he was doing as he finished getting ready. She knew all the sounds by heart: the gargle of mouthwash, the clink of his belt being buckled, the snap of his watchband closing, the spritz of the same brand of cologne he'd been wearing since college. Almost everything about him was predictable and steady, which, except for last night, had served them both well for the past sixteen-plus years. Part of her wanted to fling back the covers and hug him from behind as he brushed his desperately thinning hair in the mirror, but she didn't. She played dead as he walked around to her side of the mattress, lifted the pillow to kiss her on the cheek, then carefully put it back. Only when she heard his car pull out of the driveway did she finally heave herself out of bed.

Martha reached into the jumble of underwear in her drawer for a bra and bumped the sharp paper corner of the DVD sleeve. She snatched her hand back as though she'd touched a hot burner. After she'd watched it the day before, she realized she hadn't planned what to do with it. Destroy it? Toss it? Keep it? She certainly hadn't expected that she'd have to return the thing. If it had been John and another woman, she'd have probably burned it. Or maybe cut it up into small pieces and then burned it, just to be sure no lawyer or former lover would be able to get their hands on it. In the meantime, her underwear drawer had seemed the safest and most apropos place to stash a sex tape.

If she wasn't so hungover, so fragile-feeling, she'd wait until Minnie and John had left for work and rush the DVD back over to their house this very morning. But she didn't trust herself to pull off a reverse heist at the moment, even though it was urgent that she did so as soon as possible. Obviously, it was sentimental to John, and maybe—probably—to Minnie, too. Why else would he keep it under lock and key? Perhaps they watched it together occasionally, to remind them of a special moment between them. Or maybe to get into the mood. Although such a physically perfect, happily married couple probably didn't need porn, even homemade porn, to get into the mood.

She shoved the DVD to the back of her drawer and regarded the bra in her hand. It had been a pretty, pinkish-nude color when she bought it—six, seven years ago?—but now it was the dull, utilitarian gray of an old rubber band and about as stretched out as one, too. She put it on and looked at herself in the mirror as long as she could stand to, then closed her eyes and turned around. No wonder Lewis wasn't inspired to try anything risqué.

She slammed the drawer closed and heard the DVD slide hard against the back. Well, she imagined it anyway. It made her think about that Poe short story, "The Tell-Tale Heart," in which the narrator was driven mad by hearing the imagined heartbeat of an old man he'd killed and abruptly confessed in order to make it stop. Martha certainly would never admit what she'd done, no matter how terrible it made her feel. Instead, she'd find a time to sneak back into the Wrights' house a second time, put the DVD back where it belonged, then forget she'd ever seen it. Or try to.

~

It was Friday, so she put on her overalls and went outside to mow the lawn. It was already miserably hot, but maybe she deserved to suffer. At the very least, she'd sweat out some of the toxins from the night before. She was just about to pull the starter cord when she heard Mrs. Kashuba call to her from across the street.

"Martha!"

Oh no, she thought. What if Mrs. Kashuba had seen her going into the Wrights' house yesterday? What if she wanted an explanation? Should she deny it? Or admit only that she'd gone into the backyard, maybe to retrieve something? But what? A tennis ball from Frank Devlin's stupid Nerf blaster? She felt a cold sweat break out underneath her sun hat. Why hadn't she practiced an answer for such an inevitable question?

"Martha, dear!"

Instead of acknowledging her neighbor, Martha yanked the cord and the lawn mower roared to life. Maybe if she pretended she couldn't hear her, Mrs. Kashuba would give up and go away. But as she started to push, the mower sputtered and died. She tried again and the same thing happened. "Crap," she muttered. But by the time she realized that she'd forgotten to open the throttle, Mrs. Kashuba had crossed the street and was standing in front of Martha, waving.

"Oh, I didn't see you there," Martha said, forcing herself to smile. She'd just have to take whatever lumps were coming.

"I'm glad I caught you working outside today," she said, and sighed. "I'm afraid I've got some bad news."

Martha closed the throttle, then glanced left and right, looking for the police car that was surely going to arrive any moment to take her away. "What is it?"

"Those nasty slugs have really gotten to you, haven't they?"

Nasty slugs! What a thing to call the Wrights. "How did you know?" Martha asked.

Mrs. Kashuba picked a leaf from a potted marigold and held it out to her. It was full of holes.

"Oh, you mean actual slugs." Martha wiped the sweat from her brow.

"They're all over my yard, too. I didn't have the heart to put out any of those violent traps with beer or salt, but now they're devouring my flowers and munching the bark off my fruit trees. Actually, I'm thinking of getting a chicken to help control the population. I should've done it years ago, but I figured Mrs. Fancy-pants Mickelsen would have a fit and so I decided to save myself the heartburn. Can't you just hear her complaining about the smell of chicken poop?" She burst into a throaty laugh that betrayed her long-ago smoking habit. "Now that I think about it, maybe I'll get two. Anyway, that's not what I came over here to tell you." She pointed at Martha's crape myrtles. "I don't know if you've noticed, but you've got another little infestation. See that discoloration on the bark there?"

Martha turned and was dismayed to see that there was indeed a dark, powdery coating on some of the branches. "Sooty mold," she said, shaking her head. "How did I miss that?" She'd been busy lately, sure, but maintaining her yard had always been a point of pride. Now she had something else to add to her list of embarrassments.

"It's not extensive—yet," Mrs. Kashuba said, and patted Martha on the arm. "But it's a good thing we caught it now. The aphids are bad this year, so we've got to deal with them first. They're what's causing the soot. I'll bring over some neem oil to get rid of the bugs, and then all you have to do is spray down the trees with a dishwashing soap solution to remove the mold. I'll bring my chickens over, too, and see if we can get rid of your slugs." She laughed again and turned, waving over her shoulder as she crossed the street again.

After dealing with the lawn, Martha took a shower, and was resentful of the low water pressure. She looked with disdain at the ancient bathroom that was so narrow she and Lewis had to suck in their sagging stomachs to pass each other between the bath and the toilet. She thought about their sagging stomachs and the dreary overfamiliarity that had grown between them.

She ate lunch and put a pot roast in the slow cooker. Normally she didn't listen to music, but she turned on the radio and blasted the country station just to drown out the throbbing presence of the DVD in her drawer and all the negative thoughts swirling in her head. She stared at the bedroom walls for a while and noticed the paint was peeling again, despite her previous efforts to scrape and repair it, because Houston's humidity was too much for their antiquated compressor. She flopped onto the bed and stared at the ceiling, where she noticed how dingy the vent covers were. Was there sooty mold inside the house as well as on the crape myrtles?

She went into the utility room, which had, presumably, once been part of a sunny screen porch in an era before washing machines became ubiquitous. Now there was an old Maytag set—bought on clearance in the dinged-and-dented section of the appliance store when Martha was waddling pregnant with Harry—along the wall abutting the driveway, shaking and shimmying on peeling linoleum in a room that wasn't even air-conditioned. She took some cleaning rags from the bucket where she kept them and went into the kitchen, which had been updated exactly once since it was built in 1940, to wet them. She looked at the cracks in the old subway tile on the counter and the oven that was off by forty degrees. The leaky faucet and sticky drawers. Martha had looked it up after they'd moved in: there'd been seven owners listed on the Harris County Appraisal District website before them. A total of eight families had lived under this roof, shedding hair and dead skin and saliva into the duct system that circulated and recirculated hot, dank air. How many people in the past eighty years had left their waste and fingerprints and stench and secrets to seep into the walls and plumbing and duct system?

She scrubbed at the grime on the vent cover, but it wouldn't come off. She tried again, harder and harder, until she was nearly in tears.

~

Martha passed the rest of that day and the weekend in a funk. Lewis seemed fine but was distracted by the pressure he was under to prepare for the upcoming quarterly review at work. He settled into his easy chair with his computer and the TV remote, and moved only to use the bathroom or go to bed. For that reason, she spent most of those three days in her office, working, looking out the window into the Wrights' backyard, and sending emails to Harry at camp. She wished he were home. Even if he shut himself in his room half the day, she'd have something to focus on, someone to talk to.

After Thursday night's sexual debacle, she'd put the peridot necklace back on and hadn't taken it off since, even though all she'd worn with it were overalls and grubby old T-shirts. Ostensibly, she wore it to show Lewis her appreciation, but it was also a sort of penance, an albatross hung around her neck to remind her to be grateful for what she had instead of trying to emulate her neighbors. She reminded herself that the peridot necklace had real value, both monetary and sentimental. It was something she would keep forever, perhaps pass down to her future daughter-in-law or maybe a granddaughter if she were to have one. The pearl necklace that John had given Minnie would've been simply washed down the shower drain. It wasn't real, it didn't last. It was, in fact, more than a little bit gross. Yet she made herself miserable with both frustration and shame by continuing to think about it, especially when it caused a distracting tingling sensation between her legs. She didn't mention again to Lewis the idea of their going away together; it would be humiliating to bring it up after what happened. Plus, she didn't want him to think she had something lewd in mind. All weekend, she made sure to keep their interactions pleasant and chaste, to prove that everything was normal between them. That she was normal.

But no matter what she did to occupy herself, her mind kept returning to unwanted thoughts, and she felt her mood and self-esteem sinking lower and lower until finally, by Monday morning, she'd had enough.

She looked sternly at herself in the bathroom mirror. "Martha Bethany Pagnell Hale," she said, in a voice that sounded exactly like her mother, "it's time to get a grip on yourself." Evelyn had always had a very low tolerance for moping. Also for whining, complaining, and self-indulgent excuse-making. *Pull yourself up by your bootstraps!* she'd say, whether the crisis was a bad grade, a social mishap, or a foul mood. She was more sympathetic if Martha or her sister were suffering from an actual illness or injury—except for premenstrual syndrome, which Evelyn said was mostly in their heads. Three days was the maximum that Evelyn allowed anyone in her household to complain about something before they had to formulate a plan of action, and by force of imposed habit, Martha's internal timer had dinged.

"Here's what you're going to do. First, you are going to dry your hair and put on a decent outfit. Then you're going to call your mother." She began a mental list, starting with tangible, short-term to-dos and gradually adding more existential goals such as saving her trees, being a better wife and neighbor, and losing fifteen pounds.

~

"Well, well. Isn't this a nice surprise?" Evelyn said, sounding more reproachful than pleased. Through the phone, Martha could hear the clink of her mother's teacup being placed back on its saucer. She'd been given a nice set of china for her wedding to Martha's father, but over the years, everything but one cup, two saucers, and the gravy bowl had been chipped or broken. If anything happened to that final cup, Martha thought Evelyn would probably give up drinking coffee altogether. "You're always so busy, but you've finally made some time for your dear old mom."

"Mom, you make it sound like I never call you. Besides, I literally saw you a week ago at Harry's graduation lunch."

"I just think it would be nice to hear from you more often, especially since you're not really working. Your sister called yesterday on her way to Portland. Even Thomas called a few days ago from London."

Martha remembered her vow of self-improvement and resisted the urge to tell her mother that she'd call more often if she wasn't chastised each time for not doing it more frequently and if she wasn't constantly being compared to her oncologist sister and her financier stepbrother. "I know it's last minute, but I was wondering if you wanted to have lunch today. My treat."

Evelyn's voice dropped an octave. "Is something the matter?"

"No, of course not. Does something have to be wrong for me to invite you to lunch?" Why had she thought calling Evelyn might make her feel better?

"Certainly not! In fact, I think we should do it regularly," Evelyn said, her voice back to its normal pitch. "And since you're buying, how about that fabulous upscale American place off Kirby? Ethyl's, isn't it?

Then maybe we could go to the Menil. There's a new exhibit my friend Irene told me was to die for. And we should probably leave some time for the Rothko Chapel, too. You sound stressed, Martha. Fifteen minutes at the Rothko will do wonders. Plus, it's free."

Martha spent more time doing her makeup for lunch with her mother than she had for her anniversary dinner with her husband. Evelyn never missed an opportunity to get dressed up, and she felt that everyone else should, too, even though her own husband could rarely be persuaded to wear anything other than a rotating selection of well-worn overalls. Martha much preferred her stepfather's sense of style to her mother's, but today she made the effort to put herself together in a manner befitting the occasion.

"Don't you look nice?" Evelyn said before grabbing Martha into a hug with a force that belied her petite stature. Several other patrons in the lobby waiting for their tables looked on with detached admiration.

"Thanks, Mom. You look nice, too. That color is pretty on you."

Evelyn smoothed the front of her turquoise silk top, then looked at her reflection in the restaurant's double-door glass and sighed. "If only I weren't so fat." She looked back at Martha expectantly.

Martha forced herself not to roll her eyes. "You're not fat, Mom." This exact call-and-response had long been a ritual between them, and was as reflexive and meaningless as asking a passing stranger, *how are you?* Martha could vividly remember watching her mother get ready for one of her first dates with Henry, the man who would eventually become Martha's stepfather, thinking how glamorous Evelyn looked in her formfitting dress and sparkly shoes, then being shocked by Evelyn's reaction to her own reflection in the mirror. "I can't wear this!" she'd said. "I look enormous. When did I get so huge?" Seven-year-old Martha had desperately tried to convince her mother that she looked beautiful, but Evelyn countered every compliment, insisting over and over that she looked awful. She reached into her impressive vocabulary and hurled colorful insults at herself, using words like *beastly* and *revolting* along with others that Martha had never heard before. Her mother finally settled on an outfit that she said made her look the least hideous and then went on to have a lovely evening with Henry. But Martha remained deeply unsettled. If her slim, attractive mother was "hideous," then maybe Martha's understanding of beauty was all wrong. That moment was the first of countless similar exchanges over the years designed to boost Evelyn's self-image—and also the beginning of Martha's lifelong struggle with her own.

Evelyn slipped her arm into Martha's as they followed the hostess to their table. "This is just wonderful, having lunch with you. Tell me everything. How's Harry getting along at camp? Has he written any letters? Tell him that I expect to receive at least one from him, that little stinker." They sat down, and after thanking the hostess, Evelyn adjusted her place setting, moving the paper placemat so that it lined up with the edge of the table, shifting her water glass slightly to the right. She squinted at the fork, then scrubbed at it with the paper napkin in her lap, her bangle bracelets jangling noisily. "Make sure your fork is clean. Mine had spots." Then she reached into her purse and rummaged around. "Now where are my glasses? I swear I put them in my handbag before I left. Martha, you might have to read the menu to me." She turned in her chair and held the menu aloft, trying to catch it under the light. "Maybe this'll work. Ooh," she said, lowering her voice and peering at Martha. "It's pricier than I thought." Then she laughed and waved her hand, jangling again. "But that's okay. Your husband makes plenty of money."

The server hadn't even brought over their basket of bread and already Martha was exhausted.

"Speaking of which, that's a gorgeous necklace. I assume it's from Lewis?"

Martha made a snorting sound. "Well, of course it's from Lewis, Mom. Who else would it be from?"

Evelyn raised a hand in surrender. "I'm not accusing you of having a lover, dear. No offense, but I think men who take mistresses tend to choose them for their youth and"—she pantomimed an exaggerated hourglass—"sex appeal."

"Now why would I be offended by that?" This time Martha couldn't restrain an eye roll.

"Come on. You know how most men are. I was lucky to've found two good ones in my life: your father, God rest his soul, and your pop. Neither one so much as glanced at another woman after they laid eyes on me. Why would they when they were in thrall with this?" She laughed and struck a dramatic pose with her hand under her chin. "Of course, all bets are off with Henry now that I've gotten so fat."

"Mom, stop."

The waiter came to take their order, giving Martha a too-brief reprieve from her mother.

"Is the butter-braised wild quail as delicious as it sounds?" Evelyn asked.

"Better," he said.

"Perfect. I'll have that and a Caesar salad, no croutons, please and thank you."

"And the crispy chicken sandwich and side of mac and cheese for me," Martha said.

"Don't you want something a little more exciting?" her mother said. "What about the Gulf fried oysters with pine nuts and spinach? Or the Wagyu burger at least? You can make mac and cheese at home, for heaven's sake."

Martha looked at the waiter, hoping for some sympathy, but he only pursed his lips and waited. "Okay, fine, I'll have the burger. Medium rare. And a side of truffle fries." She forced a smile and handed the menu back to him.

"That's better. If we're going out, we should enjoy it, right? Anyway, you're lucky to have a man like Lewis. Smart, loyal, a good provider.

Plenty of women would stand in line for someone like that, even if he's not the best looking." Martha didn't disagree with her mother's assessment of Lewis, but she felt defensive of him hearing it come out of Evelyn's mouth so casually. She leaned forward to interject, but her mother continued without pause. "Men can get away with aging, have you noticed that? Just look around. They can grow a belly the size of Santa Claus's, go gray or bald, wear nothing but dungarees, but if they have an income and a decent personality then women will still throw themselves at them. I don't understand it, frankly. But god forbid a woman should gain an ounce or develop a wrinkle on her face. No matter how intelligent she is or how hard she's worked raising her family or at a career, suddenly she's nothing but a sad old cow." She shook her head, emphasizing the tragedy of it. "I've seen it happen to my friends, Martha, and I'm telling you now: you've got to be careful. In fact, I think we should forgo the Menil after lunch and go shopping for a few new outfits for you instead. Maybe some new underwear?"

Martha glanced from side to side, worried that someone had over-heard her mother. "Jeez, Mom, no."

"I'm just saying, I remember when you were a little girl, you'd wear your underwear until it fell apart. I finally started throwing it out. Do you remember that? You'd get so upset, which I could never understand. Who doesn't like a brand-new pair of underpants?"

"That was one pair. It was my lucky underwear, which is why I didn't want to throw it out. It's not like I never update my wardrobe, Mom. I get rid of old clothes all the time." She made a mental note to buy those new bras immediately.

"Well, good. You need to do whatever you can to hang on to that husband of yours. We can go pick out a few new things. It wouldn't hurt to wear a dress now and then. What's close by?"

Martha bought most of her clothes at designer discount outlets, same as her mother. It took Martha a long time to understand that even though her mother liked to appear well off and actually was financially secure since she married Pop thirty years ago, she still didn't feel that way. When she was little, they went clothes shopping exactly twice a year: just before school started and during spring break. Her mother went through her and Bessie's closets with them, discarding old or ill-fitting clothes, then made a list of items they each needed to complete their wardrobes. Evelyn purchased only what she'd deemed necessary; anything extra, Martha had to pay for with her own money. "Well, if you're buying, we can go to Lolli's. It's right across the street."

Evelyn snorted. "Very funny. You could buy a house for what it would cost to get a new wardrobe there." She leaned forward and lowered her voice. "Did I ever tell you I went in there once? This was before I met your pop and I was working as a seamstress doing alterations for a high-end tailor. We had regular customers who brought in these incredibly gorgeous clothes from Lolli's to be let out, sometimes by as much as two sizes. For whatever reason, they refused to buy a dress that fit, so they'd pay *two* fortunes: first to Lolli's, and then to us so I could take it apart and remake it. So, one day I decided to go over there and see what the fuss was all about. Maybe they didn't have clothes bigger than size four, who knew? But when I went in, the salesgirl rushed over and made it clear I 'wouldn't find anything suitable' as she was herding me out like I was cattle that'd wandered in by mistake. It was mortifying. I could feel all these other women watching and judging me." She closed her eyes and raised her hand to jangle away the memory. "You couldn't pay me to step foot in there ever again."

"I remember the story," Martha said, softening her voice. "And I was only kidding about going there. I'm sorry."

"Oh, it's fine. After all these years, it shouldn't bother me."

"I don't know, it's hard to let those things go sometimes. But anyway, you don't need to take me shopping, I'm fine."

"So says you." Evelyn took a deep breath and straightened up her shoulders. "Tell me, how are you getting along with your new neighbor?

Not that I'm suggesting anything, but didn't you mention that she was young and gorgeous? You don't think Lewis has noticed, do you?"

"I think you're embellishing it a bit. I said she was beautiful—for her age. And I'm literally less than a month older than her."

"Than 'she.'"

Martha sighed. "I'm less than a month older than she. And no, he hasn't noticed." She hoped. That particular thought hadn't occurred to her until just then. She felt for the teardrop pendant and fingered the peridots dotting the front, tangible proof of his devotion to her. Wasn't it? She thought about John and the rumors. Even though the video she'd found was of him and Minnie, that didn't mean there wasn't another one of him with someone else.

The waiter appeared with their food, and Evelyn clapped her fingertips together and beamed. "Oh, this looks divine, doesn't it, Martha?" She turned to the waiter. "It looks simply divine. Thank you."

Martha offered her mother the bread basket, but Evelyn refused. "I'm cutting down on the carbs," she said. "You might consider it. Your sister says it really works."

Martha took a big bite of her cheeseburger. There was no way she would ever stop eating bread. "Maybe," she mumbled.

"Oh, dear, don't talk with your mouth full," she said. Martha noticed an oily dribble rolling down her mother's chin as she spoke. "This quail is to die for. Would you like to try it? Look how the meat just falls off the bones. And the flavor is so rich and delicate. We had partridge a few weeks ago at a neighbor's, and it was gamy enough to make your hair curl."

Martha glanced at her mother's plate. "No, thank you." It was one thing to eat meat that had been ground or cut up into something that didn't resemble its original form, but the three braised little birds lying on their bed of greens looked too recognizable to be appealing.

"Speaking of neighbors, what did you say her name was? Minnie? Or something peculiar like that?"

"Yes, Minnie. Short for Melanie." At least that's what Martha assumed, remembering that John had called her that the night she overheard them arguing in the backyard.

"I never liked the name Melanie," Evelyn said. "It sounds like 'melanoma.'" By the way she took a long inhale through her nose and raised her eyebrows at her food, Martha knew Evelyn was thinking about her mother, who'd died of anal melanoma the year Harry had turned two. It had been quite a shock, as no one else in their family had ever developed cancer before. It was more than a little ironic, too, as Martha's grandmother had always been fond of telling people to stick their opinions *where the sun don't shine*. As a consequence, Evelyn developed a wariness of doing or saying anything that might invite similar karmic trouble. "Plus, it means *dark*. Like a dark-and-stormy night. Why would anyone name a child something with such a negative connotation?"

Martha shrugged, feeling defensive again, this time of Minnie's parents, whom she'd never met. "Maybe that's why she goes by Minnie. She's not dark at all. She's the opposite, really. All light and sunshine."

"So, you've become friendly with her?"

Martha resented the suspicious-looking expression on her mother's face. "As a matter of fact, I have. We've gotten together a number of times already and we've made plans to do it again." It wasn't a lie, exactly; she was just describing a future truth.

"That's terrific, honey. You know I worry about you sometimes. You get so focused on Harry and keeping house and your little picture business that you seem to be missing out on some bigger things like having girlfriends. You know I don't know what I'd do without my friends. Of course, I adore your pop, but sometimes he's just such . . . a man, I don't know. I need a little girl time now and then. Like this," she said, and patted Martha's hand. "It makes me happy to know that you're making time for a female friend instead of devoting all your efforts to the men in your life."

Martha considered that idea. Perhaps her mother was right, that the reason she didn't have a lot of women friends was because she'd been so focused on being a wife and mother. "But there's certainly no crime in that, is there?"

"No, of course not, dear. But Harry's growing up, and he's not going to need you the same way he did when he was little, which means you're going to have plenty of free time to fill. That's why I say it's good that you have a new girlfriend—and right next door, too!" Evelyn took a tiny bite of quail meat and added another stripped bone to the tidy, delicate stack on the edge of her plate. "But remember, proximity alone won't support a relationship. You can't take your friendship with Minnie for granted; you've got to work on it just like you do your marriage. You need to 'put yourself out there,' as the young people say. Take some calculated risks, be brave."

"Mom, jeez. I'm thirty-eight years old, not ten. I know how friendships work, okay?" Martha could hear the petulance in her own voice and knew that she sounded like the teenager she'd hated being. Worse, she knew that her mother was right.

Evelyn lifted a shoulder and pursed her lips into a smile, the fine lines radiating around them like a sun. "Let's don't squabble, Martha. We're having such a nice time."

Fifteen

Martha couldn't get out of the restaurant fast enough. She feigned a small drama featuring an imaginary deadline from one of the photographers she worked with. "Can you believe this?" she said to Evelyn, holding her phone up for her mother to see. It was actually open to a text thread between her and Lewis, but without her glasses, Evelyn wouldn't know the difference. "It's from Charles. He needs me to process a subset of images from a wedding last weekend by tonight. I'm so sorry, Mom. I hate that I won't be able to go to the museum or shopping with you after all."

"Oh, what a shame. Is it really that important, though? A new bride and groom should be wrapped in each other's arms, for heaven's sake, not looking at pictures of themselves. Can't they wait until morning?"

Under the table, Martha gripped her knees to keep herself from saying—or perhaps screaming—what she really wanted to, and forced her voice under control. "I really can't say no to Charles, much as I'd like to. He's my biggest client."

"Well, if duty calls, then we'll just have to do it another time."

In the parking lot, after enduring another of her mother's vigorous and lingering hugs, Martha trot-walked to her own car, anticipating the relief of Evelyn's absence. She heard her mother call out loudly after her, "Shoulders back, Martha! You'll lose ten pounds just by standing up straight!" Martha flung herself into the minivan and drove past her mother without so much as a wave.

She was so infuriated on the way home that when another car moved into her lane, Martha laid on the horn, then gesticulated wildly with alternating middle fingers at the other driver. Normally she avoided provocative behavior on Houston's roadways—especially toward trucks with lift kits or gun racks, and sports cars, both of which she assumed were likely to be driven by aggressive men—but since the offending vehicle in this case was a slow and nondescript sedan, Martha took the opportunity to unload her frustrations. She jerked her minivan into the adjacent lane and sped up so that she was next to the sedan, screwed her face into the fiercest expression she could muster, and shook her fist at the driver, who turned out to be an exceedingly elderly-looking man flaring his eyes in terror as she passed.

Ashamed of herself, Martha was instantly subdued. She drove calmly the rest of the way home, sending thoughts of apology both to the poor old man and to her mother. This was exactly the opposite of the self-improvement she'd earlier set out to achieve. She changed her clothes, washed her face, and sat down at her computer to order three new bras and matching briefs in one size larger than the last time she'd bought any.

~

Four days had passed since Martha had taken the DVD from John Wright's office, and so far—with the exception of the fleeting scare instigated by the amateur arborist, Mrs. Kashuba—it seemed nobody had realized what she'd done. Still, the presence of it in her underwear drawer haunted her. Before she could put it back where it belonged, however, she wanted to talk to Lupe, the Wrights' housekeeper. Martha knew how watchful good housekeepers could be. She thought back to the early days of Harry's childhood, when she would take him to the park. If there wasn't someone for her to talk to, she'd sometimes just sit on the bench alongside the nannies, most of whom spoke Spanish, and eavesdrop on their conversations. It was one of the few times Martha didn't mind being an outsider; because the women seemed to assume she didn't understand them, they often shared salacious gossip about their employers. She remembered hearing one tell another that she knew the husband was cheating on his wife because she found a condom in a side pocket of the suitcase he'd taken on a recent business trip and had asked her to empty. Martha had been struck by the foolishness of that husband—both for his infidelity and for leaving such a sloppy trail—and also by the unintended intimacy that could develop between someone hired to work in a house and the family who lived there. Who knew what sorts of secrets a housekeeper or nanny might be able to discern without her employers realizing it? So, even if the neighbors hadn't seen Martha and the Wrights hadn't noticed that anyone had been in their house, there was still a chance that Lupe would. Martha didn't know what clues she may have left behind, but she couldn't think about going back until it was clear that Lupe didn't suspect her of any wrongdoing.

She worked nervously all the next day, interrupting her own concentration to glance out the window and into Minnie's backyard, wondering what Lupe was doing. At one point, she heard the door open and close, and jumped up to watch. Her heart was thrumming in her chest as Lupe stood with her hands on her hips and looked around. Had Martha dropped something during her mad escape? Left a messy footprint on the porch? But after a moment, Lupe pulled a pack of cigarettes from her back pocket and sat down on one of the chaises to smoke. Martha felt guilty watching her take deep, satisfied-looking inhales, and then carefully exhale downwind, fanning the air in front of her, presumably to keep the smoke from attaching itself to her clothing. When she was finished, she dug a small hole in the grass and fed the cigarette butt into it, patting the grass back down to conceal the mark.

Martha relaxed a bit after witnessing that small transgression, but she wouldn't feel completely relieved until later that evening, when she could greet Lupe on her way home for the day and gauge her reaction. Lupe usually left by five thirty, so at quarter till, Martha went outside to water her bushes and wait.

When Lupe saw Martha, she waved. "Hello, lady!"

Martha, her nerves rooting her to the ground, said, "Hi, Lupe."

Lupe walked toward her, her face full of concern. "You doing okay?"

Martha swallowed and dropped the hose. She turned to face Lupe as though squaring off against an opponent in a street fight. "I'm fine. How are you?" She could hear the edge in her own voice.

"I'm tired. Miss Minnie having me clean all the closets today. Lots of work." She smiled and rubbed her lower back. "I'm getting old again!"

Martha knew she was in the clear. Relief flooded her system like she'd just drunk half a bottle of wine, and she smiled back. "You take care of yourself, Lupe. Get some rest."

"Thank you, lady. See you." Lupe waved again and headed off. Martha turned off the water and rolled the hose back up. She would take the sex tape back to Minnie's the next day.

~

After Lewis had gone to work, and as soon as John and then Minnie had left their own house the next morning, Martha crept out onto her front porch, peered up and down the street to be sure the coast was clear, then sprinted as fast as she could in her gardening clogs to Minnie's gate, kicked her shoes off once she reached the porch, and let herself in. After entering the house, she said hello to Bonnie, who once again watched her with what seemed like curiosity. She went straight to the staircase, pausing only to glance out the big picture window, hopeful that nobody was watching. Nobody was.

Once upstairs, she felt compelled to explore her friend's home a bit more. Being inside, especially alone, was a particular thrill, simultaneously dangerous and intimate. Her hand, which gripped the DVD in its sleeve, grew damp, and her heart rate increased as she thought about what she'd seen on the video, about what she might find if she looked in other locked drawers or private areas. Just as quickly, she admonished herself for having such shameful thoughts. Hadn't she been intrusive enough already? It did bother her, though, that she'd only found the one DVD. What if there really were more? Why else would there have been a rumor? Perhaps he kept the one with his wife in his filing cabinet, but one showcasing his indiscretions in a safety-deposit box somewhere? No, she decided. That was just the West U gossips being nasty. She should've known better; John had plenty to enjoy right there at home.

Newly contrite, Martha got the key from the book and put the DVD back into its hanging folder without allowing herself to look at any other files or anything on John's desk. She returned the key and checked that everything looked as pristine as it had when she'd gotten there. Lupe really was a terrific housekeeper, she thought. Either that, or Minnie and John didn't actually touch their own things.

She speed-walked through the house and was about to open the back door when Bonnie called gently out. Minnie had said that was her happy sound, and now Martha was reminded how stunned Minnie had been that Bonnie hadn't squawked or thrashed about when Martha had entered the first time. She'd been flattered then, and was again now.

She turned around and spoke to her in a singsong voice. "Hi, pretty girl. Are you singing to me?" Bonnie cocked her head from side to side as she chirped and trilled, never taking her eyes off Martha. Martha went to the cage and noticed the latch on the little door was unlocked; it moved so easily when she pulled it that the cage itself seemed merely symbolic—the bird could probably open it herself if she were inclined to do so. Bonnie immediately hopped onto Martha's extended finger. "You're such a sweet girl," Martha cooed, and stroked Bonnie's tiny talons with her thumb. After a while Bonnie grew quiet, and the two of them just looked at each other. "Are you lonely here when your mom's gone?" Martha wondered if she should offer to keep Bonnie at her house while Minnie was at work each day. It seemed sad to leave her there all alone. She looked into her cage to see if there was anything for her to play with. Did birds play?

She noticed that the little water bowl was almost empty, so she decided to fill it up. Not all the way, not so much that it would be noticeable, but enough that she'd be able to drink if she was thirsty. At the kitchen sink, she didn't dare spill a drop of water. Everything was picture perfect; even the sink was spotless. When she put the bowl back into the cage, Bonnie hopped to it and put her beak in.

"Oh, you poor little thing. Were you thirsty? It's a good thing I stopped by, wasn't it? Are you hungry, too?" There was a little plate but nothing on it. Martha went back to the kitchen to see what she might offer her. "How about a banana?" she called out, as though it were Harry she was talking to instead of a bird. There was a huge bunch of them in the fruit bowl in the center of the island; surely Minnie wouldn't notice if one were missing. "A banana's probably a good idea. But just a little bit, okay?" She pinched off several tiny pieces and fed them to Bonnie, then took a large bite herself. "Good, isn't it?"

When Bonnie seemed to have eaten her fill, Martha finished it off, closed Bonnie's cage, then went back to the kitchen to throw the peel away. Unlike the Hales', the Wrights' kitchen was spacious enough to have a drawer in which to hide a large trash can. Martha had always hated the fact that theirs was right out in the open. It had a lid, of course, but it was unsightly. What a luxury it must be not to have to look at your own garbage. Just as she started to pull open the drawer, she had a thought. Minnie might not notice a missing banana, but she would most certainly notice a discarded peel in her garbage can, especially since Lupe would have taken out the trash the day before. Well, if there was enough in there, perhaps she could bury it underneath.

Otherwise, she'd have to take it home and dispose of it there. She opened the drawer to check, and what she saw inside made her gasp.

Underneath a half-eaten container of fancy yogurt, runny scraps of egg, and some toast crumbs were Martha's photographs of Bonnie, each one torn in half and stained. Disbelieving, Martha slowly reached in and took them out of the can. "No," she whispered. "No, no, no."

She stared at the pile in her hands for a moment, just feeling the weight of the paper, the expensive archival paper, trying to make sense of the situation. Then she slowly shuffled through them, becoming nauseated as she did so. Each of the prints was ripped right across the bird's little neck. Martha's favorite, the one where Bonnie and Minnie appeared to be kissing, had been ripped twice: first vertically, tearing the two of them apart, and then horizontally on the half featuring Bonnie, beheading her again. Martha counted the pieces. All twelve of the prints that she'd carefully, lovingly made, had been trashed.

Martha looked across the room to Bonnie, as if she might find an explanation there. But of course she wouldn't. Bonnie just looked back at her, then cocked her head and trilled her happy sound. Martha looked around Minnie's immaculate kitchen, her magazine-ready living room. She looked at the sophisticated art on the walls, the elegant arrangements of books and ornaments, the understated opulence of the furniture. The hidden garbage can. How could Martha have thought that anything she made would be good enough to be hung up in a house like this one? Or admired by someone who curated visuals for a living, whose whole life was like a work of art? The shock and disappointment of seeing her work ripped into pieces was overshadowed by self-doubt and embarrassment. She'd been so proud of those photographs, the composition, the postproduction. And although she didn't want to feel cheap, she'd spent a lot on the printing. The prints had been a gift, but she'd never have wasted the money if she'd known they'd end up in the trash. But of course, that was the point; she'd actually thought they were good, and she'd believed Minnie was being truthful when she told Martha that she loved them.

Behind her, the bird chirped and trilled. Martha glanced at her and had an eerie feeling of being exposed, caught. There might not have been a security camera, but there was a witness. Bonnie knew she'd been there.

Now Martha just wanted to get out, fast, and never return. She wanted to take the photos home with her and burn them, to forget that she'd ever taken them, to forget even that she'd ever tried to be friends with Minnie. She wanted to throw the banana peel at the wall and leave it where it landed. Fuck her, she thought. "Fuck you," she said aloud, and then said it again.

But she couldn't do any of that. She didn't want Minnie to know she'd been there that day or before. Nor did she want to give her the satisfaction of knowing she'd hurt Martha's feelings. So, as much as it pained her to do so, she put the destroyed images back into the garbage can, more or less the way she found them. She grabbed the banana peel, used a paper towel to wipe the evidence of it off the counter, then balled them up together to throw away at home. Being distraught and angry made her unsteady on her feet, and when she stepped off Minnie's back porch, she slipped and fell into the flower beds, crushing a huge cluster of creamy white mophead hydrangeas. She dusted herself off, hastily fluffed up the injured bushes, and rushed home before anyone could see her or hear her crying.

~

Lewis called in the afternoon to let her know he'd be late. He was working on his presentation for the quarterly review on Monday and needed his large monitor to make the slides. "Tom and I are just going to order dinner and eat here. I hope you didn't cook anything special," he said.

"No, I haven't even started thinking about dinner yet," she said.

"You okay? You sound funny."

She paused. "I ate a clown for lunch," she said, an old inside joke she hoped would satisfy him. As much as she wished she could tell him everything, have him come home and put his meaty arms around her and tell her everything was going to be okay, she'd gone too far without him on this exploit to involve him now. Not only that, but he would severely disapprove. At least she'd gotten rid of the physical evidence of her trespassing, so he wouldn't ever have to know what she'd done. All that remained of her actions were the emotional consequences, and like the rest of it, she'd handle that on her own. "I'm going to do a little work here, too, then probably go to bed early. Good luck getting everything done."

Martha tried to do as she'd said, but she kept second-guessing her edits on the batch of wedding photos she was trying to work through. Were they too dark? Too light? The contrast too high or not high enough? She'd thought Bonnie's photos were perfect, having worked on them for hours and hours, and clearly, she'd been wrong. Maybe she was delusional. Maybe she wasn't any good at photography after all.

But then why did she have so many—allegedly—satisfied clients? She had more work than she could keep up with. If she were so terrible, then nobody would hire her, right? Surely there were enough postproduction experts that they could find someone else if they didn't like what she put out. So then why did Minnie tear up her pictures?

She opened a new browser window and navigated to the social media platform she hated the most and scrolled. How was it that absolutely everyone she followed had such perfect lives? Families on expensive-looking vacations, promoting charitable causes, honoring their fathers and grandfathers for Memorial Day. Lillian's posts were usually of her not-at-all-fat girls posing with each other or their friends or dates or herself, always dressed and made up, on a "date night" with Daniel, but there was a new one of Willy, looking less diabolical than he did in real life, playing with Beignet. Minnie's account was new and devoted to her business. She posted only images of the artwork she acquired for her clients, but there was one photo of her from early March with her then-new boss, announcing that she'd joined Steinbauer Art Advisory & Appraisals. Martha saved a copy and opened it in her editing program.

Usually, she whittled a bride's waistline, brightened subjects' eyes, and evened out skin tones. But now, she did the reverse. With the precision and subtlety of a digital plastic surgeon, she bloated Minnie's cheeks, widened her nose, darkened the skin beneath her eyes. She added bulk to her neck and calves, and expanded her midsection until Minnie looked like an exhausted, middle-aged politician. Martha leaned back in her chair and admired her work. How fun it would be to post it somewhere public, like tossing raw meat out for the lions to tear into. She couldn't, of course, but decided the act of turning Minnie into a monster had been time well spent.

She looked out the window into the Wrights' yard. The pool lights threw up their shimmery turquoise glow, but there was nothing else out there but the sound of katydids chirping in the humid dark. Then she noticed a shadow crossing the Wrights' bedroom window. Minnie paused, parted the curtains, and stood there. Something about her posture made her look upset, though it was too dark to read her expression. Was she looking at Martha? She felt a hot shiver run up her back, and quickly ducked out of sight. What if Minnie knew she'd been inside the house and that's why she was angry enough to destroy the images? And if she was that angry, what else might she do? She went back and forth, trying to parse out all the possibilities, until she decided that there was no way she could know unless she saw Minnie face-to-face.

With trembling hands, she pulled out her phone and sent a text: I have a bottle of delicious homemade limoncello I made with lemons from my tree. Want to come over? We can have that cocktail we talked about the other day. Remember? She paused, then added: When you said you loved the portraits of Bonnie.

Through the curtains, she could see Minnie's phone light up in her hand, and watched her look at it. Martha was surprised to see, almost immediately, the telltale ellipsis appear on her own screen, indicating a response was forthcoming. But then it disappeared, and there was no text. Martha closed the message app, opened it again. She stared at the screen, willing Minnie's reply to appear. Minnie was still at her window, holding her phone as though engaged with it. A minute later, the ellipsis appeared again, those tantalizing dots like a dopamine shot to Martha's heart. But again, nothing afterward. Confused, Martha refreshed her screen over and over again. Was it a technological problem? A glitch in the time-space continuum between their two houses? A third time, the dots appeared, and that time a message did follow—a single line with no emojis, no explanation.

I can't tonight, sorry.

Martha watched as Minnie appeared to toss her phone behind her—on the bed, perhaps. She stood awhile longer at the window, then disappeared. Frank Devlin must've gone outside with his dog because for the next twenty minutes or so, Martha could hear the thunking sound of tennis balls being fired from his Nerf gun. Thunk. Thunk. Thunk. She could sense the new fence weakening with each hit. In her imagination, she had an elaborate vision of marching over to his house, snatching the plastic toy from him, and banging him over the head with it so she'd never again have to listen to the maddening sound of balls repeatedly striking wood. She imagined screaming in his face, calling him a child, a moron, an idiot, or worse, standing so close that he could feel the heat of her anger, the vitriol on her breath. She imagined him stumbling backward to get away from her, tripping on a patch of turf, holding up his shaking hands to protect himself from her vigor, her might. Who was he to ruin fences, to constantly disrupt their days and nights? And who was Minnie to reject her so plainly, in the open view of anyone who cared to see? What was she doing that was so important she couldn't show her face to the person she'd insulted so profoundly?

The light in Minnie's bedroom stayed on for another hour. Martha knew it because even though her knees ached from kneeling on the floor, she remained where she was that whole time, watching.

Sixteen

Martha woke up to another day that would likely be filled with nothing much more than hours of solitary work that would remind her of her own failings, so she decided to stay in the house and bake. Already she'd made two cinnamon coffee cakes, one of which she planned to take over to Mrs. Kashuba and one she would deliver to her mother over the weekend; an extra-large batch of chocolate chip cookies for Lewis to take to work; and a tray of fudge that she might give away, but would probably keep.

As she flipped through her favorite dessert recipe book, Martha considered the fact that she might lose the weight she'd been wanting to lose for ten years if she didn't tend to eat her feelings, especially the hurt ones. She'd sampled everything generously without really tasting it, and now, as dinnertime approached, she had a craving for tiramisu. Lewis was working late yet again, so she had no reason to cook a real meal. She grabbed her keys and purse, and drove off to buy the ladyfingers she would need to make her fancy dessert instead.

She was nearly to the grocery store when she stopped at a red light behind a white SUV with Washington license plates. In spite of the fact that she'd been thinking about Minnie nearly nonstop since their text exchange the night before, it took her a moment to realize that it was her behind the wheel. The light turned green, but Minnie didn't move. Seconds passed, and finally the car behind Martha honked. Martha could see Minnie's head jerk up, like she'd been startled from looking at her phone. She glanced in the rearview mirror and waved before taking off.

Without any hesitation, Martha followed Minnie eastbound toward the museum district instead of turning left into the parking lot of the store. The ladyfingers could wait.

What were the chances she'd see Minnie just then? Martha hadn't ever run into her anywhere but her house or driveway. She'd never seen her buying groceries or picking up dry cleaning or filling a prescription at the pharmacy, and now she was overcome with curiosity. She wanted to watch Minnie in situ, the way she had back in high school, like she'd suddenly encountered a clouded leopard and would finally get to see what it did when nobody was looking.

One thing Martha saw right away was that Minnie wasn't a very good driver, which surprised her. It made her seem reckless and real, less than perfect. She hugged the right side of the left lane, like she was going to take her half of the road out of the middle. She sped toward a yellow light, then slammed on her brakes just a bit too close to the car in front of her. She turned right on red just as a pedestrian, who had the right of way, was about to step into the crosswalk. Martha felt like she'd been on a roller coaster by the time she eased onto the side street where Minnie was trying to parallel park. This was clearly someone who'd never had children. Ever since their drive home from the hospital after Harry's birth, where every dip, fissure, and pothole felt like a threat to the integrity of their brand-new minivan and every other motorist seemed out to run them and their brand-new baby off the road, Martha had become an exceedingly cautious driver.

She pulled alongside the curb several car lengths behind Minnie and put her van into park, letting the engine idle beneath the over-hanging oak branches. The sun was low behind her, casting its last gleaming light of the day such that Martha could see Minnie using her rearview mirror to apply lipstick. She stepped out of her car and into a ray of light that made her hair look so much like spun gold that Martha actually gasped. She sank low in her seat and watched as Minnie adjusted the complicated belt on her formfitting, off-white dress, which looked somehow both tailored and flowing. To Martha's dismay, she looked nothing like a middle-aged politician. Tucking her clutch under her arm, Minnie looked for traffic from both directions, then strode toward the single-story building across the street.

Martha had never been to this part of town before, even though she'd been adjacent to it forever. It was literally yards away from the edge of West U and a world apart from Martha's. She squinted at the sign in front of the building: MONTOYA FOYE GALLERY. Minnie swung open the door and disappeared inside.

Martha waited, unsure what she should do. Looking around, she saw there were other galleries nearby. A few people wandered in and out of them. Could anyone go in and look around? For minutes, Martha watched the door, debating whether she should go inside. She could just sneak in—she was getting good at that—and check out the art. And maybe speak to Minnie. Martha's feelings were terribly hurt, but she wasn't one for holding grudges. All Minnie had to do was ask her to, and Martha would forgive her. She thought of what her mother had said, that women had to work on female friendships as much as they did their marriages, that she should take some calculated risks, be brave. Maybe if she'd spoken to Minnie right after the choir incident so many years ago, they might've been able to forge the kind of relationship Martha had imagined. They might've gone through high school as best friends. Maybe Martha, though she loved Houston, would've been persuaded to go away to college, or maybe she'd have convinced Minnie to stay there. They could've been roommates, been maids of honor in each other's weddings, gone through infertility together. They'd have ended up neighbors intentionally rather than accidentally. And she'd have gone into the Montoya Foye Gallery with Minnie a few minutes ago instead of sitting outside the building in her minivan, alone.

Maybe the torn photos had been an accident. Somehow. Maybe Minnie was tearing up junk mail or old bank statements and she'd torn them by mistake. Something like that was definitely possible, considering her driving skills. And of course, she wouldn't be able to say anything about it, and that's why she was embarrassed when Martha texted her about coming over for drinks. Martha was suddenly enlivened, galvanized by her magical, what-if thinking. Friends made mistakes, she knew that. She'd made plenty. Now she was prepared to accept Minnie's apology and offer her own, and move on from the incident, happily ever after. She turned off the car and stepped out into the wavy heat that radiated off the pavement, and jog-walked to the gallery's front door.

Inside was quiet. Martha stepped into a large, open room with concrete floors and white walls with small canvases hung at intervals that seemed disproportionately large for the space. The stark atmosphere was uncomfortable, as if she'd wandered into a place of worship whose religion was unfamiliar. There were a few people scattered throughout the room, standing in front of paintings, sipping wine. Politely reverent, Martha tiptoed over to a pedestal and picked up a brochure about the art on exhibit.

> J. C. Martin's work is concerned with artistic identity and utility, investigating what it means to self-identify as a creator in the current age of ever-expanding artistic pluralism. Observations of mass-produced consumer goods, culturally specific aesthetics, social structure, pop culture, and institutionalized education inform the work and raise questions about historical accuracy and social hierarchy. Rather than taking a specific position, this body of work embodies a sense of cultural confusion through humor and visual ingenuity.

Martha read the paragraph three times and still wasn't sure what it meant. She tiptoed farther into the room, peering down a hallway where she thought Minnie must've gone. Not wanting to appear over-eager, she helped herself to a glass of wine and approached the nearest painting, which was titled *First Pancake*. Half the background was the color of pureed asparagus, and the other a Pepto-Bismol pink, blended toward each other in a rough-looking manner. On top were haphazardly placed dabs—smears, really—of other, brighter colors that may or may not have resembled shapes found in the kitchen, where pancakes would likely be made. She leaned in for a better look, trying to connect the image with the title. Perhaps that wasn't the way to consider it, however. She stepped back, tilted her head first one way, then the other. She could appreciate the skill required to paint a canvas so that it looked like a photograph, but it was much harder for her to discern the artistry of work like this, which would've been impressive only if it had been finger-painted by a chimpanzee. She moved to the next, *Roofer Madness*. It featured a similarly confusing combination of colors—browns and grays stained with neon splotches—and an unidentifiable connection to its title. Martha was looking very closely at another piece, *Festive Mouse*, when someone approached her from behind.

"You there! Please don't touch the artwork." The voice was firm, but not unkind.

"Oh!" Martha hopped backward, an apology forming before she could even turn around.

"Martha?" Minnie said.

"Minnie, hi. I, uh"—she pulled the brochure out from underneath her arm and held it aloft—"was just looking at the paintings. But I wasn't touching it. I was counting the eggs, or the babies, or whatever those yellow dots are."

"It's just that the artist is here and he'd be very upset if anyone were to touch his work."

Martha distanced herself from the wall by taking a long step toward Minnie. "I know. I mean, of course I know better than to touch someone's artwork." She was reminded of why she was there and felt a rush of anger. "I know how I'd feel if someone were to ruin something I created."

Martha thought she saw Minnie flinch before she smiled and changed the subject. "Well, it's nice to see you. What brings you to the opening? Are you interested in J. C. Martin's work?"

"Oh, I was just in the area and thought I'd check it out. How about you?" She congratulated herself on coming up with a relevant but neutral reply. This way, Minnie could see her as an equal, someone who visited art galleries. Someone who she could be friends with.

"My boss and I are looking at some pieces to present to a client." Minnie took a step forward and softened her voice. "If you're thinking of adding to your own collection, J. C. is an up-and-coming local artist. I could introduce you to him if you'd like."

Martha didn't know what to make of Minnie's comment. She wanted to believe it was sincere, but did she actually think that Martha was the type of person to have an art collection? Was she being sarcastic? And did she really think that these paintings were worth looking at, much less owning?

Before Martha could think of what to say, the door opened and an elegant-looking man in a seersucker suit floated in on a waft of hot, dank air. Martha recognized him from the photo she'd doctored. He picked up a brochure and swished it back and forth in front of his face as he looked around the room. His posture was impossibly correct. "There you are," he called out to Minnie in a thick British accent. The slight graying at his temples suggested he was older, but with his smooth forehead, trim build, and well-tailored suit, it was impossible to tell his age. And although Martha never would've thought to pair a magenta tie and socks with seersucker, he could've stepped right off a New York runway. He leaned down and kissed Minnie on both cheeks. "I'll never get used to this god-awful heat, darling. I don't know how you manage it. You look positively gelid in that glorious dress—and I mean that in the best possible way." Despite his complaint, there wasn't even a hint of perspiration at his hairline. His hair, too, remained perfectly in place even as he fanned the air in front of him.

"Thank you," she said in a shy voice that Martha didn't recognize. "Lawrence, this is my neighbor, Martha Hale. She came by to see J. C.'s work."

Martha prickled at being called "neighbor" instead of "friend," but she decided to let it go. This was a professional setting after all; perhaps Minnie didn't think having a friend at work was appropriate.

Martha offered her hand, which Lawrence—reluctantly, it seemed—shook with his fingertips, as if he didn't want his hand to fully meet hers. His eyes traveled from her face to her hair, then down and up the length of her. Martha felt herself heating up underneath his gaze. "That is certainly an unusual ensemble," he said, leaning back on his heels.

That morning, she'd put on a sleeveless maternity dress with a teddy bear print. Keeping it was a guilty pleasure; it was a *maternity* dress, after all, and not at all flattering, but it was so comfortable she could forget that she was wearing it, which she had. The light fabric and loose fit made the summer heat and her warm kitchen more bearable. Also, it was an outfit that didn't admonish her: nothing pinched or bound her at the waist. She could sample all the treats she baked and if her stomach bloated, there was plenty of room to accommodate the swell. Now she looked down at her front, seeing herself through Lawrence's eyes. The bits of dough sticking to her terrible dress, the butter and chocolate stains, the smears of flour. She looked like an even less artful version of J. C.'s *Festive Mouse*. To make things worse, she was wearing her gardening clogs, which had been the nearest pair of shoes she'd stepped into when she'd decided to make a quick run to the grocery store. Of course Lawrence was looking at her like she didn't belong—she didn't.

Martha looked up at Minnie, silently pleading with her to say something kind, to save her from Lawrence's awful grimace of a smile. But Minnie only stared back at her. The horrified expression on her face suggested that Minnie was either embarrassed by Martha or for her. Or maybe both.

Then Lawrence tapped the brochure against his palm and said to Minnie, "We need to go, darling. J. C.'s time is valuable and I want to have a look at those pieces in the back." He turned to Martha and dipped his head with old-fashioned formality. "Lovely to meet you. Do have a nice evening. Come on now, Minnie."

And Minnie, without so much as a smile or a nod, turned her back to Martha and followed Lawrence out of the room.

Martha watched them go, too mortified to move. When they were out of sight, she looked around to see if there'd been any other witnesses to her humiliation. Thankfully, there weren't. The few people that had been there were either in another room or gone. Martha put down her wine and walked as fast as she could to her car. She didn't want to give anyone the satisfaction of watching or hearing her cry.

As she sobbed into a wad of extra fast-food napkins she found in her glove compartment, she admonished herself for not taking better care with her appearance. Why didn't she take after her mother in that regard? Evelyn had probably donated all her maternity clothes the day after she brought Bessie home from the hospital, and she wouldn't be caught dead wearing gardening clogs and a stained shift into an art gallery, even an art gallery filled with atrocious finger paintings. Martha vowed to throw her dress into the trash the instant she got home.

But why hadn't Minnie stood up for her? Why couldn't she have told Lawrence to hush, to keep his opinions to himself? That's what women were supposed to do for each other. Martha had hoped that Minnie might be different from so many of the other women in West U, who couldn't seem to see past Martha's weight or her house or her lack of panache or whatever it was that kept her always outside the community, like a starving child with her nose pressed against the glass of a bakery window.

She wiped her eyes and blew her nose, then she rolled down her window and tossed the used napkins onto the street. "Take that," she said. All the way home, she thought of insults and retorts she might've issued at Lawrence and Minnie even though the opportunity to deliver them had long passed. But imagining a different outcome did nothing to alleviate her affront at being snubbed.

Upon entering the house, she yanked off her shift and jammed it into the trash can. Since she hadn't gone to the grocery store as planned, there would be no tiramisu for dinner. Standing alone in her ugly old underwear in the silent kitchen, she stuffed herself full of the fudge she'd made, wondering how she was going to get even.

Seventeen

The next time Martha went into Minnie's house, she almost didn't care if she'd be caught. She'd lain awake most of the night, unable to reconcile Minnie's behavior at the gallery. Over and over she replayed the scenario, alternating between feeling mortified and furious. Minnie could've sent her a text, offering an explanation if not an apology, but she hadn't. She gave herself a headache juxtaposing the memories of the ripped prints and Minnie's apparently false praise. *Oh, I love the photos you took of Bonnie and me,* Martha thought, mocking Minnie's voice. *You're so talented, so artistic. What a good eye you have.*

The better to see through you with, Martha retorted to herself.

She was tired of contemplating the vast and myriad ways that Minnie was superior to Martha, tired of wondering why she wasn't good enough for her. So she decided to put herself literally in Minnie's place. She didn't know what she planned to do, exactly, just that Minnie deserved to have her mind messed with a little bit.

Bonnie trilled—happily, it seemed—when Martha entered later that morning after Lewis and the Wrights had all left for their various jobs, but Martha's response to the bird was perfunctory. She wasn't in a playful mood, and besides, what had being friendly with Bonnie gotten her so far? The idea occurred to her that maybe the reason Minnie had torn up the photos wasn't because they weren't good enough, but because Minnie was jealous of how "into Martha" Bonnie had been. At the time, Martha had been proud of it, but now it made sense. Minnie wanted to be the primary object of everyone's affection. Maybe that's why she'd played so hard to get on the porch that night weeks ago, when John had been trying to coax her out of her funk, plainly trying to sweep her off her feet by offering to take her away for a weekend. He'd probably been working a lot, maybe not giving her the attention she wanted. What did she expect? He was a busy man, a doctor. What had he said to her when she refused to soften toward him? *Don't forget how lovely you are.* How could she continue to pout with her husband showering her with gifts and compliments? And hadn't Martha showered her with the same? There was no point in trying to guess what made Minnie treat her—or anyone else—the way she did; that's why Martha decided to investigate.

She started in the kitchen. What was inside Minnie's refrigerator? What did thin, beautiful people keep in their cupboards? What did they snack on, if they snacked at all? Martha opened the door to the enormous walk-in pantry and burst out laughing. Of course, she wasn't surprised to see that it was perfectly organized, like the "after" picture of a professional organizing project. It's just that she'd never actually seen such an elaborately coordinated and cataloged storage room up close. The immaculate rows of clear containers lining the shelves had printed labels for each type of pasta, sugar, flour, and grain imaginable. The spices, all in matching jars, were alphabetized. There was an entire section dedicated to a variety of protein powders, bars, and supplements. Baskets along the floor held paper towels, bottled waters, and sugar-free sparkling sodas.

Where were the boxes of cereal? The cartons of mac and cheese and pancake mixes? The bags of cookies and pretzels and tortilla chips? Martha's pantry was clean and tidy, but nothing like this. Also, it was less than half the size of Minnie's and probably contained twice as many calories—and not the right kind, apparently.

The Wrights' refrigerator was just as irritatingly fabulous, stocked with healthful-looking items: fresh—probably organic—fruits and vegetables, cartons of egg whites, hummus, a variety of nut butters, a quart of pea milk—whatever god-awful nonsense that was—and a ceramic bowl of brown eggs that had probably come from hens that roamed free in the Texas Hill Country and had been gathered at dawn by a milkmaid who only spoke in whispers. Martha helped herself to one of the little containers of Icelandic yogurt, the same kind that had been thrown into the garbage can on top of the torn photos of Bonnie. She peeled back the lid and licked it. It was absolutely delicious, thick and creamy. Nothing like the flavored store-brand yogurts she was used to eating. Not bothering with a spoon, she slurped at it like melted ice cream, then used her fingers to scoop out what she couldn't reach with her tongue. She tossed the container in the trash. She hoped Minnie would see it and find it perplexing. Even concerning. Or maybe not; Martha didn't know which of them ate what for breakfast. But she liked the idea of an extra empty yogurt container being out of the ordinary, of Minnie standing there staring into the garbage can trying to recall having eaten it, perhaps worrying that her calorie count had accidentally been thrown off. Martha licked her fingers clean and wiped them thoroughly on the tea towel that hung on the oven door, then carefully adjusted the fabric so that nobody would realize that it was now crawling with her proletarian germs.

She took her time strolling through the foyer, picking up and looking closely at the items and their arrangements. They were actually quite ugly, some of them. Especially that hideous moss ball. It didn't even look like real moss. Above that was a giant abstract painting, at least four feet by four feet, of what looked like olive-colored waves crashing into hot-pink clouds. It had struck Martha as being merely pretty the few times she'd seen it, but now that she could really peer at the layers of paint and marvel at the ambiguous, organic-looking shapes that seemed to float and sink amid the brushstrokes, she decided it was stupid. Hot-pink clouds! She reached up and tilted the heavy painting in its silver frame off level by about three quarters of an inch, then she sauntered up the stairs.

She'd seen Minnie's bedroom only from outside, through the window, but she'd assumed that it looked as stylish as the rest of the house, and she'd been right. The walls and ceiling—Martha had never thought to paint a ceiling anything other than white—were a calm sky blue. Like Martha, Minnie—or maybe it was John, who knew—made her bed in the morning. But unlike Martha's, Minnie's bed looked like it belonged in a château somewhere in the French Alps. *Sumptuous* was the word that popped into her mind as she ran her hand along the bedding. She'd never seen a California king but decided this must be one; the padded headboard stretched almost across the entire wall. Underneath was an Oriental rug, and on either side were matching lamps on charmingly mismatched nightstands. Martha assumed John's was the sturdy wood one and Minnie's was the gilded one with curves. That meant her side was the one closest to the window. Martha noted, too, that their bed faced east, toward the Hales' house, and the Hales' bed faced west. So, on any given night, Martha and Minnie fell asleep facing each other. She made a mental note to flip the bird at Minnie when she went to bed that night.

There were two closets, of course. The first she looked into was John's, which looked like it could've been a fancy man's boutique. Except for the stock of scrubs and starched lab coats embroidered with his name, it was otherwise fairly boring. All the many suits and other clothing probably looked really good on him, but hanging here, they revealed little about their owner except that he was precise, which was a reasonable quality for a plastic surgeon.

Martha opened Minnie's walk-in closet, fully expecting it to be as organized and uncluttered as John's and the rest of the house, with her shoes in clear boxes and labels on all the shelves. But it wasn't. It was enormous, of course, with plenty of built-in shelves and drawers and hanging space to accommodate a fashion maven's wardrobe. Yet somehow, even though it wasn't full to bursting, it looked like there wasn't enough room for everything. Evening dresses were mixed in with T-shirts, shoes were scattered around like they'd been kicked into a general direction and left there, handbags and scarves lay in jumbled piles. All over the floor, there were empty shoeboxes, wads of plastic dry cleaner bags, discarded tissues, torn-off store tags. Martha ignored a fleeting instinct to find a bag and fill it with the trash, to pair the shoes, to rearrange Minnie's clothing into categories for easier access. Why would her closet—and apparently only her closet—be such a disgrace? Martha, who owned almost nothing nice, kept even her shabby clothes clean and pressed, all hung facing the same direction and in rainbow color order. Minnie hadn't even bothered to swap out the metal hangers for the velvet ones that were stashed on one end of her hanging rod. Didn't she know that sweaters hung on pants hangers would lose their shape?

It occurred to her that someone's personal closet was like the home equivalent of her mind: mostly hidden, private, containing things that were deeply personal. Minnie worked so hard making everything look perfect on the outside, but here, deep inside the house, was a total mess. Martha snickered, enjoying a thrill of schadenfreude. At least Martha's closet—and her head—was put right. She almost pitied Minnie. But only a very tiny bit, and only for a moment. If Minnie didn't want Martha's friendship or photographs, which she very clearly did not, then she certainly didn't deserve her concern. Not anymore.

And since Minnie didn't seem to care about her own clothing, despite her chic appearance, why should Martha? She kicked a sequined stiletto and watched it crash into a designer duffel bag in the corner. Why on earth would anyone wear such uncomfortable footwear? Martha had never even tried on a pair of stilettos as high as those.

"Why the hell not?" she said aloud. She retrieved the shoe, sat down in the middle of the closet, and put it on. Then she searched around for its mate and put it on, too. They hurt her feet even before she stood, reminding her of Cinderella's ugly stepsisters trying to cram their horse hooves into the delicate glass slipper. Martha checked the size on one of them: eight and a half, same as what Martha wore, even though Minnie was several inches taller. For some reason that made her feel a little better. She clawed her way to a standing position, using whatever was nearby for assistance. She pulled several dresses off their hangers trying to use them for leverage, and left them there on the closet floor in heaps. It didn't seem to make the mess look any worse than it already did.

In the full-length mirror, her reflection wobbled back at her as she angled herself this way and that. Despite her humiliation at the gallery yesterday, she hadn't felt the need to dress up for a break-in. But the combination of sequins with bulky overalls and her husband's ancient college T-shirt would not do. Heels like that required something equally slinky. She kicked them back off in opposite directions, and decided to look through Minnie's clothes.

Martha didn't recognize the names on any of the labels except for the one pair of vintage Levi's. Come to think of it, they'd probably become vintage while being in Minnie's possession; if Martha's memory served, Minnie was wearing jeans just like this the first day she'd strutted into Stonewall Jackson High. She was as thin now as she'd been back then, so maybe she'd just kept them all these years. Martha laughed, thinking of all the delicious foods Minnie had probably missed out on all those years, just so she could fit into a pair of old jeans.

They seemed to be the only thing that wasn't new. A lot of the stuff hanging up—and even some of what was on the floor—looked barely worn. It was all beautiful; even the T-shirts were made of thicker, nicer cotton than the ones Martha owned. There were many, many luxurious silk tops, kimonos, and caftans. Martha searched for the Minniest of all the caftans, and she found it half off its hanger, hiding between an overcoat and a pair of suede jeans. Martha held it out, sliding the fabric between her fingers. It was so fine that she could feel the roughness of her own fingerprints against it. The background was a pale blush pink with parakeets sitting on disembodied branches, some featuring pale-violet flowers. The parakeets didn't match Bonnie's coloring; they were mostly black and white with aqua breasts. The print must've been hand-painted because it seemed no two of the birds or branches were just alike. Martha couldn't believe that Minnie wasn't wearing this exquisite item right then, no matter where she was or what she was doing. How could she not want to wear it all the time, day and night? Yet impossibly, it seemed to Martha, she hadn't worn it at all—the tag was still attached. Wait, how could it have only cost $17.95? And from Lolli's? According to her mother, Lolli's probably didn't even sell a pair of underwear for that little. She squinted again at the tag and gasped. She'd misread the tag; the price of the caftan was actually $1,795. What must it be like to wear clothes that cost the equivalent of a week at sleepaway camp?

Martha unhooked her overalls and let them drop onto the floor, kicking them into a nearby pile. She rather enjoyed seeing them there among Minnie's unkempt treasures. She took off her T-shirt and her old, ugly bra, then she pulled on the caftan, feeling it slide down her skin like cool water. Her nipples grew taut at the sensation. She took out the barrette she often wore at her left temple, twisted her coarse, frizzy hair into a loose bun, and used the barrette to secure it underneath into the closest approximation of Minnie's hairstyle she could.

She twirled first one direction, then the other, letting the silk catch the air and billow out before settling back down against her like a second skin. In the mirror, she looked magnificent. *Soignée*, as her mother sometimes said, though Evelyn pronounced it *swan-YAY* in her heavy Texan accent. She wished her mother could see her now. The hand-painted birds hid all of Martha's lumps and imperfections, and made her suddenly wish that she, too, could afford to dress like this and had a house and a life that wouldn't make swishing around in silk caf-tans like a goddess in the middle of the day seem ridiculous. Maybe if she looked and dressed more like Minnie or the women she was always photographed standing next to in *SpaceTown Magazine*, she, too, could have exciting sex, a glamorous job, and resplendent surroundings. People would want to be near her, sharing her rarefied air. Birds of a feather, flocking together.

"Now skin care," she told her reflection, and wandered barefoot into the en suite. The bathroom was tidy; towels and spare sheets all folded the same way in neat stacks in the cabinet, apothecary jars were filled to the top with cotton balls and Q-tips, a mirrored tray corralled a vast medley of candles. It was probably John who liked things that way; at least Minnie cared enough about him to keep a decent home beyond her closet.

Since the countertops were clear of personal items, Martha had to look into the drawers to see which side belonged to whom. Minnie's was a trove of expensive-looking creams and lotions, makeup and perfumes. Martha pulled out the velvet-covered stool in front of the vanity mirror and sat down. Which products should she put on and in what order? Oh, what the hell, she thought, it probably didn't even matter. She picked up a shiny tube of retinol serum, which she knew from reading women's magazines was expensive and also youth-inducing, and rubbed a generous amount onto her face and neck, careful not to get any on the silk. Then she applied a very liberal coat of moisturizing cream that was so fancy it was called crème. "Crème de Lumière," she said aloud in her mother's voice as she dug another fingerful out of the little pot. "Well, la-di-da."

Minnie didn't seem to wear much makeup, at least not day-to-day, which Martha had assumed was just her natural glow, the kind that went with messy hair and flowy kimonos. But looking into her makeup drawer, it appeared that Minnie's effortless-looking beauty was in fact an effect of some artistic mastery on her part, that her true face was actually buried under layers of foundation and concealer and bronzer, which possibly covered up the same dark circles, fine lines, and occasional acne that Martha had. Whatever her plastic surgeon husband couldn't fix with Botox and fillers. This discovery filled Martha with no small amount of glee.

She shuffled through another of Minnie's drawers, examining her hair balms and sunscreens and other miscellany. The bottom drawer was where she kept her medicines and first-aid supplies. There were large bottles of acetaminophen and ibuprofen, bandages of various sizes, eye drops, rolls of gauze, tweezers, antibiotic ointment, arnica gel. She made a note to buy some arnica next time she was at the store; it had actually helped her knees the time Minnie had shared some with her, and Harry was always coming home with bruises on his shins. He'd probably be covered with them when he came home from camp next week. There were three packs of birth control pills, too, which surprised Martha. Maybe they'd decided to stop trying to conceive after all. There were a few prescription bottles with drug names she didn't recognize and one she did for the same kind of sleeping pills Martha had taken for a while after she and Lewis decided to stop trying for another baby and she went through a period of sleeplessness and depression.

She went over to the window and looked out, first at the beautiful backyard that looked like a destination, then at her own little office window above the garage. It seemed so sad and small—not unlike her life, she guessed. She was relieved that she couldn't actually see through the panes into her office. Perhaps because of the way the light was reflecting off it, it just looked dark inside. She wouldn't want Minnie—or anyone—to know how often she peered out at the same view from the other side. Then she noticed Frank Devlin outside in his underwear, shooting the tennis ball gun in various directions for his dog to chase. Martha had never actually been able to see over the fence in the Devlins' yard before now, and was—perhaps for the only time since Minnie's house was built—grateful to have such a limited view from her own home. Mostly the dog just sat there looking at Frank and his flaccid body and what hair was left on his head going in every direction at once, seemingly apathetic about the balls that were whizzing past it. No wonder so many of them banged into the fence. She had half a mind to open the window and yell at Frank to quit trying to get his dog to chase ballistic-speed projectiles and also to put on a damn shirt. But then she realized something: she couldn't hear the balls. The same fine construction that kept Minnie's house cooler than Martha's also kept out the vexing neighborhood noises. She wondered if the soundproofing worked the other way, too. Hiding behind the curtain, she shouted, "Hey, Frank, you old fart!" He didn't seem to have heard her, so she tried again, loud enough to startle herself. He was unmoved. She could probably scream bloody murder and nobody would even know.

She turned back to Minnie's bed. Short-sheeting it would be obvious. What could she put under the covers? Nothing traumatizing like the severed head of a thoroughbred horse, of course. But something subtle and disturbing. She smiled. How about herself? She was already there anyway, like Goldilocks, trying out all the bears' things, wearing Minnie's clothing, her stomach full of their food. Besides, wouldn't it be nice to know what it felt like to sleep in this glorious bed, her feet pointing east instead of west? She noted the arrangement of the throw pillows before she moved them to the floor, then peeled back the duvet and slipped in between the sheets that were nearly as soft as the caftan. Snuggling in, she plumped Minnie's pillow, which released a faint puff of scent—shampoo or laundry detergent or perfume, she didn't know, but she liked it. She scrubbed her head back and forth against it, as much to pick up Minnie's odor as to deposit some of her own. That she hadn't showered made her snicker.

She looked at her phone to check the time. It wasn't even noon. She had plenty of time before anyone came home. She didn't really intend to fall asleep, not deeply anyway, but still, she set an alarm for three o'clock just in case.

Eighteen

Martha was yanked from the depths of sleep by the erratic screech of her phone alarm. She reached for the device, struggling to orient herself to the correct time and space, and frantically stabbed at it to make the noise stop. It didn't stop because it wasn't her alarm making the racket; it was Bonnie, though she'd never heard the bird make such excruciating, unpleasant noise. Had she hurt herself somehow? Was she in pain? Martha was about to run down to see what was the matter when she heard a man's fearsome, growling voice.

"Goddamn you, you stupid fucking bird. I've had enough of your squawking." It was John. Oh god, it was John. Martha looked at her phone to see the time. It was 4:02 p.m. How the hell did that happen? Why didn't her alarm go off? It didn't matter, she'd worry about that later—after she figured out how to get out of his bed and his house before he found her.

Bonnie screeched again, louder. Martha flung back the sheets and dove underneath the bed. But just as she shimmied to the centermost bit of floor, she realized that she couldn't leave the covers undone. If John came into the room, he'd instantly know something was amiss. And given the mood he sounded to be in, she didn't imagine he'd be very happy to discover that Goldilocks had been sleeping in his bed.

"I said enough!"

Martha crawled out and, quick as she could, pulled the sheets up tight, smoothed the duvet, stacked the sleeping pillows, and returned the decorative ones to their rightful place. The whole time, Bonnie continued to squawk.

Martha began to tremble as she stared at the Wrights' bed. Had she remembered the pillow arrangement correctly? Did the dark-blue ones go in front of the ivory, or the other way around? She heard a metallic clanging from downstairs that sounded like it might've been Bonnie's cage rattling, because the bird let out an even wilder cry. The sounds quieted, then stopped. Surely, John wouldn't hurt the bird, would he?

Martha tiptoe-ran to Minnie's closet to retrieve her T-shirt and bra and overalls. Should she stay in here until she could leave? Could she crouch in a corner and hope for the best? No, because she'd have to close the door the way she'd found it, and maybe she wouldn't be able to hear when it was safe to make a run for it. Minnie would be home before six, and then what? As soon as she went into her closet, she'd see Martha for sure. The piles of clothes weren't that big. No, beneath the bed was the safest place to hide. Clutching her clothes, she dove back under it. She tried to make herself as small as she could, scooting under the very center of the mattress and as close as possible to the wall.

The adrenaline pumping through her body made her tremble, but she forced herself to be still. She didn't know if her movements could be heard from downstairs. What if he'd already heard creaks from up above? Being caught would be bad enough, but what if he had a gun? In Texas, homeowners could shoot intruders with impunity. No, she thought. He'd never do anything like that. Would he? Oh god, what should she do?

Something moved in her peripheral vision and she jerked her head toward it. There, a mere foot away from her face, less even, was a huge brown cockroach, the kind that sought refuge inside Houston homes usually after a downpour, the kind that feasted on every kind of household item—crumbs, leather, the starch in book bindings, potted plants, dirty clothing. Martha clamped her hand over her mouth to keep from screaming, and felt her panic rise even further. She hated cockroaches. *Hated* them. Their flat, glossy bodies, their droppings, their awful, searching antennae. Lewis laughed at her whenever she leaped out of the way of a roach and demanded that he kill it. Now this one seemed to be staring at her, its antennae stretched out toward her, waving. She couldn't stay under the bed with it. She could not. Slowly, it moved toward her, then stopped. What was it doing? Why wasn't it running away like a normal cockroach? What if it crawled on her? Her flesh broke out in goose bumps at the thought. But she couldn't think about it because now her mind was racing against the tap, tap of John's dress shoes climbing up the hardwood stairs.

The roach continued its march. Martha tucked her arms underneath her and blew at the insect to keep it from touching her. The taps on the hardwood grew louder as the roach moved, and it was as if the roach was wearing the shoes, not John. They both were getting closer to her. She closed her eyes, not able to bear the proximity, not wanting to see whatever was going to happen next. She could feel her blood pressure in her ears. As her heart rate increased, time seemed to slow down, to tilt on a strange axis. She could no longer feel her body touching the rug beneath the bed, but she sensed the air around her moving as though the room itself was breathing. How could she have been so cavalier, so careless?

He walked into the bedroom. Martha held her breath, waiting for her discovery. "Filthy creature," John said, and stomped his foot on the floor. Martha's eyes flew open, and she could see the cockroach, now squashed and oozing, just past the edge of the rug. He stepped out of his shoes, picked them up, and walked away. A moment later he returned and bent down to clean up the mess with some tissues. What if he looked under the bed for more bugs?

Miraculously, he walked away again. She heard the sound of the toilet flush, and then the sound of a door slamming. "How hard is it to close a fucking door?" Martha cringed. She'd left Minnie's closet door open in her haste. He opened his own closet and turned on the light. Martha could smell her own sweat, and worried that he might, too. What was that fairy tale? "Fee, fie, foe, fum, I smell the blood of an Englishman." Martha, you idiot, she thought. Concentrate. She watched his now-bare feet walking back toward the bed. What if he took a nap? What day was it again? Friday. Shit. She didn't know what the Wrights did after John swam in their pool on those nights, just that they didn't usually leave. How was she ever going to get out of there? A terror descended upon her like she'd never experienced before. She bit her lip to keep herself still.

His phone rang. Wait—where was *her* phone? Was it in her bundle of clothes? Had she dropped it in Minnie's closet? Or, more likely, still on Minnie's bedside table? She felt her face go clammy, a metallic taste underneath her tongue. She worried she might lose control of her bowels.

"Dr. Wright here." Instantly, his voice changed from seething to calm and caramel-smooth. A doctor voice. "Yes . . . don't apologize . . . of course you're worried, but I'm one hundred percent sure you don't have cellulitis. Flushing of the skin on the lower half of the breast is completely normal . . . well, the sensitivity is the nerves waking back up, which is a good thing." From her hiding spot, Martha could see him slowly pacing around the bedroom. She kept wondering when he was going to notice her phone on Minnie's nightstand. "Listen, your breasts look perfect, if I do say so myself. If there'd been any sign of necrosis we'd have seen it by now. You're a beautiful woman and you're going to have beautiful breasts to go with the rest of you. All right . . . okay, we'll see you in a few weeks. Take care."

When he hung up, he muttered, "Why does every fucking tits-for-brains with a computer think she's smarter than an MD?" He paused, then spoke in a dark, slow, low voice as though directly to Martha: "Cunt."

Martha felt a chill go through her body. Had he really called one of his patients that terrible name? She watched his feet, trying to figure out what he was going to do. What she was going to do. What if she had to stay under the bed all night? She thought of Lewis, how she could close her eyes and see his every movement just from the sounds he made. She was gripped by the idea that she might not make it home, not before he got there, anyway. Lewis would be puzzled at first, it being so unlike her not to be home when he arrived, unless she'd told him ahead of time that she'd be gone. He would call her, certainly. And if her phone rang? Oh god, please don't let the phone ring. For once, she was relieved that she hardly had any friends, because she got so few calls and texts.

John went back into his closet and when he emerged, his feet were shod in sneakers. She heard a slap against his light switch and saw his closet light go out just before he closed the door. Then he strode out of the bedroom and closed that door, too, trapping her inside with only her fear and intuition to guide her.

She waited, unmoving so that she might be able to hear what John was doing. The air conditioner clicked on, adding a layer of faint white noise that made it even harder. Very slowly, in case he was downstairs and could hear her moving, she inched toward the edge of the bed and snatched her phone off the table and immediately switched it to silent mode. She checked the alarm: she'd set it for 3:00 a.m., not p.m. What if she'd just slept on and on, and been awakened by one of them shaking her shoulder? Thank goodness Bonnie had made such a racket; at least she had a little warning.

How long should she wait? It was now 4:36 p.m. Minnie would be coming home. Lewis would be coming home. Should she text him and say she was out? But her car was in the driveway. Maybe she could say that her mother had picked her up for a shopping trip? He'd think it was highly unusual, but he probably wouldn't disbelieve her. She should turn off her phone so he couldn't track her location. But then if she couldn't escape, what would he think? Oh god, what if she really couldn't?

Then she could hear music, loud and percussive. Obnoxious. She hardly had to strain to listen to recognize it: "Enter Sandman" by Metallica. Martha had always hated heavy metal, but her older step-brother, Thomas, used to love it, and when they all lived together at home, she had to endure hours of it seeping out from underneath his door. When Metallica came out, Thomas had just turned sixteen and seemed to be full of hormones and venom, and he played it over and over until even eleven-year-old Martha and nine-year-old Bessie knew all the lyrics by heart. The air conditioner turned off, and she could tell the music was coming from down the hall, probably from John's home gym. Of course. Why else would he have put on his tennis shoes? He was working out.

This was her chance, maybe her only one. There was no time for her to change out of Minnie's caftan; she'd have to deal with that later. Clutching her clothes, she went to the bedroom door and pressed her ear against it. John evidently liked the doors kept closed; with any luck, the gym door would be, too. She took a breath, cracked the door, and peeked out. The music was quite loud; the line about the beast under the bed floated down the hall, eerily coincidental. This is it, she told herself. Go.

Closing the door behind her, she ran-walked out into the hall and down the stairs, glancing over her shoulder to make sure John hadn't seen her. As soon as she got downstairs, she sprinted through the foyer. She slowed enough to check on Bonnie, who appeared unhurt and set-tled. From the back porch, she grabbed her clogs—thank god he hadn't seen them—and ran the now-familiar path between the Wrights' back door and her own, barely breathing, the caftan billowing behind her.

~

Inside her own closet, she yanked off Minnie's dress with trembling hands, berating herself for being so reckless, so stupid. She went into the bathroom and turned the shower on, letting the water run as hot as their old water heater would allow. Her skin felt filthy, her whole body, her mind—filthy. The memory of the cockroach and Minnie's closet and the rug under the bed made her itch. The memory of John's footsteps on the hardwood, the expletive he'd muttered low and sharp, the fear of him catching her, sent a cold chill through her. She stepped into the shower and let the water pound against her face until it hurt. Irrationally, she decided if anyone were to show up at her door, John or another neighbor, she'd be able to deny her actions. *I've been in the shower. My hair is wet, you see?* But what about video cameras? She still didn't know who in her immediate area kept surveillance systems or what they'd be able to capture. Stupid, stupid, stupid. She stayed in the shower until the water ran cold, then stayed some more, only relenting after she started to shiver.

She put on her pajamas and curled up on Harry's bed, hugging his pillow to her chest and staring out his window at the Wrights' fence. She wasn't tired; her mind was racing, racing with regrets and what-ifs and what-nows. She should get up and make dinner for Lewis, who'd be home any moment. He'd eaten takeout the past few nights at the office, but she couldn't bear the thought of cooking; she didn't think she'd be able to concentrate enough to make anything edible. Still lying down, she called the Chinese restaurant they liked and placed a delivery order.

"Marty, why are you in here? Are you sick?"

She pushed herself up, ran her fingers through her tangled hair, cleared her throat. "I'm a little tired. I miss Harry. How are you?"

"Busy. I've got a lot to do tonight. Harry'll be home soon, don't worry."

"I know. I'll be okay."

"What's for dinner? I didn't see anything in the kitchen."

"I ordered Chinese."

"Ugh. I've had Chinese the past two nights."

"I guess I'm not feeling all that well."

At almost the same time, Lewis said, "I suppose one more night of lo mein won't kill me."

He bent down and kissed her dryly on her cheek. She climbed off Harry's bed and straightened the pillows. It occurred to her that this was the second time in one day she'd been lying in someone else's bed.

Lewis changed his clothes and turned on the news. Martha poured herself a large glass of wine and sat down next to him. He peered over the top of his glasses at her.

"I thought you weren't feeling well."

"I thought this'll help me sleep."

They ate their dinner in front of the TV, then Lewis announced that he was going to work on his report. Martha put away the leftovers and wiped down the table so he could spread out his computer and papers.

"I think I'll go work a little, too," she told him, pouring herself another glass.

"Have a good time," he said without looking up. She always knew he was distracted when he said that. She could say she was going to the grocery store or the hair salon or the gynecologist, and he'd tell her to have a good time. She didn't bother responding.

The wine did help calm her down. The sense of impending doom receded, and even though the events of the afternoon were far from forgotten, Martha's mind seemed not to be spinning quite as fast. She turned on her computer, intending to process some of the images she'd fallen behind on, hoping the work would distract her even more.

She was in the process of subtly narrowing a bride's waistline when she heard a door slam. She went to the window and looked down into the Wrights' yard.

Minnie was standing near the edge of the pool with her arms crossed, staring hard into the turquoise water. She must've just come from work; she was barefoot under a gorgeous sleeveless pantsuit. It looked like she was shaking, but Martha couldn't be sure. Minnie looked like an empty vessel or a blank canvas reflecting the shimmer of light from the pool. A moment later, John came outside, carrying a martini glass.

He approached her, tacking this way and that. She twisted away from him. Minnie said something that Martha couldn't hear, but it was very clear when John said, slurring, "Don't you dare call me a drunk." Minnie spun around to face him, took the martini glass out of his hand, and tossed the contents at him. John's arms flew up, startled, as liquid splashed his neck, face, chest. Two olives landed on the concrete by his feet. Time seemed to stop as they stood there, both of them looking stunned at what Minnie had done. Martha, too, was shocked into stillness.

Then John said, "You bitch!" as he lunged toward Minnie.

"No!" Martha said.

Still holding the glass, Minnie sidestepped him and ran inside the house. Instead of following her, John turned toward the Hales' garage and looked up at the window out of which Martha was watching. She gasped and dropped into a crouch, her heart ramming against her rib cage.

She waited on her hands and knees for minutes, unmoving except to breathe, her back rigid, joints beginning to ache. She thought she heard a door close, but heard nothing else from the Wrights' yard. There was a rush of wind, the sound of a car going down the street, and then another. The unique bark of a dog: woof-yap-yap-yap. Beignet, probably out for his evening pee. She crawled away from the window and stood, then peered out from the very edge of the frame. There was nothing by the Wrights' pool but a wet spot and two olives. Their bedroom was dark, and of course she couldn't hear anything. Unlike her own, their house was airtight.

She went back into her house and found Lewis on the couch, hunched over his computer. "I think something's going on next door."

Without looking up, he said, "What?"

Martha sat down next to him. "I saw Minnie and her husband out there. It looked like they were arguing."

"Okay?"

"I think he was drunk."

Lewis leaned back and removed his glasses. He pinched the bridge of his nose and sighed. "People get drunk, Marty. It happens." He looked at her with one eyebrow hitched up. "Even to you. Remember the gala? It's not a crime."

"Jeez, Lewis. Why'd you have to bring that up?"

"I'm just saying it's not a big deal. Anyway, why are you spying on them?"

"I wasn't spying. I overheard them and looked out the window, okay? I got concerned. I think maybe we should call the police."

"That's ridiculous. It's none of our business. Besides, you'd have to admit you were spying."

"I wasn't *spying*, Lewis."

He sighed again. "So what if the neighbors are having a spat? It's their business."

"But what if it's more than a spat?"

"I'm sure it's not. Look, Marty. I can't worry about the neighbors right now. I've got work to do tonight and I'm tired."

"Fine," she said. She stood, indignant, but didn't know what to do. "I won't interrupt you anymore." It was only a little after nine o'clock. Should she go to bed? Go for a walk? Pour another glass of wine? Lewis had already returned his attention to his report. "Fine," she said again.

She went back upstairs to her office, pulled not to her computer but to the window. John was back outside, sitting on the edge of the pool, his bare legs dangling in the water. He held a handle of Tito's vodka in his lap and appeared to be smiling, like he didn't have a care in the world. She envied him for that. She picked up her glass of wine and finished it. He did look quite drunk, though.

Where was Minnie now? What was she doing, thinking? A month ago, Martha couldn't have imagined Minnie and John fighting. But now she was starting to question her judgment of him. She was still angry with Minnie, but witnessing her interaction with John inspired a sense of commiseration. At the moment at least, they were both alone. Isolated inside their marriages, their homes. She looked again at John, who was drinking straight from the bottle, swaying with his head tipped backward.

This was exactly why women needed each other, Martha thought. Even if they didn't get along.

Nineteen

The next morning, Saturday, Lewis banged his hand on the kitchen table so hard that his coffee sloshed over the rim of his mug. "Damn it!" he said, and snatched up his laptop to keep it from getting wet.

"For crying out loud, Lewis." Martha met him at the table with a dishrag.

"I'm trying to get something off the company's intranet for this report and the stupid Wi-Fi connection keeps going out. It was doing it last night, too. It's driving me crazy."

Martha cleaned up the mess, then refilled his mug. "Yeah, it's definitely gotten slower lately. It takes a long time for me to upload my processed files. Even Harry was complaining about it before he left for camp, saying he was always getting kicked out of his video games."

"If he was home, I'd just assume it was that—that he was using all the bandwidth. But he's not and it's still bad. The quarterly review is Monday and I have to finish this presentation and get it to the team by tomorrow so we can go over it. I really don't want to have to go back to the office." He dragged his palm over his face and sighed. "I'm going to reboot the modem and see if it helps."

Martha finished cleaning up the breakfast dishes, moving slowly. She was exhausted again. Still. She'd woken up many times throughout the night, her thoughts and emotions constantly returning to the terrifying memory of being trapped under Minnie's bed, fearing the worst. Had John really called someone a cunt, or had she only imagined that? She'd been startled out of a very deep sleep after all. It was like trying to recount a nightmare; the harder she tried, the faster the details seemed to fall away. But he must've said it; she wouldn't have dreamed up something as misogynistic and nasty as that.

"That's not it," Lewis said. "The connection still sucks."

"Could it be the weather?" A tropical disturbance moving through the Gulf of Mexico overnight had dragged in air that was hot and thick with moisture. Martha could tell because their air-conditioning was chugging constantly.

"No, it's not even raining. It's got to be something else. Didn't we have the cable company come out recently?"

Despite her distraction, Martha stiffened at his use of the word *we*. Usually she hardly noticed it when Lewis said things like that—*what did we get my mother for her birthday* or *did we get any microwave popcorn at the grocery store* or *where did we put the ibuprofen*. Maybe she was still agitated by John's behavior. "Yes, we did. At the end of March. The tech who came out checked everything inside the house and said it was okay. He did something with the wiring outside at the terminal or whatever it's called, and that seemed to help."

"Well, we're going to have to call them to come back out. I can't work like this."

"It's Saturday. I can call but they're not going to send anyone out on such short notice. Even if I tell them it's an emergency, they probably won't come until Wednesday at the earliest."

"Damn it." He slammed his laptop closed and slumped in his chair. A moment later, he opened it again. "I have an idea."

Martha poured herself another cup of coffee. It was either that or go back to bed, but even as tired as she was, she knew she wouldn't actually be able to fall asleep. Her mind would just continue to circle the events of the day before. Lewis's grumpy muttering and typing were small diversions at least.

"Look at this. Absolutely ridiculous."

Martha moved to look over his shoulder at the screen, which displayed a graph of some kind that made absolutely no sense to her. "What is it?" she said.

"It's a network scanner." He pointed to the first column in the table. "These are all the Wi-Fi networks in the area. And these are the frequency bands and channels they're using. And this shows how strong they are. I was just going to look for a clear channel and switch our router to that so we'd get a better signal, but there aren't any."

Martha leaned in closer. "Why are there so many that start with 'BadassDoc'?"

"Apparently some jackass—excuse my language—has a mesh network installed or a bunch of extenders and named all his access points after his main router." Lewis glanced through the window at the Wrights' fence. "It must be them. He's a doctor, right? And it's the only house close enough for the scanner to pick up that would even remotely need that many access points. How much Wi-Fi coverage do two people need?"

Martha nodded. She had no idea what an access point was, so if the house had been full of them, she wouldn't have known.

"It's just ridiculous. And they're all broadcasting on such a high power that it's interfering with our network. You know why?" Martha shrugged. "He's jamming up all the channels because their house is too big for one router. That greedy asshole."

Before, she might've stuck up for John. Not anymore. "So, can't you just change the channel anyway and see what happens?"

Lewis shook his head. "I've tried. Look. It doesn't matter: channel 1 or 6 or 11, the SNR is so low I can't keep a connection."

"SNR?"

He sighed. "Signal-to-noise ratio. We use it to measure the level of the desired signal against the level of background noise. It's complicated."

This time, Martha understood that Lewis's *we* most definitely excluded her. In this case, *we* encompassed all the scientists and engineers and scholars with advanced degrees, a cadre of which he considered himself a member. For some reason, his ivory-tower talk was getting under her skin this morning.

"I'm going to have to go over there and talk to John."

"What? No. Why would you do that?" Martha hadn't fully processed what she'd witnessed yesterday, but she was immediately alarmed at the idea of Lewis interacting with John for any reason. For one thing, Lewis was much more irritable than usual. She could hardly imagine him doing it, but what if he went over there and started spouting off his imperious information about SNRs and frequency bands? If John was still in the same mood he'd been in yesterday, who knew what might happen? Lewis was hardly in a position to defend himself against someone who called himself "Badass Doc."

"I'm just going to explain to him what's going on with the network congestion, and ask him if he'll free up a channel for me to use." He patted her hand and stood up. "Don't worry, Marty, it'll be fine." He turned to go.

"Wait!" Martha turned out from the pan the loaf of banana bread she'd just baked and was letting cool. "Don't go over there empty-handed." She ripped off a sheet of aluminum foil and wrapped up the bread, and around that, she tied the nicest tea towel she had. She handed it to Lewis. "This'll help smooth things."

He was nearly to the door when she called out, "And tell Minnie hello for me if you see her."

$\sim$

Lewis had only been gone ten minutes or so, but it seemed long enough to Martha that she began to worry. She paced aimlessly around her small house, returning several times to the living room window that yielded a view of the Wrights' driveway. Her mind raced with possibilities, most of them dreadful, but to calm herself, she decided that Lewis had probably offered to change whatever settings were necessary to the Wrights' Wi-Fi network so that everyone would end up happy.

But when Lewis came running across their yard from Minnie's, a grave expression on his face, she gave back in to her worst fears.

She flung open the door and Lewis sprinted inside. She followed him into the kitchen, where he grabbed his phone off the charger with trembling hands. "What is it? Lewis? What's happened?"

He looked at her, his eyes wide. "John Wright's dead."

Twenty

W hat?" Martha clutched Lewis's forearm. "What do you mean, 'dead'?" She checked her husband for blood or other signs of an altercation as he dialed 9-1-1. "What about Minnie? Is she okay?"

"I'd like to report a . . . death. My next-door neighbor. I mean, I think he's dead. He looks pretty dead. Oh right, 5818 Alcott Street. Me? I'm Lewis Hale. Yes, 5812. Okay. Sure, okay. Thank you."

Lewis put the phone down, looked at Martha for a moment, then ran into the bathroom. Through the door, Martha could hear him vomiting. Before he'd even finished, the police had arrived, followed by an ambulance and a fire engine, their lights and sirens blaring into the humid, overcast morning.

Martha rushed to the living room window and watched two uniformed officers and a firefighter go into Minnie's house, the paramedics rolling a gurney in after them. Lewis joined her at the window.

"It was awful," he said, still trembling.

Martha spun around and took his hands. She was too shocked to form all the questions she had, but he knew to tell her anyway.

"I knocked at the door first, but nobody answered. Then I rang the doorbell, thinking they had to be up—it was past eight o'clock. I almost gave up waiting, and then Minnie opened the door and said, 'Come in.' Then she turned and started walking, like I was supposed to follow her. So I did, even though I thought it was strange. I've never even been inside their house before. We go into the kitchen and she just stood there, not even looking at me, like she didn't know what to do next. She didn't offer me any coffee, or to sit down. I put down the banana bread, but she didn't even say thank you. It was warm in there, too, like the air conditioner wasn't working. Then I noticed that the back door was standing open. I pointed it out to her, but she just shrugged and said, 'Yes.' I guessed John might've stepped outside and left it ajar, so I said, 'I'm here to talk to John.'

"And then she laughed. I guess you'd call it a laugh. So I said, 'Can I see John?' 'No,' she said, but in a dull voice. I asked her, 'He's not home?' Then she looked at me and said, 'Yes, he's home.' I was running out of patience with her now, so I asked her, 'Then why can't I see him?' ''Cause he's dead,' she said, and started picking at her cuticles. I said, 'Dead?' like you do when you don't really understand what you've just heard, and she just nodded.

"I didn't know what to say, so I just asked where he was. She pointed outside, like this." Lewis jabbed his thumb over his shoulder. "I said, 'What did he die of?' and she just kind of shrugged and said, 'Drowning, maybe.'"

"No," Martha whispered. "How? I mean, did you . . . see?"

Lewis nodded. "I thought maybe he wasn't really dead, so I felt I should check on him. She didn't go with me, just sat there picking at her fingers. I went outside and there he was. There was a bottle of vodka on the edge, nearly gone, and him, facedown in the—" At this, he sprinted back to the bathroom and retched again.

Martha looked out the window. The emergency vehicles still had their lights spinning, although the sirens now were off. Neighbors had started to gather outside. Mrs. Kashuba in her bathrobe; Daniel Mickelsen and his wife, Lillian, who was clutching Beignet like a stuffed animal; Beatriz, along with her triplets, whom she was trying to keep from running to the truck, snatching one back onto her yard only to have to dash after another. Other neighbors Martha knew by name, even more she didn't. Joggers and walkers stopped to gawk, people in cars. Soon there was a substantial crowd gravitating together toward the Mickelsens' lawn, which was directly in front of Minnie's house. Lillian seemed to be taking the whole thing very personally, leaning into different clusters of people with a worried expression while probably claiming to know what, precisely, had happened at the Wrights'.

John had *drowned*? The morning after she, Martha, had snuck into his house, dug around inside his and Minnie's closets, their bathroom? Slept in his bed? The coincidence was more than disconcerting. Now she thought she might be sick, too.

"Lewis," she called. He went into the living room and sat down on the couch, his head in his hands. She sat next to him. "What else did Minnie say?" She could hear the hysteria in her own voice, but he didn't seem to notice. Their neighbor had just been found dead; of course she'd be hysterical. He might think something was wrong if she weren't.

"Not much. She must've been in a state of shock."

"Oh god, look." Martha stood up. The paramedics had emerged with an empty gurney and rolled it down the driveway to the ambulance. They loaded it and their other equipment, and left. The firefighters climbed back onto the engine and left, too. "They didn't take away the body, Lewis. What does that mean?"

He shook his head. "It's just awful, whatever it is."

Soon two more police vehicles pulled up to the curb and plainclothes officials stepped out. One of them hitched his pants up over his belly and surveilled the Wrights' house and surroundings, ignoring the crowd across the street. Another began taking photographs.

Immediately after, an SUV marked MEDICAL EXAMINER arrived. They took a different gurney into the house, and even from her place at the window, Martha could sense an eerie silence descend after they'd all gone inside. A few of the onlookers drifted away, but a knot of curious people remained across the street. Martha rushed outside and up to her office to look out her window. John's body, fully dressed, had been pulled from the pool and was lying supine on the edge, his head tilted at a strange angle. She felt her legs go slack and held on to the sill for support as two men lifted him onto a black body bag. One of them zipped up the bag as casually as if it were a suitcase. Where was Minnie?

Martha went back to the house, and again to the living room window to watch the medical examiner and others emerge with John's bagged body on the gurney. As they were loading it into the coroner's vehicle, Martha saw Mrs. Kashuba drop to her knees in the Mickelsens' yard. Nobody else seemed to notice.

Aghast, Martha hurried across the street to her friend. Only then did others turn to watch or offer assistance. "Are you all right? Here, let's get you up," Martha said, helping her to stand. "Do you want to go inside?"

Mrs. Kashuba leaned against her. "No, dear. I'll be fine. Thank you. I was just overcome for a moment thinking about who's in that bag."

"It's John," Martha said.

Everyone spun around to her.

"Are you sure? How do you know?" someone asked.

"Lewis went over there this morning to talk to him, and Minnie told him," she said.

"Oh my god."

"Where's Minnie?"

"Still inside, presumably," Martha said. The cluster of spectators was pulsating, shifting around so that Martha was the new center of their attention.

"Did she do it?"

"Don't be ridiculous," someone else said. "We don't even know what happened. He might have had a heart attack or something."

"Do you know, Martha?" Everyone looked at her, wide-eyed, hopeful. Expectant.

She looked around at the crowd. Even Lillian was leaning forward, anticipating her answer. Martha had wished her whole life to be the kind of person that others would lean toward or lean on. The kind of person who was invited to be part of things, who was sought out as a source of information or support or fun. Now, finally, she had some valuable social currency to spend.

Martha made eye contact with several of her neighbors, savoring the moment. When she spoke, her voice was solemn. "Apparently, he drowned."

There was a collective gasp as everyone sucked in the hot air among them. Mrs. Kashuba sagged against Martha, her hand pressing against her own heart.

"Dios mío," Beatriz said, covering the ears of her nearest triplet. She quickly herded them all back inside her house.

After a brief moment of silence, everyone seemed to speak at once, a volley of questions directed at Martha.

"Did she say how?"

"Does she even know?"

"When did it happen?"

"Did you hear anything?"

"Was it an accident?"

Martha patted the air in front of her as if to lower their voices. "I know the back door was open and that he was discovered in the pool, fully dressed. He may have been drinking, so I assume it was accidental." Even the sudden recollection that she'd been in their house only some hours before John's death didn't diminish the thrilling satisfaction of being the neighbors' primary source of information. "And Minnie's okay, considering her husband's just been found dead."

"I heard he swims regularly. How on earth could he accidentally drown?"

"She said he was drunk, that's how."

"I actually said he *may have been*." Martha was proud of herself for remembering to sound neutral about that detail; she was only supposed to know what Lewis had told her.

"So then someone might've killed him."

"Oh my god, y'all—there's a murderer on the loose in West U," Lillian said, clutching Beignet so tightly he yelped.

"We've had a couple packages stolen off our front porch recently. What if criminals have been casing the neighborhood?"

"I've heard about package theft from some other people, too. Crime has definitely gotten worse lately—but *murder*?"

"Have y'all noticed there's more foot traffic here than usual? Not neighbors, I mean," said a middle-aged blonde woman who had a sign warning people not to let their dogs do their business on her lawn. She leaned in and lowered her voice. "Strangers."

"I've seen a few walking around who definitely look like they don't belong here."

"This makes me want to get security cameras for my house. I've always felt like West U is such a nice, safe neighborhood. That's why we moved here. I can't believe this is happening here—to people like us."

"Martha said the back door was open. It definitely could've been a burglary gone bad."

"It might've been her maid. Maybe she left the door open on purpose and went back and got him drunk and—" The speaker pantomimed shoving a body backward.

"She's illegal, you know. I bet they never find her."

"All these criminals coming across the border." The man who said this cast a disparaging glance at Beatriz's house.

"Lupe is a kind and respectable woman," Martha said, indignant. "Besides, she has a bad back."

"They say it's usually the spouse," Daniel Mickelsen said with authority, raising an eyebrow while mindlessly adjusting his privates through the pocket of his golf shorts.

"Have you seen his wife?" asked the neighbor from the end of the block who played defense for the Houston Texans. "She's a tiny little thing, light as a feather. She might be able to shoot the guy, but no way she could drown him."

Mrs. Kashuba said, "She's also kind of timid and . . . fluttery."

"They always seem so happy together," Lillian added. "I've been to their house. They're very much in love."

Martha's jealousy flared at Lillian's comment. She tried to steer the conversation to keep herself in a position of authority. "Minnie is an innocent, grieving widow. She deserves our support—not accusations," Martha said.

"Well, I heard that he was a philanderer."

"Yeah, he supposedly had a pissed-off ex-lover. Maybe it was her. Or her husband."

"Revenge murder!"

"Didn't he have some big medical malpractice issue? From what I understand, his lawyers were able to bury it enough to keep it out of the news, but I think that's why they moved here—his reputation was destroyed. Maybe it had something to do with that?"

"You play with the bull, you get the horns."

Martha noticed a uniformed police officer walking across her lawn. When he began to climb the steps to her house, she said, to no one in particular, "I have to go."

~

"Officer," she said, breathless. "Hi. I live here. Can I help you?"

He looked at his clipboard. "Are you Mrs. Lewis Hale?"

"I'm Martha Hale, yes."

"I'm Officer Peters. I wonder if I could have a word with you and your husband. Is he home?"

She stepped past him and opened the front door. "Of course," she said. "He's home but he might be in the bathroom." She shook her head. "I don't mean *in the bathroom* if you know what I'm saying. Just that he might be vomiting."

Officer Peters took a backward step. "Should I come back?"

Martha waved at the air between them. "No, no, sorry. I just mean he's had a rough morning, finding John's body and all. Come on in."

The three of them sat down at the kitchen table, Officer Peters having refused all Martha's offers of food or beverage. He turned to Lewis. "I wonder if you'd mind going over the events of this morning."

Although the pallor of his face suggested that yes, in fact, he minded very much, Lewis shook his head no. He was the mild kind of man who yielded easily to the upper ranks. Martha had never quite understood why; his own father was hardly an authoritarian, and among his peers Lewis was quite composed, competitive even. Well, it didn't much matter why. The problem was that he could be a little bit too solicitous. Lewis sometimes wandered along and got things mixed up in a story. Martha hoped he would tell this one straight, and not say any unnecessary things that would just make things harder for Minnie.

He didn't begin at once, and Martha, leaning forward in her chair, had that sinking feeling of the mother whose child is about to perform.

"Yes, Mr. Hale?" Officer Peters reminded.

Lewis took a deep breath like he was filling a bellows, and started. "This morning, I noticed that we were having some Wi-Fi troubles, so I decided to do a little investigating of my own. See, there's something called a network scanner that lets you view all the networks in the immediate vicinity—"

Now, there he was, saying things he didn't need to say. Martha tried to catch her husband's eye, but fortunately the officer interrupted with: "Let's talk about that a little later, Mr. Hale. I do want to talk about it, but I'm anxious now to get along to just what happened when you got there."

"Oh," Lewis said. "All right." And he recounted the story that he'd told Martha earlier.

"And after you saw the body, what happened?"

"Once I realized he was dead, I thought I'd better not touch anything and I went back inside. Minnie was sitting that same way. I asked her, 'Has anyone been notified?' and she said, 'No.'"

Officer Peters's expression betrayed none of his thoughts, but he nodded to Lewis as if to encourage him to continue, which he did.

"I thought it was strange how she said it, like she wasn't too concerned. So, I asked her, kind of businesslike, 'How did it happen, Minnie?' She stopped picking at her fingernails and said, 'I don't know.' I said, 'You don't *know*? Where were you?'"

Martha leaned forward even more. Officer Peters simply waited, his light-blue eyes focused on Lewis.

"She said, 'I was sleeping in the guest bedroom last night.' I found that strange, but then again, there was that bottle of vodka out there. Maybe she was put off by the smell of it, I don't know. Or—"

"Lewis," Martha said, more sharply than she intended.

"Anyway, I said to Minnie, 'You're saying he was out there in the pool and drowned, and you didn't wake up?' She said, 'I didn't wake up.' Then after a minute, she said, 'I'm a deep sleeper.'"

Officer Peters nodded. Then, to Martha's surprise, he turned his intense gaze on her. "Have you known Mrs. Wright awhile?" he asked.

Martha took a breath. Why had he asked about Minnie and not John? She glanced around her kitchen, taking in what some might consider the breadth of her life. She was a woman. Minnie was a woman. Maybe that's all it was. "I've known her since high school."

The policeman raised his brows and made a strange sort of frown. He jotted something down on his clipboard, then looked back up at her. The severity of his countenance made her feel vulnerable in a way she didn't like, as though she were being slowly forced backward toward the precipice of something. Her instinct was to dodge his line of questioning—to defend herself and Minnie both. "We weren't exactly friends back then, but I knew her well. She's a lovely person. And she's been wonderful since she moved in. Really wonderful."

"So you're friends now, then?"

Martha took a breath. She'd gone this far; she needed to be firm. She'd been in Minnie's house—both with and without permission.

"Yes, actually. We're friends."

"Do you see her regularly?"

Martha wondered if watching her drive in and out of her garage counted. "I guess I wouldn't call it regularly."

"Tell me about the last time you visited with her."

"Oh, let me think." She looked up at the ceiling, away from the pressure of his stare, and calculated. It had been two days since Martha had actually spoken to Minnie at the gallery. She winced, remembering that humiliating experience and all that ensued from there.

Officer Peters must've noticed a change in her expression because he cocked his head to one side. "How did she seem to you?"

She really didn't want to talk about the gallery, especially not in front of Lewis. But what if he'd asked Minnie the same question? What would *she* have said? No, it wasn't even relevant. Her husband was dead; why would they bother Minnie with questions about Martha of all people? Unless, of course, they knew what she'd done. Martha pressed her damp palms against her jeans and forced herself to smile. "She seemed good. She was busy, so we only chatted for a minute. We talked about getting together soon for a girls' night." It wasn't a total lie; she'd just selected facts from different and more pleasant interactions.

Lewis looked at Martha with a puzzled expression. "I didn't know about that," he said.

Martha glared at him. "It wasn't a big deal."

"I just mean you usually mention things like that."

"Lewis, I don't have to tell you about every little thing I do."

Officer Peters cleared his throat. "I only have a few more questions for you folks, then I'll let you get on with your day." He looked at Martha again. "Have you noticed any unusual goings-on next door?"

She stole a glance at Lewis, who seemed to be staring at Officer Peters's badge. Should she admit that she'd seen John arguing with Minnie by the pool the night before? The police already knew that John had been drinking. Did an argument matter? All Minnie had done was throw a drink at her husband, nothing more. Lewis's expression remained blank. Maybe he was right, that it was none of her business. She shook her head no.

"Seen anyone going in or out?"

Her face flushed. "Um, no, I don't think so. Just Lupe, their housekeeper."

"Nobody else?"

Martha swallowed. "And the lawn and pool maintenance crews, of course." It occurred to her then how lucky she'd been that the pool crew hadn't been there yesterday as she ran out their back door. They usually arrived just around that time on Friday afternoons. Could they have had something to do with John's death? A fatal chemical imbalance in the water?

"I didn't notice any surveillance equipment out front. You don't happen to have video we could review, do you?"

"No," she said. Then, in a flash of cunning: "What about our other neighbors? Do they have any?"

"The other officers are checking, but so far, no."

"Why are you asking these things?" Martha blurted out. "Are you suggesting John Wright was . . . murdered?"

Officer Peters seemed to soften, albeit very slightly. "I can understand why you'd be concerned about that, living right next door. We won't know the manner or cause of death until the medical examiner completes his investigation."

She looked down at her lap and noticed one of her coarse, strawberry-blonde hairs stuck to her dark T-shirt. She plucked it off the fabric and let it fall to the floor. She was always shedding hair.

Oh no.

Oh no oh no oh no. What if she'd left any of her unmistakably not-Minnie hairs in their bed? If they thought John was murdered, they'd be looking for evidence to identify the killer. Fingerprints. DNA. She felt a thin sweat rise up against her hairline, and wiped it away with the back of her hand.

"So you're going to be looking for clues?" Even if John's drowning was an accident, could she somehow be considered—an accessory?

He misunderstood her again. "Don't worry, Mrs. Hale. We're taking this very seriously. We'll investigate it as a homicide, unless or until it's ruled a natural or accidental death or suicide."

"What does that entail, exactly?" She bit off the hangnail she'd been picking at.

Officer Peters gave her a small smile. "To start, we'll process the scene, gather any evidence, and interview potential witnesses. Like with any major crime, we have to consider motive, means, and opportunity. That's about all I'm at liberty to say." He pushed his chair back from the table and stood, then handed her a business card. He looked carefully at each of them. "I appreciate your time today. Let me know if you can think of anything that might help us with the investigation."

Martha heard herself say that she would, but all she could think was that unless it was an accidental death or a suicide, then someone had gone into the Wrights' home sometime last night and killed John. And her own DNA was all over the place.

Lewis led Officer Peters to the front door and he and Martha followed him out onto the tiny porch just as Minnie was being escorted out of her house by a man whose magenta suit and straw fedora suggested he wasn't a member of the police force. Minnie's boss. One arm was around Minnie, and in the other he carried a duffel bag. The few neighbors that were still gathered on the Mickelsens' lawn were quiet as he and Minnie walked toward his car.

"You'll stay with us as long as you want. Oscar and I have plenty of room," Lawrence said in his booming British-accented voice.

Minnie said nothing, just leaned against him and let him help her inside the car. From what Martha could see, Minnie looked just as terrible as she must've felt. Officer Peters thanked them again and turned to go as Minnie and Lawrence drove away.

"Oh!" Martha called out to Officer Peters, briefly snapped out of her panicked thinking. "What about Bonnie?"

"I'm sorry?" he said.

"Bonnie's her pet parakeet. Minnie just left without her. She must be terribly overwrought—she adores that bird. She'd never leave her behind on purpose. Can you let me into the house? I'll get her and drive her over to wherever Minnie's staying."

"Nobody's allowed into the house right now. But don't worry— Mrs. Wright didn't leave anything behind. I noticed the cages in the house and on the porch were both empty and asked her about them. She said the bird had recently escaped. Got out of the one inside, apparently, and flew out through an open door."

"Oh no!" Martha pressed her hands to her cheeks. Poor Minnie had lost her husband and beloved pet at the same time? No wonder she'd seemed catatonic when Lewis spoke to her.

"It's a real shame," Officer Peters said. "But maybe it didn't go too far. You could keep your eye out for it, I guess, in case it comes back."

Twenty-One

Martha didn't know what to do with herself or how to stop her mind from spinning. She wasn't guilty of killing John, of course, so she wasn't terribly worried about being implicated in his death. What she couldn't stop thinking about was the investigators finding her hair and fingerprints and wanting to know why. The idea of being publicly exposed for being in the Wrights' house—in their *bed*—was pure anguish. They'd have to leave West U. It would be impossible to live here with that kind of shame. She could only imagine what Lillian and the rest of them would say about her. And Harry! How would he cope with the humiliation? A scandal like that could keep the rumor mill churning for years.

She was too exhausted to nap, too distracted to work. She'd made Lewis a sandwich for lunch, but when she sat down with him, the smell of the meat nauseated her. She went out into the backyard, searching the trees over the fence line for Bonnie.

"Hey, pretty girl," she called uncertainly to the leaves. "Bonnie, are you there?"

The only answer she got was a salvo of tennis ball thwacks against the other fence. She went back inside, too distracted to be irritated by a Nerf gun.

Lewis met her in the utility room, carrying his briefcase. He held his free arm open, inviting or offering a hug. "Are you okay?" they asked each other at the same time. Neither responded to the question as they clung to each other for a moment, but in the way of people who've been together for many years, they understood what the other was thinking. Or, at least, Martha understood Lewis. He'd been shocked that morning, of course, but almost as soon as Officer Peters was gone, his one-track mind had drifted back to work. As for what he assumed she was feeling, he probably thought she was just disconcerted by a death so close by, as anyone would be; he had absolutely no idea about the panic she was trying to conceal.

"I still have to finish this damn report. The analysts aren't going to care about a death—even my own. I'm going to the office and I have to warn you: I might be there awhile. Maybe even all night, I'm so far behind."

Martha was relieved. Seeing him moping around wasn't helping her process what had happened. The idea of being alone was actually appealing. Maybe then she could figure out what, if anything, she should do.

Lewis pulled away and looked at her. "I feel terrible about leaving you here, though. Do you want to come with me? It might be boring, but at least you wouldn't be alone."

"It's okay," she said. "I'll be fine."

"What about calling your mother? Or mine. I hate the idea of you suffering on your own."

"Lewis, I said I'm okay." She appreciated his concern but was starting to feel stifled by it, too. "Besides, I'm sure they're both going to be calling me as soon as the five o'clock news comes on. Did you notice the crews outside? I'm surprised nobody's knocked on our door."

She waved at him through the window as he backed out of the driveway, thinking she'd feel a sense of relief once he was gone. But she didn't. Lewis wasn't the problem. The problem was that she'd left her DNA all over Minnie's house the day before her husband was found murdered.

Martha wondered what the police had asked Minnie about her. Certainly, her interaction with Lewis would've been discussed, but would they have asked her if she and Martha were friends? Probably not; there'd have been no reason to—yet. Martha still wasn't sure why Officer Peters had asked *her* about their relationship. She wished he'd been more forthcoming about the investigation procedures. What would they look at, take, test? Would they take the Wrights' kitchen trash? Had they already? If so, they'd find the yogurt container Martha had eaten from. Her fingerprints on the refrigerator handle, the pantry knob. She'd never been arrested for anything, had never even gotten a speeding ticket. But surely her fingerprints were in some database somewhere. She'd had to provide them to the elementary school years ago when she'd registered to volunteer for Harry's first-ever field day in kindergarten. Back then she'd been so excited to be the official class photographer that she hadn't even stopped to wonder why they'd taken such draconian measures to sign up the parent volunteers. Only later, when other parents complained about having to reregister every fall, did it strike her as excessive. But then again, so much in their neighborhood was.

Should she go back into Minnie's house and retrieve the yogurt container? Wipe down the things she'd touched? What about the sheets? Had they been slept in after Martha left? What could the police get from those, apart from any stray hairs? But that was bad enough. Another woman's hair in the bed would lead the police to think John had been with a lover there. They wouldn't even need to test the DNA on a coarse, curly, strawberry-blonde strand to suspect it was Martha. That idea would certainly complicate an investigation. How could she prove that she *hadn't* been sleeping with John? They lived right next door to each other. Theoretically, they wouldn't even have needed to use their phones to make plans to meet during the day, while Minnie and Lewis were at work.

For a strange moment, wandering around her own house, she got herself caught up in a fantasy of arranging their assignations via secret code. A certain look shared across the yard, a specific light left on in a window. The return of her recycling bins to their place by the garage. Then she would cross her lawn, carefully as she ever had, and dash unseen into the Wrights' backyard. Except John would be waiting there for her, his arm muscles rippling underneath his fitted T-shirts. She picked a shirt up from the bedroom floor and pressed it to her nose. That it smelled of Lewis jarred her back to reality, and she felt silly and ashamed. John was dead. And she hadn't ever had any intention of sleeping with him even when he wasn't. She'd even started to think he was an asshole. But that still didn't assuage her concerns about what the police—or worse, Minnie—might imagine.

For wont of something to do, she began gathering dirty clothes to start a load of laundry. There was so much less without Harry at home, it was almost an effort to fill the basket. She found a pair of Lewis's dress socks, peeled off and left in little balls by the couch. The towel he'd used that morning. Her overalls, which she'd worn yesterday. *Oh, Martha, what were you thinking?* She'd been so stupid and cavalier. And now look.

Wait, where was her T-shirt? One of Lewis's holey, old Middlebury shirts that she'd worn so often that by now it was unmistakably hers? She'd been wearing it with the overalls. She'd taken it off at Minnie's yesterday when she put on the caftan—which she hadn't known what to do with beyond folding and hiding it carefully in her dresser. Had she left her T-shirt there by accident? How would *that* be explained? Maybe she'd dropped it in her frantic hurry to leave. She ran out of the house and up to her office to look from the window, squinting at the porch, sidewalk, the hydrangea bushes for the gray T-shirt with blue lettering. It wasn't there. Had the police already found it and bagged it as evidence? Or was it still under Minnie's bed, or even in her closet?

Well, now there was simply no question: she had to go back to Minnie's house. Again. Only this time, she'd be breaking even more laws.

~

Trying to decide if it was worth the risk, she looked up the Texas Penal Code § 37.09—Tampering With or Fabricating Physical Evidence—and learned that (a) A person commits an offense if, knowing that an investigation or official proceeding is pending or in progress, he: (1) alters, destroys, or conceals any record, document, or thing with intent to impair its verity, legibility, or availability as evidence in the investigation or official proceeding. Ultimately, after debating it long enough to chew her fingernails to the quicks, Martha concluded that since what she was planning to remove wasn't really evidence since she absolutely, definitely did not murder John Wright, and what she planned to take would only complicate the real investigation by potentially distracting the authorities from finding the real murderer if there was one, then it was okay.

Obviously, she wouldn't tell anyone that. If she were caught, she planned to say that she was distraught about Bonnie's disappearance, and she was just looking for her inside the house. The bird would need to be fed and watered, if she were still there. And Lewis had said that when he got to the Wrights' that morning, the back door was standing open. Bonnie could have flown back in without Minnie noticing. In fact, the more she thought about it, the more determined Martha became that she actually had a moral duty to go over there. Besides, Officer Peters had said that nobody was allowed into the house *right now*. He didn't say definitively that nobody was allowed at all.

Still, she wasn't going to advertise her actions.

It wouldn't be dark enough to go out until ten o'clock. Lewis had called earlier to say that he was definitely staying at the office, but she also knew that he would eventually get tired, especially after the tumult of that morning. Since he preferred the comfort of their bed even to nice hotels, much less the hard floor of his office, there was a good chance that he'd pack it up in the middle of the night and come home, so she didn't want to wait too long. Ten o'clock seemed like a good time. Neighbors who'd gone to dinner would already be home by then; those who'd gone to parties would still be out. Fortunately, nobody in the immediate vicinity seemed to be hosting any gatherings, so as long as she kept to the shadows, she figured she'd go unseen.

~

Martha was watching a pot of coffee brew when the doorbell rang and jolted her out of her anxious daze. She looked at the clock—it was almost eight thirty. *Please don't let it be my mother,* she thought. She'd never be able to get to Minnie's that night if Evelyn showed up. She tiptoed to the door, careful to avoid the planks that creaked, and squinted out the peephole. Lillian Mickelsen, of all people, wearing a plain T-shirt and jeans, was standing there with her hands clasped in front of her, biting at the inside of her lip.

"Hi," Lillian said in her false drawl when Martha opened the door. She swatted at a mosquito near her face. "This feels so awkward. I mean, you and I haven't been very close. But I keep thinking about Minnie and that we should do something for her. Take her something from her house, maybe, or some food. Something to make her more comfortable."

"We?" Martha said.

Her surprise at seeing Lillian on her porch for the first and only time in the fifteen years they'd been neighbors, at being included in any sort of "we" with her must've registered on her face as something else, because Lillian shifted uncomfortably. She swatted again at a bug, and a lock of hair came loose from her ponytail. "You're right. I shouldn't have been presumptuous. It's just that I don't know her very well, and you and she are close. I thought you'd know more than I what might make her feel better. But if you're already planning something, maybe I can chip in?"

Martha scrunched her brows and shook her head, unable to decide what to process first: Lillian's suggestion, her misunderstanding, or her strange and unprecedented deference to Martha.

After a moment of awkward silence, Lillian's eyes filled and she sniffed back the first tears. "I'm sorry, I shouldn't have bothered you. It's just been such a terrible, terrible day." She started down Martha's steps. Martha watched her go. She had plenty of reasons to let Lillian slink back across the street, to revel in the unexpected reversal of their social order, to indulge in a bit of schadenfreude at her apparent dismay. But Martha had been too often in Lillian's current position to do any of that.

"We're not close, actually," Martha said. Lillian stopped and turned around. "Do you want to come in? I just made a fresh pot of coffee."

Martha offered Lillian a seat at her kitchen table, the same one Officer Peters had used earlier that day. She handed her a box of tissues, a slice of banana bread, and a cup of coffee, and watched as Lillian scooped three heaping teaspoons of sugar into her mug. This, the woman who didn't allow her children to eat candy for fear of them getting fat. She still looked good, Martha noticed. But she wasn't quite as trim as she'd once been. A small, soft roll at her waistline showed through her T-shirt. And her neck, once tight and tan, was looser and slightly creased. She was only five or six years older than Martha. Martha wondered if she still wore shorts. She wondered if underneath all Lillian's pretense and posturing and even clothes that maybe they weren't so different after all.

"This bread is delicious," Lillian said. She looked around Martha's kitchen, and Martha followed her gaze across the clean, old surfaces, the outdated appliances. Lillian didn't offer any compliments about the house, which actually made Martha trust her a little bit.

"Thank you," Martha said.

"Honestly, I thought you and Minnie were friends."

"Why would you think that?" Had Lillian seen her going to Minnie's house through her gate?

"Well, I mean, you knew about John before any of the rest of us for one thing."

Stalling with a long sip of coffee, Martha searched Lillian's face, looking for unsaid accusations. She couldn't see any. "Lewis went over there to talk to him about some tech problem. It was coincidence, really," she finally said, though she was disappointed to admit that she wasn't in any special position in Minnie's life as she'd led the neighbors to believe that morning. "What about you? You were invited to her party."

"Oh, that? No, that was because Daniel—my husband—was doing business with John. He sells medical devices to surgeons. John invited him to the party. Well, us."

"And your dog."

"What?"

Martha realized how petty she sounded. She waved her hand as if to wipe it away. "Nothing." She went to get the pot to refill their mugs, wishing that her matching ones weren't in the dishwasher. "I tried to be friends with Minnie. I even took pictures of her bird, but she—" In a rare moment of thinking before speaking, Martha stopped herself from mentioning they'd been ripped up and thrown away. How would she have explained that? "She didn't even send a thank-you note."

"Oh, she loved those pictures! She showed them to me. She said she was going to get one of them framed."

"She did?"

Lillian nodded. "They were really good, by the way."

Martha was simultaneously pleased and confused. She wanted to ask Lillian why Minnie would've destroyed them if she liked them so much, but instead said, "Sounds like you know her pretty well if she showed you the photos."

Lillian shook her head as she stared down at her coffee. "No, I ran into her at the pet store a week or so ago. She was in line in front of me and I was making small talk, asking about her bird, and she showed me the pictures. She had copies of them on her phone. Anyway, that party was the only time we socialized. I tried other times, but she always had some excuse. It's kind of embarrassing, in retrospect."

"Yeah," Martha said, meeting Lillian's eyes and recognizing a familiar vulnerability in them. "Me too."

They were quiet for a moment, then Lillian said, "I had the impression they weren't very happy, despite appearances."

Martha was cautious. She didn't want to reveal something to Lillian that she hadn't told the police. Also, she knew that couples could disagree and still be happy. "But earlier today, outside, you told everyone they were in love."

"I know, but it was because of what my husband said about it being the spouse. I didn't think he should've put that idea into anyone's mind. It didn't seem fair to her." Lillian leaned forward and lowered her voice, even though it was just the two of them there. "Daniel told me that he offered to take John hunting during the special white-winged dove days in September, but John said he had a buddy with a ranch in South Texas and why wait 'til fall. Daniel told him it was illegal, but John just laughed and called him a . . . pussy. It made Daniel really uncomfortable. And that wasn't the only thing." After a pause, she said, "He seemed like a . . . a hard man."

Martha thought about seeing Minnie throw John's martini at him, him calling her a bitch, him calling his client a cunt. "Yeah," she said, wondering what else he did behind closed doors. "You might be right."

"I kind of like the idea of her standing up to him, though, if that's what happened," Lillian said. "Not that I'm glad he's dead or anything."

"No, no," Martha said. "Of course not."

"It's just . . . you hear rumors. It's hard to know what to believe."

"I guess we mostly believe what we want to," Martha said.

"That's why I was worried about her. Even if they weren't happy, she's got to be going through an awful time." Lillian looked at her watch. "I have to run. Believe it or not, I'm taking my real estate license exam tomorrow morning." She stood up and carried her mug to the sink. "I feel like such a cliché," she said, shaking her head. "But being out of the workforce for twenty years, what else am I going to do?"

Despite everything, Martha couldn't help but feel a little bit sorry for Lillian. "I like your idea about doing something for Minnie," she said as they walked to the door. "I'll give it some thought."

Lillian nodded, then paused. "My nephew is leaving this week. He won't be getting Harry into any more trouble."

"Oh," Martha said. "Okay."

"I haven't been very nice to you," Lillian said. "And I shouldn't have let Willy get away with making your son take the blame for what happened."

Martha looked down, feeling a heaviness in her chest. "No," she finally said.

"It's not easy to do the hard thing, even when it's right," Lillian said. She looked down at her hands, then back up at Martha. "I'm sorry."

"Thank you," Martha said, and returned Lillian's shy smile. She waited until Lillian had crossed the street and gotten safely back inside before she closed her door. She'd have liked to think more about what had just happened, what it might mean, but it was getting late, and she had something even more important to do.

Twenty-Two

After Lillian left, Martha's thoughts returned to eradicating any signs that she'd been in the Wrights' house the night before John's death. She put Minnie's caftan in the dryer on a delicate cycle for a couple of minutes—only long enough to loosen the wrinkles and, hopefully, Martha's scent along with them. That she'd be able to return it to Minnie's closet, with the tag intact, was another good reason to go over there. She rolled it loosely and put it inside a satchel that she could wear slung across her torso, leaving her hands free. She didn't want to leave any more of her identifiable stray hairs anywhere by accident, so she pulled it into a tight bun and hair-sprayed it down the way her mother had done during Martha's brief childhood foray into ballet dancing. But she worried that a strong breeze or a misstep might jostle a hair from her scalp, so she put a shower cap on, too. Nor did she want to leave any more fingerprints, so she put on her dishwashing gloves. She'd done so many dishes in her lifetime that it was hardly awkward at all. Finally, in order to avoid having to turn on any lights in the Wrights' house, she took Harry's night-vision goggles from his shelf. It wasn't lost on her that he'd been wearing them the night of the penis graffiti incident. She only hoped she wouldn't get caught as he had.

In the Wrights' backyard, Martha stared at the shimmering lights under the pool's surface, imagining John drowning there. When had it happened? Why hadn't she heard anything, especially since she'd slept so fitfully? A strange sensation passed through her as she remembered watching the medical examiner casually zipping John into the body bag, any hope of him surviving gone. She crept to the door, careful to avoid the part of the porch where he'd been pulled from the water. Yet even after she had her foot on the doorstep, her hand on the knob, Martha had a moment of feeling she should not cross that threshold. She wished she'd never done it in the first place.

It was strange—and sad—not to see Bonnie in her gilded cage in the corner. She whispered hopefully out into the dark, "Hello, pretty girl! Are you there?" It occurred to her that a judge might struggle to believe she was looking for a bird while wearing night-vision goggles. But she couldn't risk turning on the lights. Anyway, unless she was apprehended right then, nobody would know she'd been using them. Officer Peters hadn't realized how relieved Martha had been to learn that their neighbors didn't have surveillance cameras all over the place.

"Bonnie! Come here, sweet girl!"

Martha crept through the living room to the cage. She looked at the little door and gasped. The latch had been unlocked before; she assumed that Minnie simply didn't bother with it. But now it looked as though the hinge had been pulled apart. Like someone had been rough with it. The water dish was nearly dry, and there wasn't any food. Martha felt strange, like something important to her had been lost—but she hadn't known how important it was until that moment. She thought maybe she should cut up some fruit, just in case, but decided it was too risky.

She went into the kitchen, and even beyond the green of the night goggles, she could see that it wasn't right. It was a total mess. It had always been perfectly clean—slicked up as if for a photo shoot. There was Martha's banana bread, still wrapped in aluminum and covered with her favorite tea towel. Her eye caught a clear canister on the counter next to it. The cover was off, and beside it was a paper bag of sugar, half-full. Minnie had probably been transferring the sugar to put away in her pantry. She must've gone to the grocery store after work. There were several paper bags folded on another counter, and a few left standing on the island with cans and jars still inside. She pulled out a jar of fancy cherry preserves and looked at it. Why had that work been left half-done? She had an urge to empty the rest of the bags and put Minnie's things away for her—incomplete things always bothered Martha—but then she realized it would be obvious to anyone who'd already seen it this way. Touching these items was something that might put her in violation of the penal code. So was removing the yogurt container from the garbage can, but she did that anyway. She used the dishrag that had been left on the island to wipe off the surfaces she'd touched the day before. Then she returned the jar of cherry preserves to the bag, careful not to disturb anything else, and looked around at things begun and, for some reason, not finished.

Martha crept up the stairs, glancing out the window as she passed, relieved to see that the street below was dark and quiet. "Bonnie," she whisper-called, in a manner of releasing herself from the disquiet. There was no sound in return but the hum of the air-conditioning.

She passed the guest bedroom and was surprised that the door was open, since the Wrights seemed normally to keep the doors to their upstairs rooms closed. One more thing left undone. And there was the bed—unmade. Minnie had told Lewis that she'd been asleep in the guest bedroom last night, and here was the proof of that. Martha wondered if it was common for her to sleep there, apart from John. Maybe he'd snored. Sometimes, when Lewis snored so loud it woke Martha up, she'd move from their bed to the couch, covering her head with a pillow to drown out the noise. Or maybe it was because of the martini and the harsh words that Minnie and John had thrown at each other before bedtime.

Martha took a step inside the room, as if her mind had tripped on something. Her eye caught sight of what looked like Minnie's treasure box sitting on the nightstand, next to the side of the bed that had been slept in. On the dresser to her left, where the box had been before, was an empty place. If she hadn't admired it so thoroughly that first time she'd seen it, perhaps she wouldn't have noticed that it had been moved. Why had Minnie put it there? Had she been lying in bed, reminiscing about the past? Even though she didn't want to disturb anything, Martha couldn't help wanting to peek again inside that box. She wasn't mad at Minnie anymore, not really, especially now that she was widowed, and Bonnie had gone missing. She wished she'd made a better effort than she had—the correct kind of effort—to get to know Minnie Foster when she'd had the chance.

With her gloved hands, she picked up the treasure box and held it a moment, then, with a little sigh, opened it.

Instantly, her hand went to her nose. There was something wrapped up in a piece of silk, a handkerchief or a scarf, but it wasn't Minnie's time-capsule treasures.

"Bonnie," Martha whispered, feeling a catch in her throat.

She pulled back the silk, and there was the bird, eyes closed and her head lying at a strange, painful-looking angle. Not like she'd been sick, but like somebody had wrung her neck.

But who would've done such a thing?

Martha stared at Bonnie's body with dawning comprehension, with growing horror. She thought about the broken hinge on the cage, like a large hand had pushed into it. She remembered the angry, predatory tone of John's voice on the phone, on their porch. *Cunt, bitch.* She thought of what Lillian had said about him being a hard man and also that Minnie had loved the photos of Bonnie. She remembered how they'd all been ripped, right across the bird's tiny neck. Minnie wouldn't have done that. How could Martha have thought that she would?

At once, Martha knew: for whatever reason, John had done this to Bonnie. He'd killed Minnie's pet bird. He was angry at his wife, and he wrung her bird's neck with his own hands. She couldn't help imagining the snapping sound, his drunken pleasure at hearing it. That was how he could hurt Minnie. Maybe the only way.

Martha looked at the dresser and noticed the top drawer was slightly ajar. Inside were all the items from Minnie's childhood that had been in the box before. Clutching the box to her chest, Martha realized that Minnie had planned to bury Bonnie in it. She thought of the unbuilt baby crib in the closet and wondered what it must've been like for the Wrights, never having had any children around. Minnie said John had wanted them. And the way Minnie had talked about it sounded like he hadn't thought of the bird as an adequate substitute. *Goddamn you, you stupid fucking bird,* Martha had heard him say to Bonnie yesterday in her sleep-drenched panic. She remembered the sound of what might've been her cage being rattled.

She felt tears begin to fill her eyes, thinking about how Minnie must've felt being married to a man like that. She wished again that she'd come over here more, ringing the front doorbell, not prowling in through the back, making sure Minnie felt the friendship that Martha had desperately wanted to share with her. That was a crime, she thought. That was a real crime. And who was going to punish that? They'd lived so close together, and also so far apart. Going through the same things—just different kinds of the same things.

A bright light from outside the window briefly illuminated Minnie's guest bedroom. Martha dropped into a crouch, feeling the pops of her knees. Her heart raced at the sudden intrusion, though it seemed to have been only a passing car. It was also a good reminder that she shouldn't be there and that she needed to hurry. She pushed the dresser drawer closed, set the box with Bonnie inside back where she'd found it, and hurried into Minnie and John's bedroom. All she wanted was to get herself and her DNA out of there as fast as possible.

The bed looked just as she'd left it yesterday; nobody seemed to have slept in it after she had, which made sense. Minnie had been in another room and John . . . in the pool. She bent down and looked underneath it, hoping to find her Middlebury T-shirt there. It wasn't. A panicky feeling rose up in her, but she reminded herself that it might still be on the floor of Minnie's closet. For now, she wondered if she might just peel back the covers and run a vacuum over the sheets and pillows. But no, she couldn't risk the noise a vacuum might make, even though the Wrights' house seemed to be entirely soundproof. More importantly, she couldn't see well enough with the night-vision goggles—what if she missed a strand that would link her to the scene? She couldn't risk it. She'd have to change the sheets.

Martha put down her satchel and went to the closet where she'd seen the extra bedding. Thankfully, there were enough sets there that probably nobody but Lupe—and possibly Minnie—would notice one was gone. Carefully, she removed the decorative pillows and duvet, then rolled the soiled sheets into a ball. She remade the bed exactly as she had before. Even if she'd gotten the order of the pillows wrong yesterday, this arrangement would match what the police had seen and, possibly, photographed.

Then she took the caftan from her satchel and hung it back as close to where she remembered finding it as she could, then pushed some other items in a way that might conceal it. She dropped to her knees, looking for her T-shirt. Her panic mushroomed as she shifted the detritus here and there, not finding it. What if it *had* fallen out of her arms on her way out? She dug deeper into the recesses, flinging items out of her way, until she found it beneath a jumble of other clothes in the remotest corner. Never had she been so happy to see such a raggedy old thing. She held it to her chest and rocked back and forth on her knees, as grateful as if her life had just been saved. After spending a moment like this, she tried to restore the mess she'd made to a semblance of its previous, less violent-looking disorder, shoving things out of the walking space at least.

Withdrawing her hand from a small heap, she felt something wet against her forearm above the edge of her glove, like she'd been licked by a strange animal. She shook it off, more frantically than necessary, and looked down at the thing. She picked it up, as though by its tail, and examined its full length. It wasn't an animal; it was the jumpsuit Minnie had been wearing the night before. It was wet.

She stood there, staring at the fabric, letting her mind go through the possibilities. There were many, but she kept returning to one. Slowly, she lifted it to her face and inhaled. It smelled very faintly briny with just a hint of natural chlorine. A wave of nausea took Martha back down to her knees.

Martha thought of how John's body looked lying poolside, his head bent at an awkward angle, not unlike Bonnie's. Minnie had loved that bird so much, it would've been awful for her after the bird was . . . gone.

Martha remembered finding a kitten on her way home from elementary school. She picked it up, thinking she'd take it home and ask her mother if she could have it for a pet. Then some older boys came along and one of them snatched it away from her, saying it belonged to him. But instead of cuddling the kitten, he began to mishandle it, and before she could get there, right in front of her . . . she couldn't even bring herself to finish the memory. But she knew that if the other two hadn't held her back, she'd have hurt that boy.

Martha felt sure that, so far, she was the only person besides Minnie and John who had an idea about what had really happened between them. John had been drunk when Minnie came home from the store after work. Something interrupted her while she was putting away the groceries, and then she went outside to the porch. Martha had seen her there, trembling, it looked like. That made sense now. John had come out. Martini, *bitch*. For some reason, he was so angry, or drunk, or both, that he'd gone in, reached into Bonnie's cage, pulled out Minnie's bird, and killed her by wringing her neck. What had he done with the poor creature then? How had Minnie discovered Bonnie's body? What did she do once she did?

Martha wondered what Minnie—in the clutches of grief at losing her beloved pet, her "child"—would've been capable of. Could she push a drunken man into a pool and watch him drown? Could she get in and hold him underwater?

Martha, still on her knees, clutched the wet jumpsuit in her rubber-gloved arms and endured the chill that ran through her body.

Obviously, the investigators hadn't thought to dig through Minnie's closet. If they'd gone in there at all, they'd have probably just observed that it was a mess—not unlike the current state of her kitchen. They might not think it was such an extraordinary thing in an otherwise perfectly ordered house. But that the police hadn't discovered Minnie's jumpsuit yet didn't mean that they wouldn't. And what would they think of that?

And if they were to also find Minnie's bird, dead in a funerary box? They wouldn't get stirred up over a little thing like a dead parakeet, not with a real human murder to contend with. Or would they? Officer Peters had talked about looking for a motive. If there was a definite thing, something to show—something to make a story about—that might connect someone to the murder, then they'd want to know about it.

If Officer Peters had found Bonnie's body and Minnie's wet jumpsuit, he'd most certainly have what he was looking for: motive, means, and opportunity.

Martha looked around the inside of Minnie's closet, feeling like she'd just come out of a spell. Everything seemed different than it had before, as though she'd been looking at it all through a mirror instead of a window, and what she'd seen was reversed: a reflection of reality that wasn't actually real.

With this new disillusionment, Martha forced herself to reconsider her earlier perceptions of Minnie and John. She wondered why they'd really moved from Seattle and why they'd had so few visitors since moving to West U. She thought of Minnie's jumpiness the afternoon Martha took photos of Bonnie when she realized John would soon be home. Through a different lens, she considered Minnie's reluctance to let Martha get close to her—and also to Lillian, apparently; perhaps those slights she'd felt hadn't been personal after all.

She thought about the sex tape. The slapping had seemed exciting to Martha at the time. Titillatingly dangerous. She'd even wished Lewis were more daring. But Lewis would never slap her, not even playfully. John's slaps had been hard enough to leave marks, to make Minnie lie still.

Minnie's excuse for the brace on her wrist was that she'd fallen off a stepladder at work, and her lip was bruised from a Botox injection. Maybe those were true, but maybe John had hurt her. Maybe he hurt her enough to keep arnica gel in her purse. Enough to take birth control pills when she'd claimed they were still trying to have a baby.

Martha recalled John's suggestion of a romantic getaway, how insistent and even pleading he'd sounded, and how dispassionate Minnie's response had been. Martha had been envious then, marveling at his devotion. But now she wondered if his gesture had been conciliatory instead of indulgent, and if it was part of a pattern—there was a file full of unsigned apology cards in his locked desk drawer after all. Maybe they'd worked in the past, but an apology wouldn't bring a bird back from the dead.

Martha felt a deep conviction taking root inside her as she knelt there in the dark. Perhaps, as she felt had happened to her so often during her life, Martha had been judging Minnie too harshly. Or not judging her correctly at all.

Martha took a long, slow breath, then wrapped Minnie's jumpsuit along with her own T-shirt into the pile of sheets. She stuffed the wad into her satchel and hoisted the handle over her shoulder and across her body. Then she went to the guest room. Whatever had happened to Minnie, she had already suffered enough.

She stood at the door, contemplating the gravity of her actions. There was no question that she'd violated the penal code at this point; there would be little favor for her if she were to be caught. But she could extend favor. She lifted the lid on the wooden box and gathered Bonnie's silk-wrapped body into her hand. With the other, she created a depression in the sheets in her bag and placed Bonnie into it, as though settling her into a nest. She refilled the box with the things that Minnie had dumped into her dresser drawer, but rather than return it to its original place, she left it on the nightstand, where the reordering of its contents would escape the investigators' notice.

Then, with the two things that would make Minnie's conviction for murder a certainty hidden away in her satchel, Martha slipped out of the Wrights' house and into the night.

Twenty-Three

Martha was strangely calm as she ripped off a sheet of aluminum foil and placed it in the pan, the way a priest might feel while performing a funeral, or a technician at a crematory. Her hands trembled slightly, but only because the washing machine behind her in the utility room was on the final spin cycle, which reverberated through the kitchen floor.

She'd clipped some low-hanging panicles from one of her crape myrtle trees and arranged the prettiest of the hot-pink blossoms into a bed on the foil. She laid Bonnie gently on top of them, straightening her neck as best she could, and after stroking the bird's blue and yellow feathers a final time, she covered her with a few more flowers. When the oven dinged, indicating it had reached 450 degrees, she put the pan inside, then went into the utility room to put the laundry into the dryer. She'd considered putting everything into the fireplace and burning it, ashes to ashes, dust to dust. But there was nothing discreet about lighting a fire in the middle of June in Houston.

Martha opened a bottle of wine, poured nearly half of it into a plastic cup she'd brought home from one of the West U Little League galas years ago, and sat down at the kitchen table where just hours and an eternity earlier, she and Lewis had sat with Officer Peters, then she again with Lillian Mickelsen.

When, for several minutes, the smell from the oven became almost pleasant, she thought of her recent lunch with her mother and Evelyn's trio of roasted quail, how her mother had raved about the flavor, devoured the tiny bits of flesh. Martha ran to the bathroom, feeling like she would be sick. She stayed there until the odor that reached her was distinctly charred. Anyone who could smell it would merely assume she'd burned her dinner.

She turned off the heat and removed the pan from the oven. Without looking directly at Bonnie's remains, she placed another sheet of foil on top and crimped the edges to form a seal. Quickly, to avoid turning it into a ceremony, because it would be a woefully inadequate one, she shoved the whole foil packet down inside the garbage can. She didn't think she'd be able to eat either fowl or yogurt ever again after this. She lifted the bag from its can, took it outside, and heaved it into the bin. Then she washed the cremation pan and set it in the rack to dry.

After the dryer cycle finished, Martha took the basket of warm laundry to her room and dumped it out onto her bed. She folded Minnie's eight-hundred-thread-count Egyptian cotton sheets and her elegant jumpsuit, then put them into a heavy-duty trash bag she'd gotten from the garage. To that, she added not just the one she'd worn yesterday but all her old Middlebury T-shirts, which she never wanted to see again. Besides, even though she knew she'd never become the kind of woman who actually wore silk caftans, maybe it really was time for her to upgrade her wardrobe a little bit. She scooped all the old bras from her drawer and dropped them in, too. From Harry's room, which made her miss him so fiercely she thought she might cry, she grabbed the pile of outgrown clothes she'd culled the day after he left for camp and put them on top. The last thing she jammed in, before knotting the bag and placing it in the back of her minivan, was the pan. She'd never be able to use that again either.

By then, it was after midnight, and she was both restless and exhausted. Now that she'd completed the tasks she'd assigned herself, the worry that had been hovering at the periphery began to creep in. She wondered if there was something else she could do—or undo. She didn't know what the police would decide about John's death, or find if they came back looking. She didn't know if she would be prosecuted for any of her wrongdoings. Or Minnie for hers. She had no idea what would happen next to any of them. In the past, she'd have been embarrassed thinking back on how she'd behaved, but already she was changing. She'd discovered an untapped well of grace in her heart, enough for everyone, including herself.

She checked her phone, which she'd inadvertently left on silent. There was a voice mail from her mother, wondering if she knew the man who'd been murdered in West U, and one from her mother-in-law, inviting them to dinner the next night. Lewis had sent her a text message, telling her good night and that he would be home in the morning. There were a dozen more from people she never typically heard from, including some whose numbers weren't even in her contacts list, asking what she knew about the Wrights, about John's death, about Minnie.

She wondered how Minnie was doing. The prayer that she usually said at Sunday dinners came to mind: "May all be fed. May all be healed. May all be loved." She hoped Minnie's boss and his partner were taking good care of her, that they had given her a good meal and made up a comfortable bed for her. She hoped that she had an excellent attorney and an even better therapist. Martha realized that she and Minnie could never get to be true friends, not now. Not after all this. In fact, they may never have a chance or a reason to speak again. But she hoped that on some level, without even knowing why, Minnie would feel from Martha those things that Martha had wanted to feel not just from Minnie but from all the other women she'd tried so hard all her life to befriend: understanding, acceptance, solidarity, protection. Love.

ACKNOWLEDGMENTS

The idea for this novel arrived unexpectedly, rich in substance and potential, like a gift bag full of Meyer lemons delivered just when I needed it most. I'm eternally grateful to those friends and colleagues who helped me develop the recipe to turn those lemons into *A Gracious Neighbor*.

My most heartfelt thanks go to Heather Montoya and Kristi Foye for helping me imagine Martha into existence, for their invaluable critiques, and for their kick-ass support. I couldn't have written this book without you. For her unwavering enthusiasm, Ten-of-Pentacles prescience, and impeccable advice about everything, I send thanks and love to Louise Marburg. Profound thanks go to these wonderful friends and early readers for their time and generous feedback: Charlie Baxter, Pamela Erens, Lee Ann Grimes, Shana Halvorsen, Jenny Johnson, Laura Moser, Marlies Schmitt, and Juliet Snowden. I'm grateful for the support and input from dear friends Lucy Chambers, Caroline Leech, and Mimi Vance, and my amazing writing group: Tobey Forney, Mark Haber, and Cameron Hammon. Thank you, Bonnie Treece, for lending your name and gentle spirit to a bird. Unlike Martha, I'm so fortunate to have so many incredible women in my life. To all the members of my various lady gangs: my Fun Friday co-mothers, my Taekwondo-practicing Curtsy Militia, my Sidelot Sisters, my book club, and my Porch friends, thank you for your sisterhood.

Countless thanks go to my brilliant agent, Jess Salky, and her fabulous team at Salky Literary Management, especially Rachel Altemose, for believing in me and working so hard on my behalf. I'm beyond grateful to my editor, Carmen Johnson, for her vision and passion for this book, and for giving me a new home at Little A. Thanks, also, to the entire team for their important contributions to the book along the way.

I'm so grateful to my family for their love and championship, especially my mom, Cindy Slator, and sister Sara Huffman for reading my early drafts with such gusto. For reasons far too numerous to list here, thanks go to my husband, Harris, and our children, Sasha and Josh. I love you with all that I am.

Special thanks go to Susan Glaspell, who wrote "A Jury of Her Peers," the story that inspired this novel, and to Sasha's Honors AP English Literature teacher, Sharon Gehbauer, for assigning Glaspell's story to her class.

BOOK CLUB DISCUSSION QUESTIONS

1. In addition to Minnie's pet parakeet, Bonnie, there are bird references throughout the novel. What do these references symbolize?

2. The epigraph is a four-part definition of the titular word *gracious*. Which of those definitions applies to each character?

3. Do you identify with any of the characters? If you noticed any shared characteristics, how did it make you feel? Would you admit those traits to your book club?

4. Several of Martha's choices are driven by her assumptions and misperceptions about Minnie. Which other characters in the book make assumptions about one another?

5. Do you recognize similarities between Martha's neighbors and members of your own community?

6. While female relationships are at the heart of this novel, the male characters play important roles in driving the women's actions and reactions. What were your initial impressions of the men in this story? Did your opinions evolve over the course of the book?

7. Do you think Martha is a reliable or unreliable narrator in her own story? Why?

8. As a photographer, Martha understands the value of perspectives and seeing things through different lenses. As a photo editor, she also understands how images can be manipulated to distort reality. Why do you think she misses these truths when it comes to her perspective and the lens through which she sees Minnie? Why does she allow her distorted perspective to become her perceived reality?

9. The idea of samaritanism comes up when Harry is caught painting graffiti, then again when Martha hears a rumor about her would-be friend. Do you think Martha's choices to act on her Good Samaritan impulses were justified? Or just that *she* thought they were? Were you still rooting for her even as she started to make some unusual choices?

10. How do Harry's summer-camp absence and looming adulthood affect Martha's emotional state?

11. We only know Minnie through Martha's few interactions with and frequent thoughts about her. How do you feel about Minnie as a person? Did you reach conclusions similar to Martha's about Minnie, or did you suspect other dynamics existed that Martha was missing?

12. Why do you think Minnie felt such a strong bond with Bonnie? In what ways are the two of them alike? What role did Bonnie serve for Minnie?

13. On the day that follows Martha's first foray into the Wrights' home and the Hales' anniversary-evening missteps, Mrs. Kashuba points out the sooty mold infecting Martha's crape myrtle trees. In what ways does the author

use natural elements to illustrate truths about the plot and/or characters?

14. In what ways are Bonnie's and John's murders foreshadowed?

15. Do you think Minnie is guilty of murder? If so, do you feel sympathetic toward her anyway? Why do you think this was purposely left open ended?

16. What do you think happens to Martha and Minnie after the last page?

ABOUT THE AUTHOR

Photo © 2021 Larry A. Pullen

Chris Cander is the *USA Today* bestselling author of the novels *The Weight of a Piano*, which was named an Indie Next Great Read; *Whisper Hollow*, also named an Indie Next Great Read, longlisted for the Great Santini Fiction Prize, and nominated for the 2015 Kirkus Prize for Fiction; and *11 Stories*, named by *Kirkus Reviews* as one of the best books of 2013, the winner of the Independent Publisher Book Award for Fiction, and a USA Best Book Award finalist. She is also the author of the Audible Original Stories "Eddies" and "Grieving Conversations." Cander's fiction has been published in twelve languages. She lives in her native Houston, Texas, with her husband and two children. For more information, visit www.chriscander.com.